SAVAGE KING
KINGS OF TEMPTATION

SIENNA CROSS

Copyright © 2023 by Sienna Cross

All rights reserved.

No part of this book may be reproduced in any form or by any electronic or mechanical means, including information storage and retrieval systems, without written permission from the author, except for the use of brief quotations in a book review.

Paperback ISBN: 9798870135816

Cover Design: Joy Design Studio

❀ Created with Vellum

To all the women who find it perfectly acceptable for a gorgeous Italian mobster to unalive anyone who's ever hurt you...
~ Sienna Cross

SAVAGE KING

CONTENTS

1. Revenge — 1
2. No Saint — 6
3. Starting Out with a Bang — 14
4. Betrayal — 21
5. Be Good — 27
6. Nothing but Trouble — 34
7. Rose Version 2.0 — 41
8. Light It Up — 46
9. Not Again — 52
10. Cruel Irony — 57
11. Bossy Mob Boss — 65
12. You Are Mine — 71
13. Sending a Message — 77
14. Questionable Life Decisions — 83
15. You Disobeyed Me — 90
16. Jury's Still Out — 95
17. Nightmares and Daydreams — 102
18. No Free Sneak Peeks — 108
19. Merry Christmas to Me — 114
20. A Special Gift — 122
21. I Should Not Be Doing This — 128
22. The Ugliest One — 136
23. Man Bun — 143
24. Self-Preservation — 150
25. Full of It — 156
26. Run — 163
27. Ruined — 170
28. Feeding the Monster — 177
29. Emotionally Unavailable Mob Boss — 184
30. Already Addicted — 190
31. Did You Bite Me? — 196
32. Use Me — 202
33. Stuck with Me — 208
34. Better than Heaven — 216
35. Beware the Fury — 222

36. Just Friends	230
37. See You in Hell	236
38. Falling for Him	243
39. I'm Not Okay	249
40. Do You Love This?	255
41. I Am Yours	261
42. It's Almost Time	270
43. Payback	276
44. A Surprise Gift	283
45. A Barely Veiled Threat	288
46. Unexpected Alliances	296
47. A Confession and an Escape	303
48. You Can't Hide	310
49. Fury is Power	315
50. Never Be Alone Again	324
51. My Queen	330
Epilogue	335
52. Sneak Peek of Brutal King	343
Also by Sienna Cross	351
Acknowledgments	353
About the Author	355

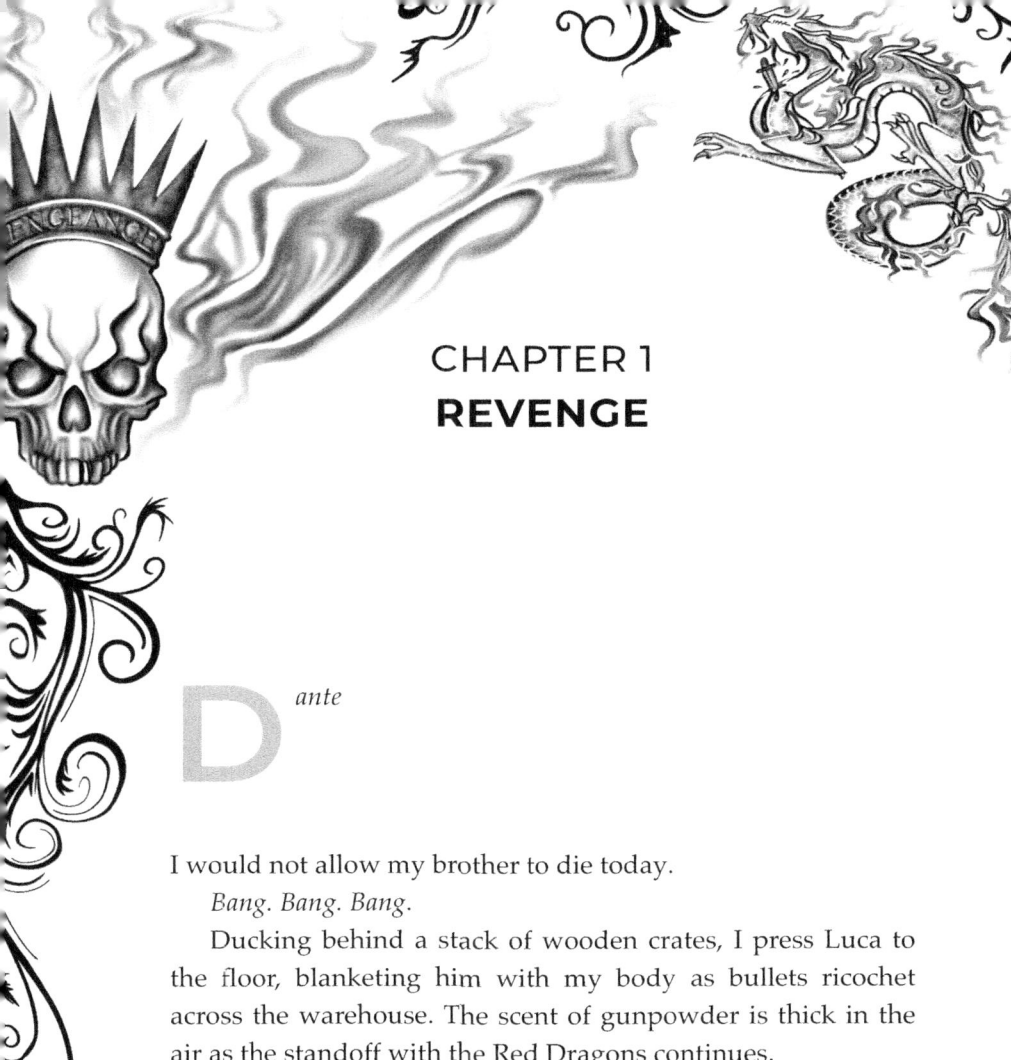

CHAPTER 1
REVENGE

D*ante*

I would not allow my brother to die today.

Bang. Bang. Bang.

Ducking behind a stack of wooden crates, I press Luca to the floor, blanketing him with my body as bullets ricochet across the warehouse. The scent of gunpowder is thick in the air as the standoff with the Red Dragons continues.

"Dante, *smettila!*" he growls from beneath my arm. "Get off me, I can fight for myself."

"No," I snarl, my finger closing around the trigger. I shoot off a hailstorm of bullets into the murky space. "Stella will kill me if anything happens to you. I already owe your fiancée enough. I don't need to add to the debt."

He remains silent for a blissful minute. My stubborn younger brother has always believed himself to be invincible. Until he met her. Now everything has changed. The idea of dying becomes much less acceptable when you're forced to leave behind someone you're fucking crazy about.

Lucky for me, I don't have that problem.

Luca shoves me off and crouches beside me, drawing out the handgun from his inside jacket pocket. As C.E.O. of King Industries, my *fratellino* doesn't have use for a weapon on most days. But today, the Triad got the drop on us.

"Where the hell are Tony and the other guys?" Luca hisses as another spray of bullets zings over our heads.

"On their way," I mutter through clenched teeth. I never should've let my brother come today. So much for a quick check on our supplies. How the fuck did Feng Zhang and his men know we'd be here? And unprotected?

"I can't believe that *figlio di puttana* is still alive," Luca grits out.

I nod and squeeze out another round before reloading. Feng was supposed to be dead, along with his cousin Bo who'd nearly killed us three months ago. Bo's father Jianjun is the head of the Chinese Triad. His bastard son captured Luca's fiancée and my brother lost his shit. We thought they were all dead, then last week a fucking ghost appears.

Feng.

The thirst for revenge changes a man.

I know this well enough. After Papà died and Luca slid into the King's throne, vengeance was all I lived for.

The sudden silence jerks me from my musings, and I glance around the dark warehouse.

"Why'd they stop?" Luca whispers.

I inch up and peer over the edge of the bullet-riddled crates. Feng stands across the sprawling space with two men at each side. They're all in red from head-to-toe, wearing the traditional Chinese warrior cuirass along with more modern hoods.

"I've come to deliver a message." Feng's voice cuts through the unnatural silence.

Luca stands, but I wrap my fingers around his wrist and jerk him back down. "Stay down," I hiss. "You're too valuable."

"Oh, fuck off, Dante."

I throw a narrowed glare at my brother. "Stella," I mouth.

He huffs out a frustrated breath and shrinks down behind the splintering crate.

"We're listening," I shout back.

Feng clears his throat, then reaches into his pocket and something silver glints beneath the dim halogen lights.

"*Merda*," Luca mutters.

He creeps closer, hands extended palm up. His men trail him on either side, guns trained at us. As he nears, I finally focus on the silver circlet. Bo's gaudy dragon ring. Feng slides it onto his middle finger and squeezes his hand into a fist.

Then he glares at me from across the room, lips twisted into a snarl. "You slaughtered my cousin and his men, nearly killed me, and now you will pay. The Chinese Triad has declared war on the Kings."

"That's bullshit—" Luca leaps up, and a bullet whizzes just past his head.

I shove him down to the floor again, muttering curses. "I told you to stay down, you *stronzo*."

A dark chuckle fills the tense air. "One more thing. The Triad has placed a price on Luca Valentino and Stella Esposito's heads. Dead or alive. One million dollars each."

"Fuck," Luca hisses.

Feng sneers, and I can feel the tension radiating off my brother in waves. "You'll have every low-life scum gunning for you and your precious fiancée."

Luca jolts up again, digging his elbow into my side when I try to stop him. "If you lay a hand on her, Feng, I'll tear you up from limb to limb, piss on your entrails and drag your remains across China Town."

"Big words from a mob boss gone soft, Luca."

"That's *Signor* Valentino," he snarls. "Or did you forget your place in the sewers, you little rat?"

"A lot has changed in the last three months, *capo*. The Kings don't rule the Lower East Side anymore. I do."

"Yeah, we'll fucking see about that," Luca spits.

"You've been warned." Feng dips his head, and his men move as one surrounding him in a red wave.

Heavy footfalls drag my attention to the opposite end of the warehouse. Tony, Mickey and half a dozen of our guys race in with guns drawn. Just as the Red Dragons slip out the back.

"That little shit, who the hell does he think he is?" Luca roars.

Tony moves in step beside my brother and gives him the once over before the tense set of his broad shoulders relax. "You okay, *capo*?"

"Yeah, I'm fine, Tony." My little bro gives his righthand man a tight smile. *Tony would be the most difficult to convince…*

I bite back the snarl on my lips. For years, Tony has coddled and fussed over Luca like he was his older brother. It pisses me off to no end.

I'm the older brother, that's my job. Sure, I might have fucked up a few things here and there along the way, but I'm on my game now. I can protect him. Which is why I know what I have to do next, no matter how much Luca will hate me for it.

The Frank Sinatra impersonator croons in the background as the guests filling my new penthouse ooh and ahh at his rendition of *My Way*. Ma's smile is so big I'm worried her lips will crack. Luca and Stella dance in the middle of the living room, the look in their eyes as they sway to the music nauseatingly sweet.

Everything is going according to plan. A dozen of my men

are stationed in the penthouse and lobby, ready for my word. With so many dignitaries in attendance, their presence isn't questioned.

Besides, my brother is so obsessed with his beautiful fiancée, his head permanently buried between her thighs, he won't see it coming until it's too late.

Just like he didn't see the Chinese Triad slowly encroaching on our territory.

That's what love does to a man. The most ruthless man in New York City has gone soft, and now it's time for me to step in.

CHAPTER 2
NO SAINT

D*ante*

"Sorry I'm late!" A bubbly voice fills the apartment, cutting through the soft tunes, and I spin toward the sweet sound.

Rose barges in like a bull in a china shop, whizzing past the commissioner and his mistress, and the mayor and his escort. Both men are married, of course, but given their intimate dealings with King Industries, they're free to let loose in a party like this.

Stella's best friend barrels right past me with a quick wave. "Hey, D!" Then wraps my future sister-in-law in a hug. My brother tenses the moment his fiancée is out of his arms. *Dio*, he's completely *impazzito*. Fucking crazy.

I saunter over, the beautiful blonde always fun for a laugh. She and Stella attend NYU together. While my brother's future wife studies business, Rose is an aspiring psychologist. The girl is batshit crazy, hot as fuck, and definitely has a wild streak.

Once she peels herself off Stella, she turns to me and offers a mischievous smile. "Where's Caroline, D? I thought she'd be here tonight for sure."

Stella rolls her eyes, and her lip curls in distaste. My on-again, off-again female companion had a thing for my brother before Stella came into the picture. The software company heiress was dying to get her claws into Manhattan's most eligible bachelor. For a while, I thought she was my ticket to finally getting out from behind Luca's glowing shadow.

But now fate has other plans for us.

"Ugh, thank *Dio* she didn't come," Stella mumbles.

Luca smirks and tucks her into his side. "You're not still jealous of her, are you, *amore*?"

"No," she snaps. "I just don't like her. She looks at me like I'm hired help."

"She's the one who's jealous," says Rose as a waiter walks by and offers a tray of champagne flutes. She grabs the fullest one and gulps it down in one go.

I went all out for this affair. It was the only way to avoid my brother's suspicions.

"Geez, take it easy, Rose." Stella eyes her friend.

"I'll be fine." She waves a nonchalant hand. "Rough day at the office."

"Is that crazy guy still calling you?" Stella asks.

My mind flickers back to the first time I met Rose a few months ago. She'd been dating a patient from the psychology practice from which she interns.

"Yup." She pops the P and reaches for another glass when the waiter reappears.

"Do you want me to scare him off?" Luca offers. "I can send Tony or Mickey."

"As tempting as that sounds, I don't want Dr. Winchester to find out about my extra-curricular activities, and if I lash out, I'm worried he'll spill about us. Then I'll lose my job."

"I told you not to date patients!" Stella scolds her friend.

"Dr. Mark might be crazy, but he's hotter than Hades." She takes another sip. "Obviously, I've learned my lesson, and I'll never date a patient again."

Stella rolls her eyes and Luca grins, like everything the woman does is the most adorable thing ever.

I'm not entirely sure I believe Rose either. From what Luca told me, this was her third or fourth patient. I smirk as I watch her pretty pink lips close around the rim of the crystal. Mmm. I'd love to have that mouth closed around my cock. I can practically picture her head bobbing up and down as she takes all of me in. Rose would be a fucking tiger in bed, I just know it.

I've had a few chances to test my theory over the last couple of months but ultimately decided it was better to stay away from Stella's best friend. She's overly protective of the girl, and given our tainted past, I'm certain she's warned her away from me.

I couldn't blame her really. I'd been a total asshole when I first met Stella.

We've come to an understanding now. She realized I did what I had to in order to protect my brother, but that doesn't mean she wants a man like me involved with her closest friend.

My phone buzzes, drawing my attention away from the vivacious blonde. I draw it out of my jacket pocket and stare at the screen.

Aldo: *Everything's ready, just give us the word. I'm worried about Tony though. He still seems conflicted.*

I swallow thickly and glance up at my brother and his fiancée. He nuzzles her ear, whispering something that has her cheeks flaming a deep crimson. A swirl of guilt lashes at my insides, but I shove it down. Papà would want this. It's the only way.

I type out a quick response and pocket my phone. I need to find Tony and make sure he's on board before this goes down.

The singer is on his last set, and before long, it'll be time to make my move.

Lifting my gaze to the happy couple and Rose, who's slurping down another glass of champagne, I offer a tight smile. "Excuse me, I have to check on something. Be right back."

"Who knew you'd make such a great host?" Luca teases. "From now on, we're holding all the fundraisers at your place instead of mine."

"We'll see about that, *fratellino*." I spin on my heel and march toward the library.

The powder room door whips open, and I nearly slam into the pale white oak. "*Cazzo*," I growl.

"Dante!" Mamma peers out from behind the door, and I snap my jaw shut.

"*Scusi*, Ma." *Dio*, I'm twenty-nine years old, and one glare from my mother has me shrinking back like a beaten dog. I clear my throat, force a smile and glance down at the feisty Italian woman who raised us on her own after Papà passed. "Are you enjoying the party?"

"*Certo, sì*. It's just lovely, Dante." She rises to her toes and scans the packed living room. "I thought Caroline would be here."

Ugh. My meddlesome mother. "Ma, things with Caroline aren't serious."

"*Grazie a Dio*," she mumbles under her breath. Thank God?

My brows shoot up to my hairline. Mamma is always after Luca and me to settle down. "You don't like her?"

She cups my scruffy cheek and offers a warm smile. "She's not for you, *figlio mio*. But I'm certain you'll find the right woman soon, just like Luca." She stares past me to my brother and his fiancée who are dancing again. Or rather fucking with their clothes on. Those two are like animals.

"Sure, Ma," I finally answer. "Anyway, go enjoy the music while you can. The singer is on his last set."

With a smile, she releases me and hurries back to the great room. I watch her for a long minute before I tear my gaze away. She'll be angry too, but she'll have to get over it.

I heave out a breath and continue my march down the hallway. The further I move, the faster my pulse pounds. The soothing sounds of Frank Sinatra grow fainter beneath the roar of my thundering heartbeat across my eardrums.

By the time I reach the library, sweat coats my skin and I'm a second away from ripping my jacket off. I whip the door open and find Tony in the corner. He's flipping through an old copy of *Jack the Ripper*.

"You good?" I ask as soon as the door shuts behind me.

"I don't know if I can do this, Dante. Luca's going to be furious."

I stalk closer and level my brother's old friend with a steely glare. "We're doing this for him, remember?"

"He's not going to see it that way." He shakes his head, wrenching his hands.

"It's not like he's going to kill you for this."

Tony scoffs. "You don't think so? He'll see this as a fucking betrayal, and you know it."

I close the distance between us and jab my finger into his barrel chest. "What would you rather have: Luca pissed or dead?"

His lips press into a tight line.

"And what about Stella? If anything happens to her, Luca would be devastated. Everything we've all worked for would crumble. This is the only answer, Tony."

He nods slowly and releases a frustrated breath. "It just feels wrong."

"I know." That pang of guilt returns, spearing me in the chest. I will it back and focus on what comes next. "Trust me, it's for the best."

"Right." His head dips, and he thumbs through the worn pages of the book again.

"Keep your phone handy. I'll text you when it's time."

"Got it, *capo*."

My lips twist at the title. It's belonged to my brother for five long years. He's been the boss, he's called all the shots of our underground dealings, and as C.E.O., he's made King Industries the powerhouse it is today.

A seed of doubt wiggles its way into my gut. What if I can't do this? I growl and squash it down before it takes root. This is my birthright, and I will claim it.

Running my hand through my wild, dark locks, I heave in a breath as I attempt a casual stroll back into the thick of the party. Scanning the crowd, I search for my brother and his fiancée. They're gone.

I move through the crowd, weaving between CEOs and Congressmen and women. Barely anyone looks at me. Everyone knows Luca, the golden boy. I bite down on the envy and search every corner of the great room before I move onto the balcony.

Nothing.

"Fuck," I snarl.

"Yup, that." Rose appears from behind one of the burly guards stationed on the terrace. She wobbles a little as she saunters toward me.

"What?"

"Luca and Stella. They're probably fucking. They disappeared a few minutes ago after they were getting all hot and heavy on the dancefloor."

I draw in a breath to steady the rising panic. "Thanks." Spinning on my heel, I head back inside to search the bedrooms. That *bastardo* better not be screwing his fiancée on my bed. I pass the first guest bedroom and press my ear to the door. *Niente*.

Then I move past my room to the final spare one at the end of the hall. A faint moan makes my dick twitch. I creep closer and linger for an instant at the door as the unmistakable sounds seep through the cracks in the white-washed oak.

Merda. This is going to set my plan back by at least a half hour. Once those two start, they're at it forever.

Soft footsteps echo behind me, and I spin around to find Rose grinning like mad. "Oh, my gawd, I was right, wasn't I?" She presses her ear to the door and covers her mouth.

I hover behind her, torn between waiting for them to finish and barging in.

More moans fill the air between us, and my damned cock starts to harden. Clearly, I've been watching too much porn and not getting laid enough.

Rose giggles and spins around, and her mouth is suddenly an inch from my own. She stumbles and her hands wrap around my waist to steady herself.

Looking up at me, she bats long lashes. "Sorry." The scent of champagne mingles between our lips. She inches closer and presses her body flush against mine.

Cazzo, now I'm hard. And she's rubbing her hot little body against me.

"Rose...," I growl.

She cocks her head to the side innocently. "What?"

"Don't do that."

Her hands tighten around my waist, and she slips a few fingers beneath my shirt, touching my bare skin. "Come on, D. Don't tell me that doesn't turn you on." She ticks her head at the moans still seeping through the doorway.

It shouldn't because it's my goddamned brother and his future wife, but my dick is too stupid to understand. I press my lips into a hard line as her fingers dance across my skin, moving toward my belt buckle.

"Don't tell me you've never wanted to?" Her eyes are shiny, the scent of alcohol thick between us.

She's drunk. And I'm not.

Rose cups my cock over my slacks, and I let out a hiss. "Just one time, D. It'll be our little secret."

I wrap my hand around her wrist and drag her to my bedroom.

I'm also no fucking saint.

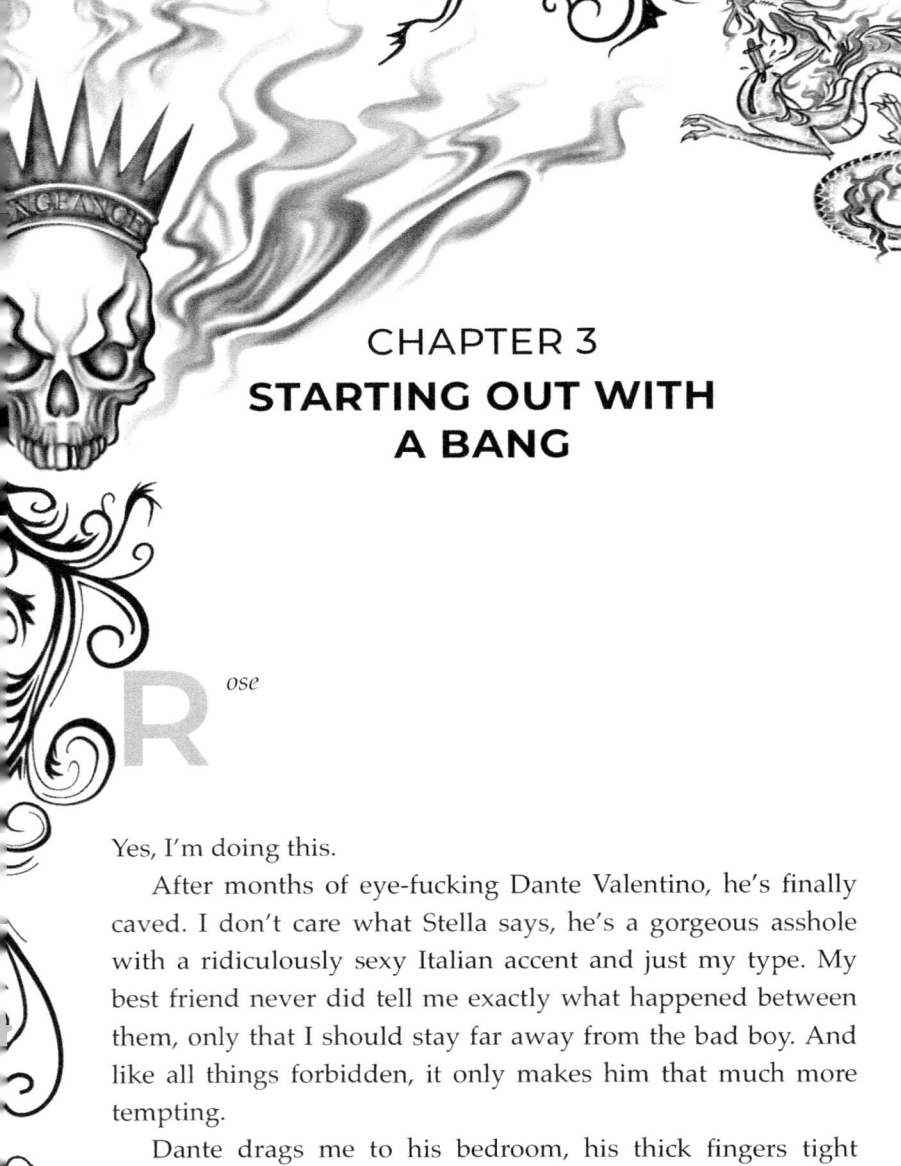

CHAPTER 3
STARTING OUT WITH A BANG

R *ose*

Yes, I'm doing this.

After months of eye-fucking Dante Valentino, he's finally caved. I don't care what Stella says, he's a gorgeous asshole with a ridiculously sexy Italian accent and just my type. My best friend never did tell me exactly what happened between them, only that I should stay far away from the bad boy. And like all things forbidden, it only makes him that much more tempting.

Dante drags me to his bedroom, his thick fingers tight around my wrist. My pulse flutters like mad beneath his touch. He whips the door open, and my breath catches as he yanks me across the threshold. A blast of cold air wafts over me and my nipples harden, poking through my silk blouse. Or maybe it's the adrenaline rushing through my veins at the idea of finally hooking up with the mafia enforcer.

Dante slams the door and shoves me against the thick

timber. A faint gasp escapes as he presses the full length of his body against mine. Gawd, he's already so fucking hard. His erection lifts up my mini-skirt and settles between my legs. His eyes chase down my body, zeroing in on my peaked nipples. A feral smile curls his lips.

"Are you ready for me, sweetheart?"

"D, I've been ready for you since the first time I heard a dreamy Italian word spill from those sexy lips."

A rough chuckle tumbles from those sexy lips. His hand skates down my hip and toward the apex of my thighs. He cups my pussy, and fire rages through my core.

"Mmm, you *are* ready for me. Soaked." He slips his finger across my lacey panties, and heat pulses across my clit. Another groan echoes between us. His? Mine? Who the hell can tell?

His mouth claims mine, teeth gnashing against my own. His fingers dig into my hair, and he wraps the long locks around his fingers. Fisting them, he jerks my head back and bares my throat.

"That's a good girl," he whispers as his tongue glides across my jaw line then down my neck.

I reach for his slacks and make quick work of the belt buckle, button and zipper. I slide his pants down his slim hips and take in his fully tented boxer briefs. The outline of his huge cock has my tipsy pussy pulsing with need. Gawd, she has no shame.

As Dante's mouth ravages my neck, one hand slips up my top. He squeezes my bare breast, and an appreciative growl vibrates his throat. "Just perfect," he murmurs.

"Really? I always feel like they're too small. Like once I make it big with my celebrity psychology practice, I'll go up a size or two--"

Dante's hand slaps across my mouth, smothering my words. His eyes meet mine, and an unfamiliar twinge pinches in my chest. "I said they're perfect. Now stop talking." His mouth finds mine again, his tongue punishing, teeth nibbling until my lower lip is puffy and swollen.

Good gawd, he's an animal. I match him stroke for stroke, digging my own fingers into his silky hair. I'm about a second from humping him against the door. Why should my best friend be the only one getting laid tonight? Besides, after Dr. Mark, the stalker from Dr. Winchester's practice, I deserve a little fun.

Dante shrugs off his jacket, and my hands move down his crisp, button-down shirt, then my fingers slip between the buttons. A swirl of tattoos dance beneath my fingertips, and damn, I'm so tempted to rip his shirt right off, Superman style. As I undo the buttons, I explore the dips and valleys of his ripped torso, and I imagine licking every inch of his cut abs. My hand glides over a patch of puckered skin, and he tenses beneath me.

My fingers freeze over the scar.

Dante may be an asshole, but he saved his brother and my best friend's life by taking a barrage of bullets meant for them only three months ago. Stella would've been dead if it wasn't for him. Which is why she forgave him for whatever the hell he did to piss her off in the first place.

He releases a shuddering breath drawing my attention back to the towering male looming over me.

"Sorry," I mumble. "Is it still sensitive?"

"No," he growls. Those dark eyes lance into me for another endless moment before the curtain of darkness lifts. He jerks my skirt up to my waist and latches a finger under the waistband of my panties. The sharp rip of fabric rings out over our haggard breaths.

"Damn, D, you could've just told me to take them off. This is my lucky thong." From this day forward.

The corner of his lip twitches, but he doesn't reveal that elusive smile. Instead, his arms come around my torso and for a second, I'm completely weightless. A squeal bursts free as he tosses me over his shoulder.

"Oh, shit," I squeak.

He smacks me on the bare ass, the crack echoing across the quiet room. "You've got a dirty little mouth, sweetheart."

"You have no idea." I press my lips together the moment the words are out. Damn, those champagne bubbles went straight to my head. I sound like a total slut. *Stop it, Rose.* Even if this is just a one-night stand, I'm going to have to see this man a lot in the next few months. I'm Stella's maid of honor and he's Luca's best man, obvi. I cannot let this get awkward.

Dante drops me onto the bed face down. "So you like it dirty? You want me to smack your ass like a naughty whore?" He climbs on top of me, his erection pressing against my ass through his boxers, and I cant my head back to steal a look at him.

"Maybe…" I cock a mischievous brow. There's a reason I always end up with fucked-up men. Which is why I've chosen my profession. If I can't figure out how to fix myself then who can?

He drags his boxers down his powerful thighs, and his cock springs free. Good gawd, he's huge. A shiver of excitement races up my spine. He slides his thick head between my ass cheeks then across my center, and every nerve ending throbs with anticipation.

"Good, drenched and ready, just like I'd imagined it."

I slant him a teasing grin. "Naughty Dante, you've imagined fucking me?"

A dark laugh tumbles from those pouty lips. "Only every damn night, sweetheart." He grabs a handful of my ass and kneads the sensitive skin. "Now spread your legs wide for me like a good girl." He runs his hand up the inside of my thigh, and I clench in anticipation. His finger dips inside me, and I roll my hips for him, so my clit brushes his palm. "You feel so good," he groans as he curls his finger inside me. "That sweet pussy is just begging for my cock."

"Umhmm…" My head tips back, resting on his shoulder as he finger fucks me until my knees start to tremble.

With his free hand he jerks my mouth to his, claiming it in rhythm with each thrust of his finger. My hips buck against his hand, desperate for the friction. Fuck, I'm close, so close already. I want that cock inside me.

I reach around and wrap my fingers around his erection. A bead of moisture trickles into my palm as I slide up and down his silky shaft. He pumps his hips, and a swirl of pleasure races through me. It's stupid, but Dante has always seemed so unattainable. All the women I've met hanging from his arm are not only gorgeous, but successful and wealthy beyond my wildest dreams. I guess you can never take the awkward little fat girl out of the woman. Sex is my weapon, one I use frequently and with little abandon, my own personal revenge against all the jerks in high school who rejected me.

It gave me the illusion of control after….

Burying the dismal thoughts to the far fucked-up corners of my psyche, I focus on the sheer pleasure raging through my lower half. "I'm ready," I rasp out.

He plunges a second finger inside me, and I cry out. "Not yet. I want you to come on my cock, but you have to be ready to take all of me in."

Oh gawd, I'm ready.

I rub my clit against his palm like a freaking dog in heat. I need this so badly from him, and I don't even know why. There's something about Dante, the power he represents, the savage darkness buried just under the gorgeous surface. He slips his fingers out, and I let out a frustrated squeal.

"Sorry." He chuckles. "Gotta get a condom." He reaches over me to his bedside table and fumbles through the drawer. "We don't need any little Dantes running around Manhattan."

"No, definitely not." My chest is heaving, raging heat coursing through my center. "Hurry up."

"Dirty and demanding." He smirks. "Who would've thought?"

"Oh, D, you have no idea."

Dante rips through the little silver package with his teeth, a snarl curling his lips. I watch expectantly as he rolls the condom over his impressive length. My breath catches as I imagine him filling me.

A sharp ding has my racing heart catapulting up my throat.

"Shit," Dante mutters, and the condom slips to the floor. He darts across the room to his discarded slacks and rummages through the pocket.

"Are you serious right now?" I snap.

"Sorry, this is important." He doesn't even look up at me as he scans the text message.

What a dick.

He stares at the screen, an unreadable expression carved into his strong jaw. The tendon flutters beneath the dark layer of scruff, and he squeezes his eyes closed. As if he's ultimately made up his mind about something, he releases a frustrated breath. His gaze finally lifts to mine. "Sorry, sweetheart, I have to go."

"You're joking?"

He shakes his head. "Wish I was. You know what they say, business before pleasure." He spears his legs through his pants, foregoing his underwear all together and buttons up the top of his shirt. "Another time, *Rosa*."

Gawd, I hate how sexy my name sounds on his lips. *And in Italian*! My fiery insides just liquified into a puddle of lust. He tosses me a wink as he buckles his belt, but with every second that passes with me kneeling on his bed and my skirt hiked up my waist, the lust morphs to anger. No, I wouldn't let this guy just walk out on me. Not like all the others….

"This is your only chance." The words pop out before I can stop them.

His dark brows furrow, and he meets my glare. "Excuse me?"

"This was a one-time deal, Dante." I plant my hands on my hips and steel my spine. "Stella has sworn me off you for good reason, I'm sure. If this doesn't happen tonight, it doesn't happen at all."

A thick vein in his forehead pulses as he regards me. His eyes darken, nostrils flared. For a second, a whisper of fear snaps my spine straighter. The Kings and the ruthless brothers who rule Manhattan are notorious, but I've never seen this dark side of them, of Dante.

He closes the space between us in two long strides. With me kneeling on the bed, he's half a body taller than me. And scary as fuck when he stares me down. "Are you threatening me, sweetheart?"

I swallow hard. "No." I pause and nibble on my swollen lower lip. "It's a promise."

His eyes narrow, darkness churning within those pitch orbs. "It's probably for the best then," he finally whispers. "I would've ruined you for any other man."

CHAPTER 4
BETRAYAL

Dante

Cazzo. It takes every last ounce of willpower to march out of my bedroom with Rose glaring up at me, half-naked on my bed. My dick is so hard it hurts. I'd imagined sinking into the sweet pussy of hers at least a hundred times since I met her all those months ago at the Met Gala. I never thought it would happen either. Stella must not have let her in on our murky past. I squeeze my eyes shut, chasing away the dark images of what happened that day. I never would've done it. I'm an asshole, but I would never force myself on a woman, no matter how much I wanted her out of Luca's life. I'd only been trying to scare the truth out of Stella, because I was certain she was using my brother.

Still, I fucked up big time, and I didn't think I'd ever be able to make it up to Stella.

But of course, my damned little brother had to ruin my one shot with Rose.

It probably is for the best though. Relationships aren't my thing and having to see Rose on the regular may have proven awkward in the long run. She doesn't strike me as the clingy type of girl, but you never can tell.

I run my hand through my dark curls, and her musky scent reaches my nostrils. Her natural perfume still coats my fingers. Fuck. Shaking my head out, I toss the lusty thoughts to the furthest corners of my mind. No pussy, no matter how good, is worth my brother's life. I must focus.

I march down the corridor and find Aldo pacing at the foot of the foyer. Behind him the singer belts out the last song. The party is winding down and in a second, I would've missed my chance.

"Where the hell were you, boss?" Aldo grumbles.

"None of your damned business. Where's Luca?"

"He and Stella are with Tony in the garage. You better hurry up. Luca's no fool."

"Thanks, *stronzo*, like I don't know my own brother." I shoot past Aldo and sneak out into the hall before any of the guests notice. Because my absence would be easy to explain, but not Luca's … I am merely a shadow; he's the king.

Aldo slips into the elevator behind me, and we remain in a tense silence for the entire descent. My heart riots in my chest, the manic beats more than enough to contend with. Guilt entwines with years of anger and resentment. This is it.

The elevator doors slide open, and Luca and Stella stand beside my brother's newest toy, a tomato red Lamborghini. My future sister-in-law's hair is wild, her cheeks flushed. Yup, my *fratellino* fucked her good. A swirl of irritation writhes low in my gut. That could've been Rose if we hadn't been interrupted. But this couldn't wait, not with the million-dollar price tags on their heads.

Tony stands beside Luca, a face of pure guilt. How the guy made it so far as my brother's righthand man baffles me. The guy's got no poker face.

"What's the hold up?" Luca asks. His eyes are bright and clear, the permanent scowl he used to wear erased by the woman on his arm. Isn't love fucking grand?

Half a dozen of my men emerge from the shadows, and my heart kicks up a beat.

Luca's gaze darts to mine as his arm instinctively tugs Stella closer. "What's going on, Dante?"

"You're going on an extended vacation, *fratellino*."

"What the fuck are you talking about?"

I glance at my watch, and a hint of anxiety unfurls. What if the drugs don't take hold in time? What if he tries something?

Right on cue, Stella stumbles back against the sleek sports car.

Luca holds her tight against his body before his eyes sear into me, a murderous glare stealing the air from my lungs. "What did you do?" he grits out. He blinks quickly and wobbles.

Tony is by his side in an instant. "I'm sorry, *capo*."

Luca shoves him off, the look of betrayal so sharp, his righthand man staggers back a step. "Whatever the hell you're doing, Dante, stop." He pulls Stella closer, running his hand up and down her trembling arm. "It's okay, *amore*."

"I can't, Luca. I made a promise to Papà a long time ago, and I intend to keep it."

"By doing what?" he shouts. He leans against the car, the sedative I had slipped into his drink finally taking hold.

"Keeping you safe," I bark.

"By murdering me and my fiancée?"

Surprise hits me like a lightning strike, illuminating the depths of my brother's mistrust. "*Cazzo*, Luca, do you really think I would do that?"

"I don't really know what you're capable of."

Those words spear right through my heart, nearly piercing my soul. I screwed up big time with Stella, and I may have been envious of my brother, but to hurt my own blood? "I would never…"

"You're going to steal my throne then?"

"Yes! If that's what it takes." I grit my teeth and try to shove down the rage. "I swear I'm only doing this for you, *fratellino*. Have I been jealous of you for the majority of our lives? Fuck, yes. But this isn't about that. You're about to be married." I hazard a glance at Stella. I've given her every reason to hate me, but in this moment, I don't see the loathing I expect. It spurs me on, inflating air into my sagging lungs. I knew he'd hate me for this, but he would just have to get over it. "You both have bounties on your heads. Manhattan isn't safe for either of you. I know you, Luca. You'd never run, so I'm doing it for you. Take a few months off, enjoy your engagement. Fuck your fiancée in peace and quiet before reality rolls in. I'll take care of the Red Dragons and when you come back, I promise your throne will be waiting."

"*Sei un pezzo di merda*, Dante." Yeah, maybe I am a piece of shit, but the hint of a smile curls my brother's lip, and for a blessed instant, I'm relieved. He'll forgive me for this, just like he's forgiven me for all my sins. "You didn't have to drug us, you *imbecile*."

"Um, yeah, he probably did." Stella grins at her fiancé and wraps her slender arm around his waist. Somehow, they keep each other upright. "No way you'd be going this easily if it wasn't for the sedatives."

A loopy smile parts my brother's lips. "Perhaps."

I take a wary step closer, still not certain my brother won't pull out a gun and shoot me in the face for betraying him. "Now let Tony take you to the car before you pass out, and we have to carry your heavy asses."

"Where are you sending us?" Stella asks.

I glance around the garage filled with my men. I've known most of these guys for years, but I didn't trust anyone with my brother's life. "You'll find out when you get there. Just do me a favor and stay put, okay?"

"It better be nice," Luca mutters.

"Only the best for the king." I throw my brother a smirk. "Oh, and Ma will be meeting up with you shortly. She was much easier to convince."

"Mamma knew about this?"

"More or less."

"She didn't know you were forcing us."

I nod, my gaze chasing to the floor. I'm not sure if it's the drugs or something else, but the hard set of Luca's jaw softens. I hate it when he looks at me like that. Like maybe I'm not only the heartless monster everyone assumes I am.

He stumbles closer and wraps his arm around my back. He sways against me, but somehow remains standing. As I hug Luca, I glance at Stella over his shoulder. "Take care of my little brother."

"Till death do us part." She rewards me with a smile I know I don't deserve after the shit I put her through. "And you keep an eye on Rose for me, okay?"

"Rose?" I choke out.

"Yeah, you know, my best friend who has terrible taste in men?"

Ah, yes, that one. True assessment. "Umhmm," I mutter as Luca steps back to lean against the car again.

Stella sinks into his embrace. "If that crazy guy gives her more trouble, will you help her out?"

I nod slowly. "Sure, Stella, I'll watch out for her."

"Thanks."

He presses a kiss to his *amore*'s lips, and the vast chasm in my chest deepens. I look away, but my brother's voice forces my gaze back up. "Dante, you know what King Industries means to me." His unfocused eyes dance across my face.

"I do."

He presses his lips together, dark brows furrowing. "I know it'll be in good hands."

I swallow hard, unexpected emotion thickening my throat. I expected cursing, a fight, endless vows of retribution, but this—I never expected this.

"Prove to everyone how much you deserve your birthright,

fratello." Luca flashes me a smile, a genuine one he typically only reserves for Stella. "And don't die."

A rueful chuckle slides out. "Same to you."

Tony leads Luca and Stella to a black Town Car parked behind the Lambo. *Maybe I'll take that bad boy for a spin while he's gone.* I toss aside the errant thought as my gaze trails after them for a long moment. Whispers and quiet laughter pass between the pair. Again, an odd sensation tightens my chest.

Feng was right; love has made my brother soft.

And now it is my turn to return the Kings to their glory.

CHAPTER 5
BE GOOD

R*ose*

Gawd, I hate Mondays.

My nose twitches, and I spin my head away from the armpit of a man crammed beside me on the subway. *Bleh*. It's Christmas break, but Dr. Winchester insists we remain open for the few days leading up to the holidays. Apparently, it's the time of the year when our patients need us the most. Figures a happy little fat man in a red suit bringing presents to kids would coincide with depression and psychotic breaks being at their all-time peaks. Which means I'm stuck underground heading to the Upper East Side when I should be enjoying my well-deserved time-off from classes.

Who am I kidding? I don't have time for a break, even from a barely paid internship. At least the occasional twenties Dr. Winchester slips me for coffee helps. Unlike my bestie with an uber-rich fiancé, I have to pay my way through NYU.

My thoughts flicker back to Friday night and those devilish

fingers dancing across my center. Fucking Dante. I still can't believe that asshole just walked out on me like that. I was so close.... And as much as I hated to admit it, a part of me knew he was right. If we'd screwed, he would have ruined me for any other man.

There was something about him that had my insides in a tangle of chaos.

Maybe I read something hidden in his eyes, something beyond that smart mouth and wicked tongue that I was desperately familiar with.

The subway grinds to a halt, and I barely get my hand around the metal pole fast enough. My nose is about an inch away from Mr. I Need Better Deodorant before I stop the forward momentum of my body.

The doors glide open, and I race out of there, holding my breath until I reach the light of the East 79th Street exit. A blast of icy air cools my face and I exhale, blowing out the stale oxygen of the underground and drawing in the winter chill.

I head up the block toward Dr. Winchester's practice, the elegant townhouses and pre-war apartment buildings lining the impeccably maintained sidewalks. The tree-lined avenues provide shade and a sense of tranquility, contrasting with the bustling city I left just blocks away. The sharp sound of Taylor Swift's latest song blasts from my phone. Scanning the screen, I let out a happy squeal. Stella. Finally! "Where have you been, girl?"

"Well, actually, Luca surprised me with a last-minute trip."

"Where?" I squeak.

"Um, this is going to sound really weird, but I can't tell you."

I freeze in my tracks and stare at the phone like it could somehow deliver my glare directly to my best friend. "Excuse me?"

She sighs, her tone suddenly weary and exhausted. "It's about Luca's business. It's probably for the best you don't know the specifics. No one knows where we are, not even Dante."

"Shiiit."

"Yeah."

"How long are you going to be gone for?"

"I don't know yet, but I'll keep you posted." She releases another frustrated breath. "I mean it's not that awful here in all honesty. I just don't like leaving you by yourself with that guy still screwing with you."

"Please, don't worry about me. Dr. Mark is old news. Honestly, he started backing off ever since that night Dante scared the shit out of him over the phone." An unexpected laugh bubbles out. *No, you do not find the dickhead amusing. He walked out on you with your panties around your ankles, remember? Awesome, now I'm talking to myself.*

"Good." Stella's voice drags me back to the present. "Promise me you'll go to Dante if he pops up again."

"I promise," I groan.

"And I'm sorry I didn't get to say goodbye to you the other night. Where'd you run off to anyway?"

Heat surges down below my bellybutton as Dante's hot mouth ghosts over mine. Then a wave of guilt splashes over the brewing lusty tornado. I'd also promised my friend to stay far away from her fiancé's brother months ago. *Bad, Rose!*

"Rose?"

"Huh? Oh right, I don't know how we missed each other. I was belting it out with the singer all night."

Stella laughs, and I try to focus on the fact that for the first time since I met her, she's actually happy. Dante may be a dick, but Luca treats her like she's bathed in gold and propped atop a marble pedestal. That's the kind of guy I need to put a ring on my finger.

Then again, I'm not exactly the marrying type. The idea of being tied down to one man for the rest of my life is terrifying, and kids are completely horrifying. Guess I'll stick with my hot assholes for now. And buy my own rings. As soon as I can afford one.

Crap, that reminds me. I need to find a paying part-time job ASAP.

"Rose, are you listening to me?"

I still my rambling thoughts and focus on my friend. "Yeah, sorry, I'm just walking up to Dr. Winchester's office. Can I call you later?"

"Sure, but not too late. I'm like six hours ahead of you." She pauses and lets out a curse. "Don't try to calculate where I am please."

"I won't, even though now it's all I want to do."

"You just can't resist the forbidden fruit, can you?"

"Damn right, girl." I blow her a kiss into the phone. "Ciao, *bella*. Enjoy your fiancé and remember, no Italian babies! You must at least walk down the aisle with that gorgeous and insanely expensive white gown Luca's going to buy you before you start popping out kids."

She laughs again. "Right, love you, Rose. Be good."

"Same to you, Stel. Byeee!" I slip my phone into my jacket pocket and whip the front door of Dr. Winchester's practice open. She scored a ground level office which means her patients don't have to trudge through the main entrance of the building. Privacy is key. Some of her clients are in the upper echelons of Manhattan's elite: doctors, lawyers, even senators.

I know this because I'd screwed around with quite a few before Dr. Mark, the stalker. Now, I've sworn off all patients, and I intend to stick with it.

"Morning, Rose." The receptionist offers me a smile as I shrug out of my hot pink puffer jacket.

"Hey, Mary." I hang it up and sneak by the one patient already sitting in the waiting room. Then I slip behind the door into the back and start chatting with the girl. Dr. Winchester hasn't arrived yet. It's my job to onboard the new patient, scan over the forms and present my initial observations. It's all part of my fabulous internship experience. As much as I complain, I know I lucked out with the doc. She's pretty chill and lets me get away with a lot.

"Here's her paperwork." Mary ticks her head toward the thick, double-paned frosted glass window, and I glance out into the waiting room at the new patient. I open it a crack and study the young woman scrolling through her phone. Most of our patients are older, but this girl looks about my age, mid-twenties at most.

Who am I to be judgey? I've been in therapy for years.

I glance at the name in the file and open the window all the way. "Come on in, Ms. Jordan, we can get started."

The young woman pushes back the curtain of auburn locks and bright green eyes find mine. "Great, thanks."

I lead her down the quiet hallway to the room Dr. Winchester has set up to look like a cozy sitting room. There's a fireplace, a worn leather couch and a steady flow of lavender and chamomile pumped into the space for maximum relaxation.

"You're awfully young to be a psychologist, aren't you?" The woman glances up at me thoughtfully.

"Oh, I'm not Dr. Winchester." I give her a reassuring smile and adjust the pink scrubs I've formally made my uniform. "My name is Rose Holloway. I'm interning with the doc for the semester."

"Oh!" She claps her hand over her mouth.

"But don't worry, all that doctor-patient confidentiality stuff applies to me too."

"Okay, great because oh my goodness, I was about a second away from spilling all my deepest, darkest secrets." A nervous laugh bubbles out.

"Don't worry, Ms. Jordan, you're in good hands."

The day flies by in a blur, and the best part is that I got a lead for a job that I'm actually thrilled about. As it turns out, the doc's new patient, Ms. Jordan works for the head of human resources at Palestra, one of the fanciest gyms in Manhattan. A couple years back, I'd taken a few yoga classes to deal with stress, and I'd ended up loving it so much I got certified as an instructor.

A job at Palestra would be everything.

And all I have to do is show up tomorrow for an interview.

A swirl of excitement simmers through my veins as I head for the subway downtown. No happy hour for me tonight. I'll need to prepare for the interview and pretend I haven't been living in sweats and hiding out in my tiny midtown studio since summer ended.

I sink into an empty seat on the subway car, my mind racing with the possibilities. I should run by Lulu Lemon on the way home and buy something cute. Wouldn't I do the same for any job interview? Yes, yes, I would. It's totally worth the extra expense.

Tomorrow will be my lucky day. From the sound of it, the job would pay well, and I'd be surrounded by gorgeous Manhattan socialites. No more mentally unstable losers for me!

I dig through my purse for my wallet and let out a curse as I find the empty credit card slots. Damn it. I'd completely forgotten I'd frozen my only remaining credit card in a block of ice to keep from spending. I stare at my sorry debit card and picture the measly balance. Definitely not enough for a new yoga top and pants.

I hurry off the subway at Grand Central Station and weave through the mass of tourists. I'll just stop by my place, defrost the damned credit card with my blow dryer and run out before the store closes. I'm totally good.

I'm practically sprinting by the time I reach my building on East 51st Street. The pungent scent of curry is thick in the air, and my stomach grumbles as I unlock the entrance door. My little apartment is nestled between an amazing Indian restaurant and a twenty-four-hour laundromat. What else could a single girl need?

I race up the stairs to the third floor because the elevator is always broken and let's be honest, I could use the exercise now that I'll be rocking a skimpy yoga outfit. As I walk down the narrow corridor, a faint odor fills my nostrils. I glance down the hall and spot something outside my door.

What the hell?

I creep closer, a chill snaking up my spine. I draw in a breath as my heart rams against my ribcage, growing more frantic with each step. A black vase filled with wilted yellow roses leans against my door. A white notecard pokes out of the arrangement, sending fear cascading through every inch of my body. *It's just a note. Pick it up and read it.*

The smell of ammonia and rotting garbage reaches my nostrils. I pinch my nose as I bend down and pluck the notecard with trembling fingers. Three words steal the remaining air from my lungs.

Miss me yet?

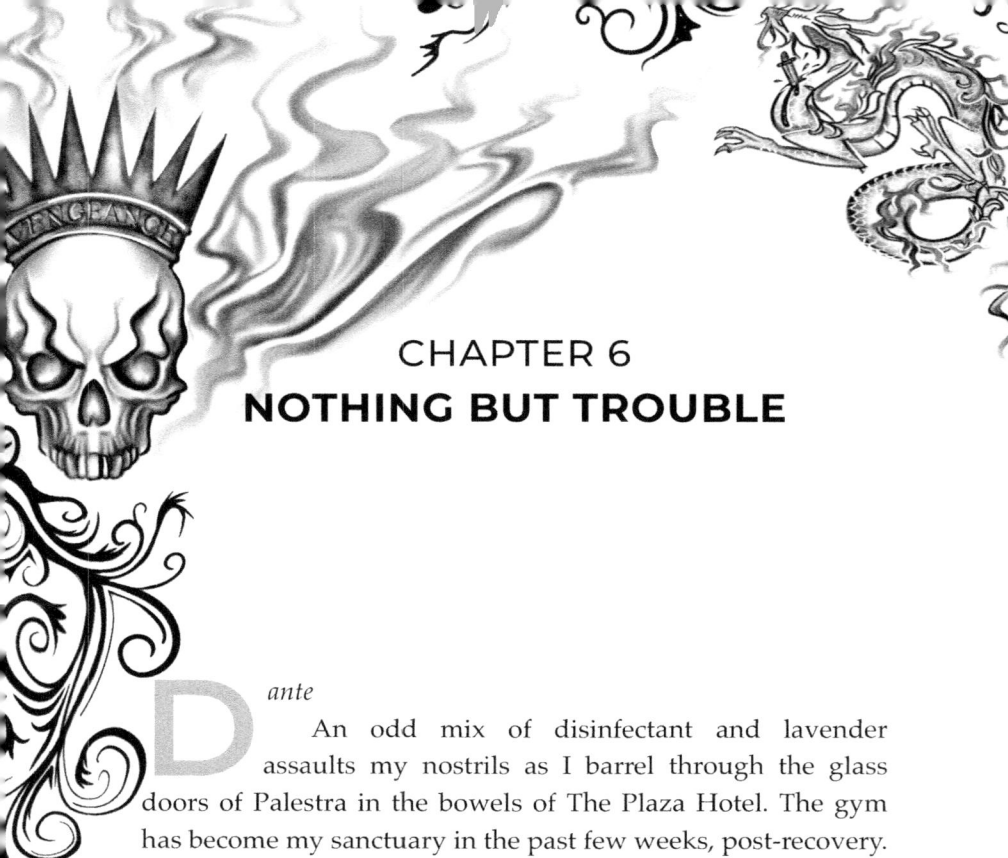

CHAPTER 6
NOTHING BUT TROUBLE

Dante

An odd mix of disinfectant and lavender assaults my nostrils as I barrel through the glass doors of Palestra in the bowels of The Plaza Hotel. The gym has become my sanctuary in the past few weeks, post-recovery. I'd only joined at first to irritate my little brother and find an in with the female socialites of Manhattan, but now, if I didn't get a workout in first thing in the morning I was frustrated as hell all day. It's only been four days since I forced Luca on vacation, and already the stress is getting to me.

How did he manage running King Industries by day and the Kings by night? Maybe I'd underestimated my *fratellino*. The seeds of doubt take hold, the ones sown all those years ago when I was just a teenager. I grit my teeth and keep my head down as I pass the front desk with my duffle bag hitched over my shoulder.

"Excuse me, membership card please?"

I lift my gaze to the brunette in front of the neon Palestra sign, an angry growl ready to erupt. My eyes immediately dart past her, drawn to the familiar blonde standing beside a redhead.

"Rose?"

Her head spins around, and she tucks the clipboard she's holding to her chest. Her lips thin out, and a hint of guilt creeps into my chest. Walking out on her the other night had been unexpectedly difficult. It had to be because I hadn't gotten laid in a while, and I was hard up. Yes, had to be that.

Still, I can't look away from her, or that sexy cropped top, exposing a milky white shoulder and perfectly toned abs. My gaze drifts lower to the tight yoga pants, and my thoughts whirl back to that night. To those legs wrapped around my waist, that hot pussy rubbing against my cock. I squeeze my eyes shut, banishing the heated memories. *Not the time, coglione.*

The redhead nudges her in the ribs. "Take your time filling out the questionnaire, and I'll be back for you in a few." She ticks her head at the seating area in front of the entrance.

"Right, thanks, Ms. Jordan."

"Please, call me Maisy. Ms. Jordan is my mother, and God help me if I ever turn out like her!"

Rose nods and walks right past me before settling onto the black leather chair.

The cute brunette behind the counter watches the exchange, and I realize I still haven't shown her my damned membership card. I yank it out of the pocket of my duffle bag and flash it an inch from her nose.

"Oh, Mr. Valentino, I'm so sorry I didn't recognize you." Her cheeks flush. She probably thinks I'm Luca. Papà's blood runs strong; our dark hair, Roman noses, and wide jaws are characteristic of the Valentino men. I debate correcting her, but what's the point of beating a dead horse? Besides, there's something about Rose's complete dismissal that has my temper flaring.

Bypassing the girl, I slip into the seat beside Rose and drop my workout bag on the floor at my feet. "You're not even going to say hi?" I whisper-hiss.

"Oh, sorry, D, I didn't see you there." She doesn't even look up.

"Rosa..." I growl.

Her eyes lift to mine, and I know my gut is right. There's something wrong with her. Besides the annoyance with me, the typical light in her lively green eyes has dimmed. "What?" she hisses.

"Are you all right?"

"Yes." Her lower lip quivers ever so slightly. "Why wouldn't I be?"

"You just don't seem like your usual bubbly self." I shoot her a smirk, but not even the corners of her lip twitch.

"I'm here for an interview, Dante. I can't fuck this up. I need the job."

I look up and scan the entrance foyer for the redhead in the skirt suit. The Valentino name goes far in Manhattan, even when it's spoken from my lips. King Industries has funded and donated to nearly every important enterprise in the city. Including Palestra's holding company. "Is that redhead the girl in charge? I can put in a good word if you want."

She stares up at me incredulously. "It's really not necessary. And no, that's Maisy, she's the one that got me the interview, but she's just the HR assistant."

"Then I'll find the head of Human Resources." I attempt to stand, but Rose's hand closes around my tattooed forearm.

"I don't need your help, D."

"*Dio*, Rosa, just let me do something—"

"To make up for walking out on me the other night?" she grits out. "And don't call me *Rosa*. My name is Rose."

My eyes chase to the floor, and I release a frustrated breath. "I already told you I was doing you a favor. Just leave it at that. Now, I promised Stella I'd look out for you while she and Luca are gone, and the last thing I need to do is fuck that up. My future sister-in-law has more than enough reasons to hate me."

"Well, she shouldn't have asked you to do that. I don't need a babysitter." She jerks the pen from beneath the metal clip and starts to scribble on the questionnaire.

I slide my hand into her purse and grab her phone.

"What are you doing?" she barks, and the girl at the desk glances over before clearing her throat.

Before Rose can steal it back, I input my number and press send. "There, now you have my phone number."

She snatches her cell back and tucks it into her purse. "I'm deleting it as soon as I'm done with this."

I snort on a laugh. Feisty little thing. I sit there for a long minute, but her pen strokes only become more agitated with each second I linger. With an irritated grunt, I finally stand up and grab my duffle bag. "Call me if you need anything."

"Don't hold your breath."

I can't help the wicked chuckle that rumbles my chest. Maybe it wasn't just a good thing for *her* that we didn't screw. I have a feeling that little firecracker and I would've been nothing but trouble.

Tony glances up at me from the chair in the corner of my office at King Industries like a lost puppy. The guy is struggling without my brother to dote on. I should have just sent him away with Luca and Stella, but a part of me was hesitant to lose my brother's righthand man. He knows almost as much as Luca about the illegitimate side of the business and because of my estranged relationship with my *fratellino* I'd fallen behind on the inner workings.

"You want to come with me to the Red Dragon?" I offer.

His dark eyes sparkle as he glances up from his twitchy fingers. "Yeah, sure, *capo*. What's the plan?"

"First of all, don't call me that. Dante is fine. Save that *capo* shit for Luca."

"Right, sorry, *ca*—Dante."

"And the plan is to talk to Jianjun Zhang to see if we can come to a civilized agreement. The leader of the Chinese Triad should be more levelheaded than his nephew. I need those bounties removed from Luca and Stella's heads."

Tony slides to the edge of the chair and clucks his tongue. "I don't know, D. We killed his son only a few months ago. You really think he's going to go for this diplomatic crap?"

I shrug. *Hell, no.* "You know my brother likes to do things the gentlemanly way, so I'll give it a try." Then if things go south, I'll fuck shit up.

"Whatever you say, *ca*—" Tony cuts himself off when I shoot him a narrowed glare.

Two sharp knocks send my heart leaping up my throat. *Cazzo.* Damned PTSD still hasn't quite faded. I'd spent the better half of my twenty-nine years avoiding bullets, nothing like getting battered by half a dozen to fuck with your head.

"Come in," I call out.

Clara, my brother's executive assistant, saunters in with a stack of folders pressed to her chest. I inherited her, just like I did this office with the sweeping views of Central Park. I'd offered to take another office, but Luca had insisted it was all about the optics. If I was to be the interim CEO of King Industries, I had to play the part. My little brother was suited for all the political intrigue and power plays. *You're way out of your league, Dante,* a taunting voice echoes in the dark corners of my mind.

No. For years, I'd taken a backseat in the business. It's my time.

She dumps the pile of folders on my desk and smooths down her silk blouse, then turns her scrutinizing gaze on the untouched mountain beside it.

"What's up?" I finally ask when her stare becomes uncomfortable.

"Dante, I need you to sign all of these documents before you leave the office tonight."

I cock a skeptical brow. There must be hundreds of pages within those folders. "*Veramente?*"

"Yes, really." She huffs out a breath and flips through the first few. "This is the contract for the gambling cruise. This one is the new docks project in the Lower East Side. This one is the blueprint for the new King's tower in the Financial District." Her words blur in the background as she flips through countless files.

"How did Luca find time to do all this shit?"

"Your brother worked hard for everything he has, Dante. He lived in the office for months when he was building this business. If you think you can just come in here and take over without putting in an ounce of effort—"

I lift my hand, cutting her off. "*Basta.*" If this woman wasn't like a second mother to my brother, I would've had her carted out of here. That is the fundamental problem in this arrangement. My power as interim CEO is limited. And maybe that's a good thing. Maybe Luca was right all along, and I wasn't cut out for this white-collar nonsense. Maybe Papà knew it too, and all that bullshit he fed me was just an excuse.

She bites her tongue and looses a frustrated sigh, drawing me from my thoughts. "*Scusi.*"

I wave a nonchalant hand. "It's fine. It's going to take us all a little while to adapt to this new situation."

"How long do you think Luca will have to stay away?"

"Until those Triad fuckers bend to my will." And the sooner the better. I rise and tick my head at Tony. "Come on, let's go to China Town."

Clara trails behind me with an armful of files. "But Dante, you have to sign these."

"I will when I get back." I lengthen my strides and even Tony has to hurry to catch up as I flee the mountain of paperwork.

"Swear it, Dante."

"*Lo giuro,*" I call out over my shoulder.

CHAPTER 7
ROSE VERSION 2.0

R*ose*

"Are you done for the day?" Mary spins away from the computer and leans back in her chair as I scroll through messages on my phone.

"I am with job number one." I slip my cell back into my purse, and an unexpected smile works its way across my mouth. I'm actually really excited about my first day at Palestra. I couldn't believe it when I'd gotten the call from HR yesterday. The whole process had only taken twenty-four hours. That had to have been a record of some sort. "Now I'm off to my second. I'm teaching my first yoga class today."

"Oh, so exciting!" Mary claps her hands. "If I could ever afford a gym like that, I'd totally go support you."

"Thanks, Mary, you're the best." I really lucked out meeting Maisy in the office. Otherwise, there was no way I would've gotten the gig. I swing my purse onto one shoulder and my backpack onto the other. "Wish me luck."

"Good luck," she calls out as I step into the waiting room.

The front door creaks open, and a familiar pair of blue eyes catch mine from across the space. My stomach sinks. Mark.

I dart across the room, weaving around him, and barrel

through the door. My chest is heaving by the time the crisp fall air fills my lungs. A horn blares, and I spin around to a cab racing toward me. Shit! I sprint back onto the sidewalk and clap my hand over my heart. It launches itself at my ribcage, thundering out a rapid beat. Gawd, I just ran into the middle of the street for fuck's sake!

"You okay, Rose?"

That deep, gruff timbre lifts the hair on the back of my neck. I cant my head over my shoulder and nearly graze Mark's nose. I leap forward a step then whirl around. "Dammit, you scared me," I hiss.

"Sorry. You ran out of the office so quickly I thought something might be wrong." A slimy smile curls his mouth.

How did I ever find this guy attractive? Oh right, it was probably the beautiful blue eyes, tussled blonde hair, and the totally in age gap. The M.D. at the end of his name didn't hurt either. My thoughts flicker back to the vase of dead roses. It couldn't be him ... He'd been annoying and slightly stalkerish, but never that creepy.

"Nope, nothing, just in a hurry," I finally force out.

"Where are you going?" His eyes narrow as they slowly scan over my body, inch by inch. His measured scrutiny has nausea creeping up my throat. Thank gawd I hadn't changed into my skimpy yoga outfit yet.

"Class," I blurt.

His light brows slam together, and he drags his hand through his dirty blonde curls. "Rose, why would you lie to me? It's Christmas break." He cracks his knuckles, the snap of bone sending goosebumps spilling across my flesh.

"Yoga class," I amend.

"Oh." His practiced smile returns, and that older man charm I'd found irresistible finds its way back to the surface.

Why hadn't I looked into his file more closely? Narcissistic personality disorder hadn't sounded that bad at the time.

"Anyway, I have to run." I jerk my thumb over my shoulder at the subway entrance up the block.

"You know I love yoga. What studio do you go to?" he calls out as I start to back pedal.

"Sonic Yoga." I blurt out the first name that comes to mind. No way in hell I'm telling this guy about Palestra. He's crazy enough to follow me and rich and well-connected enough to get in.

I spin around and jog up the block. If I waste another minute with this guy, I really will be late.

I'm smiling like a lunatic as a few men approach at the end of class to thank me. Even a few females shoot me their praise. My heart feels so full I'm scared it's going to burst. For years, yoga has been my escape, and to be able to share that with others fills me with a happiness I never thought I'd experience.

A super attractive guy with light hair pulled into a sexy man bun walks up as I dab a towel across my forehead. Beads of sweat glimmer over every inch of me, and Mr. Hot Yoga is making me feel each and every one.

"Hey," he whispers. "Great class."

"Thanks. I was so nervous." An embarrassing giggle spills out.

"You shouldn't be. You were amazing." He smiles, his parted lips revealing perfect white teeth. "I was wondering if you could teach a private lesson at my penthouse?"

Heat races up my neck and blossoms across my cheeks. Hell, yes. *Wait.* My thoughts fly back to Mark and the mess that turned into. What does Dr. Winchester always say about the definition of insanity? Oh right, repeating the same actions over and over again and expecting different results.

Steeling my resolve, I force the words out of my mouth. "I'm sorry, but it's against Palestra policy. I'd be happy to schedule a private lesson here on property though." It is also against Palestra policy to have relationships with clients, but according to Maisy it happens on the down low all the time.

I resolve to not be that employee this time. No matter how tempting.

"Sounds good. I'll schedule it with the front desk." Mr. Hot Yoga offers me a goodbye, and I give myself an internal high five for staying strong. Once the studio has emptied out, I grab my mat and water bottle and saunter into the hallway.

The workout floor is filled with half-naked men pumping iron, and damn, I could get used to this view. I bring my water bottle to my lips and slurp down a big mouthful of cool water. If I stand here any longer, I'm going to need a cold shower.

Across the room, a broad tattooed back catches my eye. Swirling black ink paints the male's flesh, the intricate patterns too difficult to make out from this distance, but damn, it's hot. The guy sits on a bench curling massive weights, more ink spiraling around his thick arms. Dark wavy hair falls in wild tumbles and sweat glistens across muscled shoulders.

Hot damn.

A tall, blonde with a cute bob creeps into the periphery of my vision, and I hiss out a curse. Caroline. Which means … *No*! I inch closer as she approaches the tattooed god sprawled on the bench.

He turns toward her, revealing a familiar profile. That Roman nose, sculpted cheekbones, scruffy jaw. Dammit. Dante. Why did I have to land a job in the one place I'd be forced to see that asshole every day?

Her perfectly manicured hand runs over his shoulder, and a bout of jealousy carves at my insides. First Luca and now Dante. Can't that damned heiress find another set of hot Italian brothers to fondle?

I'm filled with the most ridiculous urge to stomp over there and physically remove her hand from his body. Which is completely insane. Sure, Dante is hot as sin, but so is half the population of this gym. Not only had he walked out on me mid-hook up, but I'd also promised Stella I'd stay away from him.

Dante Valentino is nothing but trouble.

And I need to work on Rose Holloway version 2.0. The new Rose would be responsible, mindful, and self-aware and would certainly not date toxic men.

As if Dante hears his calling card, his dark gaze pivots toward me. Caroline's hand curls around his jaw, pulling for his attention, but his eyes remain pinned to mine. That piercing stare has heat pooling between my legs, and my heart kicking at my ribs. He runs his tongue across his bottom lip, and memories of that wicked thing in my mouth, along the column of my throat and across my collarbone spring to the forefront of my mind. I shiver at the fiery images.

An agonizing moment later, I tear my eyes away from his and force my feet to move toward the locker room. I really need a cold shower now.

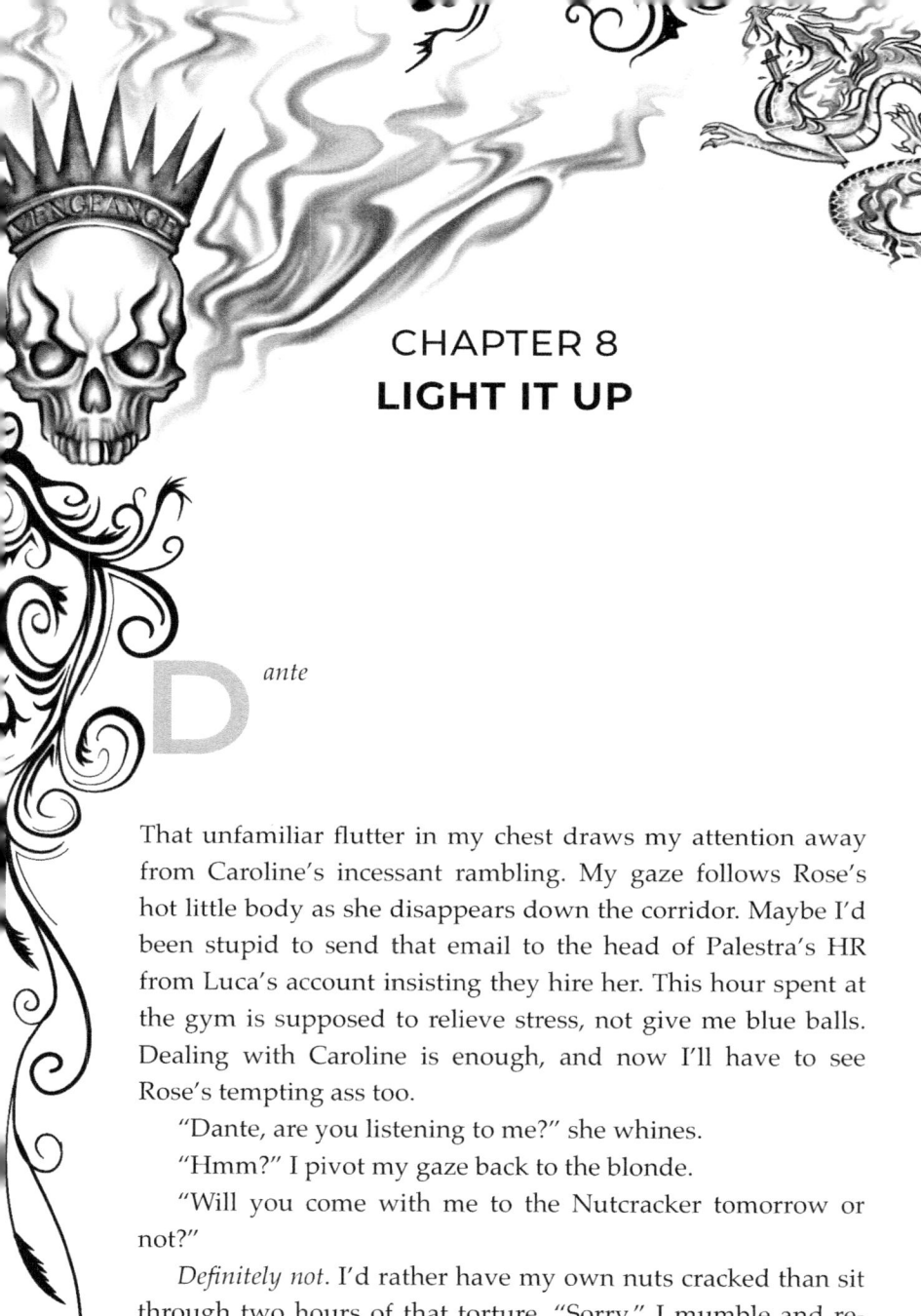

CHAPTER 8
LIGHT IT UP

D*ante*

That unfamiliar flutter in my chest draws my attention away from Caroline's incessant rambling. My gaze follows Rose's hot little body as she disappears down the corridor. Maybe I'd been stupid to send that email to the head of Palestra's HR from Luca's account insisting they hire her. This hour spent at the gym is supposed to relieve stress, not give me blue balls. Dealing with Caroline is enough, and now I'll have to see Rose's tempting ass too.

"Dante, are you listening to me?" she whines.

"Hmm?" I pivot my gaze back to the blonde.

"Will you come with me to the Nutcracker tomorrow or not?"

Definitely not. I'd rather have my own nuts cracked than sit through two hours of that torture. "Sorry," I mumble and re-rack the dumbbells. "I've got a work thing that night."

"What work thing?"

I heave out a breath and channel my brother's impeccable bedside manner. "Caroline, Luca's on an extended vacation with his fiancée so I'm taking the helm at King Industries. I don't know that I'll have much time for outings in the near future."

"Does that mean you're breaking up with me?" Her big eyes widen.

I wasn't aware we were officially dating. I decide to keep that little tidbit to myself. The last thing I need is Caroline Dumphries making a scene in front of the who's who of Manhattan. "Of course not, darling," I grit out. The term of endearment tastes bitter on my tongue. I picked it up from her, but I still couldn't quite get used to it. "I'll call you when things settle down."

She pushes her lower lip into a pout, and I remember a time when that little expression would make me go immediately hard. But right now? *Niente*.

I rise from the bench, drag a towel over my face and press a quick kiss to her cheek. "We'll talk soon."

"Dante, come on, baby...," she whines. Her arms lace across her chest, forcing the swell of her breasts to spill over the top of her sports bra. Again, something that should've driven me mad. Instead, only irritation flares because every minute longer I spend with her is another one I'm delaying my confrontation with Jianjun. The leader of the Chinese Triad was mysteriously absent on my last visit. Today, I'll be sure to pop in without warning. It's time to settle this business with the old man and the bounties on my brother and future sister-in-law's heads for good.

Warm breath tickles the shell of my ear, snapping me from my thoughts. "Maybe I can come over later tonight and help you work out some of that stress." Caroline's fingers dig into my shoulder, and she massages away the knot. She leans closer and slides her hand between our bodies. Her slender fingers close around my dick.

Cazzo. There are three men working out within mere feet from us.

"Caroline…," I growl. Her father would not be pleased if word of this inappropriate behavior reaches his ears. And my brother would have my ass if Mr. Dumphries reneged on the building contract with King Industries. It would cost the company billions. "Maybe," I mutter and casually remove her hand from my cock. "But I have to go now. I'll call you later tonight if I get home at a decent hour."

"It doesn't have to be decent, Mr. Valentino." She shoots me a wink, and I finally wriggle free of her hold.

Gritting my teeth, I force a smile before spinning away and practically sprinting out of the weight room. If I don't get out of here now, she'll follow me into the men's locker area. It wouldn't be the first time. I'd fucked her in the men's shower just a few weeks ago, but somehow things had changed in the short time since I'd sent Luca away.

Or maybe it was something else….

"Rose!" Her name bursts from my lips as she rounds the corner in nothing but a towel. I soak her in, a smattering of freckles on her shoulder, her cheeks rosy and those full lips. Water drips from her long hair, disappearing between her perky breasts.

That insatiable hunger ignites, and I clench my teeth to keep from saying something completely inappropriate.

"Oh, hey, D." She offers a tight smile. "I think I got a little turned around in this maze. Any idea where the staff changing room is? I'm sure you've had an illicit romp or two with one of the other instructors."

My brows slam together as I regard her. She's not wrong, but shit, is that what everyone thinks of me?

"Word gets around." She arches a challenging brow.

I refuse to rise to the baiting, and instead, draw in a steadying breath. "So you got the job?" I ask innocently.

"Yup." She wraps the towel tighter under her arms, and I

find myself praying for it to fall. Images of our heated hook-up rise to the surface. I'd never gotten to see her fully bare form in the rush, and my imagination painted a very vivid picture of what lay beneath that towel. "So are you going to keep eye-fucking me, or are you going to show me where the staff area is?" She smiles sweetly baring her teeth.

Dio, this woman would be my undoing. I'd never met a woman I couldn't have. That must be what is driving me crazy. Would she seriously stick to her vow?

Clearing my throat, I point to the corridor on the right. "It's that way. Last door on the left."

"Thank you." She saunters past me, the outline of her bubbly, perfect ass swaying beneath the white towel.

"You know," I call out. "I've been thinking about taking up yoga."

She turns her head over her shoulder and throws me a wicked grin. "I'd twist you into a pretzel, Dante Valentino."

God, I hope so.

Turning toward the locker room, I catch a glimpse of myself in the mirror. A stupid smile stretches across my face. *Dio*, what is wrong with me?

Tony stands outside of *Nonna Maria*'s scarfing down a cannolo, like he thinks I'm not going to see the powdered sugar all over his lips. I eat up the last few yards down the block as he wipes his mouth with a napkin.

"Really, Tony?"

"What? I was hungry, and you were late."

I eye my gold wristwatch. Fuck, he's right. That little interaction with Rose had my head spinning and my dick so hard I'd had to let off some steam in the shower. It was her face I'd seen, her name that had exploded from my lips as I came in my hand.

I needed to fuck her and get her out of my head, or I'd be useless.

I unleash a frustrated breath and turn to Tony. "Well, if you're done with your snack, we've got some Red Dragon assholes to put in their place."

"Ready when you are, *cap*—Dante." Tony hides a sheepish smile beneath the napkin before tossing it in the trash. Then he moves into step beside me, and we march the remaining two blocks to the Red Dragon in silence.

The scent of fried dumplings and sweet and sour sauce assault the air as we cross into China Town. Little Italy has been invaded by the Triad fuckers, and it's time someone taught them a lesson. My little brother is too diplomatic, too politically inclined. What we need is to break bones and shoot some shit up. That's the language these *bastardi* understand.

The cool metal of my gun presses against my torso as I take the steps up to the restaurant that serves as a front for the Chinese Triad. Jianjun, as the eldest, is the leader of the organization that encompasses the entire island of Manhattan and parts of the Bronx and Brooklyn. His Red Dragons prowl lower Manhattan, while Qian Guo and the Four Seas take the Upper East and West Sides, and Hao Wei's gang covers the outer boroughs.

Jianjun is the head of the snake and if I succeed in cutting it off, the others *will* fall. Then they'll all be at my mercy, and the Kings will once again reign supreme.

Tony reaches for his revolver, his finger on the trigger as I whip the door open. A hailstorm of bullets pierces the air as we storm in. I squeeze off an entire round, shooting up the empty dining room. The hostess at the entrance screams and ducks behind the podium.

"Don't even think about it, honey." I drop to the ground beside the woman reaching for the phone and train my gun at her head. "I don't think your boss would like it if we got the cops involved. This is between him and me."

Straightening, I turn to Tony. "Light it up, *amico*."

Gunshots reverberate in the air, ricocheting across the golden lanterns hung from the ceiling, ripping holes through the pink tablecloths and piercing the oversized fish tank in the back of the space.

A shit-eating grin curls my lips. It's about time this *figlio di puttana* understands what happens when you mess with the Kings.

"What the devil is going on out here?" Jianjun appears from the back of the restaurant with half a dozen guards wearing red from head to toe surrounding him.

"Time for retribution, old man."

CHAPTER 9
NOT AGAIN

R*ose*

I'm still smiling from the high of teaching my first yoga class as I ride the subway back home, not to mention imagining the paycheck I'll get in two weeks. Even part time, the pay is going to be more than what I make with Dr. Winchester. If I can just hold down this job, my internship, and classes in the spring, I'll be golden.

The subway grinds to a halt and I jump up, throw my backpack on my shoulder and race through the sliding doors. I'm starved after that workout. And to celebrate, I'm going to defrost my credit card and hit up Tandoori Express right below my apartment. I pull out my phone as I resurface in midtown and search the delivery app. A text message catches my eye, and I click on the blue bubble.

Maisy: *How was your first day?*

Smiling, I type up a response.

Me: *It was fantastic! Thank you so much for getting me the job.*

Maisy: *I didn't do anything. It was all you. Want to celebrate with a drink?*

Me: *Hell, yes. I'm almost home so I'll run in and get changed, then we can meet up?*

Maisy: *Perfect, I'll text you the details in a sec.*

Closing out the delivery app, I race up the steps to my apartment. Happy hour is way better than Indian takeout. With Stella gone, I missed having a girlfriend. Maisy seems perfect. From the little I'd discovered about her, she was twenty-three and recently divorced. Apparently, she'd married a total dickhead when she was only nineteen.

And since I am now Rose 2.0, I even checked with Dr. Winchester to make sure it was okay for me to hang out with a patient. She'd agreed as long as I no longer consulted on her case. Luckily, the doc had more than enough patients for me to help out with.

By the time I reach the third floor, I get another text from Maisy confirming the trendy spot in the West Village, and now I'm super excited. This day is getting better and better by the minute. If it wasn't for that awkward encounter with Dante at Palestra, it was really quite perf—

My happy thoughts grind to a halt when I reach the door to my apartment. The *open* door. The wood is splintered, and the lock is all scratched up, like someone tried really hard to jimmy it before resorting to a crowbar and forcing it.

I peer through the opening, and my heart smashes against my ribs. My chest feels too tight, like my lungs have suddenly tripled in size. I suck in a haggard breath and force my feet forward. "I've got a gun, and I'm not afraid to use it," I shout through the crack. I freeze, listening for any sign of the intruder. Every nerve ending is on edge as I wait an endless moment.

Nothing.

Releasing a breath, I fumble for my phone and dial 911. I pace the quiet hallway as I wait for a response from the dispatcher.

Ten minutes later, I'm finally off the phone and still waiting. Where the hell are they?

I shoot another message to Maisy with a lame excuse about period cramps. There's no way I'm telling my new friend about my possible stalker. If this is Mark, he's gone too fucking far. With every lap I pace, I grow angrier. How dare that asshole break into my apartment? He's not going to scare me. I refuse to let him get to me.

I'd never let any man have that power over me again.

Steeling my nerves, I march back to my door and slowly push it open. I expect to find the place ransacked, but instead, my little living room seems untouched. My sorry little Christmas tree stands in the corner, the colorful throw pillows are all in place, the remote control sits on the coffee table just where I left it, and— a familiar sickly odor fills my nostrils. My head spins toward the kitchenette and the tiny island. A single dead yellow rose sits atop the counter.

No, this isn't happening. My stomach clenches, and fear wraps around my lungs and squeezes. A clunk from across the studio freezes the blood in my veins. I creep toward the wood partition that separates my bed from the living area, my pulse hammering across my eardrums.

"Is anyone there?" I shout, instilling venom in my tone. I grab the umbrella by the door and hold it up like a baseball bat.

I round the white wood paneling and peer into the dim room. My bed is unmade just like I left it, my closet door closed, but my armoire… The top drawer is open. Had I left it like that in my rush to get out this morning? No, I don't think so.

My fingers squeeze around the umbrella handle, and I inch inside. The framed picture of my family sits atop the dresser, our smiling faces giving me an added burst of courage. Standing on my tiptoes, I peer over the top of the drawer. All my underwear and bras are neatly arranged by color.

Shit. Now I know I didn't do that.

A sharp creak stops my heart. I spin around, and a gloved hand covers my mouth. I stare at the freaky *Scream* mask and jab the umbrella into my attacker's stomach. "Bitch!" he growls, something off about his voice, and a biting sting races across my face.

He squeezes my hand so hard I drop the umbrella. I try to scream but his hand is back on my mouth again, and my voice is muffled against the fabric. A hood drops over my head, and panic shreds into my heart. I scream and cry as strong hands shove me onto the mattress face down. "Let go of me!" I kick and squirm, but he's too strong.

Darkness edges my vision, and I'm hurtled to the past. Two firm hands holding me down, a familiar voice telling me it's okay as a hand moves between my legs. No, no, not now. I couldn't let the past drag me under. I had to fight.

I buck against the mattress, but the man's hold only tightens. *No, not again.*

"Don't fight me, Rose, it'll only make things worse for you." An eerie robotic voice, like the one all serial killers in movies use, whispers across my ear.

My lungs burn as I try to drag in a breath through the blinding terror. Fingers dig into my hips and grope for my yoga pants. "No! No!" My assailant's knee digs into my back as he drags my pants and panties down. Chilly air races over my bare cheeks, and nausea claws its way up my throat. "Don't do this!" I screech. Tears burn my eyes, but I refuse to let them fall, not like with *him*. I'd only been sixteen then, naïve and innocent.

A gloved hand cups my ass.

My entire body tenses.

"Don't pretend you don't like this, Rose. I know what sort of depraved fantasies fill that dirty mind."

Oh God, that robotic voice. A shudder races up my spine.

The whine of a zipper sends another wave of panic crashing over me. The man wraps his hands around my thighs and jerks me to the edge of the mattress. He shoves himself between my legs and the feel of his limp dick against my ass makes my stomach revolt.

"No, please no," I yell. My fingers tear at the sheets, desperate to get away.

"I'm going to fuck you good, you little bitch. Once I'm done with you, you'll wish you never—"

The wail of a siren stops him mid-sentence.

"Fuck," he grumbles. "I guess we'll just have to wait until next time, my lovely rose." He jumps up and his retreating footfalls echo all around me. I rip the hood off my head and catch only a glimpse of the masked man as he sprints out of my room before the tears begin to fall.

CHAPTER 10
CRUEL IRONY

D*ante*

"I already told you I don't know where Feng is." Jianjun is a lying *pezzo di merda*. No way that piece of shit has no idea where his nephew is.

I press the muzzle of my gun harder against his temple, and asshole in red number one flinches. Six of the red-hooded bastards surround their leader. "Then call off the bounties on my brother and his fiancée."

"I cannot do that either."

"Why the fuck not?" I tick my head at Tony, and he trains his gun on the dragon beside Jianjun. "How about I give you some motivation?"

Tony cocks the pistol.

"I'll have Tony here get some target practice in until you figure out how to stop this."

"I didn't put out the hit, Dante," the old man snarls. "You

know how it works. Only the one who set the price can renege on the deal."

"You're the fucking head of the Triad, Jianjun. Don't feed me that bullshit, *vecchio*."

"My hands are tied." A sneer curls the corner of his lip, and my finger tightens around the trigger. Just a tiny bit more pressure… I squeeze my eyes closed and imagine the blood splatter all across the pink table linens. So satisfying. Drawing in a breath, I force myself to think things through. This was exactly what my brother warned me about, flying off the handle half-cocked. I had to prove him wrong, prove to him I could handle this job.

"Then let's do this, old man, until Feng shows his face here, I'll take out one of your men every hour."

"That seems a bit rash," he bites out. "What would the *capo* say?" His grin grows wider.

"Keep my little bro out of this. I'm in charge now because your asshole nephew took a hit out on Luca and his future wife. You know that's unacceptable. So now you're stuck with me, and I'll do whatever I see fit to ensure the future of the Kings."

He scoffs.

My phone vibrates in my jacket pocket, drawing my attention from the string of curses poised on my lips. I'm tired of this arrogant bastard. I slide the phone out, glance at the screen, and my heart kicks at my ribs so hard I nearly drop the cell.

Rose: *I need you.*

"Shit," I grumble. My pulse fires up, red-hot fury singeing my veins.

"What's wrong?" Tony eyes me, his gun still pointed at one of Jianjun's thugs.

"*Andiamo, adesso,*" I hiss out. We have to get the fuck out of here right now.

He nods quickly, no questions.

I race to the door with Tony at my heels and call out over my shoulder. "You're right. I should give you a little more time. I'm a rational man, after all. The countdown has started, Jianjun, find Feng and deliver him to me or you'll lose one man a *day.*"

Police? What the fuck? The cops drive off, and I shout at Mickey to pull over in front of Rose's apartment. I texted her about a dozen times during the ride over and each unanswered message drove my blood pressure up a hundred points. A lethal mix of dread and rage twist in my gut as I shove the car door open and sprint across the sidewalk.

"Hey, D, you want me to come?" Tony calls out.

"No, stay there. I'll let you know if I need you."

Some woman opens the door to the building, and I barrel by her nearly knocking the grocery bag from her shoulder.

"Hey, watch it!" She yells from behind me, but I barely make out her words over the roar of my pulse.

Cazzo, Rose should not be living in a building like this. No doorman? No security? Any asshole can just barge in.

When I reach the third floor, sweat already soaks my shirt, sticking to my jacket. Since the moment I got that text, irrational fear has been carving at my insides. Rose was so pissed at me. Whatever happened must be bad for her to reach out.

Apartment 3D stands at the end of the hall and even from this distance I can make out the splintered wood. *Cazzo.* It was a good thing Stella had given me her best friend's address when she made me vow to keep an eye on her, otherwise I never would've found the place.

I sprint the last few feet and barrel through the teetering door. "Rose?"

She sits on the couch, knees tucked to her chest. Her eyes are puffy and red, and a swollen welt mars her left cheek. Fury soaks my being, surging through every inch of me. "Who did this to you?" My voice isn't my own, it belongs to the monster I keep buried deep inside. I fall to my knees in front of her and wrap my hands around her bare ankles. "Rose, please, tell me what happened?"

A tear streams down her cheek, and she swats it away. "I—I don't know." She glances toward the kitchenette, and I spot a withered yellow rose on the counter, then an entire vase full of them.

"Rose, talk to me." I force my voice to soften, but a tremor of rage laces my tone. I cant my head toward the dead flowers. "Who are those from?"

She shakes her head and swallows hard, the delicate column of her throat bobbing. Her shoulders heave, and she sucks in a ragged sob.

My fingers clench into fists, my nails digging into my palms. I'm fairly certain I've drawn blood. Wouldn't be the first time and sure as hell wouldn't be the last. I jump up and cross the small living room to the wilted bouquet. My nostrils flare at the pungent odor of death and decay. I pluck the notecard from the vase and scan the dark scrawling.

Crumpling the card in my fist, I slam it onto the countertop. The entire damned kitchenette trembles. "That *pezzo di merda*! It was that patient from your office, wasn't it? Did he come here? Did he hurt you, Rose?" I eat up the space between us and fold onto the couch beside her. "Tell me, damn it!" No one threatens what's mine and lives. And while Luca and Stella are gone, Rose is mine.

Her lips screw into a pout and more tears spill down her

cheeks. They race a track across the bruise beginning to form on her left side. "He... he was in my apartment when I got home," she stammers.

"When did he send those roses?" I didn't know much about flowers, but they seemed dead as shit.

"A couple days ago," she whispers.

"When exactly, Rose?" If the cops were here, they must have asked the same.

"The night before my interview at Palestra."

"*Cazzo*, Rose! Why didn't you tell me?" I leap up and drag my hand through my hair. I knew something was off when I saw her that morning at the gym.

"I'm not your problem, Dante. And I didn't think it was such a big deal. I can handle myself."

"Obviously you can't," I hiss. I pace the short length of the studio, and my gaze catches on a pile of discarded clothes beside her bed. Her yoga pants, the ones I'd seen her in earlier today and her panties. Torn.

Deep crimson consumes my vision, and I spin back toward her, my heart a battering ram against my ribs. "Did he--?" I can't even say the words. Raw fury consumes my chest, and I can barely drag in a breath.

Rose draws her legs tighter against her chest, and she dips her chin to her knees, squeezing her eyes closed.

"Rose," I roar, and another tremor zips up my spine. "Did he rape you?"

"Stop yelling at me!" she cries. "He didn't...." She pauses and nibbles on her lower lip. "He tried, but the police got here, and he ran off."

Grazie a Dio. I drag in a shuddering breath, forcing my lungs to inflate. God, how is this happening? I swore to Stella I'd take care of her friend and she was nearly raped, of all things, under my watch? *Merda.* This is the cruelest of ironies. I inch closer, focusing on my breath like my therapist insists on to calm the rage.

"I'm sorry," I whisper as I sink onto the opposite side of the sofa. "*Cazzo*, I'm so sorry this happened."

"I—I need a shower."

My head dips, and I mutter another string of curses. I'm going to flay the man alive. My fingers cramp with the desire to wrap around the *figlio di puttana*'s throat.

She slides to the edge of the cushion and staggers as she stands. I jump up in time to catch her before she falls back. My hands are hesitant as they steady her around the waist. What if she doesn't want to be touched? *Dio*, I can't imagine what she's feeling right now. Guilt's claws tear into me, and Stella's panicked face fills my vision. I put her through this very same thing. Fuck, I *am* a monster.

Rose leans against me, and I slowly bend, giving her time to deny me. When she doesn't, I lace one arm beneath her shoulders and the other under her thighs and scoop her into my chest. She's tall and willowy but right now, she feels so fragile against me.

I carry her toward the bathroom in a few long strides. The studio is so tiny, the entire thing could fit in my master bedroom, and the bathroom is so small I can barely turn around while holding her. I gently place her on the toilet and spin the faucets on all the way.

My eyes fall on her clothes for the first time since I barged in here, fear and rage clouding all else. She's in an oversized t-shirt and men's boxers. An irrational wave of jealousy pummels me in the gut. Who do they belong to? Is she dating someone new?

Warm steam fills the small space, drawing me from my insane thoughts. "I'll leave you to it."

She nods and lifts her arms over her head as I turn toward the door. A sharp hiss escapes, and I spin back. Her lips are pressed together, and she's rubbing her shoulder.

"What's wrong?"

"Nothing, I think I just twisted something when he had me pinned to the mattress."

"Fuck!" I snarl, another wave of anger burning anew. I'm going to find that fucker and tear him to bits.

"Can you just help me get my shirt over my head?"

I swallow hard as a wave of desire crashes below my belt. *Idiota*. My dick is a fool. I dip my chin and reach for the hem of her shirt, keeping my eyes fixed to the top of her head. I slide one arm free, and my gaze catches her bare shoulder. *No bra*. Great, now I'm hard. Dispelling the completely inappropriate thoughts, I tug the shirt over her head and pin my eyes to the wall behind her.

"Um, do you need help with anything else?"

"No, I got it, thanks." She rises, one arm across her breasts and wiggles out of the boxers.

Every bone in my body urges me to look down. Just one quick glance. Gritting my teeth, I fight against the overpowering sensations and whirl toward the door. "I'll be right outside if you need anything."

The shower curtain slides closed, and my fingers wrap around the handle, but before I twist, Rose's voice stops me.

"Can you just stay in here until I'm done?"

The fragile edge to her tone nearly undoes me.

"Yeah, sure," I mumble.

It's the longest five-minute shower in history. Every trickle of water, every touch of skin, every faint groan goes straight to my cock. *Dio*, I'm a *coglione*. How can I even be imagining her like that after what she's been through? I'm such a fucking ass.

Rose finally appears, peering out from behind the pink curtain, her long blonde hair dripping down her shoulders. "Can you hand me the towel and the bathrobe?"

I reach for the fluffy pink things and hand them over, diverting my eyes. Once she's all wrapped up, she draws the curtain back and I offer my hand. "How's your shoulder?"

She gently wiggles it around and winces. "A little sore but it feels better after the hot shower."

"Good." I lead her through the sitting area and back behind the small partition where her bedroom lies, and my gaze falls on the torn thong on the floor. My fingernails dig into my palm again, and I barely suppress another growl.

She releases a breath and slowly blinks, as if she's clearing her vision of something awful. Then she turns away from the armoire, apparently changing her mind about getting dressed and releases another slow breath. I follow her as she returns to the living room and plops down on the sofa.

Grazie a Dio the police interrupted that fucker before he--. I squeeze my eyes shut and chase away the horrific thoughts. Relief floods my chest as I thank the God Mamma so fervently believes in. Me? I don't believe in a higher power, except for maybe Satan. I've seen enough bad shit in my life to believe he's real all right. Hell, I've seen the devil in myself.

Rose's puffy eyes lift to the broken door. "I should probably call someone about that."

"I'll handle it; I've got a guy. And by the way, Tony's already standing guard outside. No one's getting in here tonight, sweetheart."

She nods, a glossy sheen to her lifeless eyes.

Dio, I hate seeing her like this. "What did you tell the cops?"

Her gaze flickers to the small window to the fire escape. "I didn't tell them about Mark."

"Why the fuck not?"

"Because I can't lose my job, Dante! We're not all super wealthy gangsters around here."

The corner of my lip twitches, a hint of amusement for the first time tonight settling over my scowl. I pause, considering her words. "Good. If you didn't tell the cops about him then no one will think twice when they find his mutilated body."

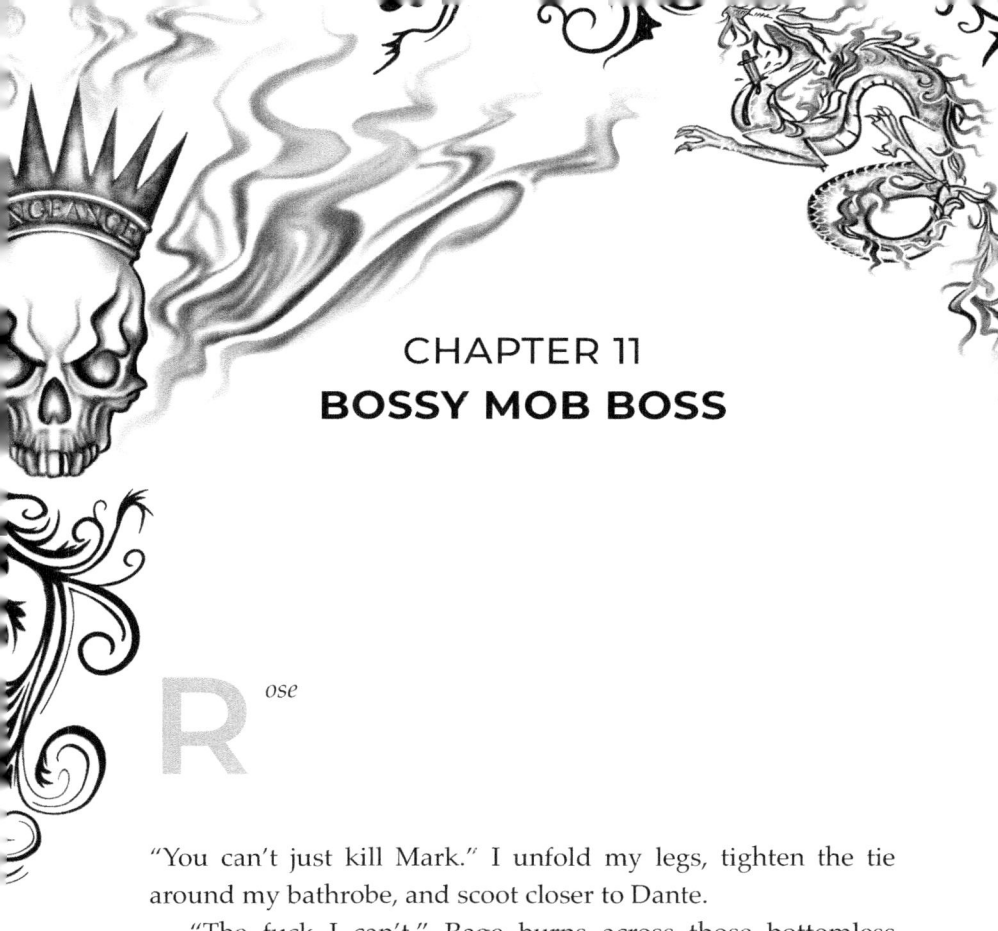

CHAPTER 11
BOSSY MOB BOSS

R*ose*

"You can't just kill Mark." I unfold my legs, tighten the tie around my bathrobe, and scoot closer to Dante.

"The fuck I can't." Rage burns across those bottomless irises, and something else too. Worry? Did the great Dante Valentino actually care about me?

I don't even know why I texted him. I could've called my dad, my brother or Maisy. Hell, even Stella might have answered if I calculated the time zones right. But my fingers had zipped over my phone on autopilot. Thank gawd I didn't delete his number like I'd fully intended on doing. "I'm not even a hundred percent sure it's him."

"Sixty percent? Seventy? I'll take anything over fifty, sweetheart." A wicked gleam flashes through those midnight orbs.

Heat radiates from his form, and I can't help but lean into him. A chill has settled into my bones, one so deep even the shower didn't help much, but for the first time all night, it's starting to dissipate. Dante is untouchable, indestructible. I know if I said the word, Mark would be nothing but a pulpy mess by tomorrow morning. That sort of power is alluring, addictive.

"Rosa, please."

My name on his lips is enough to chase away every dark memory. I glance up and meet smoldering irises. He cups my cheek, running a calloused thumb over the tear stains. Half-moon circles are carved into his palm, fresh blood along the cuts.

"Say the word, and I'll gut the *bastardo* from throat to tailbone."

As tempting as it sounds, I remind myself I'm Rose 2.0 now. I can't sentence a man to death without proof. Did the dickhead deserve it for his stalkerish tendencies? Maybe. Either way, I couldn't stomach the thought of condemning an innocent man.

I slowly shake my head. "He was wearing a mask, had a creepy voice disguiser and put a hood over my head."

He lets out another string of curses, his warm hand falling from my cheek. "If it wasn't Mark, I *will* find out who it was. I'll have every rapist tracked down and questioned until I have the *pezzo di merda* in my hands."

"Thank you," I murmur, and my fingers wrap around his hand. I'm careful not to touch the fresh cuts.

His eyes dart to mine, and something unreadable flashes through the never-ending darkness. "Never keep something like that from me again, Rose. Do you understand?"

I nod.

"I made Stella a promise, and I intend to keep it. Please don't make me a liar. I've fucked up enough with my future sister-in-law."

"You know, Stel never told me what you did…."

His lips press into a tight line, and the tendon beneath the layer of dark stubble tenses. "I'm surprised," he finally mutters.

I want to ask so badly. I just need a distraction from my own fucked up life right now. I've drilled Stella about it for months, and she always refused to spill. I suppose it's because she feels some sort of loyalty toward her future brother-in-law for saving her and Luca's lives.

A wave of exhaustion suddenly splashes over me, and my head lolls on Dante's shoulder. His arm settles around me, and a yawn parts my lips.

"*Dormi, Rosa, sei al sicuro con me. Nessuno ti farà mai più del male.*" Dante's whispered words float like a prayer in the background as I drift to sleep.

My eyes snap open as a phantom gloved hand closes over my mouth. I gasp and jolt up off the couch. Scanning my light-filled apartment, I heave in a breath. *It was just a dream.*

The creak of a door opening sends my heart spasming again until I focus on the half-naked Roman god emerging from my bathroom. "Dante," I rasp out. The early morning sunlight bathes his perfect form in a golden glow, highlighting each dip and valley of his torso, the intricate patterns of black inked across his chest, and the faint scars buried within.

Gawd, he's like an Italian masterpiece.

"You stayed?"

"Mmm." He nods and wraps the towel tighter across his narrow hips. My eyes drop to the deep V disappearing beneath the white terry cloth. "I hope you don't mind I helped myself to a shower."

"No, not at all. Sorry you had to sleep on the couch. You didn't have to—"

He raises a hand, cutting me off. "I don't do anything I don't want to, Rosa."

Noted.

My eyes lock on the massive tattoo printed across his chest in bold gothic writing: Vengeance Is King. A creepy skull with a spiked crown spreads across his muscled pecs. I latch onto the words, almost obsessively, because in that moment there's nothing I want more than revenge on the asshole who crept into my sanctuary and stole my peace of mind.

"I already spoke to Dr. Winchester and the HR assistant at Palestra." Dante's deep tenor pulls me from the dark thoughts. "You're taking the day off."

"What? No, I can't, Dante. I just got the job at Palestra, and I cannot risk losing it." I shoot to my feet, and my robe slides off my shoulder. I yank it up and tighten the tie around my waist. I need to get some clothes on, but the idea of going into my bedroom has nausea crawling up my throat.

"Rosa, it's December twenty-third. People aren't taking yoga classes. They're buying last minute Christmas presents. You need a few days to recover, and besides, the gym will be closed until the twenty-sixth. It's just one extra day off."

"But Dr. Winchester...."

"She said you deserve a break, and she'll see you bright and early on the twenty-sixth." He ticks his head at the kitchen counter. The roses are gone and in their place are a fresh set of clothes. A comfy oversized t-shirt and my yoga pants. Tears burn my eyes, but I quickly blink them back. "Get dressed."

He's right. I refuse to spend the day wallowing in self-pity. So, I was attacked? I survived, and the asshole won't get away with it. Between Dante and the cops, they'll find whoever did this and he'll be punished. I must believe that.

"You can't stay here, sweetheart. Where are you spending the holidays? I can have Mickey drive you there a day early."

My chin dips to my chest, and I wrap my arms around my middle. I *was* going to Long Island to spend it with my dad and stepmom until I found out my uncle was in town from Florida. A shudder surges up my spine at the thought of seeing him, especially now. "I'm not going anywhere," I finally admit.

"Don't your parents live in Long Island?"

Gawd, how does he know so much about me? After my recent stalker streak, you'd think I'd find it unnerving, but with Dante, it's quite the opposite. "Not my parents, plural. My dad and step-mom do, but I thought I'd be working so I didn't plan on going out there."

"Then change your plans."

I glare up at the bossy new mob boss. "I'm *not* going to Long Island."

"Why?"

"It's personal, Dante, and I don't owe you an explanation."

He scowls and reaches for his black button-down shirt. The same one I drooled on all night. He spears his tattooed arms through the sleeves and eyes me. "You can't stay here by yourself."

"You just said you're going to find the guy, right? And the police are on it. I'll be fine." I tighten my hold around myself. If I didn't hate my uncle so much, I'd go running home. The idea of spending the night alone in this place has fear strangling my insides.

Dante closes the distance between us in two long strides and looms over me. Gawd, he's tall. "I will find him, but until I do, you cannot stay here alone."

"Fine, then I'll go to one of my friends'." Only everyone I knew had already left the city for Christmas break. Except for Maisy ... maybe I could text her.

"Very well." He hands me my phone. "Send me her name, number and address."

"Dante...."

"No buts, sweetheart. I made a vow to Stella, and I intend to keep it."

A swirl of disappointment blossoms in my chest, and I want to kick myself for being so blind. This has nothing to do with me. This is all about his promise to Stella. Gawd, how could I be so stupid to think he actually cared about *me*?

Dante Valentino made it very clear he didn't care about anyone.

"Rose, I'm waiting." He ticks his head at my frozen fingers.

I don't even know where Maisy lives, and sure, I could ask her to hang out, but we aren't close enough to ask her for a place to crash for the next few nights. It's Christmas. She must have plans like every other normal person in the world. "I can't remember her address. I'll send it to you later."

He crosses his arms over his barrel chest and cocks a dark brow. "You're not lying to me, are you?"

That look is intimidating as fuck, but instead of fear only desire blossoms low in my gut. Dammit, what is wrong with me?

"No," I snap. I punch in her name and phone number and press send. "There, you happy?"

"Ecstatic."

"Don't call her," I warn.

He shoots me another pointed glare that has the blood in my veins bubbling.

"At least give me a chance to talk to her. I don't want her to think I'm giving out her number to random strangers."

"Whatever you say, Rose." He reaches for his pants and heads for the bathroom. "Get ready, I have an appointment to get to in an hour, and I'm not leaving here without you."

The bathroom door barely closes before he drops his towel, and I get an eyeful of his perfect ass.

Too bad he is one.

CHAPTER 12
YOU ARE MINE

R*ose*

Dante sits across from me in the sprawling back seat of the Town Car. He scowls at the stack of papers in his lap as he scribbles a signature, then moves onto the next. When the driver, Aldo, came to pick us up, he arrived with a fresh suit and tie for his boss. Dante dragged the jacket on, pouting like my two-year-old nephew when my sister-in-law makes him put on his shoes.

Focusing on this, something so trivial, is easier than dwelling on last night. Besides, the look on Dante's face as he tugs on the knot of his tie would pick up anyone's mood. He's as out of place in that fancy three-piece suit as I'd be in one.

Scrubs and yoga pants, now that's the type of practice I'll have one day.

If I don't find you first. That eerie robotic voice echoes in my mind, and a shudder surges up my spine.

"What's the matter with you?" Dante barks from across the back seat.

I school my expression and wrap my arms around my middle. "Huh?"

"You just jumped or something." His darting eyes land on my breasts. Of course, my nipples are poking through the soft material of my sports bra and top because of that damned chill.

"Nothing, I'm just cold." I reach for my jacket I'd tossed on the seat and wrap it around my shoulders.

Dante knocks at the small window behind his head, and the glass slides open.

"What's up, boss?" Aldo's thick New York accent invades the silence.

"Rose is cold, turn up the heat."

"Will do."

He slides the partition closed and refocuses his attention on the papers piled on his lap. A curse hisses out, and though my Italian is weak at best, I recognize it for what it is. In the short amount of time I've spent with Dante, I've learned the Italian word for shit, *merda*. He uses it about every third word. That and *cazzo* which Stella translated loosely as fuck.

"You know, you could just get an electronic signature and have your assistant sign all that stuff for you."

Dark eyes lift to mine and thick brows jump so high they nearly reach the wild tumbles of midnight hair. "You're shitting me?"

"Nope. I do it all the time for Dr. Winchester."

"Why wouldn't Clara tell me—" Dante bites off the end of his sentence with another curse. "That woman is purposely trying to torture me." He pauses, shoves the pen between his teeth and chews on the end. "No, this is Luca. He probably told her to keep me busy so I wouldn't get into any trouble. That sneaky *bastardo*. If he thinks burying me in a pile of paperwork is going to keep me in check, he's got another thing coming."

It takes every ounce of restraint I have to keep the smile from stretching across my face as he dumps the stack of papers on the floor. Dante in a business suit is bad enough but forced to sit behind a mountain of files at a desk? His brother really must be punishing him for something.

The elder Valentino is like a wild animal, a ruthless, savage lion on the prowl. Forcing him to sit in an office all day is like chopping the king of the jungle's balls off and throwing him in a cage at the zoo. No wonder he's been so pissy lately.

He pulls out his phone and growls something in Italian I definitely can't make out. Then he glances up at me. "What's this Dr. Mark's last name?"

My heart stops beating with just the mention of my possible attacker. It takes me at least a solid minute to force it to start pumping again. "Dante, I don't want this getting out...."

"I understand your concerns, but I already told you, this piece of shit will not go unpunished. No one touches what's mine and lives. This is not up for discussion." He slides to the end of the seat and spears me with those midnight orbs. "Until Luca and Stella return, You. Are. Mine." He punctuates each word with a snarl, and fuck me, it's the sexiest thing I've ever heard. Because I'm clearly a mental case.

Heat pulses at the apex of my thighs, and I'm about a second from spreading my legs for this man. Which is insane and wrong on so many levels. Especially because I'd sworn he'd lost his chance with me. Going back on her word for an incredible fuck would be something the old Rose would do, but not Rose 2.0. No, I'd have to rein in the crazed sex kitten and buy a better vibrator.

"Rose?" Dante perches his elbows on his knees, and he leans closer. His legs are so long, his knees nearly brush against mine, despite the huge back seat. "Trust me when I tell you that whatever happens to the good doc, no one will ever know this had anything to do with you."

"Okay." My chin dips to my chest, and the hint of a smile creeps across my lips. "You promise not to kill him unless you're sure he was the one that attacked me?"

His gorgeous mouth twists, and he releases a frustrated growl. "Fine, Rosa, I promise."

Shit, did I just indirectly agree to letting him kill the guy if it *was* him? "How will you find out?" I blurt.

Dante cracks his knuckles, and a wicked grin splits his lips. "I have my ways, sweetheart."

My eyes fix on his mouth, on the naughty twist, and I inch closer until our knees do touch. Our eyes meet, and my heart staggers for a completely different reason this time. Dante's gaze dips to his legs, then slides to my thighs. That heated gaze crawls up the inside of my leg until I feel it on my throbbing pussy. That one dark look has me clenching with need.

Which gives me a hope like no other I've ever felt. I thought after last night ... but no, that asshole couldn't steal this from me. I wouldn't give him that control.

"Fuck," Dante grits out. Then he draws in a breath and shakes his head before scooting back in the seat.

Aldo whips around a corner, and I tumble forward. Splaying my hands out for purchase, I grab two handfuls of Dante's fine suit and land between his legs. Something hard and thick presses against my belly, and heat floods my lower half.

"*Cazzo*, Rosa..." he hisses as I scramble on top of him, grazing his cock.

"Sorry." I can feel the burn on my cheeks as his big hands wrap around my hips to steady me. He plops me onto the seat beside him like I weigh nothing. I can't help but glance at his lap and the outline of his massive erection. I also can't help the ridiculous giddiness at seeing him hard for me. Dante Valentino can have any woman in New York City, and I just gave him a hard on when I fell into his lap. Point for the crazy girl.

Aldo pulls the limo over, and I glance out the tinted window to the upscale West Village neighborhood. A cute brownstone sits in front of us with colorful flowers on every windowsill. I lucked out that Maisy answered my text, otherwise I would've been shit out of luck.

Before messaging her, I'd gone through my paltry list of friends, and I'd been right, everyone was out of town for the holiday. If it wasn't so last minute, I could have hopped on a plane to crash at my brother's place in Florida, but the flights were expensive as hell two days before Christmas. So here I am.

Aldo opens the car door for us, and Dante slides out first, then offers me a hand. Chivalry? I so did not see that coming from the rough, tattooed mob boss. He eyes the three-story townhouse before turning to me. "I had this Maisy woman checked out so you should be safe for now."

"Checked out?" I squeak. No wonder he wanted all her personal details.

"You didn't think I'd let you stay with just anyone, did you, sweetheart?" He smirks, revealing that elusive dimple.

"I never knew you'd make such a devoted bodyguard, D." I jab an elbow into his side and bat flirty lashes. "You're a real-life fucking Kevin Costner."

He glances down at me, the amusement ebbing into the darkness. "Are you sure you're okay?" His voice deepens, and the fear I've been trying to smother all day comes rushing back.

I blink quickly, the rough edge to his tone shooting cracks through the wall I built years ago and reinforced last night with everything I have. "Yeah, I'm fine," I finally manage. "Maisy and I will have a girl's night—"

Dante raises his hand. "At home. All night."

"Yes, yes, of course. We'll watch a movie and eat popcorn or something totally PG."

He grunts. "Why do I have a feeling you're more of a rated-R kind of girl, Rosa?"

Damn, it's freaky how well this man knows me. "Guess you'll never know now, will you, D?"

The corners of his lips curl, and that wicked glimmer lights up his dark eyes. "Take care of yourself, sweetheart." He turns toward the car before spinning back. "Oh, one more thing, if I find out something happened with that psycho and you don't call me immediately, it won't just be him who will get punished."

A shiver races down my spine at the violent edge to his tone, and it has nothing to do with fear.

"Do you understand, Rosa?"

I nod, chomping down on my bottom lip to keep myself from saying something completely inappropriate. Like how much I want him to spank me.

"And Merry Christmas."

"You too, D. Although, I didn't think they let the devil celebrate." I shoot him a cheeky grin, and he rewards me with a heart-stopping smile. Damn that man for being so gorgeous.

His scalding gaze trails after me as I dart up the brick steps and press the buzzer. Maisy appears with a smile, and the tension eating away at my insides starts to dissipate at her reassuring grin. I glance back over my shoulder as Maisy escorts me in, and those dark eyes are still pinned to mine. They remain locked on their target until the door finally closes behind me.

CHAPTER 13
SENDING A MESSAGE

D *ante*

"That's right, Dr. Mark Rattinger." I hiss out the *figlio di puttana*'s name to another colleague of mine over the phone as I walk up Park Avenue. I have every lowlife in the city looking out for the motherfucker. His practice is closed for the holidays, he hasn't been home since yesterday, and every second that passes with the guy in the wind has my blood pressure skyrocketing.

The nail marks in my palm have become permanent engravings in the twenty-four hours since Rose was attacked. I don't know what pisses me off more: that I can't find the asshole or that I'm actually considering keeping my vow to Rose. I never should've promised I wouldn't kill the slimy bastard. Because the truth is, I want to paint that man's fancy uptown practice in his blood.

I eye the luxurious building across the street. I've been camped outside his office for hours and no luck. According to my sources, the good doctor owns the penthouse on the top floor while his practice sits on the third. He hasn't been in or out.

Even if Mark wasn't the one who attempted to rape her, he's still been a freaky fuck stalking her for weeks. My fingers curl into fists again, ripping open the scabs on my palm. I should've done something all those months ago when Rose first told us about the guy. She played it off like she does all things she doesn't want to deal with, and I'd bought into it.

I'd seen it firsthand today, that desire in her eyes when we were in the car. It was all a coping mechanism. Rose uses sex as a distraction, much like I do. Ha, and my therapist thinks I never listen to anything she says.

My cock stirs at the memory of her warm body pressed against mine. Damn, why'd I pick out that scandalous workout top and those curve-hugging yoga pants from her dresser? Just one look at her bouncy ass had me hard as shit. I keep picturing her folded over my bed, my cock driving into her pussy from behind as I palm those perfect cheeks. *Dio*, if I only hadn't fucked everything up with her that night.

My phone buzzes, jerking me from the heated memories, and I yank it out of my pocket and scan the screen.

Tony: *Nothing from Feng. You sure you want to start this?*

Fuck. As if I don't have enough problems with the Red Dragons. I should be dealing with Jianjun instead of surveilling a sketchy surgeon.

Me: *Yes. I'm not going back on my word. Everyone needs to know what happens when you fuck with the Kings. One Red Dragon every day. Start tonight.*

Tony: *Will do, D.*

Before I tuck my phone back into my jacket, I shoot off a quick text message to Aldo. I need someone else to take over surveillance duty. I've got more pressing matters to attend to.

Only a few days as interim CEO of King Industries and already I want to gouge my eyes out. The quicker I deal with Feng, the faster I can get Luca back here. I may want to sit on the King's throne, but my little bro can take the boardroom.

"Dante, I thought that was you." An irritatingly sweet voice rings out down the street, and I mutter a curse as she approaches.

"Ah, Caroline." I drop a quick kiss to her cheek when she leaps for me. "What a lovely surprise."

"Why have you been avoiding me?" Her eyes narrow, and she backs me into a delivery entrance door. For such a lithe thing, she's surprisingly strong.

I clear my throat as she presses her chest against mine. She's wearing one of those Chanel power suits that remind me of Hillary Clinton. Not exactly my style. "What? Avoiding you?" I offer her a charming smile. "I've been doing no such thing."

She slides her hand between us and cups my cock over my slacks. "I've got needs too, Dante. I came by your place last night and your guard said you weren't home." Her hand tightens around my flaccid dick.

"Late night at the office," I mutter.

"Really?" Her eyes lift to mine, insecurity flashing through those pale hazel orbs. I used to find them so appealing, but they're nothing compared to Rose's lively, brilliant blue. "Because I thought maybe there was someone else." She runs her hand up and down my dick, coaxing it up.

"No, of course not, darling." The term of endearment tastes bitter just like this whole arrangement. What we had was good, until it wasn't anymore. But how do I end things with her without costing King Industries millions? Would her father pull his money from Luca's development out of revenge? I wouldn't think he'd be that petty, but who knew with these touchy billionaires.

A groan slips from my lips as she continues to stroke my

stupid dick. "Caroline…," I warn. We're in the middle of the fucking streets.

"Come on, Dante, haven't you ever dreamed of me on my knees for you in a dark alley?"

Actually, yes.

But that was before….

She pushes me back a few steps, until we're in the shadows of the narrow alleyway. She slides her hand beneath my pants, and a hiss escapes as her fingers wrap around my dick.

After the earlier encounter with Rose, I have major blue balls and coming in her hand sure as hell would help with the tension. I squeeze my eyes closed, and all I see are shimmering blue ones. Blonde hair piled high in a messy bun. That tight ass body in yoga pants. I imagine that soft hand is Rose's pussy, tight and wet taking my cock in and in *and in*.

"Yes, Dante, yes. That's right, come for me." That shrill voice snaps my eyes wide open.

Fuck. "I can't do this." I wrap my hand around Caroline's wrist and jerk it away.

Her eyes grow to twice their size, and hurt flashes across that perfectly preserved face. "What's wrong?"

Clearing my throat, I buy myself a second to come up with an excuse. What idiot wouldn't want a beautiful woman to jerk him off in the middle of the day? "If someone sees us, the tabloids will have a field day," I blurt. "Your father would not be pleased."

She nods, pushing out her bottom lip. The lips I used to love wrapped around my dick. "You're no fun anymore now that you're the boss, Dante."

"No shit." I shrug and hold her out to arm's length. "On that note, I have a meeting I'm late for."

"Can I come by your place and finish this tonight?"

I nod because I can't think of another fucking excuse on the spot. I'll have to text her with one later. "Sure, that would be great, darling." *Cazzo*, I sound like a fake fool. With another quick kiss to the cheek, I take off down the block.

I've got to find a way to break things off with Caroline without costing my brother a fortune.

I glance down at the body, blood pooling around the ruby shirt and pants of the low-level Red Dragon. I may want to make my point with the Triad, but I know better than to start at the top. A couple of dead lackeys won't ignite Jianjun's full retribution, but hopefully, it will be enough to drive home the message.

Tony holsters his revolver and glances between Aldo and me. "We have to be prepared for payback."

"We will be." I nod. "If the old man has any sense, he'll hand over his nephew."

"You really think he'll give up Feng that easily?" Tony kicks at the lifeless corpse.

"Probably not. But maybe after a week, or two...."

"You're serious about one man a day?" Aldo's dark brows furrow.

"Serious as a fucking heart attack, *amico mio*."

"Luca wouldn't—"

I cut off Tony before he gets another word out. "Luca's not in charge. I am. If you've got a problem with how I run things, you're free to go."

His lips twist into a frown. Tony's been my brother's right-hand man since he took over for Papà. His father worked for mine, starting the long legacy. Tony's the only man alive who knows the real reason why Luca took the King's throne instead of me.

"You know I didn't mean any disrespect, D."

I nod. "Just trust me, okay?"

"Of course, whatever you say."

I roll the motionless body over with the tip of my boot and meet a pair of vacant eyes. *Pezzo di merda.* "Make sure you leave the corpse at the door of the Red Dragon. I want to make sure Jianjun knows who's responsible."

"Done, boss." Aldo pulls out his phone and types a quick message to the clean-up crew.

I close my eyes and instead of this man, I picture that blonde doctor, the one who dared lay a hand on what's mine. When I find the asshole that hurt Rose, there won't be a face left to recognize.

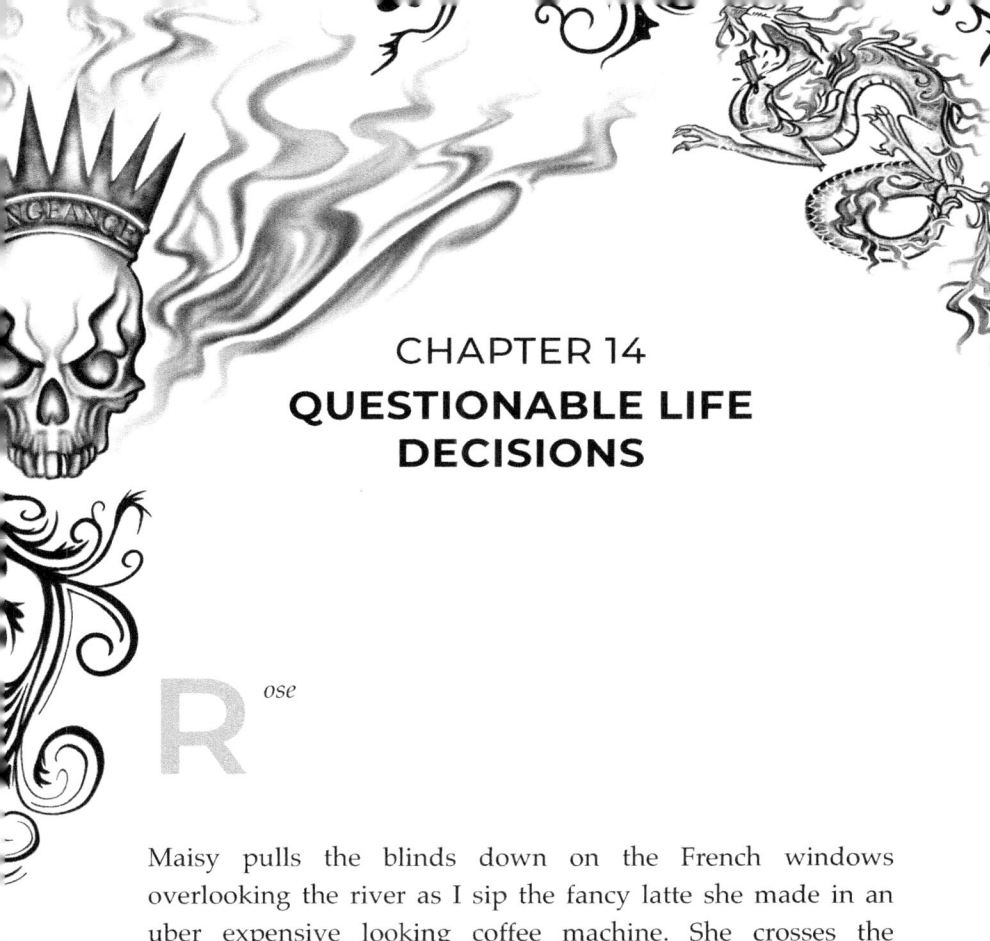

CHAPTER 14
QUESTIONABLE LIFE DECISIONS

Rose

Maisy pulls the blinds down on the French windows overlooking the river as I sip the fancy latte she made in an uber expensive looking coffee machine. She crosses the immense sitting room and slides into the chair in the cute breakfast nook. A deep purple orchid sits on the table, its light fragrance lingering in the air. Everything is perfect. When I woke up this morning, fresh avocado toast was already waiting for me on the table. Talk about five-star service.

"I still can't believe that was the notorious Dante Valentino that dropped you off last night." She smirks as she takes a big bite of her toast.

I still can't believe that Maisy held out on me. She never mentioned she was super rich. When Dante's driver pulled up to the brownstone, I assumed my new friend lived in one of the apartments, not that she owned the whole building.

I take another careful sip and shrug. Stella had sworn me to secrecy when it came to all things her fiancé and that meant Dante by extension. Most people have heard of King Industries, but their shady, underground dealings are nothing but speculation. "How do you know about him anyway?" Before Stella met Luca, I knew little about the Valentinos or their multi-billion-dollar company.

"My ex, Jasper, the douchebag." Maisy winces. "They ran in the same circles, and then later I'd see the brothers around Palestra."

That explains the gorgeous brownstone. All of Manhattan's wealthy elite frequent the same gyms, clubs, galas, and fundraisers. I'd learned that from my year interning with Dr. Winchester and my resulting questionable dating history.

I want to ask her more about the man who'd sent her into therapy, but the haunted look in her eye at the mention of his name stills my tongue.

"I can't believe your best friend is engaged to Luca Valentino. He is just wow...." Her eyes take on that glossy, dreamy quality all the women get around Stella's future husband. The younger Valentino is nothing like rugged, foul-mouthed, unpredictable Dante.

The hint of a smile crawls across my lips at the memory of him in the limo yesterday. Shit, I'd been way too hasty with that ultimatum the night of the party. If I hadn't, would he have fucked me in the back seat? Gawd, I wanted him to in that moment.

"What are you smiling about?" Maisy's cute little singsong wipes the smile right off my face.

Dante is not the type of man to be daydreaming about. There'd be no sweet nothings whispered in my ear, no declarations of undying love. If I let Dante have me, it would be brutal, rough and dirty.

"Oh my, do you have a thing for bad boy Dante Valentino?" Maisy's mouth curves into a capital O. "How could you not mention that last night?"

We'd spent all night in, just like I'd promised Dante, chitchatting, scarfing down tacos and ice cream. It was as close to heaven as you could get without an orgasm. "I do not," I blurt. "We're friends—kind of."

Like how a lion is friends with a lamb.

"That man is gorgeous," she purrs. "I've seen him around the gym, those tattoos...."

"You should see him without his shirt on." The confession slips out without my approval.

"Dang, girl, tell me everything, you little tease!"

I wave a nonchalant hand. "It was one time. Clearly a drunken mistake. We didn't even have sex because the asshole walked out on me when he got some super important text message."

Maisy's eyes widen, and she drops her coffee mug. "Get out! He did not."

"Yup. Total dick move." I shake my head, dispelling the heated memories threatening to bubble up to the surface. "Anyway, that was the old Rose. The new and improved version will never have anything to do with Dante Valentino."

"Good for you." She lifts her cup and clinks it against mine.

I still haven't asked Maisy about her Christmas plans. It's awkward and embarrassing as all hell. What kind of loser doesn't have anyone to spend the holidays with?

"Thanks again for letting me crash here last night. My supe said the heater should be up and running soon, but with the holiday, I'm not sure when it'll happen."

"No problem, I had a lot of fun yesterday. I hadn't realized how badly I needed a girls' night."

"Same." I give her a smile before bringing my coffee up to smother the shame. "So ... what are you up to tonight?"

She lets out a breath, blowing the bangs up off her forehead. "I'm driving up to Connecticut in a few hours to spend Christmas with my sister and her perfect family." She rolls her eyes. "White picket fence, two-point-two kids and a lawyer husband who worships the ground she walks on."

"Sounds like torture." I force my smile in place despite the disappointment. Now where would I stay tonight?

She laughs. "It is. Especially with my life crumbling around me."

"I'm really sorry."

"Nah, don't be. I'll muddle through somehow." She finishes off her coffee and glances back up at me. "What about you?"

"Oh, um, heading to Long Island to visit my dad and step-mom." I couldn't sound like a total loser to my new friend.

"Where does your mom live?" She eyes me curiously as I pick at my toast.

"She passed away a few years back." The dark memories threaten to rise, but I stuff a chunk of avocado in my mouth and choke it down.

"Oh gosh, I'm sorry, I had no idea."

"It's okay. I mean it's not, but what can you do?"

Maisy nods and glances out the window, the choppy waves of the Hudson blending with the gray skies overhead. "It sucks getting older, huh? I never thought I'd be divorced at twenty-three, and I bet you never imagined Christmases without your mom."

Or having a stalker…

My head dips slowly, and I pray to all the gods she doesn't ask what happened. Could a broken heart kill you? Because I'm fairly certain that's what happened to my mom. And this had nothing to do with love.

I pop out of my seat before Maisy can ask any more questions. "I should probably head out and let you get ready for your trip."

"I don't have to leave for another hour so there's no rush."

"I wish I could stay longer, but I need to get some last-minute presents." *Lie.*

"Oh, okay." She rises and surprises me with a hug. Her slender arms wrap around my neck, and my throat tightens at the reassuring touch. "Thanks for last night, I really needed it."

"Me too."

Maisy releases me and escorts me to the door. My bags are already packed and ready to go. Not that I'd brought much in my desperate escape from my studio. Would I ever be able to go back there again? Just the idea of sleeping in my bed has my stomach churning and nausea creeping up my throat.

So where would I go? Maybe I shouldn't have been in such a hurry to get out of that conversation.

I throw my tote bag over my shoulder, and Maisy gives me another smile. "Merry Christmas! I'll see you back at Palestra in a few days?"

Hope unfurls in my chest, and a huge smile splits my lips. *Palestra*! Why hadn't I thought of it sooner? The Plaza Hotel is always open which means I could easily slip into the gym with my all-access employee key card. I could spend the night on the couch in the employee lounge, if I could manage any sleep that is. Sure, it isn't ideal, but it's my best option for now.

I spin back and throw my arms around my new friend. "Merry Christmas, Maisy. I hope you have a great one."

Sneaking into the gym at the basement of the Plaza Hotel was much easier than I imagined. The hotel staff was already used to seeing me after only a few days of working there, and I was able to slip right in no questions asked.

What I hadn't counted on? No lights. They must have been on a timer or something.

I use the flashlight on my cell phone to navigate the dark hallways until I finally reach the employee lounge. *It isn't at all creepy.* I release a sigh of relief when I slide my keycard over the scanner and the door clicks open. *I'm fine, totally fine.* Now safely tucked away in my hideout, I check out the large space. *I can do this.* I have my phone for entertainment and a roof over my head. No one would ever think to look for me here. I'm perfectly safe.

My stomach growls, reminding me I'd completely forgotten about food in my mad dash. What a sad Christmas Eve this would be. Unless…. I dart toward the fridge and pray no one cleaned it out for the holiday weekend.

Whipping the door open, my eyes land on a sad Lunchable, an apple and a mini bag of baby carrots. Beggars can't be choosers, but seriously, a Lunchable? Who over the age of five eats those?

I do. That's who.

Reaching for the paltry contents, I load them up in my arms and trudge toward the couch. Besides the refrigerator and coffee machine, a few tables and the couch, there's not much in the lounge. There is the shower though.

At least that would kill some time after my sad dinner. And maybe, just maybe I'd be able to sleep tonight without the nightmares. I slowly eat all my snacks, then watch a few funny cat videos before I'm fidgety again. Time for that shower.

Rifling through my tote bag, I grab a fresh pair of yoga pants and an old Christmas t-shirt and head toward the shower.

Merry Christmas Eve to me.

I stand under the steamy spray, contemplating the life decisions that brought me here. Unwanted emotion thickens my throat as I think about my shitty past, and I barely hold back the tears. Or maybe I don't, but no one will ever know beneath the steady stream of hot water.

Finally, I draw in a breath and twist the handles until the steady drizzle tapers off. If it weren't for my damned uncle, I would be on my way to Long Island right now instead of spending Christmas Eve in an empty gym. And if it weren't for being an idiot and dating patients, the same would be true.

Or would it? I still don't know for sure if Mark really was my attacker. I wonder if Dante had gotten anywhere in his investigation.

I very briefly contemplate texting him but toss the desperate thoughts aside. It's Christmas Eve, no one's working right now. *You got this, Rose.* It's just two days stuck in this dark, empty gym. After the holiday, maybe the police or Dante will have found my attacker, and everything could go back to normal.

I wrap the towel around myself, dabbing at my wet skin and then reach for my clothes. Dammit. Of course, I forgot my underwear in my bag. Cinching the towel under my armpits, I tiptoe back out into the lounge, my wet flipflops squeaking with each step.

A dark shadow catches my eye by the doorway, and a scream rips from my throat.

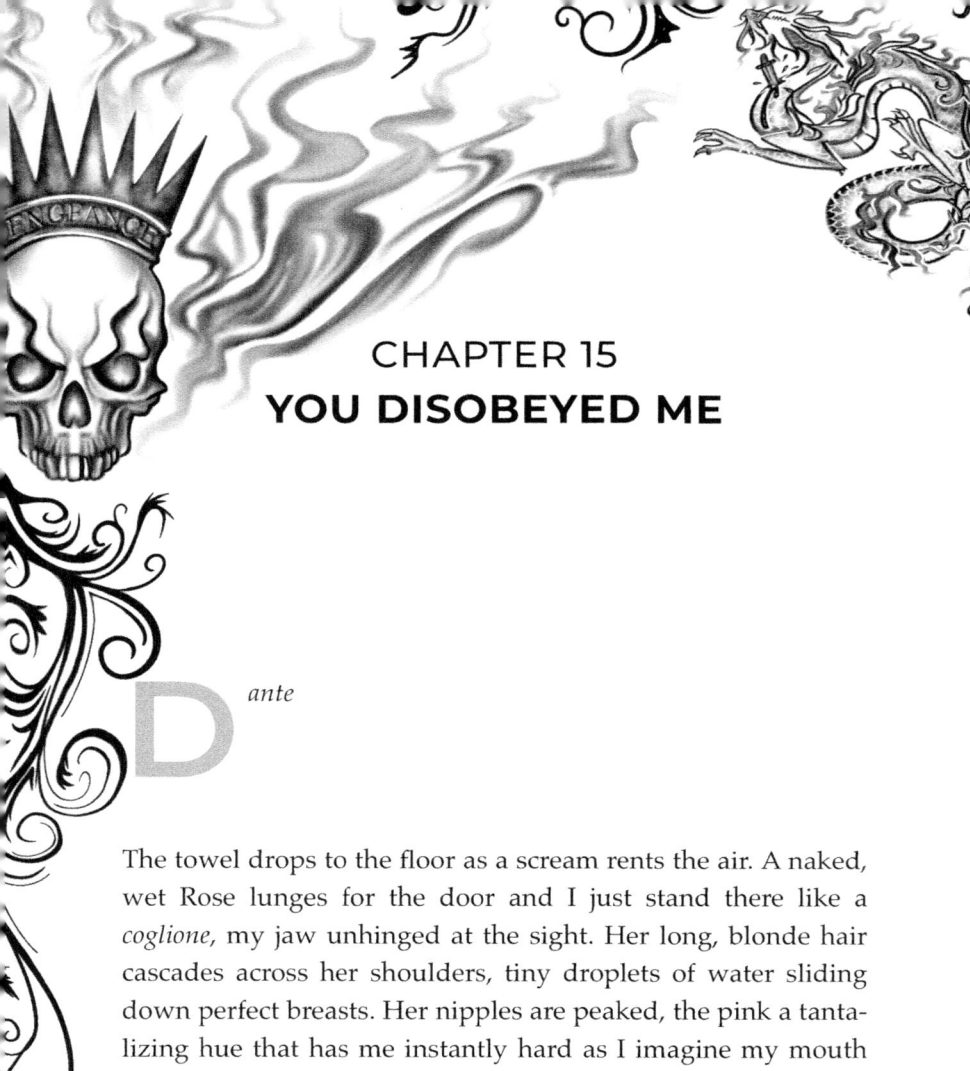

CHAPTER 15
YOU DISOBEYED ME

D*ante*

The towel drops to the floor as a scream rents the air. A naked, wet Rose lunges for the door and I just stand there like a *coglione*, my jaw unhinged at the sight. Her long, blonde hair cascades across her shoulders, tiny droplets of water sliding down perfect breasts. Her nipples are peaked, the pink a tantalizing hue that has me instantly hard as I imagine my mouth devouring them.

I barely get it together in time to throw my arm out as she races by. "It's me, Rosa," I whisper, my arm winding around her waist. She's trembling and tremors shake her entire body.

"Dante?" She glances up at me, squinting in the dark room.

"What the hell are you doing here?" I snarl, unable to keep the barely contained anger at bay. When Aldo told me he'd trailed her to The Plaza, I'd assumed she'd come for an after-hours workout. Strange but not completely bizarre. But when I had one of my guys hack into the Palestra security system, and

I saw her getting comfy on Christmas Eve in the sorry employee lounge, I nearly lost my shit.

My fingers dig into her soft, bare curves as she stares up at me innocently. Long lashes bat across big, blue, enchanting eyes. Those tantalizing drops of water skate down her flesh, and I want to trail them down her torso with my tongue. My cock is so hard it hurts as it strains against my zipper and digs into her stomach. *Cazzo*, what is it about this girl?

"Rose, why are you here?" I repeat, masking the blossoming desire with that swirl of anger.

"Can't a girl shower?" She leans into me, those damned perky breasts rubbing up against my jacket.

"At a closed gym?"

Rose throws her shoulders back, grim determination set on those fuckable lips. "I work here, so technically, I'm not doing anything wrong."

It blows my mind that this girl is still standing naked in front of me without batting an eye, even with the murderous scowl carved into my face. This look would have half of the guys on my payroll shitting themselves. She's got *palle*, that's for sure.

"But why? Why are you at Palestra instead of at your friend's place where you promised you'd stay?" *Merda*, she disobeyed me again.

"It's none of your business." The corners of her eyes taper as she regards me. "How *did* you find me anyway?"

"You think I would just leave you alone with her?"

"Um, yeah."

"Because you're proving to be so trustworthy...." I tighten my hold around her waist, and a whimper escapes her lips. "Tell me why you didn't stay with Maisy. Did something happen?"

"No," she hisses.

"Then tell me."

"She had Christmas plans, okay? Is that what you want to

hear? That I'm so fucking sad I don't have anywhere to go tonight?" The false bravado vanishes, leaving an unmasked, vulnerable, naked woman.

Her words spear through my chest and sink right into my heart because I feel the same every damned day. Alone as shit. Even with family nearby. A brother who can do no wrong, a mother who thinks he hung the moon and a part-time girlfriend who settled for second best.

"You should've told me." At least she's not trembling anymore which makes this next part easier. It has to be done, despite the pang of guilt stabbing at my insides. She must learn if she wants to survive this. "You disobeyed me, Rosa. And I warned you what would happen, didn't I?"

The hurt and embarrassment from a second ago recede, and a flash of mischief streaks across those luminous eyes as she glares up at me. "Are you going to punish me, Dante?" She draws her lower lip between her teeth, and damn, I want to be those teeth.

My hand twitches where it lays just above the curve of her ass. "Is that what you want, sweetheart?" That raspy edge laces my tone, despite my best efforts to restrain it. Electricity sizzles in the minute air between us, and all the blood rushes to my cock. It throbs with the overwhelming need to take this naked woman, bend her over the couch and fuck her until she moans my name.

Her head dips, mischief curving her lips. "I guess it's what I deserve, right?"

Excitement races through every inch of me, and my dick feels like a steel pole. I'll spank her perfect ass raw, then drag my tongue over the soft, rosy flesh and fuck the disobedience right out of her.

"Oh, Rosa, you have no idea what you're in for." My fingers dance down the small of her back and grab a handful of that perfect ass. A faint groan slips out, and she rocks her hips against me, that sweet pussy grinding at my slacks. I can feel her wetness through the fine material. Is it from the shower or her arousal? Fuck if I know or care.

Closing my hands around Rose's hips, I toss her over my shoulder. She lets out a squeal when I smack her fine ass, the sting on my palm only heightening the raw energy sizzling through every nerve ending.

"That's only the beginning. When we're done you won't be able to sit for a week." I close the distance between us and the couch in three long strides and sink into the rigid cushion. How the hell did she think she was going to sleep here?

I flip her across my lap, her perky ass spread over my legs. A tremor races up my spine at the effort to contain myself. I'm like a fucking horny virgin around this girl. My thoughts flicker back in time to Luca and me as kids. The first time I'd….

Shit, I can't do this. I swore to Stella I'd take care of her best friend and impaling her into the sofa until morning wouldn't sit well with my future sister-in-law. And Luca would kill me. He'd cut me off again, and I could not handle that.

"Just do it, already," Rose murmurs, her face pressed into the couch cushion.

I lift my hand, my heart raging against my ribs. Warm wetness seeps into my slacks. *Dio*, she wants this as much as I do. "You're soaked and ready for me, aren't you, sweetheart?"

Her head spins around, and a different kind of fire rages. "Fuck you, Dante. Damn it, what am I doing?" she hisses and runs her hand through her wet hair. "I swore you lost your chance when you walked out on me that night, and I'm not going back on my word. I'll take your fucking punishment, and then I'll finish myself off when you leave."

"Well, shit, you just sucked the fun right out of it, Rosa."

"And don't call me that! My name is Rose." She leaps up and snatches the discarded towel from the floor.

"Where the hell do you think you're going?" I snarl.

"To get dressed."

"Your punishment isn't over," I shout and jump up to stop her. What the hell is she thinking, walking away from me like that?

She shoots me the middle finger over her shoulder and slips into the bathroom.

All the pent-up sexual frustration morphs into rage. I stomp around the lounge, my anger intensifying with each passing second. How did I get sucked into this? The last thing I need right now is to be playing bodyguard to an infuriating woman who has my balls in a chokehold.

Fuck this, I'm out of here. I stomp toward the door, and my hand closes around the handle. *If you open that door, you'll never get it ... the one thing you want more than anything.* An annoying voice niggles at the back of my mind. When the hell had I developed a conscience? A frustrated grunt vibrates my throat, and I let out a string of curses.

I walk my ass back to the couch and slump down on the stiff cushion. When Rose finally emerges from the employee restroom, my fingers are curled into my palms, nails drawing blood. "Let's go," I growl.

"Go where? Did you not hear the part when I said I had nowhere to go tonight?"

"I'm taking you home."

A chill skitters up her spine as she clearly misunderstands my intent. The reaction is so violent, her entire body shudders.

"To *my* home."

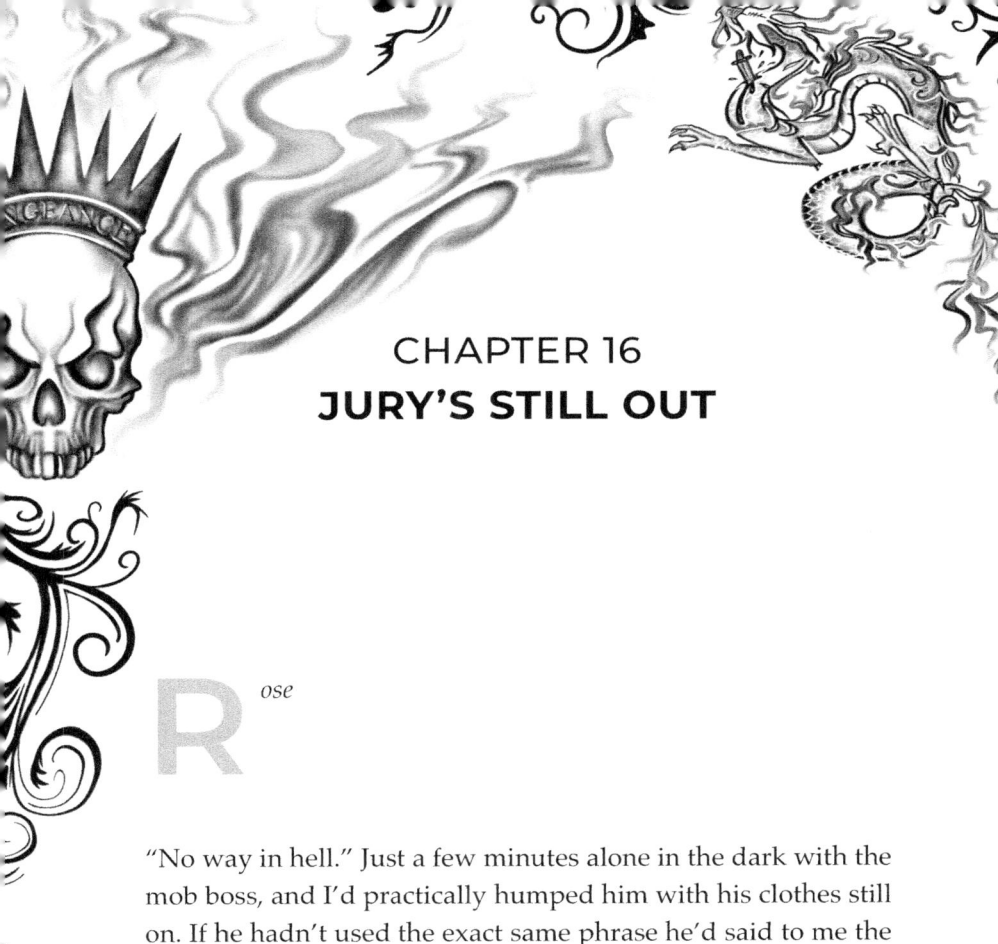

CHAPTER 16
JURY'S STILL OUT

R *ose*

"No way in hell." Just a few minutes alone in the dark with the mob boss, and I'd practically humped him with his clothes still on. If he hadn't used the exact same phrase he'd said to me the night we'd almost fucked, triggering memories of the mortifying moment, I would've let him do whatever he wanted to me. No way I'd survive an entire night in his penthouse. If I really wanted to give Rose 2.0 a shot, I had to hold strong. A night with Dante would be like leading a gazelle to the lion's den and expecting it *not* to get devoured.

I have *some* willpower but come on.

"I'm not asking." He closes the space between us, and that damnable musky, animal scent envelops me. "I already fucked up once since my brother left you in my care, and I'll be damned if I do it again."

Right, because this is all about Luca and Stella. How could I forget?

"Are you ever going to tell me what you did to my best friend? I don't get how you could still be acting like her bitch even after you literally saved her life." It's a low blow and I know it, but I also don't give a fuck right now. I'm exhausted and embarrassed, and the last thing I want is to spend the night with Dante Valentino. I just hope if I piss him off enough he'll leave me alone.

"It's not my secret to tell." His expression shutters and for a second, guilt flares in my gut.

Too far with that one?

His hand closes around my wrist, fingers digging into my flesh. Piercing midnight orbs lance into me, the intensity so raw and violent, my breath hitches. "If I have to drag you to my apartment bound and gagged, I will, but I will not allow you to sleep here alone tonight."

I swallow hard, images of fuzzy pink handcuffs and silk sheets invading my fucked-up psyche. "Fine," I hiss. "But only for tonight."

"Listen to me, sweetheart." His free hand closes around my throat, thumb stroking the delicate skin. "You will stay until I say it's safe for you to go. You don't get to make the rules; I do. Are we clear?"

"Crystal," I bite out. A normal person would be terrified or at least pissed at his caveman attitude. Me? I'm fucking wetter than when he threatened to spank me.

What the hell is wrong with me?

His nostrils flare as if he can somehow smell my desire in the air. I wouldn't be surprised. Dante Valentino is more beast than man.

"Now, let's go." He releases his hold around my throat, but only tightens his fingers around my wrist.

For some screwed up reason, I like it. I haven't felt protected or cared for since that night at sixteen when my innocence was stolen.

Dante throws my oversized tote over his shoulder and

drags me out of the staff lounge. I can't help a tiny smile from forming as I sneak a peek at the towering, tattooed mob boss carrying the bright pink, sequined bag embroidered with *Yogis Do It Better*.

"If you laugh, you'll be holding it yourself." His dark gaze catches mine, and the corner of his lip twitches.

I press my mouth into a tight line, barely restraining the giggle from bursting free, and follow him through the dark halls.

The penthouse is surprisingly bright with city lights dotting the floor-to-ceiling glass windows. Sprawling views of the west side of Central Park stretch as far as the eye can see as I walk into the great room. If I squint, I can make out Luca and Stella's condo just across the park in the Upper East Side. It's almost as if the brothers were taunting each other from across the green divide. Unlike his younger brother's place, which is OCD immaculate, discarded shoes lie at the entrance, unopened mail sits on the kitchen countertop and a collection of used glasses wait in the sink. I take in all the little details as Dante gives me the grand tour. The one thing the two penthouses share is the clean lines of the furniture and modern décor.

It's a huge step up from my tiny studio. Still, I'm not sure how this arrangement could possibly work out.

I'd only been to his place the one time. The infamous night of the party when I'd either made the best or worst decision of my life. Jury's still out on that one. I walk through the quiet hallway, trailing a few steps behind my new roommate when his words echo in my mind, *It's probably for the best then, I would've ruined you for any other man.* For an instant, I'm sprawled on that bed again as he stares down on me, heat burning my cheeks.

Too late, buddy.

I'd been ruined long ago.

"This is the guest room." Dante pauses in front of the door beside his bedroom and swings it open.

Flashes of that night surge to the forefront of my mind again. My fingers clenching his sheets as he runs his thick cock across my pulsing center from behind, then slides a finger inside me. I shudder. Heat pools between my legs, and I squeeze my eyes shut to chase away the much too vivid images.

"You okay?" He moves closer, his warm breath spilling over the shell of my ear and goosebumps ripple across my arms. "Why do you always shiver like that?"

I shrug and take a gigantic step back, putting some distance between us. "Always cold, I guess."

"Well, start wearing more clothes or something. I like my place at a comfortable sixty-nine degrees."

"Of course you would." I shoot him a smirk.

He rolls his eyes, but the ghost of a grin tickles his lips. Gawd, he's just unfairly good-looking when he smiles. He motions through the doorway. "Well, go ahead and make yourself comfortable. If you need anything else from your apartment, I'll have Aldo get it."

I nod. "You don't even give your guys a break for Christmas?" Which reminds me it's freakin' Christmas Eve and Dante doesn't even have a tree up in the living room. This really is the worst Christmas ever.

"They get paid well so I don't get any complaints."

"They're probably scared you'd shoot them if they did." I curl my arms across my chest, lean against the doorframe and throw him a cheeky grin.

"Rose, *cazzo*, you can't just blurt shit like that. What if it slips out in front of someone who doesn't know about the Kings?"

"Relax, Dante. I've kept my mouth shut for months, ever

since Stella spilled all your dirty little secrets. Why would I out you guys now?"

He shakes his head. "Things are going to be different now with you staying here. You might overhear or see things you shouldn't. It's absolutely necessary, more for your sake than my own, that you forget all of it. Do you understand?"

Staying here? He makes it sound like a permanent arrangement. "Yes, I get it," I finally grumble.

Dante marches into my new bedroom and drops my bag on the bed. "There's a bathroom through that door and that's the closet."

"Great." I eye the light gray walls and interior designer touches. No way he put this place together by himself. Nothing about the penthouse says Dante. "Any luck finding the guy?" My voice hitches a notch.

"No," he snarls. "And your Dr. Mark coincidentally seems to have disappeared too."

"What?" A twinge of icy fear ripples up my spine.

"I've been trying to find him myself, but the good doctor has vanished."

"It's Christmas break, D. There's hardly anyone in the city besides tourists. That must be it, right?"

His jaw ticks and that tendon beneath the scruffy jaw rages. "Could be."

Oh God, Mark could be out there somewhere looking for me... A strange choking sound slips through my clenched teeth. Dante surges forward, his massive body suddenly surrounding me. His gaze darkens as he regards me, brows furrowed. "I swore to you that no one would hurt you again, and I meant it." He points back and forth between our chests. "This shit between us doesn't matter. I will protect you no matter what, understand, Rosa?"

My chin dips, the intensity in his gaze too piercing to hold.

His hands close around my shoulders and squeeze. "No one fucks with what's mine and lives."

My head bounces up and down. I don't know why but I need to hear it. And somehow Dante knows. That violence, that darkness, it calls to me.

He releases me, and my body sags forward, instantly missing his touch. "I have to make some calls. I've had my guys scouring the city for any lowlife women-abusing scum just in case it isn't your ex."

"Thanks for this." I tick my head at the neatly made bed. "You didn't have to—"

"I already told you I'm not in the habit of doing things I don't want to. I'm also not some fucking knight in shining armor so manage your expectations, sweetheart."

"Right." I bite down on my lower lip as a wave of exhaustion takes hold. It's not even nine yet, and there's nothing I want more than to sleep and forget all about the last few days.

Dante moves toward the door, and it takes all my willpower not to beg him to stay until I fall asleep. If it hadn't been for my sleepover with Maisy last night, I never would've slept a wink. As soon as my eyes close, I see him. I hear that voice.

Dante pauses in the doorway, dark eyes scrutinizing. I don't know how this man can possibly read me so well. We barely know each other. "You all right?"

I fiddle with my fingers, twisting them into a pretzel. "I—it's just—"

"Spit it out, Rose, I have things to do."

"Nothing, never mind." I slump onto the bed.

He heaves out an exasperated sigh and jabs his fingers through his dark hair. "Just tell me."

"I—I haven't been able to sleep alone since that night…." I allow my words to fall off as embarrassment burns my cheeks. I don't dare look up.

The sound of retreating footfalls a long minute later finally jerks my eyes to the doorway. The bastard is gone.

A twinge of hurt bubbles up in my chest, and I will the

ridiculous pain down. Gawd, you're so stupid, Rose. This is Dante fucking Valentino, not prince charming. What did you think the bad boy gangster was going to do, tuck you in? Hold you in bed all night long? As I internally curse myself from here until next Tuesday, the sound of approaching footsteps sends my heart into cartwheels.

Dante fills the doorway in a soft tee and low-slung sweats with his laptop in one hand and phone in the other. Without saying a word, he sinks into the chair in the corner of the room and whips open the MacBook.

I watch him for a long minute, but his eyes never find mine.

When I'm tired of waiting, I crawl across the bed and pull the covers up to my chin. The cotton is so soft and the comforter so warm I barely suppress a groan. The faint scent of lavender tinges the sheets, reminding me of the sweet undercurrents of Dante's musky fragrance. Burying my head in the feather pillow, I curl up into a ball and watch the surly Italian across the room.

Until I fall asleep.

CHAPTER 17
NIGHTMARES AND DAYDREAMS

D*ante*

Aldo: *It's done, another Red Dragon is dead, boss.*
Me: *Good.*
Aldo: *You sure you want the guys to pop a guy tomorrow? It's Christmas.*
Me: *I know what fucking day it is. Just keep to the schedule. Until Feng shows his face, I'm not backing down.*
Aldo: *Okay, boss.*

I shove the cell phone back into my pocket and heave out a breath. Those damned Red Dragons are drawing this out much longer than I'd imagined. I was certain Feng would show his ugly ass face by now.

Refocusing my attention to the glowing computer screen, I skim the report Clara sent over. There's some new player in town, Gemini Corp, and they're buying up all the land along the west side docks. My turf. I stare at the document for a few seconds longer, but all the words blur.

Blinking quickly, I glance up over the top of my MacBook as Rose's quiet breaths fill the room. I was sure she was going to bust my balls all night, but instead she fell asleep in minutes. So much for not being able to sleep.... Silky blonde hair splays across the pillow like a freaking halo. Shit, do I want to knock that angelic ring right off and defile every inch of her. I inhale a deep breath as if I can somehow smell the intoxicating vanilla scent of her shampoo from this distance.

She squirms in her sleep, and her crop top rises, revealing her smooth torso and a hint of her breast. *Madonna mia.* My eyes laser on the soft cotton and the sharp peaks of her nipples poking through. That damned electric bill is going to be worth every penny for the length of Rose's stay.

I trail the soft curves of her body until I reach those tight ass yoga pants. How she wears those things in public is beyond me. I'd never let her out of *my* house looking like that. They're practically painted on, leaving nothing to the imagination. I can practically see every curve of her pussy right through that damned material, and I'm not the only one. I've seen every hotblooded male at Palestra eye-fucking her when she walks by. And it sets my veins on fire. Something changed the day Luca and Stella left her in my hands. Whether Rose likes it or not, she's mine. Mine to protect, mine to tease, mine to ruin.

My cock hardens, tenting my sweatpants at the thought of all the things I'd do to her. All the things she'd *let* me do. A few days with her and already I know she'd be nothing like uptight, frigid Caroline. No, she'd be wild, and I'd fuck that naughty streak right out of her until she got down on her knees for me.

Great, now I'm so damned hard my laptop teeters on my dick. I shove it aside and wrap my hand around my cock. I'd better shoot off a quick one, or I'll never get any work done.

Not with the sexy Rose sprawled across the bed just begging for me to wake her up and fuck her to kingdom come.

God, I'm a complete *coglione* for even thinking those things after what she's been through. Only a monster would. But … would she let me?

I throttle my cock, imagining her warm pussy tightening around me, drawing me in, and I barely repress the moan building in my throat. I focus on her hard nipples and envision my tongue swirling around the sensitive flesh, teasing them to tight peaks. Then I'd move down her torso, dragging my tongue down that perfect body, tasting her salty sweetness until I reach the altar between her thighs. *Dio*, I am not a religious man, but I'd fall to my knees to worship her sweet cunt.

Cum pools at the tip of my cock, and I'm practically dripping just thinking about her. *Cazzo*, I can't imagine what it would be like to actually have her. I'd blow my load the second I shoved inside.

A groan escapes through my clenched teeth, and I pump my shaft harder, faster. Squeezing my eyes closed, I picture my cock sliding into Rose's pussy, in and in and in, spreading her open until I'm balls deep inside her. I can almost see the flush of her cheeks, the curve of her mouth as she calls out my name when I nail her to the bed board.

One last pump and the orgasm rips through me. Fiery pleasure tears through every inch of me with those brilliant blue eyes plastered across my vision. A spray of warmth fills my fist as I finish myself off with my gaze fixed on Rose's innocent face. Damn, I could just imagine that dirty little mouth filled with my cock and my cum dripping down her chin. I squeeze my eyes closed again as I ride out the last waves of pleasure.

One day, sweetheart. One day I'll have you, when all this shit is behind us.

Grabbing a tissue box from the nightstand, I wipe myself off before dipping into the bathroom.

When I emerge, feeling slightly less strung tight, I force

myself back into the chair and prop the MacBook on my lap. Compelling my gaze to the overflowing email inbox, I sort through the first twenty, deleting most. I can't believe my brother deals with this bullshit all the time. Since assuming the roll as interim CEO, I must have gotten a million emails. This bureaucratic bull is enough to send anyone to an early grave. Hell, I'd dig it up and jump in myself.

Give me the thrill of the streets any day.

A soft sigh sends my gaze shooting over the screen again. Rose murmurs something in her sleep. I close my laptop again and set it on the nightstand. Fuck it, I'm not getting anything done tonight. Then I kneel on the mattress, leaning over her like a *pazzo* trying to make out her incoherent mutterings.

"Dante...."

That one word on her lips, and I'm hard again. All that work for nothing.

"Dante, please help...."

A cry rips through her lips, and her eyes snap open. I'm leaning over her like a real-life psychopath, and I half expect her to scream again. Only she doesn't. It's so much worse.

Her arms wind around my neck and coax me into the bed beside her. With a sleepy yawn, she takes my arm and places it beneath her neck and then curls the other around her waist, pressing her ass into my quickly returning erection.

Damn it.

"Thank you," she murmurs as she weaves her fingers between mine, trapping me against her body. Her soft exhales fill the minute space between us a second later.

I remain perfectly still, mentally cursing my brother for placing this woman's life in my hands. I'm not cut out for this shit. As soon as I'm certain she's asleep, I try to wriggle my arm out from under her head, but the moment I move, she groans, then sinks her ass deeper against my cock.

Mannaggia alla miseria.

Looks like I'll be the only one not getting any sleep tonight.

I rub my eyes and stare at the computer screen, cursing the hundreds of emails that appeared overnight. Clara would have my head if I didn't at least pretend to read them. Contracts from the commissioner, the mayor, reports from the zoning committee. Ugh, it's a nightmare of paperwork. Only Luca could handle this bureaucratic B.S.

My thoughts whirl to the past, to the conversation I had with Papà that changed everything all those years ago.

"Swear to me, Dante. Swear it now." Papà's thick accent fills the dark kitchen as he jabs a big finger into my chest. It's just past midnight and Ma and Luca are already asleep. I'd come home for the weekend from Cornell so Mamma could do my laundry.

"No," I bark. *"You worked so hard to build Re Industries, why would you want us to give it up?"*

"You know very well why, figlio mio.*"*

Papà had long been the right-hand man to the Esposito crime family. Coincidentally, Stella's grandfather. They ruled all of Manhattan, long before the Red Dragons, the Irish, the Russians, any of them. Then the old man died, and without any male heirs, the field was left wide open. Papà stepped in, using the company he'd started back in Italy as a front for the operation. And so, the Kings were born.

I'd begged Papà to let me in on the family business, but I'd just been accepted to Cornell, on a scholarship no less, so he shipped me off to college. Back then, I wasn't just a smartass. Papà had such high hopes for me.

"I can do it, Papà. I can make a legitimate business out of it."

"No, it's too late. The name Re Industries will always be tainted with rumors of the mob. I do not want that for you or Luca. You both deserve better. When I'm gone, let the company die with me."

My lips twist, a pang of pity for my father and everything he'd accomplished rising to the surface. He fought so hard when he arrived in New York City to provide a better life for his family. And he had.

"Promise me, Dante." He frames my cheeks with his warm, calloused hands, raw emotion streaking across his dark eyes. "Swear it on my grave, that you will never assume your roll as heir. I don't want this for you. You're capable of so much more."

"Lo giuro, Papà," I grit out.

"It's the only way to keep you and your brother safe. I have many regrets in this life, figlio. I've done things I'm not proud of and I only hope you'll never discover half of them. If some day you do, just know I did awful things for what I thought were the right reasons. For you, your brother and your mother. I love you all more than anything in this godforsaken world."

I nod, unable to summon a single word.

"When I'm gone, it'll be your job to keep our family safe. Capisci?"

My head dips again.

Dio, how I'd fucked that one up.

CHAPTER 18
NO FREE SNEAK PEEKS

D*ante*

I'd kept my promise to Papà that day, but in doing so, Luca had stepped in, assuming the role he thought I was too much of a coward to take. I'd stuck to my word, but I hadn't kept Luca safe. Quite the opposite. I threw him into the mouth of the lion, and at the time, I was too fucked up to realize what my silence would cost.

"Um, hello, Dante?"

I blink quickly, burying the dark thoughts of the past and focus on the woman sprawled across the bed waving at me. From the tight knit of her light brows, she must have been trying to get my attention for a while.

"Morning, sweetheart," I grumble.

"I can't believe you slept on that chair all night." She sits up and stretches, her long arms extending her slim torso and revealing another peek of the underside of her breasts.

Oh *Dio*, not this again.

It takes me a second to process her words with the overwhelming distraction of her half-naked body. She doesn't remember dragging me into bed with her?

"How'd you sleep?" I decide skimming over the truth is my best bet.

"Shockingly well." Her brows knit as she regards the crumpled pillow beside her.

"No nightmares?" *Dio*, I'm a masochist. Why even bring it up?

Her lips screw into an irresistible pout. "I don't think so. I just remember feeling safe for the first time in days."

An unexpected pang of emotion streaks through my chest. I massage the foreign feeling settling at the hollow of my ribcage. Clearing my throat, I mutter, "Glad you slept well. At least one of us did."

Her cheeks flush an enticing crimson, the tantalizing hue I imagine she'd turn if my cock was thrusting deep inside her.

"Yeah, um, sorry about that." She slides off the mattress and starts to make the bed. "Maybe I should just go back to my place—"

"No," I bark.

Her head whips toward me, electric blue eyes wide.

"It's fine. I slept just fine right here. Anyway, I had to get work done."

She nods and continues folding the blanket over the top of the pillows.

"You don't have to do that. Maria will come in later and take care of it."

Curiosity flickers across those lively eyes. "I didn't know you had a housekeeper."

"She only comes for a few hours a day. Tidies up the place and does my laundry. I don't need a live-in lady like my OCD brother."

"Clearly." She smirks, and it goes right to my damned cock. "You said you were working over night?"

Sure. I nod, closing the laptop, and shove it aside.

"Did you find anything on the guy?"

Irrational anger floods my veins. When I checked with Aldo again this morning there was still no word on the good doctor. My guys had brought in a few dirt bag rapists and pumped them for info, but so far, we'd come up empty. "No," I grit out.

Her cheery expression falters, and it's like a damned knife in the gut. "Okay, well I'm going to jump in the shower." She throws her thumb over her shoulder.

I watch her as she rifles through that pink tote bag and pulls out something red, but I'm too distracted by the lacy bra and thong that accompany it. She straightens, and I force my gaze away from her ass as she marches toward the bathroom.

When she reaches the door, she twists her head back and tosses me a smile. "Merry Christmas, D."

The door closes behind her before I can respond. Shit, in all the turmoil, I'd completely forgotten about Christmas. *Cazzo*, Caroline... I was supposed to do brunch with her and her family today.

I drag my phone out of my pocket as indecision wars in my gut. Earning the Dumphries' displeasure is the last thing I need with my precarious hold on King Industries. The rush of water jerks my attention to the bathroom door. A clear voice seeps through the door, singing some song I've heard on the radio a million times. The corner of my lip hitches up as Rose belts it out. My gaze darts between the bathroom door and my phone. Fuck it.

I type out a lame excuse to Caroline about being sick and shove the phone back in my pocket. Unexpected relief blossoms in my chest the moment I hit the send button. I must end things with that woman somehow.

My phone vibrates and I pull it out again, scanning the message from Aldo. Still nothing from Dr. Mark. The guy has completely disappeared which only serves as confirmation he's behind it. When I get my hands on the asshole, I'll tear him to shreds.

Before I can put my phone away, my eye catches the number of unopened emails in my inbox, and I hiss out a curse. I stare at the screen for a few minutes before giving up. It's fucking Christmas Day, don't I at least get one day off? I chuck the phone across the bed as the door to the bathroom creaks open.

My eyes dart in the direction of the sound and find Rose peering through the crack in the door, wrapped in an indecent towel. "Uh, I need my body lotion. Could you hand it to me?" She points at the pink bag atop the bed.

"Christ, what am I, your maid, sweetheart?" The corner of my lip flips up despite my best effort at surly. "Come out here and get it yourself."

Her eyes taper at the edges as she regards me. "You're just hoping my towel slips off again, aren't you, you dirty old man?"

A laugh squeezes out, shaking my entire damned chest. "Old man? I'm not even thirty yet."

"You're practically ancient compared to my fresh twenty-two years."

"Don't test me, Rosa. Even I have my limits."

"Hard limits?" She smirks. "Because I know a few great safe words—"

I throw my hand up cutting her off before she has me hard again. "Fine, I'll get it." I slowly rise and march to the bed, rifling through her bag until I find the lotion. Tahitian vanilla. Of course. Gripping the purple bottle, I saunter toward her at a snail's pace, taking in the tiny droplets of water dripping down her chest and disappearing beneath the plush towel.

I will it to fall.

Fall. Fall, damn it.

When I finally reach her, I let out a frustrated growl.

"What?" She eyes me, full lips puckered.

"It pisses me off when things don't go my way."

"What are you talking about?"

"Nothing," I grumble and hold out the lotion.

She reaches for it, but I snatch it away at the last instant forcing her to stumble out into the bedroom. "Dante...."

"What?" I give her an innocent smile.

"Give it to me." She tightens the towel around her, cinching it beneath her underarms.

"What do I get in return?" A wicked grin curls at the edges of my mouth.

"I'll smell nice." She smiles sweetly.

"Oh, Rosa, your natural female scent is more than enough for me." I snap my jaw closed an instant too late. *Fuck, this is not the plan, Dante.* She reaches for the lotion again, but I dart back another step. "Come and get it, sweetheart." Fuck the plan. Impulse control was never my strong suit.

She lunges for it, but I drop it into my sweatpants where it remains suspended at the stretchy waistband. A naughty grin twitches her lips.

"You want me to come get that, in there?" She points at my thickening erection.

"No, I want you to drop your towel. Then I'll give it to you."

"No way," she shrieks. "No free sneak peeks."

"Think of it as a Christmas present."

She snorts on a laugh, tucking the towel tighter around her chest. "You're out of your mind."

"Come on, Rosa. I need a good visual to get off on when I go shower, and your hot little naked body would be perfect."

Her cheeks burn a deep ruby red. "Dante!"

"Come on...." I inch closer. "You already deprived me of sleep all night, don't deprive me of this pleasure." I woke up hard as a rock with that ass pressed against me all night.

Those cobalt eyes sparkle with mischief as she takes a step toward me. "This is a one-time deal, Dante. A very special

Christmas present. I meant what I said that night. When you walked out on me, you lost your chance to have *all* this." She drops the towel, and my jaw nearly hits the floor alongside it.

I never thought she'd do it, but damn this girl has *palle*. Big, huge balls. And *Dio*, that body. My gaze rakes over every inch of her, saliva pooling in my mouth. Her nipples are so hard they could cut glass, and that pussy, shaved to a neat landing strip. I want to drag my tongue across those sweet folds and devour her.

As I stand there mesmerized, she sneaks her hand into my sweatpants and curls her fingers around my cock. "Oops." She glances up at me with a wicked grin. "Wrong one." Yanking her hand back, she grabs the bottle of lotion and sashays into the bathroom, wiggling that perfect ass, taunting me.

"Mark my words, I will make you go back on your vow, Rosa," I rasp out, my tone pathetically breathy. "In fact, I'll make you beg for it."

"Not in this lifetime, Dante Valentino."

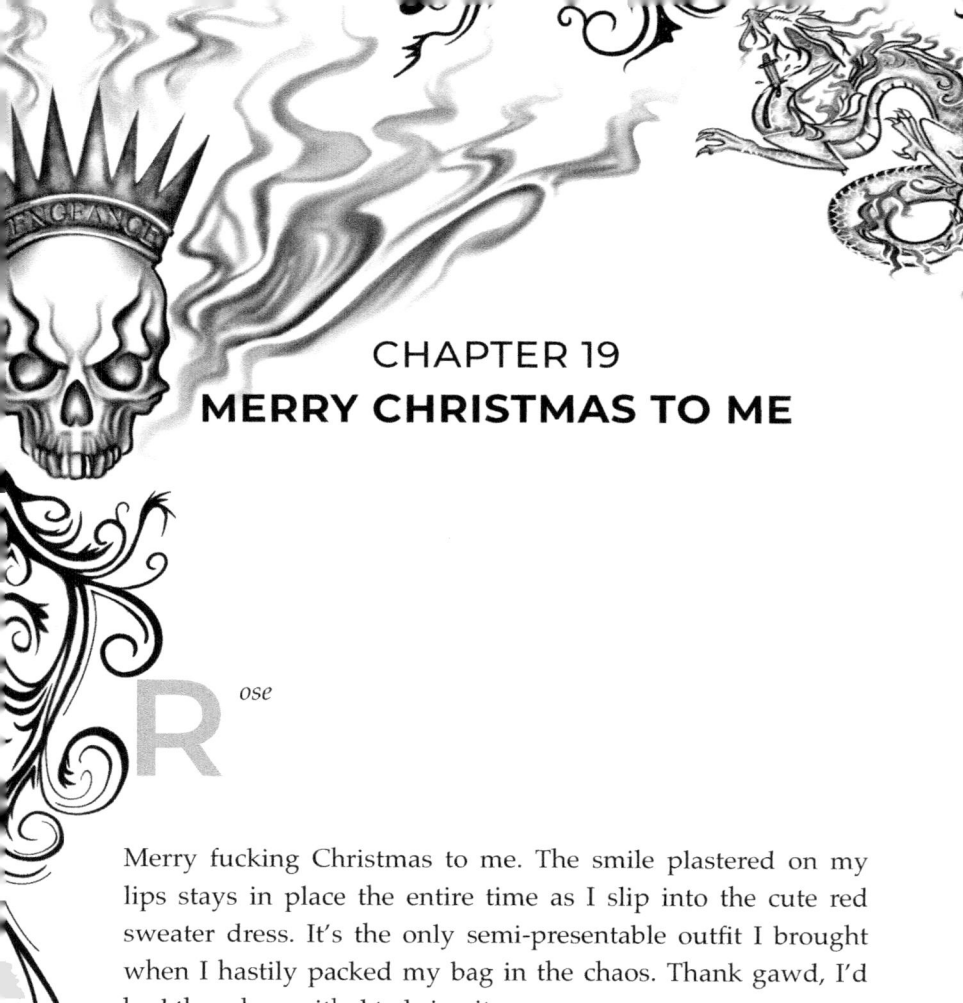

CHAPTER 19
MERRY CHRISTMAS TO ME

R ose

Merry fucking Christmas to me. The smile plastered on my lips stays in place the entire time as I slip into the cute red sweater dress. It's the only semi-presentable outfit I brought when I hastily packed my bag in the chaos. Thank gawd, I'd had the wherewithal to bring it.

In the wake of the worst few days of my adult life, I have the great Dante Valentino lusting after *me*.

This is just the distraction I need.

After he smashed my ego to pieces that night when he rejected me, I sure as hell was going to make him work for it. I sweep the mascara over my lashes, then dab some cherry red lip gloss across my lips. It's game time.

When I finally emerge from the bathroom, a hint of disappointment streaks through my chest at the sight of the empty bedroom. Tossing it aside, I slip on my strappy heals, steal one more glance in the mirror, run my hand through my freshly blown-out locks and step out into the hallway. Dante did say he had to shower…. The idea of his hand wrapped around his thick cock with naked images of me on his mind sends a thrill up my spine.

Whispered voices echo down the hallway, a familiar female one raising my hackles. I pause before I reach the foyer and lean against the doorframe. Totally eavesdropping.

"I just came to make sure you were okay, Dante." Fucking Caroline. "It's Christmas, what did you expect, that I'd leave you here sick and alone?"

"I'm fine. It's really not necessary," he whisper-hisses.

"Then why aren't you at brunch with Daddy and me?"

"I don't want to risk getting either of you sick. It's not worth it." He shrugs, and his dark gaze sails in my direction. I jump back out of his line of sight just in time.

"And why are you whispering?" she shrieks.

"My throat hurts."

What a stinking liar. Nausea roils in my gut at thoughts of our earlier encounter. How could I be so stupid? There he was flirting with me, proposing indecent arrangements, while he was supposed to be having Christmas brunch with his girlfriend and her family. I'm such a fucking idiot.

My feet move before I can stop them, my heels slapping against the marble floor in time with my escalating heartbeat.

Caroline's head whips toward me, fury twisting her heavily botoxed face. "Who the hell are you?" She spins toward Dante. "Who is this woman?"

"Relax, Caroline, this is just Rose."

"Just Rose?" What the actual fuck? I chomp down on my tongue to keep from spilling a string of curses at the two-timing bastard.

"Caroline, darling…"

That pet name sounds so fake, so forced, I nearly spew the measly contents of my stomach.

He rubs her shoulder, sliding his hand down her arm.

"Rose is Luca's fiancée's best friend. Surely, you remember her from the Met Gala?"

Her eyes taper as she regards me. Now I know why Stella hates her so much. She does look at everyone like they're covered in dog shit. "And what is she doing here?"

"She needed a place to stay. I'm just doing Luca a favor."

Every word is like a knife to my stupid heart. How could I have forgotten? I was only Dante's to babysit. I was his duty, his responsibility. Sure, maybe he wanted to fuck me, but that was just a bonus.

"And on that note, I'm out of here." I spin toward the door as heat pricks at the back of of my eyes. Rose 2.0 is a total disaster.

"No, Rose, stop!" Dante's footfalls echo behind me as I make a mad dash.

I finally reach the hallway just outside his penthouse, but the damned elevator crawls up to the top floor. I jab my finger at the button as he races toward me. My chest is heaving, and I wish I could say it was from the run, but I'm not *that* out of shape.

"You're not going anywhere, sweetheart." He reaches for me, but I squirm away from his grabby fingers.

"The hell I'm not."

His gaze turns murderous, midnight orbs pulsing. "What did you just say to me?"

"I'm not staying here with you and Caroline and spending a lovely Christmas together. I'm not your friend, I'm not your responsibility, I'm not your anything."

He towers over me, pressing me against the cold steel of the elevator doors. His hand closes around my neck, and his thumb grazes the column of my throat. "You. Are. Mine," he growls, punctuating each word with more pressure against my bobbing throat. "And you will do as I say."

"You're delusional, Dante," I spit. Actually spit in his face.

He wipes the saliva from his cheek, raw fury streaking

through those midnight orbs. "I told you what would happen if you disobeyed me, didn't I?"

"You're going to fuck the naughtiness out of me, Dante?" I hiss. "With prim and proper Caroline watching?" A swirl of excitement pools low in my belly. Gawd, I am so screwed up. Even this has my stupid pussy wet with need.

And I'm not the only one.

Dante's hard-as-hell cock rubs against my belly as he pins me to the elevator doors. He dips his mouth to my ear, warm breath spilling across the sensitive shell. "I don't give a fuck about Caroline." He pauses and nibbles at the lobe. "And *cazzo*, yes, I *will* punish you for this disobedience, and you *will* take it like a good girl."

Caroline stomps into the hallway, and her gasp echoes across the marble walls. I can only imagine what we must look like.

Dante cocks his head over his shoulder. "Go home, Caroline. I have an important matter to deal with."

"But Dante...."

"Go home," he barks.

"You're choosing her over me?" Her voices hitches, and it looks like she's about to cry.

Dante's hand closes around my wrist and he drags me away from the elevator, pinning my back to his front. With his free hand, he presses his finger to a scanner on the wall. In seconds, the elevator doors open.

Dante motions to Caroline with her unanswered question still hanging in the air. "Go home," he repeats, more calmly this time.

"My father will not be happy with this, Dante Valentino."

"Fair enough."

"This is it then?" She stands between the elevator doors, her hand preventing them from closing.

"For now, yes."

"You're going to regret this, you low-class nothing." She

steps back, arms crossed so tight they're wrinkling her bougie Chanel jacket, and the doors glide closed.

The moment she's gone, Dante's shoulders round, and he heaves out a frustrated sigh. His warm breath races across my ear, sending a splash of goosebumps over my arms.

"Sorry about your girlfriend," I mumble.

"She's not my girlfriend. I don't give a shit about her, but you, you're going to be sorry all right." A feral smile curls his lips as he drags me toward his penthouse door. As soon as we cross the threshold, he tosses me over his shoulder. My sweater dress rides up, exposing my thong and half of my bare ass cheeks.

I squeal and try to wriggle out of his grasp, but his arm is like a steel vice around my waist.

"You said something about a safe word earlier?"

A roar of excitement ripples up my spine. "Umhmm," I mumble against his shirt.

"Choose one."

"Ex-squeeze me?"

He kicks the door open to his bedroom and plops me onto his bed, face down. Memories of the last time we were in this room surge to the surface, a mix of excitement and frustration tumbling through my mind. Cool air rushes over my exposed ass and another wave of goosebumps ripples over my skin. Until he climbs on top of me. Through his slacks, his thick erection skims over my ass and settles between my cheeks. Fire races up my needy pussy. Dante stretches over me and opens the drawer in his bedstand. The clink of metal jerks my attention.

Revealing two pairs of handcuffs and a sinister smile, my heart kicks at my ribcage.

"Dante … what are you doing?"

"Safe word?"

"No," I cry. A hint of fear mixes with the overwhelming lust.

"That's too easy, sweetheart. It's gotta be something better than that." His massive arms cage me in, dark ink peeking out from beneath his white muscle shirt. Those beautifully dark and twisted tattoos swirl across muscled flesh blotting out my vision.

"I mean no way in hell I'm letting you cuff me to your bed. Don't get me wrong, I'm all for the kinky shit, but I can't tell if you want to fuck me or murder me right now."

"A little of both." He smirks, revealing a hidden dimple beneath that layer of wild scruff.

I try to struggle against him, but he only drops more of his weight over me. "I said you lost your chance with me, and I meant it."

"And I fully respect your decision," he rasps against my ear. "I'm not going to fuck you sweetheart, not unless you beg for my cock. I am however going to smack that ass raw for disobeying me. I let you off once, but that's all you get. No one, and I mean no one, gets second chances with the King, so consider yourself lucky."

Oh, my gawd, he's snapped. Dante has lost his ever-loving mind.

And fuck me, a part of me is all for it.

Didn't I want the mob boss out of control? Hadn't I dreamed of that cock ravaging my pussy night after night since the first time I met the foul-mouthed Italian god?

He snaps the handcuff around my wrist and fastens the other end to the bedpost. "Dante, no!" He repeats the procedure with my other hand, despite my best efforts at squirming out of his hold. His erection rubs against my pussy with each squirm, and I'm finding it harder and harder to keep pretending this isn't driving me wild.

He presses his lips to my ear and breathes, "Safe word?"

"Fuck you," I hiss out.

"Not the most original one, but not horrible. *Fuck you* it is."

He draws his tongue over the shell of my ear before finally lifting off me. "Mmm, so sweet."

I can finally breathe, the overwhelming scent of him drifting away with his massive body.

He steps between my legs and draws my sweater dress the rest of the way over my ass and up to my waist. Then he slips his hands beneath the tight material and latches his finger through the waistband of my lace thong. Painfully slowly, he draws it down my thighs.

"Dante…," I rasp out. His name comes out way too needy. Even I can hear the desire dripping from my tone. It doesn't say, *Dante let me go before I scream bloody murder*, no, it purrs *Fuck me Dante, fuck me so damned good*.

He drapes his body over me again, his breath tickling the back of my neck. His musky scent envelops me, hints of lavender from his laundry detergent filling the air. "Let's make a deal, sweetheart."

"What?" I hiss.

"If I cup that sweetness between your legs and you're not wet for me right now, I'll stop. Deal?"

"Fuck off, Dante!" I screech.

A wicked laugh warms the air. "Should I check?"

"No!"

He palms my ass, sliding a finger between my cheeks toward my pulsing pussy. "You sure sweetheart? You sure you don't want me to finger-fuck you right now until you cry out my name?"

Yes. Hell, yes. "No," I growl, barely able to form the word with his finger so close to my fiery core.

"Okay, then, let's start." He pushes off me and stands at the foot of the bed. Electricity tingles in the air, each and every one of my nerve endings standing in attention.

His hand skates over my ass, softly, taunting. "Last chance, Rosa. I can make this much more pleasurable if you just give in."

"Fuck you, Dante!" I hiss.

"Wait, was that your safe word?" He chuckles again, and I want to strangle the bastard.

"Just do it, already."

"Four slaps, one for each time you disobeyed me. One for not telling me about those flowers that psycho sent you last week, two for sneaking off to Palestra, three for refusing to drop your towel for me earlier, and the last one for trying to leave me."

My stupid, sucker of a heart latches onto the last words. *Leave me.* Something about his tone changes in those last two syllables. Or am I imagining it?

All thoughts fly out as a sharp sting lances across my ass.

CHAPTER 20
A SPECIAL GIFT

D*ante*

"Last one, sweetheart." I stand behind that perfect ass, a tantalizing rosy hue blossoming across her soft skin. I'm hard as fuck, my cock straining against the zipper of my jeans. I would've kept my sweatpants on if I'd known.

This entire morning has been a shit show. First, Caroline appears and then Rose has the *palle* to disobey me again. I nearly lost my mind when I saw her racing for the door. I couldn't let her leave, even if it cost me the Dumphries' account.

I only hoped Luca would see it my way.

"Just do it already," Rose rasps out. The sexy, rough tone goes straight to my dick. *Dio*, it's taking every last ounce of restraint not to drop my pants, free my cock and plow into her. Every cry, every moan has me on the edge of insanity.

I bend over her, rubbing my crotch against her ass, and she

lets out another gasp. "You know, we could finish this off on a good note…."

"Never," she hisses.

I can feel her wriggling with need beneath me, but the woman is stubborn. I'll give her that. And there's nothing I like more than a challenge.

Straightening, I rub my hands together to warm up my palm and land one last glorious spank. She cries out as our bare skin meets, the sting on my hand only intensifying the tangle of lust and fury. For some fucked up reason, they've always gone hand in hand for me.

I dip my mouth to her ass cheek and drag my tongue over the sensitive flesh. She squirms beneath me, her arousal wetting my sheets. *Dio*, I knew she'd like this. "Are you sure, Rosa?"

"Yes, you bastard, now get me out of these cuffs."

I press a kiss to her rosy ass cheek and give it one last squeeze for good measure. "Your wish is my command." Moving around the edge of the bed, I uncuff her from the bed posts and examine her wrists. The metal handcuffs have a soft, fuzzy inner lining, but a slight line mars her skin. The little tiger fought hard. I drop a kiss along the faint mark, and another gasp escapes those pouty lips.

As soon as she's freed, she rolls over, revealing that beautiful pussy. Her thighs are slick with her arousal, and *cazzo*, I want a taste. I want to drag my tongue up her inner thigh and devour her sweetness.

My tongue darts out, sliding over my bottom lip. "*Merda*, sweetheart, you look good enough to eat."

"Too bad you'll never get a taste." She starts to roll her dress down her hips, but I stop her before she gets far.

"Not yet." I reach for the hem of that scandalous sweater dress, and I'm shocked when she lets me push it up over her glistening torso. "We need to soak that ass, or you won't be able to sit down later today. And we wouldn't want to ruin Christmas."

"I'm going to soak your ass," she grits out through clenched teeth. "This is the worst Christmas ever."

I've definitely had worse. In fact, it's shaping up to be a rather memorable one. I draw the tight dress up and over her head and her breasts tumble free. *Cazzo*, she's not even wearing a bra. A growl vibrates my throat, the desire to take one of those hard nipples into my mouth overwhelming.

Summoning every ounce of self-control left, I sweep her off the bed, cradling her naked body in my arms.

"What are you doing?" she squeals.

"I told you, it's bath time." I kick the bathroom door open and gently place Rose onto the marble tub. Her eyes widen as she takes in the master bath with the silver-veined marble and gold touches. It's a bit much in my opinion, but I wasn't going to argue with the ridiculously expensive interior designer Luca hired.

Gifting me this apartment was his way of mending the enormous rift between us. It had been growing since the day Papà died, and only expanded with Stella's arrival.

I turn on the faucets, then tear open a container of bath salts with my teeth, keeping one hand on Rose in case she decides to bolt, and dump the fragrant powder in the warm water.

"Well, I never expected this." Rose eyes me like I've grown a second dick.

"I can't have you whining about your ass hurting later. They're soothing essential oils and shit."

A knowing smile curls the corner of her lip, and damn it, she looks beautiful.

I pour in a cupful of the scented oil and dip my hand in the warm water. After giving it a swirl so the bubbles rise, I tug her in. She slides into the tub with a moan that has my cock straining to be freed.

Fuck it. "Can I get in with you, sweetheart?" What the hell? Did I just *ask* her?

She leans her head back and closes her eyes. Her perky tits bob above the surface, and I'm tugging at the hem of my shirt before she answers. The grinding of my zipper snaps her eyes open.

"I never said yes."

"I shouldn't have asked. This my fucking tub." I slide my pants down and spring free.

Rose's eyes widen as they scrape down my body, trailing my tattoos and abs, lingering on my cock. She's not the only one who doesn't wear underthings.

"Fine," she mutters and swallows hard. "But stay on your side."

A wicked chuckle rumbles my entire chest. This girl isn't even remotely afraid of me. I spanked her ass raw, and still, I can see the flare of lust in her eyes. She's only fighting me to prove a point, but little does she know, I never take no for an answer.

I step into the tub and the warmth of the water has nothing on the heat sizzling through my veins. If this woman really thinks I'm going to sit in this bath with her like a good little choir boy, she's got another thing coming.

I fold down and stretch out my legs. Despite the enormous size of the basin, my legs have to wrap around hers to fit. "I'm not comfortable," I grumble.

"That sounds like your problem." She leans her head back against the pillow towel and smirks.

Feisty little thing.

I dip my hands under the bubbles and blindly search. My hands close around her toes, and she lets out a satisfying squeal. Then I move up her leg, and my fingers wrap around her calves.

"What are you doing?" she cries.

"I need more room." I tug her leg toward me, and she slides down beneath the surface.

"Dante!" She pops up an instant later, her blonde hair soaked.

Before she can recover from the unexpected dunk, I grab her other foot and hitch her legs around my waist so she's straddling me. My arms wrap around her back and press her tight against my chest.

She lifts an irritated brow. "What are you doing?" she grits out.

"Don't you agree this is much more comfortable?" My hands move down her spine and cradle her ass so my cock presses against her belly. *Merda*, I'm so desperate for a taste. One night under my roof, and I've lost all control.

Okay, control has never been a strong suit of mine.

"No." She presses her lips together, but it doesn't conceal the breathy edge to her tone.

"I've got an idea." My hands cup her ass cheeks, fingers digging into her soft flesh. I press her close so my shaft glides through her wet folds.

She lets out a whimper as her hips tilt for me.

"It's Christmas, right?"

Rose nods, nibbling on her lower lip.

"So I want to give you a present, a special one, just from me to you."

She shakes her head, the ghost of a smile pulling at her lips. "Oh yeah, a special one?"

"It won't cost you anything, and it won't be going against your vow to deny me that beautiful pussy because I'm not requiring anything in return." I lift her hips and slide her up and down, along the hard ridge of my cock.

"What does that even mean?" she pants.

"I'm going to gift you the best orgasm of your life."

A laugh bursts through her clenched lips. "I don't think so—"

I dip my hand between us and press a finger to her clit, stopping her mid-sentence. Her hips squirm against the pressure.

"Come on, sweetheart, we both know you want this." I start to circle the swollen nub, and she grinds against my cock.

"I don't!"

But she keeps doing it. So, I take it as a yes.

Getting a good grip on her wet cheeks, I stand, haul her out of the water with me, and prop her on the edge of the tub.

"Dante!" she hisses as the cool air pebbles her skin and draws her nipples to tight, tempting peaks.

I can't help myself. My mouth closes around one, and she lets out a breathy moan that makes my cock twitch. Kneeling between her legs in the warm water, I spread her wide. "That's a good girl," I murmur against her breast. "Let me see that beautiful pussy."

I drag my tongue down her torso, savoring every fragrant inch of skin.

"Dante...," she mumbles.

"Just relax and enjoy it, *Rosa*. This is all on me, a once in a lifetime offer."

CHAPTER 21
I SHOULD NOT BE DOING THIS

Rose

Fuck. I should not be doing this. There is no way in hell I should be allowing Dante to do this to me. This goes against everything Rose 2.0 stands for. My head falls back as a wave of pleasure tumbles over me as Dante licks his way past my navel.

Gawd, his mouth on my nipple nearly had me coming.

I don't doubt he could give me the best orgasm of my life just with that wicked tongue.

My fingers curl around his thick, dark hair as he slowly descends. I try to focus, try to remind myself all the reasons why this is *so* wrong. Then why the hell does it feel so damned right?

My thoughts whirl back to that night in his bedroom. *This is your only chance … If this doesn't happen tonight, it doesn't happen at all.* The chubby little angel on my shoulder wags a disappointed finger at me.

Technically, I was talking about sex. Penis-inside-vagina sex. This would not be that. It's a total technicality, and I'm fully aware of it. He should stop. I should tell him to stop. But I can't force the words out of my mouth.

All I can think about is his hot tongue trailing across my inner thigh. My pussy pulses with need, anticipation burning my core. Fuck, I just need that tongue on me.

And it's like he hears my silent plea.

His tongue parts my drenched lips and drags across my throbbing center.

"Oh, Dante," I moan as he circles my clit.

"Spread those legs for me, sweetheart," he mumbles against my sensitive flesh. "I want to see all of you." The rumble of his voice nearly sends me diving over the edge.

He licks and teases, dipping his tongue so far inside me, my hips buck against his mouth. My back arches as raw pleasure races through every inch of me. But I don't want to lose control just yet. If this is my Christmas gift, I need to enjoy every last second.

As if he can feel me getting close, he pulls back and stares up at me, those bottomless midnight orbs drilling into the darkest parts of my being. "Watch me," he whispers. "I want your eyes on me when I give you the best orgasm of your life, so you never forget whose tongue was inside you when you come so hard you tiptoe across the gates of heaven."

I suck in a breath as anticipation tightens my core. "It's coming soon," I pant.

"Not yet, sweetheart. You'll come when I tell you." He lowers his mouth to my pussy keeping those eyes locked on mine. The moment is so raw, so primal, the sound of his mouth sucking, and devouring, I'm going to come from the sheer intensity.

"Dante…," I pant, my hips rocking against his mouth, desperate for the friction.

He moves one hand from my ass and plunges a finger

inside me. I cry out from the riot of sensations between my legs. He thrusts in a steady rhythm as his tongue lavishes my folds. I'm a wriggling, squirming mess.

"I need to come," I rasp.

"Not yet." He pushes a second finger inside me, and I clench around him, the feeling of fullness intoxicating.

Just when I think I can't stand another second, he extends his pinky and circles the sensitive skin around my back hole.

"Oh. My. Dante!" I cry out as the rush of sensations overtakes me.

"Now you can come, sweetheart." He sucks my clit between his teeth, and an explosion racks my core.

My eyes squeeze closed as an orgasm rips through me. He wasn't fucking exaggerating, for a second, I definitely see the heavens, the stars, the goddamned entire solar system. My hands dig into his hair as I ride the wave of pleasure, my hips bucking and straining as he continues his assault.

"That's right," he whispers against my pulsing flesh. "That's my good girl."

My head falls back, and if it weren't for Dante's hands on my thighs, I would've slid right into the water. As I sit there panting, attempting to catch my breath, he looms over me, my arousal glistening on his chin.

"Merry Christmas, sweetheart." He stands and nearly whacks me in the face with his hard-ass cock as he gets out of the tub.

"Where are you going?" I rasp out.

He pops two fingers into his mouth, the ones that were just buried inside me and sucks, his cheeks hollowing. My insides clench because holy hell it's one of the hottest things I've ever seen. A long minute later, he slowly draws them out, his tongue circling the tips. "Mmm. I need to finish myself off before my balls explode. Those noises, Rosa, I could come from them alone."

A shiver of excitement races down my spine. I have no

doubt I could come again. Just one look at that huge cock and I'm ready for him. No. No. NO. I push the lusty thoughts down. This was a one-time deal. A Christmas present which I totally deserved after the shitty week I've had.

"You should soak for a little longer," he says over his shoulder. "When you're ready, I'll see you out in the living room."

"You have another surprise for me, D?"

He scoffs. "Remember what I said about managing your expectations?"

I smirk. The truth is that the hard mob boss hasn't been at all what I'd expected.

"It's a surprise, but it's not from me."

"I'll take it then."

He closes his hand around the doorknob then pauses and slants a glance in my direction. "That was just a taste, sweetheart. If you ever decide to reconsider your ultimatum, I can promise I really would ruin you for anyone else."

Before I can get a word out, he whips the door open, slips through the crack and slams it shut behind him.

I sink into the warm water and bury my head in my hands. What the hell have I gotten myself into it?

Once I'm back in my red sweater dress, hair blown out once again, a familiar, sweet voice has me sprinting toward the living room. Dante is sitting on the leather couch with his laptop across his legs. A hint of disappointment fills my chest as I discover the source of that voice.

Dante spins the MacBook in my direction, and Stella's smiling face fills the screen.

"Merry Christmas, Rose!" She waves excitedly and despite the disappointment of not getting to see my best friend in person, I can't help the smile from stretching across my face.

I sink into the couch beside Dante and commandeer the laptop. "Stells! I've missed you so much!"

"Me too. I'm so sorry I've been MIA. I wish I could be there with you celebrating the holiday like last year."

I nod as images of our last Christmas together float to the surface. Her drunkass dad had passed out before lunch, and Stella and I had exchanged homemade gifts and eaten leftover lasagna. Thank goodness for her neighbor, Mrs. DeVito, who at least always kept us well-fed.

"It's okay," I muster. "Dante's been pretty decent."

Luca's face fills the screen, and he eyes his brother. "He has?"

"Of course, I have." His thigh brushes mine, and tiny stabs of electricity dart up my leg.

"Thank you, Dante, for taking care of my best friend."

He nods roughly then averts his gaze.

"How's everything going in New York?" Luca asks.

"Fucking fantastic." Dante rolls his eyes. "Damned Red Dragons are more stubborn than you—"

"Uh, uh, uh." Stella waggles her finger. "It's Christmas day, this is not turning into a work conversation. You guys can talk about all that crap on your own time." She smiles at her fiancé sweetly, and the man's resolve crumbles. Gawd, she really does have the retired mob boss completely wrapped around her pussy. "So, what do you guys have planned for today?"

"Well, Dante was supposed to have a date with Caroline and her rich daddy," I chime in.

He shoots me a narrowed glare over the top of the screen.

"You cancelled?" Luca asks.

"Yeah, I'm all stuffy right now, feeling a little under the weather."

I barely suppress an eye roll. He had no problem breathing when he was ravaging my pussy.

"I'm glad you two will be spending Christmas together."

"You are?" I blurt. For months, my bestie had been swearing me off her fiancé's older brother.

"Of course, I am. I'd hate for you to spend it alone." Stella is one of the few people that I've confided in about my uncle. It was the same reason I'd skipped Christmas with the family last year. But had Dante told her about my stalker?

I move off screen, pretending to shift the computer and mouth to Dante, "Do they know about the attempted assault?" I hate to worry my friend when she is so far away and there is really nothing she can do.

He slowly shakes his head. "I'm handling it, aren't I?" he mouths.

"Right."

"What are you two whispering about?" Stella asks.

"Nothing," we answer in unison. Whoa, freaky.

"And why don't I see a Christmas tree?" She scans the great room through the limited angle of the lens.

"Dante never gets a tree," Luca huffs. "He's like Scrooge."

"You only have one because your housekeeper sets it up for you every year," Dante counters.

"Can we get one this year, please, Dante?" I pivot toward my grumpy roommate. "I'll do everything, I swear."

"Wait, what do you mean *we*?" Stella's brows slam together.

Oops. Dante shoots me a panicked gaze. "Um, my heater is on the fritz, and the supe is out, you know, because of the holiday so I spent the night. But Morris should be back on the job by tomorrow, so I'll be back in my place before long."

"Oh." Stella's curious gaze darts back and forth between us. "And you called Dante of all people?"

"You're the one who told me to reach out to him if anything happened."

"I meant something dangerous...."

"I ran into her at Palestra," Dante cuts in. "She told me what happened, and I insisted."

"That's oddly gentlemanly of you, *fratello*." Luca grins at his brother. "Maybe you do have some of those hero tendencies after all."

A rueful chuckle vibrates Dante's massive chest. "I don't think so, *fratellino*." Little brother. Seeing the siblings' lighthearted banter fills me with an odd, unnamable sensation.

"So can we get the tree?" I blurt.

"Yes, yes, get her a Christmas tree, Dante, please!" Stella presses her hands together and gives him the best puppy dog eyes I've ever seen from my friend.

He huffs out a breath like buying a big ass fir is the most arduous task on the planet. "Fine, as long as it keeps you from annoying me."

I toss him a super dramatic lower lip pout.

"I guess we have shopping to do," he mutters at his brother. "Thanks for this. I'll be sure to get you two back in the near future. Those damned pine needles get everywhere."

"Oh, stop it." I clap him on the shoulder. "I said I'd take care of it."

With another round of Merry Christmases and goodbyes, Dante disconnects the call. A weird sadness descends over me the moment their smiling faces disappear. Luca and Stella are so freaking happy, and I'm so damned jealous. I mean I'm not, because I love my friend, but I want that too.

I glance up to find Dante's dark gaze on me.

"So will you wear a sexy French maid outfit when you sweep up the pine needles all over my apartment?"

"If that's what it takes to get my tree." I shoot him a mischievous smirk.

"I suppose it's a deal then." He stretches out his hand, and I warily take it. His warm fingers wrap around mine, and his thumb slowly brushes across my palm. His eyes meet mine, and a storm brews just below the dark surface. Of all the dangerously tempting things this man has done to me, this right here is the worst. Because that soft touch, that piercing stare, doesn't streak down to my lusty pussy, no, it surges right up to my vulnerable heart.

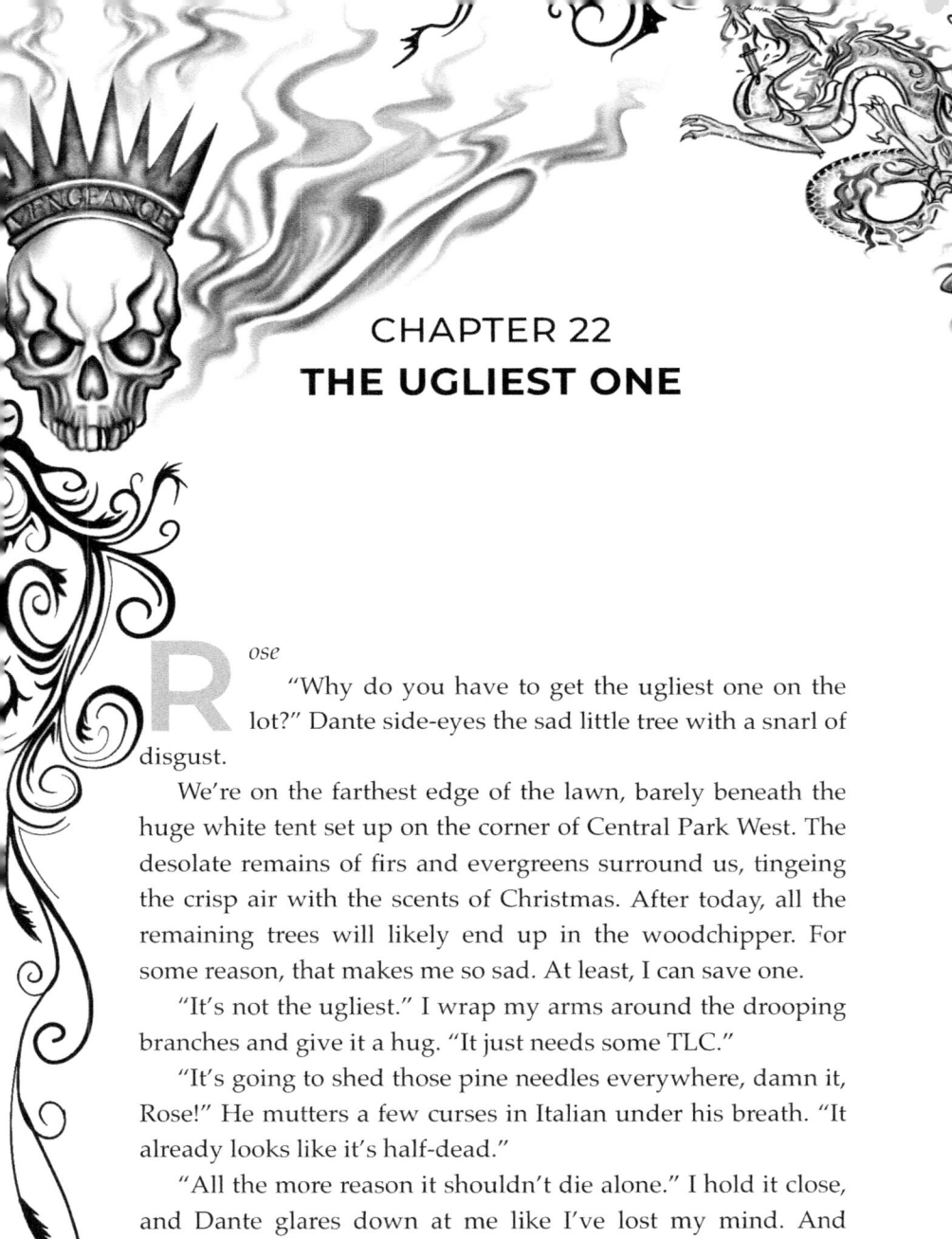

CHAPTER 22
THE UGLIEST ONE

R*ose*

"Why do you have to get the ugliest one on the lot?" Dante side-eyes the sad little tree with a snarl of disgust.

We're on the farthest edge of the lawn, barely beneath the huge white tent set up on the corner of Central Park West. The desolate remains of firs and evergreens surround us, tingeing the crisp air with the scents of Christmas. After today, all the remaining trees will likely end up in the woodchipper. For some reason, that makes me so sad. At least, I can save one.

"It's not the ugliest." I wrap my arms around the drooping branches and give it a hug. "It just needs some TLC."

"It's going to shed those pine needles everywhere, damn it, Rose!" He mutters a few curses in Italian under his breath. "It already looks like it's half-dead."

"All the more reason it shouldn't die alone." I hold it close, and Dante glares down at me like I've lost my mind. And probably I have because of that mind-blowing orgasm. I'm still tingling with aftershocks hours later. "Please, Dante. This is the one I want." I flick the red tag hanging from the sagging limb. "And look, it's on sale."

"No shit, because no sane person would ever want the hideous thing in their home."

"Well, I want it." I release the tree and clap my hands on my hips, glaring up at the bossy mob boss. His eyes lock on mine, then narrow. I can almost see the instant he realizes he's lost the battle. It's extremely empowering and satisfying.

"You're insufferable. Completely insufferable." He huffs out a breath and stalks through the tangle of trees toward the check-out counter.

I stay with my prize, arranging the limbs so it doesn't look quite so sad. The tree lot is practically a ghost town. We were lucky we found one open on Christmas Day with any supply at all. At least decorating it will give us something to do when we get home.

Decorations … crap, Dante probably doesn't have any of those.

I search the forest of trees, weaving in between towering evergreens. I thought I'd seen some when we walked in. After a few circles, I finally find the display stand with a meager collection of ornaments remaining. I grab a few boxes of colorful bulbs, stars, a string of lights and a container of red bows. Dante's right, the tree is pretty scrawny, and I doubt it'll hold much more.

Hushed voices draw my attention behind a cluster of trees.

"I already told you, the Kings don't run shit anymore in Lower Manhattan."

The hair on the back of my neck prickles, and I drop down behind the ornament display.

"That's not the word on the street." A slight Italian accent hangs on the man's words. "I heard the Red Dragons are being killed off one by one until you have the balls to show your face."

"That's just fucking Dante Valentino. This new power he's inherited has gone to his head, but he won't be trouble for long. Soon Luca will be forced to emerge from hiding and when he does—" The first man makes the sound of a gunshot. "—It'll all be over. Trust me, it's for both of our benefits to work together. When the Kings are gone, Gemini Corp will be poised to take over."

A gasp almost sneaks through my clenched lips as alarm bells go off.

"My boss doesn't want to work with you, Feng. He wants to obliterate you."

Shit. I know that name. Feng is the asshole who put the hit out on Luca and Stella. He's the reason they're in hiding and Dante's in charge. I may have done some snooping of my own. I fumble for my phone in my jacket pocket, but my gloves are too thick, and I drop it. I freeze as it sinks into the icy dirt.

I don't breathe for a long minute.

Feng scoffs. "Oh, yeah? Well, I've got a message for your boss."

The squelch of something sharp sinking into a soft and gooey mass hits my ears a second before a muffled grunt. A loud thud hits the frozen earth, and everything goes silent. I hold my breath, forcing my ragged heartbeats to slow.

The sound of footfalls crunching through fallen snow grow closer.

Shit. Shit. I reach for the fallen phone and rip my glove off with my teeth. I press my back to the stand, wishing I could disappear into the cheerful array of ornaments and jab the call button. Luckily, Dante was the last person I'd called.

A loud ring sends my heart catapulting against my ribs.

"Hello?" Feng snaps, his voice echoing just behind me. "Yes, uncle, I'll be right there. The meeting with the Gemini guy didn't go as well as planned."

The smack of approaching footsteps whirls my head toward a tattooed, raging Italian barreling through the jungle of trees. His eyes latch onto mine, and relief floods his features. Then they lift to the Red Dragon presumably standing right behind me.

"Feng!" he shouts. "Get away from her!"

I shrink further into the stand as the nephew of the leader of the Chinese Triad leans over the short stand and pins me with dark, narrowed eyes. He mutters a curse and spins around, before racing between the trees.

"Feng, you coward!" Dante yells after him. "Come back here and face me like a man."

Dante slides to the ground beside me, his strong, calloused hands cradling my face. "Are you all right, Rosa?"

My head bounces up and down. "He never saw me. I was hiding, and he had no idea I was here, not until you showed up anyway."

"*Grazie a Dio*," he mutters and pulls me into his chest. "Thank God, you're okay."

I sink into his arms, burying my nose in his shirt. His scent invades my being, bringing with it an odd sense of calm. I feel invincible with Dante's massive body enveloping me.

"*Cazzo*, Rosa, I leave you alone for a second…."

"It's not my fault."

He releases me and holds me out to arm's length. "Tell me everything."

"There's not much to tell. I was minding my own business picking out ornaments—"

Dante rolls his eyes so hard, only the whites show.

"—when I overheard him talking to some guy with an Italian accent."

"What guy?" Now they're so wide the darkness nearly eclipses the white.

"I don't know, but I think he's dead." I must be in shock because the words just spill from my mouth like it's any other Tuesday.

Dante rises and tugs me up with him. I point over the ornament display, through the trees.

"Over there."

He jerks me behind his back and creeps around the

Christmas display. Just a few yards away, a pool of deep crimson blankets the snow. Another string of curses erupts from that foul mouth. For some reason, it's so much hotter in Italian.

I try to get around Dante to see the body, but he shoves me further behind him.

"You don't have to see this."

The crazy thing is that I want to. Some sick, dark part of me wants to see the unseeing eyes, expressionless mask of death. I'd imagined it a hundred times, that same look, on my uncle's face as I stand over him with a knife in my hand.

Only I'd never had the balls to go through with it.

The crunch of approaching footfalls sends my head spinning over my shoulder. Aldo races toward us, gun drawn.

"What the hell took you so long?" Dante growls.

"Sorry, boss, I was grabbing a hot dog when you texted."

"You're fucking lucky Rose wasn't in real trouble." He grabs Aldo by his jacket collar and lifts him off the ground. Terror streaks through the man's eyes as his feet kick and find nothing but air. "If she had been hurt and you showed up late, it would've been your body left for clean up."

A strange chill of excitement at the venom lacing his words skates up my spine.

Aldo swallows hard, his gaze dipping to the snowy ground. "I'm sorry, boss. It'll never happen again, I swear."

"Clean this mess up." Releasing him, Dante ticks his head at the body. "You know who this guy is?"

Aldo shakes his head. "No idea. Never seen the man before."

"He works for Gemini Corp or something," I blurt.

"What?" Dante's dark gaze pivots in my direction.

"I heard them talking before Feng killed him."

"*Merda*," he snarls. "Tell me everything exactly as you heard it."

"Sure." I hug my arms around myself. There's something

in Dante's expression that has every hair on my body standing on end. It's not anger or fury or even annoyance. It's worse, much worse. Fear.

I flip the small silver star around in my palm and eye the highest branch of my scraggly little tree. I don't even need to stand on my tiptoes to reach it. There's no way I was letting that unexpected encounter with the Triad ruin my Christmas. When we got back to Dante's apartment, he disappeared into his study, and I got to work on the tree. The poor little thing lost half of its needles in the town car on the way home.

I offered to clean the trunk, but Dante insisted Aldo would do it. Part of his punishment for his untimely hot dog break. I wish I could say I didn't find Dante's crazy protectiveness insanely attractive, but it would be an outright lie. The way he threatened Aldo had my blood pumping and heat rushing between my legs.

Speak of the devil….

Dante stalks into the living room, eyes my sad little tree and shakes his head. Ignoring him, I clip the star onto the tallest branch. And the limb sags.

Dante's broad chest bounces with the force of his laughter. "Great pick, sweetheart."

"Oh, just shut up." I lift the sagging branch and clip three limp limbs together to hold up the star. "There." The glittering star barely hangs on, the remaining branches droop and most of the ornaments look like they're about a second away from hitting the floor, but I did it. My little tree is up.

Dante stands just behind me, the heat from his body searing into my back. "I ordered Chinese food for dinner. I wasn't exactly expecting company."

"You actually cook?" I twist my head over my shoulder to cast a shocked gaze at the big brute.

"I'm an excellent cook, actually. Maybe one day I'll show you, if you're a good girl." He smirks, then his dark gaze latches onto my little tree. "I'm scared if we turn on the lights it'll set the damn scrawny thing on fire."

"Just do it." I tick my head at the plug which lies only a few inches from the outlet on the wall.

"You're going to be severely punished if this burns down my apartment," he whispers against the shell of my ear. A feral grin parts his lips, and heat races to my core. Visions of his palm on my ass flash across my mind, and a tremor surges up my spine.

"Stop being so dramatic," I finally force out once I've banished the heated memories. There will be no more of that any time soon. "Now, stick it in."

"Mmm, Rose, I thought you'd never ask." He looms closer, pressing his front flush against my back, and I can already feel him thick and erect against me. A dangerous glimmer sparks in his eyes.

I jab my elbow into his rock-hard abs and regret it immediately as I nail my funny bone, sending electric tingles up and down my arm.

He moves away only long enough to plug in the lights, then returns to loom over me. The brilliant, twinkling lights illuminate the apartment in a golden glow and warmth floods my chest. From the corner of my eye, I catch a smile curling the corner of Dante's lips.

And for once, it's not a smirk, or a sneer, but a genuine smile, and God, it takes my breath away.

"It's beautiful," he murmurs.

I couldn't agree more.

CHAPTER 23
MAN BUN

Dante

Stop watching her sleep, you *coglione*. I pace the living room, the first rays of sun coming up over the park, and I'm not sure which is more beautiful, the deep oranges of the sunrise or the woman stretched across my couch.

Rose and I spent all night talking in front of that damned ugly ass tree, and by the time she fell asleep, I couldn't turn off the twinkling lights. Despite my legitimate fears about a fire. So, I spent most of the night with one eye open instead of getting some much-needed rest. My penthouse is perfectly decorated with all the designer touches, but nothing brought warmth like that scrawny, brown thing.

My phone vibrates, tearing my thoughts from my new roommate to my cell. As soon as Rose told me what she'd overheard at the Christmas tree lot, I had Tony find out everything he could on Gemini Corp. Clara had mentioned the name in one of those inane weekly reports that I barely skimmed. Now I had to pay attention.

I jab the call answer button. "What did you find?"

"Not much, unfortunately. Gemini Corp is a privately held company, so they're not required to publish much of anything."

"Just like King Industries."

"Yup." He pops the P and for some reason, it grates on my last sleep-deprived nerve.

"What about Feng? Any word on the street about his interaction with Rose? Does he know who she is? If he thinks she overheard something—" I bite off the rest of the sentence, the prickle of fear robbing the remaining words.

"Nothing, boss. But I've got all the guys on it. If Rose's name or even her description gets picked up in the rumor mill, we'll hear about it."

"Good." My fingers curl into fists, nails digging into my skin. "And Dr. Mark?"

"Still M.I.A., but according to the sign at his office, the practice opens on Monday, so he'll have to show up eventually."

"Stay on it, understand?"

"Sure, thing."

"And Tony, step up our game with the Red Dragons. I want two taken out every day."

"Are you serious?"

"Do I sound serious?" I growl. "That asshole is giving me the run around, and I'm tired of it."

"Dante, the Lower East Side is already a powder keg. You do that and it's going to set off—"

"I don't care," I shout. "Give the order." Rose rolls over on the couch, a soft sigh pursing her lips.

"Will do, boss."

I jab my finger into the call end button and shove my cell into my pocket.

"Good morning, sunshine." Rose's rough, sleepy voice sends the irritation dribbling right out of me.

"Sorry if I woke you," I mumble.

"I like waking up to the sound of your voice." Her brows knit, and she presses her lips into a tight line as if they'd spilled out without her consent. She straightens and brings her knees to her chest, tucking in those long, sexy bare legs. "Guess I fell asleep on the couch, huh?"

I nod. "I didn't want to move you. You seemed so comfortable."

"I was." Her brows pucker again as if she was surprised at the admission. She's not the only one. I spent most of the night with her head on my lap, though I'd be damned if I admitted that to her.

I jerk my thumb over my shoulder toward the study. "I have some work to do today, so...."

"Oh, yeah, no worries. I have to get going anyway. I have a nine o'clock class to teach."

"Today?"

"Um, yeah, it's the twenty-sixth. Palestra is open, remember?"

I mutter a curse and drag my hand through my wild hair. "Can't you postpone it for a few more days?"

"No! I just got the job, Dante. I can't ask for more days off."

I tower over her, my knees pinning her to the couch, trying my damnedest to intimidate the obstinate woman. "I'll pay you whatever they would for the class."

"No!" she squeaks. "You can't just buy me off like one of your lowlife informants."

"Why not?"

"Because I need this job, Dante. Not just for a week or a month, or however long you have it in your head that you need to protect me."

I fold my body over hers, planting a hand on either side of

the couch cushion. "Listen to me, sweetheart, I thought I'd already made this clear."

"No, you made up stupid rules you expect me to follow, but this is one I can't. I need that job, Dante. More than that, I like it." She pauses and sucks in her lower lip. "Please don't take that away from me."

A flare of guilt unfurls, a toxic mixture of pity and regret. If I hadn't failed her, like I did everyone else, if I'd been more proactive from the beginning with this stalker she wouldn't be in this shitty situation. "Fine," I grit out. "I guess I'm going to yoga then."

"What?"

"I'm not letting you walk out of this apartment by yourself. Not only is your crazy ass ex after you, but now there's Feng. I have no idea what he thinks you heard or saw, and I can't risk him retaliating. He saw us together. It won't take him long to figure out who you are to me."

I bite down on my tongue. I hadn't meant that last part to come out. *To me.* What was she to me anyway? A job, a responsibility, redemption? In a few short weeks she'd become too many things to wrap my fucked-up head around.

Fear races across those brilliant green eyes, and I want to shove my foot in my mouth for being so callous. In only a matter of days living with me, I've managed to expose her to even more trouble. *Cazzo.*

She nods slowly, tearing her eyes from mine, and focuses on her tangled fingers. "Can't you send one of your guys to follow me like before?"

"I don't have anyone I trust enough to spare." It's the gods-damned truth. There are few men I would trust with her life right now. Which leaves me on babysitting duty, again. At least I can get a workout in. Something I'm in great need of right now to let off some steam as a result of the permanent blue balls this woman has gifted me for the holidays.

Rose glances up at me, and her nose nearly brushes mine.

A tiny sigh escapes, and she drags her tongue across her bottom lip. *Dio*, I want to claim that mouth along with every inch of her. That one little taste yesterday wasn't enough, nowhere near enough.

"Okay," she murmurs. "But I'm warning you, Dante, if you think I'm going to take it easy on you, you've got another thing coming."

I scoff. "Nothing is easy with you, sweetheart. And that's what makes it interesting." I shoot her a wink and force myself to back off. Being with this woman is testing me in more ways than I ever thought possible.

I'm going to rip out pretty boy's man bun if he doesn't take his eyes off Rose's ass. I glare at the punk in the front row, rage flooding my veins. He's done nothing but stare at her for the entire hour-long yoga class.

And fuck, a part of me can't blame him with Rose wearing those curve-hugging skintight yoga pants. I can make out the exact shape of her pussy, and it has my dick raging against my sweatpants. She's in downward dog, her fine ass up in the air and breasts spilling over the top of her sports bra. I must have a word with her about her wardrobe choices, or I'm going to have a fucking coronary. And here I thought yoga was supposed to be relaxing.

All I want to do is gouge out the eyes of every man in this room.

Rose pushes off the floor and walks between the students, adjusting their positions. When she reaches man-bun and glides her hand across his lower back, I nearly lose my shit. A growl vibrates my chest, the sound so loud, the blonde beside me startles.

"Sorry," I mutter. "Indigestion."

I try to focus on the pose, on my breathing, but only deep

red consumes my vision as man-bun whispers something that has Rose giggling like a fucking schoolgirl. Are you shitting me right now?

That guy cannot be that funny. He's a twenty-something-year-old with hair like a girl.

Rose finally straightens and claps her hands. "Well done, everyone. Great job today. Looks like those two days off for the holidays has everyone nice and limber and relaxed."

Except for me. My fingers are twitching to strangle every male in this room.

I straighten and stretch out my arms over my head. Man-bun rolls up his mat and saunters toward Rose, who's chatting with some other tool in front of the studio. Why are so many men surrounding her?

Bunching my mat into a terrible roll, I slip it under my arm and stalk toward Rose.

"It's really a shame you don't do private in-home visits," says man-bun. He leans in and squeezes her shoulder. "I'm really tight in my quads, and I could use the special one-on-one attention."

Fury surges through my veins, loosening my jaw from the stiff set. "Get your fucking hand off her before I break it off," I snarl.

Rose gasps. "Dante!" I barely hear her, I'm so focused.

Man-bun's pale blue eyes widen, and he blanches, mouth curving into a capital O. "Excuse me?"

"You heard me, pretty boy. Don't you ever touch Rose again. She's mine, and I'll cut your balls off and feed them to you if you lay a hand on her just one more time."

He backs up, spins around and runs away so fast he's nothing but a distant memory.

"How could you?" Rose hisses.

I fix my eyes to hers and wrap my hand around her wrist. "He was eyeing you like you're nothing more than a piece of meat. I kept my mouth shut for the entire class. I couldn't control myself for another second."

"Then you better freaking try harder. If you can't behave, this is never going to work."

"I'm just trying to keep you safe."

"From Jack?" She ticks her head down the hallway where man-bun disappeared.

"From all of them."

She shakes her head, rolling her eyes. "I see what this is. You're jealous…." The hint of a smile curls her lips.

"I am not," I growl.

Another man approaches, inching between us. "Excuse me, Rose, I just wanted to say what a great class this was. Do you offer private lessons?"

Oh, fuck no. Pezzo di merda. My hand snakes out before I can stop it, curling around the back of Rose's neck. I yank her mouth to mine. She stares up at me, eyes wide an instant before my lips crash into hers.

CHAPTER 24
SELF-PRESERVATION

R*ose*

Dante devours me, his mouth consuming mine like my lips are the only thing standing between him and salvation. The worst part? I'm matching him stroke for stroke. My body melts into his, my soft curves fitting perfectly against his rough edges. Gawd, none of this was supposed to happen. Dante was supposed to be a drunken quickie all those weeks ago, and denying myself that has turned this into so much more. That must be it. There's no other logical reason I'd be grinding against this man's cock like this. Right in the middle of my fucking yoga studio.

A sliver of sense dribbles in between the lusty haze, and I shove him back. "What are you doing?" I snarl. Spinning around, I search for Charlie who'd asked about private lessons. I sure as hell could use the extra cash. Only he's gone. As is every other student in the room.

Fucking Dante scared them away with his growly voice and murderous, midnight eyes.

Now that we're alone, I pin him with a glare, rising to my tiptoes to come close to his eyelevel. "You can't do that shit, Dante. This is my work. How would you like it if I came into your office, insulted your co-workers and kissed you like that?"

"Sweetheart, I'd bend you over my desk, pull those indecent yoga pants down to your ankles and fuck you right up until quitting time."

My breath catches, an embarrassing squeak emitting from the back of my throat. All the blood rushes from my head down to my lusty pussy.

He winds his arm around my waist and drags me flush against his body. "All you have to do is ask."

"Never," I hiss. Even as my traitorous hips tilt to meet his rock-hard erection. *Dammit, Rose.* Pressing my palms to his chest, I attempt to push out of his hold. He must've been appeasing me last time because now, I don't move an inch and neither does he.

Dante's hold only tightens as he grinds his hips against mine. If I weren't half a foot shorter than him, he'd be stroking me right through my center. Shit, I'd never hated him for being so tall as I do in that moment. "Come on, sweetheart, just give in already." He licks his lips, dragging his tongue devastatingly slowly across that perfect bow. "I'm sorry I walked out on you that night. Is that what you want to hear? I fucked up, okay?"

A swirl of satisfaction blossoms in my chest, parting my lips into a huge smile. Yes, that was exactly what I wanted. What I needed from him.

"If I could go back in time, I would've ignored that call until after I'd plowed into that sweet, tight pussy. Because *cazzo*, Rosa, now I just can't get you out of my fucking mind.

And the idea of those assholes' hands on you makes me want to break each and every bone in their bodies."

I suck in a sharp breath, the violence in his tone stoking the burning flames raging below. I should've been repulsed by his words because a part of me knew how true they were. He wasn't bluffing. The man was a killer. Stella had always warned me to stay away, given me glimpses of the monster that lay beneath the beautiful, rugged surface, but I just never wanted to believe.

I do now. The truth is screaming at me from those bottomless, pitch irises.

He drags his thumb roughly over my bottom lip, and a sexy growl vibrates his throat. "Do I scare you, precious?"

How the heck he plucked that thought out of my mind is beyond me. I shake my head and suck his thumb into my mouth. Because obviously I've lost my fucking mind. He hisses out a curse as my tongue circles his calloused finger.

"Rosa, be careful…." The rough edge to his tone has my insides clenching. "You know what they say about monsters."

I clamp my hand around his and bring it closer to my mouth. "What's that?" I mumble around his thumb, leisurely sucking and circling.

"Once you set a monster free, there's no getting him back into his cage."

I spit out his thumb and smirk up at him, wiping the saliva from my chin. "Then I guess it's a good thing I don't want you caged." It takes every ounce of willpower in my body to turn away and walk toward the door.

"But you should."

His whispered confession is so faint, I barely hear it over my thundering pulse. I'm playing a dangerous game, and I'm all too aware.

Just one kiss left me in a puddle. If I really did let Dante in, he'd devastate me. This is more than just about Rose 2.0. It's self-preservation.

I chew my PB&J slowly in the staff lounge, none too eager to face my new roommate lingering in the hallway. Dante remained outside the door of my yoga studio all day. Those midnight eyes never strayed, pinning ominously to any male that came within five feet of me.

I wouldn't let him get to me though. Private lessons at Palestra were big money so I refused to let Dante scare away all the clientele. Shockingly, he remained fixed to the spot by the door all day and didn't threaten another soul. Maybe this could work after all.

The lounge door opens, and Maisy's smiling face fills the entry before I catch a snarling Italian behind her. He sneaks a peek into the employee lounge before the door swings shut, and I release a breath of relief. For a second, I was sure he was going to bust in here like he did on Christmas Eve when I planned on sleeping on the couch.

"Hey, Rose!" Maisy scoots into the chair beside me, then unwraps her sandwich, a grown up looking one with lettuce, tomatoes and all the fixings. Unlike my kid's meal. Dante needs to upgrade his fridge contents stat. "How was your Christmas?"

"Great," I mumble around a mouthful. Luckily the PB&J is a good excuse not to expand on the topic. "You?"

She shrugs. "Just perfect. With my perfect sister, her perfect husband and kids."

I swallow down the big bite and squeeze her hand. "I'm sorry."

"No, don't be. I'm being a total B for no reason. I'm just bitter."

I've still never asked her much about her divorce, and I'm not stupid enough to get into that right now, but I make a mental note to find out more one day when we're alone.

"How was Long Island?" she asks.

I freeze, debating whether or not to tell her the truth, or at least a version of it. I hate lying to my new friend. "I didn't end up going," I finally mutter.

Her eyes widen, and she drops her sandwich, the lettuce and tomato fly out and splatter on the floor. "Oh, sugar! Sorry, I'm such a clutz." She bends down and tries to scrape up the rest of her sandwich from under the table, then pops up with a huff. "Any who, why didn't you go?"

I mentally flail as I struggle to come up with a logical excuse. But nothing comes to mind. "Family drama." Short and sweet and true. "I'd rather not get into it."

"Sure, I get it." Maisy takes a sip from her water bottle before her brows knit. "But wait, I thought your heater was broken. Where'd you stay the night?"

Heat burns my cheeks traveling all the way to the tips of my ears. Which makes no sense. Just thinking about the savage Italian has my body in a tizzy. "Um, I actually stayed with Dante."

Maisy's pale green eyes look like they are about to burst from her head. "Oh, girl, how could you just throw that out so casually? You spent the night with the gorgeous Roman god, Dante Valentino?"

A few heads twist in our direction, and I sink down in my chair. Sometimes I forget what a big deal the Valentinos are, especially in these circles. "Nothing happened," I hiss.

"Is that why he's standing outside the lounge?" She cocks her head over her shoulder toward the door and waggles her brows.

"Huh. You noticed that?"

A ridiculous grins splits her lips. "Impossible not to ignore the huge, snarly, sinfully delicious male."

"I don't know, maybe." I wave a nonchalant hand, but even I don't buy it.

"Spill, Rose. Please!" She grabs my hands and squeezes, excitement flaring to life in her eyes. "I could use a fun distraction in my life. Please, let me live vicariously through you!"

I lean in close and drop my voice to a whisper. "Nothing. Happened."

Maisy kicks her head back and laughs. "You're a horrible tease. And a terrible liar." The door opens again as one of the spin instructors enters, and I catch Dante's murderous glare over the guy's shoulder.

Maisy must too because she spins back to me, shaking her head. "That does not look like the face of a man with whom nothing happened."

"You're right." I smirk. "If something had happened, he wouldn't be able to wipe the grin off his face." Stuffing the rest of the PB&J in my mouth, I crumple up the paper bag and toss it into the trash. I can't avoid Dante forever, and I have a feeling the longer I make him wait, the worse his wrath.

Maisy cackles again. "I just hope you know what you're doing. I've heard stories about that man…." Her smile melts away, twisting into a frown.

"He's all bark and no bite, trust me." I squeeze her shoulder as I rise. "But I appreciate you looking out for me. With Stella gone, it's nice to have a friend."

"Same! We should definitely have another sleepover soon."

"Absolutely." The word comes out forced because the truth is I probably shouldn't with my stalker still on the loose. The last thing I want to do is put Maisy in danger. If I wasn't so embarrassed about my stupid decision of dating a patient, I'd admit the truth to my new friend. Maybe one day I'd work up the courage.

I consider how I'd frame the idiotic mistake as I march over to my locker to grab my bag and mentally prepare to face the devil outside the door. I'm not sure how much longer I can fight him. Worse, I'm not sure I want to anymore. I type my code into the keypad and the metal door clicks open. A single, withered yellow rose stares up at me.

CHAPTER 25
FULL OF IT

D*ante*

Rose's scream sends my heart raging against my ribs. I barrel through the employee lounge door, crimson tainting my vision. Scanning the room, I find her in seconds, standing frozen in front of her locker. Her shoulders are trembling, her arms pulled tight across her body.

Something squeezes the remaining air from my lungs.

I push past some redhead making her way toward Rose and jerk her into my chest. "What the hell happened?" I roar, an instant before my gaze settles on the yellow rose perched atop her tote bag. "Fuck."

A few of the other instructors and staff litter the room, curious gazes lancing in our direction. "Everyone get the hell out," I bark.

Footsteps quicken toward the exit, and I turn my attention back to Rose. She buries her nose in my shirt, her chest heaving against mine. *Cazzo.* How the hell did this prick make it past Tony? Hell, past me? "Shh, I got you, Rosa," I whisper in her ear.

"He's never going to stop," she murmurs into my shirt.

Raw fury races through my veins, and I curl my fingernails into my palms as I hold Rose tight against me. "You're wrong, sweetheart. A dead man can't do shit."

"Are you okay?" The redhead appears beside her, and I finally recognize the woman. It's her friend, Maisy, the one whose house I allowed her to sleep in after a thorough background check. Her ex-husband was an abusive asshole, but he's out of the picture thanks to a restraining order. The fact that the girl didn't obey my command to leave the lounge is irritating as all hell, but I bite down on the annoyance for Rose's sake.

"Yeah, I'm okay." She tries to step out from my hold, but I only tighten my arm around her waist. *Dio*, for a terrible second, I thought I'd find Mark or worse, Feng, with a knife to her throat. The image had sent ice through my veins, stalling out my fucking heart.

"Is that a rose?" Maisy peers into Rose's locker, her brows furrowed.

Rose huffs out a breath, and her body finally relaxes against mine. "I'm sorry, I should've told you. My ex is being super creepy and sending me weird shit."

"Oh, sweety, I'm so sorry." Maisy reaches for her, and I'm filled with the most insane urge to tug Rose out of her grasp. As the woman's hand closes around Rose's shoulder, I shove the monster down to my darkest depths. She's not going to hurt her, you *coglione*. "Is there anything I can do?"

"No," I bark. "I've got her."

Maisy's eyes lift to mine, and a glint of distrust scrunches her freckled nose. She leans in close to her friend. "I'm serious, if you need anything I'm here for you, okay?"

Rose nods and offers her a tight smile. "Thanks, Maisy, I really do appreciate it."

The redhead gives me another once over before turning toward the door. I should be grateful she has a friend here, but all I feel is insulted that the woman thinks I can't handle this. Rose is mine.

You've already failed her multiple times. That dark voice scrapes through my subconscious. I hate that it's right.

Grabbing her pink tote bag with one hand, I wrap the other around Rose's palm and tug her toward the door. "Let's go home. I'll have one of my guys check the Palestra security cameras, and we'll find out exactly who did this."

Rose glances up at me, unshed tears glistening in her bright eyes. "You can do that?"

"Of course, I can."

She plants her feet, stopping a foot from the door, her fingers still entangled through mine. "Wait. So that night I was here, you were watching?"

"I was."

Her lips screw into a pout but shockingly they remain closed. She jerks me toward the exit, and I follow her like some pussy-whipped boyfriend. The most frustrating part is I haven't even gotten to enjoy the benefits of that warm pussy. I just get all the crap.

Shaking my head, I dismiss the pointless thoughts. This woman is going through hell, and all I can think about is my cock. Damn, I really am a *bastardo*.

"How is that possible?" I snarl at Tony through the phone, sinking into the leather chair in my study the next morning. I stare at the computer screen, the grainy black and white footage of the employee lounge at Palestra playing on a loop.

"Maybe it's not this doctor guy, boss? Whoever hacked the security system is on the same level as our techs."

That makes no sense. How would a run-of-the-mill plastic

surgeon have access to some of the best hackers in the business? Not to mention the fact that it seems like the guy has disappeared off the planet. And yet somehow, he got into Palestra.

Darkness coils beneath my skin; the monster I try so hard to keep buried claws its way to the surface. The urge to wring the life out of the man that torments Rose boils the blood in my veins.

I need to do something, or I'll explode. "Feng's two men, have they been eliminated yet today?"

"One down, one to go, boss."

"Good." Excitement tosses around in my gut. It's been a while since I watched the life drain out of a man. If it couldn't be Dr. Mark, one of the Red Dragons would do just fine. "Call off the second hit, I'm going to handle it myself."

"You sure?"

"Yes, Tony, I'm sure."

"But Luca said—"

"My brother's not here. Is he?" I snarl. Luca probably warned him about my tendencies. Addiction is something I've fought for years. It can come in many forms, not only drugs and alcohol. The feeling of taking a life can be as addictive as sinking your cock into a wet, tight pussy. I know because I've been a slave to it all.

"No, boss, Luca's not here."

"So that means I'm in charge, and I don't appreciate being questioned."

"Right, sorry, *Signor* Valentino." My lip curls into an unexpected smile. The title brings back memories of my father. After the vow I made to him, I never thought I'd see the day when I sat the throne of the King's empire. It's been a hell of a lot more than I bargained for, but the victory is still sweet, nonetheless.

"I'll let you know when it's done." I jab my finger into the red button on the screen and shove my phone into my pocket.

A walk across the old neighborhood will be fun, cathartic even. Then the first Red Dragon rat I come across will suffer my wrath.

I march out of my office and nearly slam into a soft body. My hands instinctively curl around Rose's waist, and she glances up at me, tears staining her cheeks. My heart clenches, and I suck in a breath at the unfamiliar sensations invading my chest.

"What's wrong?" I mumble.

She sweeps the stray tear from her cheek and drops her gaze. "Nothing. I just got something in my eye. You should really have your housekeeper come more often; there's dust everywhere."

My lip twitches, but I keep the rueful smile at bay. "Fine, if you're sure you're okay, I have to go out."

Her eyes pop up to mine. "Where?"

"I need to take care of some business."

"Dr. Mark?"

A frustrated hiss escapes through my clenched teeth. "No, that asshole has disappeared. He's not even on the damned camera footage at Palestra."

"How is that possible?"

"No clue, but I sure as hell am going to find out." I start toward the door, but she jumps in front of me again.

"Let me go with you." A crop top hangs off her shoulder, and she's wearing those indecent yoga pants. She's not going anywhere in those.

"Absolutely not," I snap and try to move around her. The last thing I need is Rose anywhere near me when I let the monster loose from his cage.

"Please, Dante." She blocks the hallway and rises to her tiptoes, batting dark lashes. "I don't want to stay here alone."

That unfamiliar feeling knots my chest again. I press my fingers into the aching spot, attempting to loosen the tangle of emotions. "You're safe here. I can't say the same out there."

"But I'll be with you."

The hope in her eyes is worse than a knee to the balls. It siphons all the air from my lungs and leaves me gaping like a complete *coglione*. This woman actually trusts me, believes in me, even after I've failed to protect her numerous times. What the hell is wrong with her?

Overwhelming anger bubbles up, crushing everything else in its path. I step into Rose and shove her against the wall, pinning her to the smooth surface. Her breath hitches, eyes widening, and her fear only urges the monster to the surface. "Do you remember what I told you that night at Luca's all those months ago after the Met Ball?"

She shakes her head, her full lower lip trapped between her teeth.

I press closer, my hardening cock straining painfully against my slacks. "When Dr. Mark kept calling you and I grabbed the phone away to tell him to fuck off?"

Understanding flashes across the deep blue depths, but she doesn't speak.

"I told you back then I was no one's hero, sweetheart, and I meant it. I'm not cut out for this knight in shining armor shit."

Her entire body tenses beneath me as I crush her against the wall. She must feel my erection digging into her belly. "For someone who's so reluctant, you're doing a damn good job," she whispers.

A rueful chuckle erupts. "If I was doing such a damned good job, that asshole would be six feet under by now, and you'd be safe back in your own cozy, little studio. Far away from me, and all this shit."

She stiffens her lower lip and sears those soulful eyes to mine. "What if I don't want to be far away from you?" Her hips tilt to meet mine, and now I'm hard as hell.

The anger tangles with the awakening desire, but I shove it down, holding onto the fury. I need it to survive. "Then you're far more stupid than I thought, sweetheart."

Rose swallows hard, the corners of her eyes tapering. Not the hint of a tear remains. *Good.* I'd rather her hate me than be upset over that psycho Dr. Mark. "And you're full of shit, Dante Valentino." Her lips claim mine, stealing the breath from my lungs.

CHAPTER 26
RUN

R*ose*

I fully comprehend I've lost my mind. The stress of having a stalker coupled with my fucked up past has finally broken me because there is no other sane reason for me to be kissing Dante right now. More than kissing, so much more.

I rise to my tiptoes and wind my arms around the back of his neck, tilting my hips to feel his cock against my throbbing center. He's still too damned tall, so I wrap my leg around his waist and his palms move to my ass, suspending me against the wall so I can get my other leg around him. A groan slips free when I finally get the friction my lusty pussy so desperately needs.

Fuck Rose 2.0. If the original version gets to ride Dante like a savage, I'm totally okay with her.

After the realization that my stalker had been inside Palestra, inside the very lounge I was going to hide out in a few nights earlier, the fear had reached monumental levels. If

Dante hadn't dragged me out of there that night, who knows what would've happened?

I could be dead. Or worse.

A chill surges up my spine, and Dante tightens his hold, his fingers digging into my ass and only increasing the delicious friction between us. Another moan escapes but Dante swallows it up, his mouth devouring my lips.

"*Cazzo*, sweetheart, those sounds," he murmurs around my tongue. "You're going to make me come from them alone."

I slip my hand between our bodies and wrap my fingers around his erection over his slacks. His cock twitches at the touch. Then he's balancing me on one palm and the other wraps around my wrist and drives my hand under the waistband of his pants.

"If you're going to do it, Rosa, do it right."

I smile against his lips as my fingers find his hard length. He's like steel wrapped in satin. I stroke him slowly, beads of cum dripping down my hand as I slide up and down his shaft.

Gawd, I want this. I've wanted Dante from the first moment I laid eyes on him with that snooty Caroline on his arm. But I'm scared. Terrified.

This man will ruin me. I'm certain his words that night weren't an idle threat. Only a few days with him, and I can feel the truth within every bone in my body. And I'm not sure I'm strong enough to survive him.

My hand must slow with my whirling thoughts because Dante spears me with a questioning gaze, his pupils blown out with desire. We remain frozen, locked in each other's eyes for an endless moment. Those piercing orbs lance into mine, prying out the dark truths.

"Run," he finally mumbles. "Run far away from me, sweetheart, if you know what's good for you."

I shake my head, my eyes still fixed to his. I'm too far gone already. I can try to fool myself all I want, but I'm falling for the savage King. "No." I stiffen my lower lip.

"Then hide. If I find you, I will fuck you."

A thrill surges up my spine as fiery heat spreads through every inch of my body. He releases me, and my feet scramble to find the floor.

"Are you serious?"

"I'll count to ten."

I nod quickly, my heart a jackhammer against my ribs. Then, I spin out of his grasp and run.

His voice booms in the background as he begins the countdown, the deep timbre vibrating my core. Fear and excitement throttle my body, and the ache between my legs only intensifies. This can't be normal. I dart around the corner, through the great room and the warm twinkle of the Christmas tree catches my eye. How did we go from sitting around the tree in a comfortable silence just less than forty-eight hours ago to this? I toss the random thoughts to the back of my mind and race toward the bedrooms. There's a laundry room beside the guestroom with a huge linen closet. If I hide behind the stacks of towels, maybe he won't find me. I doubt the man has spent more than a minute of his life doing laundry.

"Three, Two..."

I freeze mid-run as the persistent throbbing at the apex of my thighs reaches a crescendo. Wait, I want him to find me. No, I need it. I need that man's cock pounding into me to distract from all the chaos.

"One." Dante's voice echoes through the enormous penthouse.

The jagged edge to his tone sends my heart into a tailspin, and my feet take off of their own accord. I wrap my trembling hand around the laundry room doorhandle and jerk it open. The scent of fresh lavender temporarily simmers the frantic beats of my heart. Darting inside, I fumble in the darkness until I find the linen closet and crawl in.

And wait.

The silence ratchets up my fear, every second escalating the pounding rhythm of my pulse. I tuck my knees into my chest in a lame attempt at blocking the sound vibrating my entire torso.

The slap of heavy footfalls on marble stills my lungs. I hold my breath as the sound grows closer. "Oh, Rosa, when I find you, I'm going to devour you. I'm going to sink my cock into that sweet pussy until I'm balls deep, and my pulsing head punches your spine."

I clap my hand over my mouth to keep the gasp from escaping. Heat pools between my legs with each ragged breath. Gawd, that man's mouth is filthy. And nothing has ever turned me on more.

The click of a door opening sends my heart ratcheting up my throat. I shrink back and scoot behind a wicker hamper. The slats in the door reveal a dark shadow looming just outside.

"Mmm, sweetheart, are you wet for me already? I can smell that tantalizing scent from here." He sucks a finger into his mouth, the wet sounds sending a chill up my spine then he pops it out. "You know, I can still taste you on my skin. It's faint but it's still there. You taste like sweet strawberries and salvation."

Gawd, was it just two days ago he'd ravished me in the tub? So much has happened in the past forty-eight hours. So much has changed between us.

I sneak a peek beneath the crack in the door and can just make out the black tips of Dante's shoes. He's so close. I can't decide whether to creep further into the closet or jump out and throw myself at him. I'm tired of fighting him off. I've fully accepted my fate.

"Here I come, sweetheart." He stands in front of the closet door, his lips pressed to the slats. "I hope you're ready because I don't think I have the patience for any foreplay tonight. You've tortured me for days, and now it's time to pay up."

This time the gasp escapes before I can cover it. A wicked chuckle echoes in the darkness of the laundry room.

"Oh, Rosa, those sounds. I can't wait to hear every single, sexy one as I impale you to the mattress and fill you with my cum."

I've never been so turned on by the idea of cum dripping down my inner thighs. It is a damned good thing I'm on the pill. In Dante's current state, I doubt he'd waste time with a condom.

The door whips open, and his ominous form fills the doorway. Cast in shadows, darkness coils around his massive body. His chest is heaving, straining against the tight tee. My fingers itch to tear it off so I can run my hands across the map of tattoos. And scars. Those bullet wounds that prove he's not the monster he claims to be. Because a true monster would never lay down his life for his brother and fiancée.

"Come out, little mouse."

I shrink back against the wall, tucking my legs to my chest. I can already feel the arousal slickening my panties. But still, I'm frozen, a chaotic mixture of excitement and nerves paralyzing my body.

Two big hands wrap around the edges of the hamper and a second later, it's gone. It flies across the room, bounces off the wall and lands upside down. I sit on the floor, curled in the corner with a tremor dancing up my spine. It's not fear, it's so much more. The energy racing to my lower half is like nothing I've ever felt before.

"There she is." A feral grin curls Dante's lips, and gawd, it's equal parts beautiful and terrifying.

He bends down, crouching before me, and wraps a hand around my neck. My pulse flutters against his palm as he runs his thumb over the dip in my throat. "A deal's a deal, right sweetheart?"

My head bounces up and down because gawd help me, I want this. I wanted him to catch me, I need him balls deep inside me. Because I'm certain for those precious, sinful moments everything else will fade to exist.

His lips crash into mine, all-consuming. His tongue ravishes my mouth, plundering and exploring as he lifts me off the floor, spins us around, and plops me onto the washing machine. Guess we're forgoing the mattress all together. He sucks my lower lip between his teeth and bites down. Hard. I let out a squeal as the metallic taste overwhelms my tastebuds.

"Bite me," he whispers against my mouth before offering his pouty lower lip.

"Excuse me?" I rasp out.

"I want you to taste me, to know all my darkest parts so you understand exactly what you're getting into." He wraps my legs around his waist and scoots me to the edge of the washer, so his hard cock strokes my center.

I suck his lip into my mouth and nibble at the soft pillow.

"Harder, Rosa," he barks. "My world is blood and pain, and if you want to survive in it, you must be intimately acquainted with both."

That dribble of fear rises to the surface. Shit, maybe I am in over my head. Maybe I should have listened to Stella when she warned me away from the crazy heir to the King's throne.

His midnight irises sear to mine, torment flashing across the never-ending abyss. "Good, you should be scared." He rocks his hips, rubbing that rock-hard erection against my clit. Once, then twice. My entire body shudders at the friction, and then he stops. I nearly mewl my irritation. "Because once I claim you as mine, I'm not sure I'll ever be able to let you go. You've done something to me, sweetheart. When I'm around you, I can't tell my head from my ass. Self-control has never really been my thing, and once you let me loose, there's no going back. Do you understand that, Rosa?"

I dip my head to my chin, my gaze unflinching. Then I snag his lower lip and chomp down, until the taste of his coppery blood fills my mouth, mingling with my own. There's something so damned erotic about sharing blood with this man. It's like our very souls colliding and merging as one.

A sinful smile spreads his lips as he watches me.

I want Dante Valentino any way I can have him. I want the dark, twisted mob boss, the strong, protective bodyguard, and mostly, the scared, insecure little boy he allows no one to see.

My trembling hands move between us and unbuckle his belt.

CHAPTER 27
RUINED

R *ose*

Before I drag Dante's zipper down, he's yanking my shirt off and diving headfirst into my breasts. His mouth closes around a sharp peak, and my back arches from the streaks of pleasure that race straight to my core.

He lifts me off the washer long enough to tear my yoga pants and panties off in one swift move. Then he drops me back on the cold metal. Another shudder races up my spine as the chill from the lid reaches my heated flesh.

Dante snakes a hand around my back, presses a button and a chime rings out over our ragged pants. The washing machine begins to vibrate beneath me, stoking the rising heat between my sensitive folds. "Oh, gawd," I moan.

"That's right, sweetheart," he mumbles. "I am your god, but I'll be the one worshipping at your altar tonight." He spreads my legs and trails his lips across my inner thigh.

My hands wrap around his wild hair, fingers threading

through his silky locks. I'd been so consumed by his tongue I'd completely missed when he'd shed his pants and boxers. I sneak a quick peek at his cock, blood pounding through the thick veins. It stands straight and tall, and I think it's the most incredible thing I've ever seen, so powerful and intimidating. He's so much bigger than any other man I've been with, and I've seen a lot of erect dicks.

Thanks for that, Uncle John. You fucked me in the head real good.

Forcing my thoughts away from my dark past, I focus on the Italian god before me. With Dante, I'm untouchable. He fills me with a strength I've never experienced.

He's working his mouth toward my throbbing center, and I'm completely mesmerized by the dark head of hair bobbing between my legs. I scoot to the edge of the washer so I can reach his cock. The need to touch him as his tongue ravages me is overwhelming.

After teasing for endless minutes, he drags that wicked tongue through my folds. A groan of pleasure escapes, and my fingers tighten around his erection. He's silky smooth and dripping for *me*. The amount of pleasure I derive from that fact is insane.

Dante sucks my clit into his mouth, and stars dance across my vision. My core clenches as he nibbles the overstimulated bud, and my legs wrap around his hips, drawing him closer. My thighs are slick from my arousal and his saliva, the sight of it only intensifying the moment.

One hand travels up my torso, and his fingers close around my nipple. He pinches, and a squeal bursts free as the pain surges in a direct link to my pussy. Releasing the delicate peak, he palms my breast, squeezing and kneading until my hips buck against his mouth.

His tongue dives into me as his thumb circles my clit, and my head tips back, fingers scrambling for purchase across the smooth metal of the washer. Its vibrations combined with this man's skills are almost too much. He plunges a finger in next, and my insides clench around him. Oh, fuck, I'm close. The onslaught of sensations drive me closer and closer to the edge.

"Dante," I pant. "I want you inside me."

"Not yet, sweetheart." His words vibrate my clit, electrifying the taut nerve-endings. "First, I want you to come in my mouth, so I can taste your soul spilling into me."

Oh. My. Gawd.

The crude mob boss is also a fucking poet, and his words alone wring the orgasm right from my clenching apex. I ride his thick finger and his devastating tongue, hips rolling as wave after wave of pleasure crashes over me.

He holds me in place until the final rush ebbs into a faint buzz. Then he lifts his eyes to mine, and I take in the breathtaking dark depths of those blown out orbs, and my arousal slickening his chin.

"Have you ever tasted yourself, Rosa?" He runs his tongue across his bottom lip, then further down his chin until he laps all of me up.

I shake my head. It had always seemed entirely unappealing.

"I want you to taste yourself on my lips." He drags a finger across my pulsing center, and I squirm from the unexpected invasion, then he smears my arousal across his lower lip. There's something so freaking hot about it.

He wraps his hand around the back of my neck and fists his fingers in my hair. Standing over me, he brings his shiny lip to my mouth. "Now you'll know what heaven tastes like." A wild grin stretches across his scruffy jaw as he forces my mouth to his.

The musky, pungent taste is odd at first, but Dante's excitement is contagious. I suck on his lip, tugging him closer and already the fire begins to reignite below. His cock is hard between us, only inches away from my entrance. I tilt my hips to meet that thick head, but Dante pivots an inch, just enough to keep me writhing for more. My breasts rub against his bare chest, drawing the nipples to tight points.

"I'm ready," I murmur against his ear before nibbling on his soft lobe. My hands clench around his ass, forcing him closer. His thick shaft strokes my still-pulsating center.

I slip my hand between our bodies and cup his balls, gently massaging them in my palm. He hisses out a curse, his own head falling back. It's all the urging I need.

With the washer still vibrating beneath me and my ass perched on the edge of the machine, I guide his cock to my entrance. He freezes beneath my touch, and those bottomless irises fix to mine.

"Are you sure?" he rasps out, piercing orbs diving so deep into mine they nearly touch my soul.

A soft smile pulls at my lips as I regard the beautiful, scarred beast. "For a self-proclaimed monster, you sure are being considerate of my needs."

A smirk quirks his lips. "You're right. I should stop that. I don't want to give you the wrong idea, sweetheart."

He rams his cock inside me so hard, I don't just see stars but the entire damned universe. I'm so full of him I'm scared I'll tear, then I'll really be familiar with all the blood and pain of his world. Is that what he's trying to achieve?

As if he's read the fear in my eyes, or maybe it's the building tears, he slows his savage pace, fully retreating before sinking into me with renewed violence. His eyes dip between us as he slows again, pulls out nearly completely and then thrusts again. It's slow torture. In and in and in. He watches every second.

The intensity in his gaze has me trailing his eyes. He seems utterly mesmerized as his dick moves in and out of my pussy, and fuck, it's so hot.

His fingers snake around my neck, and he jerks my head forward. "I want you to watch, sweetheart. I want you to see how your greedy little pussy sucks my cock in. She weeps for it, soaking my dick with each thrust."

And damn, he was right. I couldn't get enough. I couldn't stop watching the steady in and out, the crazy wonder of how our bodies were made for each other. And not just human beings in general, but Dante and me in particular.

My lips spread for his cock, wider than I could ever imagine being comfortable. And here I was on the brink of another orgasm. His huge balls smack against me with each thrust, the additional point of contact only intensifying the raging sensations.

He is brutal as he rails into me, shaking the entire washing machine with each violent thrust, filling me until I really do feel his head against my spine. Then he slows, his gaze dips, and he just watches the slow, almost tender movements. His breath normalizes, and an awe-filled, reverent look replaces the wild glare.

I don't think I'll ever understand this man.

But he was right about one thing, he *would* ruin me for anyone else.

And I couldn't be more excited for the devastation.

"I'm going to fill you up with my cum. I want to see it spilling down your legs, coating each and every one of your holes. Are you ready, Rose?"

My head bounces up and down. Dammit, I am way too obsessed with this man already.

A deadly mix of fury and lust shines through the darkness as his eyes lance into mine. "Come for me, first." His hands clamp around my ass, and he lifts me from the washer, so I cling onto him like a baby koala. At this angle, his head finds that mythical spot and thrusts with the confidence of man who's discovered unexplored, virgin territory.

I moan as he plunges deeper, his hands guiding my hips over his shaft. Harder. Faster. The orgasm builds at an alarming rate. I wriggle and squirm, the sensations too overwhelming. "Oh, Dante…." Raging heat races to my core, filling every inch of me with liquid fire.

"I'm going to come, I'm going to—" An explosion of pleasure floods my core, and for an instant, my heart stops, my lungs fail, every part of me ceases to function. Only the fiery sensations exist. Only Dante, only his magnificent cock.

He drives harder, a savage growl vibrating his chest a second before his dick twitches inside me. My pussy clenches around him, wringing out his own pleasure. Warmth spills down my legs as he buries his face in the crook of my neck. His muffled groans shake my entire body, only intensifying the powerful release.

We remain there, motionless, for a long moment, him standing and me with my legs wrapped around his hips, holding on for dear life. It's a damned good thing my thighs are strong from years of yoga because right now, they are the only things keeping me upright. My chest rises and falls in a rapid rhythm, matching the erratic one beneath me. Dante's tattoos seem to come to life with each ragged pant.

My fingers trace the dark whorls before stalling at a light pink scar. The man's body is riddled with them, different shapes and sizes, but this one is fresh, and it matches the other eight lining his torso.

Hot tears burn my eyes, and I have no idea why. My emotions are all over the place from that mind-blowing orgasm. Or maybe it's the devastating thought of these bullets having hit their mark and me missing out on this intense moment with this man.

If Dante had died….

My throat closes up, and I swallow hard, forcing the knot of emotion down. Blinking quickly, I chase away the completely inappropriate thoughts. I have no doubt Dante's made women cry while he brutally fucked them, but these tears are for a completely different and much more terrifying reason.

"Don't." The sound of Dante's gruff voice stills my roving fingers. "Don't make this more than what it is."

My eyes dart to his, and I pray to a god I'm not sure exists, that they're not filled to the brim with tears. "What are you saying?" I force out, impressed by how calm I sound.

His finger tips my chin up, locking it to his cold gaze. The fire and passion from a second ago are gone. "This was just a good fuck, understand? We can keep doing it as long as it suits both of us, but there won't be anything more."

A tiny sliver of my stupid heart breaks right off.

Dante must notice because the hard set of his jaw softens. "Love is weakness, a frailty, and in our world only the strong survive. I was wrong before when I said I would ruin you. *You* would be my utter undoing Rose, and I cannot have that."

He pulls out from inside me, and that gaping hole spreads all the way to my chest. Unraveling my legs from his waist, he drops me onto the washing machine and spins toward the door. He stalks out before I can process what just happened.

CHAPTER 28
FEEDING THE MONSTER

D*ante*

Cazzo, I'll never get used to this shit paperwork. I stare at the mountain of files on my desk and groan. No, not today. I push off from the grand mahogany desk that still doesn't feel like mine, and the wingback leather chair jerks back. I can't spend another second hiding out from Rose in this office.

For days, I've been sneaking out of the apartment before she wakes and burying myself in mounds of papers just to avoid her. Because the goddamned truth is I can't get her out of my mind. Her sweet scent still lingers on my pants from that night, which I haven't washed because I'm clearly insane, but worse, its permanently carved into my memory. Every time I close my eyes, she's all I see. Her head tipped back, cheeks flushed, and lips parted as I sink my cock inside her over and over again.

But then those tears… *Dio*, I wasn't expecting that. It shook me to my core.

And what is even more absurd is that when I let the monster free, thrusting inside her with the violence that I try so hard to keep buried, she took it. More than that, she *liked* it.

Whenever I let loose like that on Caroline, she grits her teeth and bears it because she's a whore for my cock, but I know she doesn't like it. I can feel her pussy slamming closed, unwilling to take me. But not Rose, no, she loved every fucking minute.

And *merda*, all I can think about is how badly I want to claim her all over my damned penthouse. On the kitchen counter, on the balcony, splayed out across the dining room table, and the living room, especially there in front of that ugly ass tree. I'd nail her against it if I didn't think it would collapse beneath us and set the entire damned apartment on fire.

But *cazzo*, I'd been wrong, so wrong when I thought Rose and I could just be a fling. The tornado of emotions that woman ignites inside me is dangerous. Just one taste and I am already addicted. If we keep it up, or *Dio*, if it turns into more, I'd never be able to control myself.

Which is why I ran afterward, like a complete fucking coward.

Last night as I sat in this damned desk staring at the video surveillance of Rose in my apartment, I almost picked up the phone and called that frosty bitch, Caroline. I'd jacked off twice watching Rose sitting in front of that stupid Christmas tree, and still, it hadn't been enough. I thought maybe, just maybe, Caroline's lips on my cock would be the distraction I needed. Only I couldn't even get my fingers to punch out her number.

The idea of being with anyone else had my dick so soft it was embarrassing. So, I just sat there for hours like a *coglione* watching Rose on the monitor as she read her Psych textbook.

I have to do something. My hands curl into fists as I stare out the floor-to-ceiling windows at the bustling streets of Park Avenue. My fingernails dig into my palms, the pain grounding me. I refuse to become a slave to my addictions again. I'd struggled for years to overcome those demons.

My ribcage tightens, the unwanted swell of emotions more than I want to deal with right now. I need a release, and if I can't have sex, alcohol or drugs, there is only one other logical answer. The corners of my lips lift as I stalk out of the office with Clara cursing me out in Italian. The shareholder's meeting can wait. I have something more pressing to attend to.

I stand in the shadows of the small alleyway in China Town, only a stone's throw away from the Red Dragon. Two of Feng's men had already been taken down today, but I owe him another from a few days ago when I'd let Rose convince me to stay and fuck her instead of taking care of business.

Huge mistake. One I would not be repeating any time soon. If only I could get my dick on board.

My fingers tighten around the knife in my pocket as muffled footsteps grow closer. No one said it would be a healthy release. The monster inside me craves violence. If it has its fill, I can stave off my other desires. Odd that this choice seems the best of all evils.

I creep to the edge of the alley and press my back to the graffitied wall. Drawing in a deep breath, I attempt to still my quickening pulse. I search for the calm, that icy peace that takes over my body during the thrill of the hunt. I'd felt the same stillness when I'd searched for Rose in the penthouse, only that little mouse had my throbbing cock as a guide. This time, a different sort of lust fills my veins.

My hand snakes out as the red-shirted dragon rounds the corner. Grabbing him by the throat, I drag him into the murky recess. He coughs and splutters when I slam him against the wall, his eyes going impossibly wide.

The man shakes his head quickly, mouth gaping, desperate to draw in breath he won't find.

"Do you know who I am?" I growl, my fingers tightening around his throat.

His Adam's apple jogs up and down the column, pulse raging, then his head bobs up and down.

"Good."

I have no idea who this asshole is, just some sewer rat I followed from the subway station. I watched as he knocked an old lady with a cane to the floor just to steal her purse. The *figlio di puttana* deserves so much worse than the punishment I'm about to inflict.

When Luca took over for *Papà*, there were certain rules he'd put into place. Rules that our father had ground into us as kids, and we passed on to every male and female that served the Kings. Never lay a hand on a woman, a kid or the elderly. Everyone else is fair game. This guy just broke one of those cardinal rules, and now, he'd pay.

And man, am I looking forward to it.

I jerk the knife from my pocket, and a scream erupts from the man's mouth. Only with my hand crushing his windpipe, it's barely more than a whisper.

I cluck my tongue at the asshole and sear him with a narrowed glare. "I saw what you did to that old woman back there." I tick my head toward the Canal Street entrance. "Have you no shame? What if that was your ninety-year-old grandma?"

I loosen my grip just enough so he can answer.

"I—I...."

"You what, *pezzo di merda*?" *Dio*, this man truly is a piece of shit. Not only had he done the despicable deed, but he couldn't even own up to it.

"Feng said we each had to bring in a thousand dollars today, and I didn't have it, all right?"

"So, you thought the old lady would be easy pickings?"

He tried to nod, but my hand prohibited much movement.

"Well, it's your lucky day, dickhead, because now instead of Feng, you have me to deal with." I drag the knife across his chest and another muffled scream rushes out. Blood oozes down his shirt, matching the vibrant red of the fabric. "Uh, uh." I shake my head at him. If you're going to scream, I'll have to gag you."

Torturing him in the middle of an alley in China Town probably isn't the smartest move on my end, but a tiny part of me wants to get caught. More than anything, I want to draw that fucker Feng out. Once I snap his neck, Luca and Stella can finally come back and things can go back to normal.

Or at least, somewhat normal.

Now that I'd had a taste of the King's throne, I wasn't sure if I could let that power go. Sure, I'd pass on all the administrative and corporate crap, but this, the stuff on the streets, I loved. I was born to be the king in the shadows.

Pulling my arm back, I let it loose, smashing my fist into the guy's face. The crunch of bone beneath my knuckles feeds the monster within. More. More pain. More destruction. Blood trickles down from his nostrils and onto his lips. He tries to spit, but I slowly shake my head. "Don't even think about it." I tug at my silk button down shirt with my clean hand. "This is Armani."

Loosening my tie, I jerk it free from my collar and tie it over his mouth. The guy kicks and squirms, but I have at least a hundred pounds on the dragon. Once he's nice and quiet, I take a moment to roll up my sleeves. Black ink crawls up and down my forearms, a map of skulls, wicked beasts and tribal markings I've added over the years. My personal favorite is the Chinese dragon with a dagger through its heart. I pause when I reach the detailed art, making sure he sees it.

"If you behave, I'll make it quick and honorable."

He mutters what I think is a "please don't," but I can't be

sure beneath the gag. Nor do I really give a fuck. The guy dies tonight, and that's the end of it.

I throw another punch, just because it feels so damned good. Nothing releases the rage like the feel of skin on skin and the sick crunch of bone. The knife is quicker and more expedient but just doesn't hold as much satisfaction.

Just to test my theory, I slice another gash across his chest, creating an X. More blood gushes down his shredded shirt. Nope, not as good as the punch. I deliver another blow to the center of the X I've crafted, and my fist comes away covered in crimson.

Another muffled gasp echoes through the hallway. He's biting at the gag, swinging his head from side to side. The cuts are shallow like Papà taught me, the perfect way to extend the torture. I sink the next one in deeper, just between the third and fourth ribs and dangerously close to his liver.

The thrill is waning, the monster retreating to the dark depths, and a part of me just wants to get this over with. Which is very odd. The usual gratification is missing.

And now I'm pissed.

Jerking the knife out, I wave it in front of his face. Beads of sweat roll down his forehead into his glossy eyes. Tears and snot snake down his cheeks, and I can't seem to derive a single ounce of the usual pleasure.

A trickle of water draws my attention to the crumbling asphalt. A pool of piss collects between the man's feet. The crotch of his cargo pants darkens, and the pungent odor of urine reaches my nostrils.

My nose crinkles, nothing but disgust filling my black heart.

I take a step back and revel in the fear carving up the man's features. I pause for an endless moment, waiting for that high I usually feel, the excitement of taking a life, of holding something so precious in the palm of my hand. But I feel nothing.

Nothing but empty.

And I know there's only one thing that will fill that void.

Now I'm fucking terrified.

My fingers tighten around the worn wooden handle, and I slice the blade across the guy's throat. A fountain of blood spurts out when I sever the carotid artery, and I barely jerk back in time to avoid the splatter.

The Red Dragon sags to the ground, the light in his dark eyes extinguishing almost instantly. By the time he hits the floor, vacant orbs stare into the pitch sky.

"Save a seat for me in hell, *bastardo*."

CHAPTER 29
EMOTIONALLY UNAVAILABLE MOB BOSS

R *ose*

For someone who was so concerned with my safety before he fucked me, Dante sure as hell seems mighty fine with passing me off to someone else after the fact. I huff out a breath as I stare at the text message from my dad, standing in front of my new locker in the employee lounge at Palestra. I'd begged the manager to assign me a new one after the dead rose incident, but I'd had to make up some stupid excuse about it smelling funny. I don't need everyone at my place of work to know how screwed up my life is. Maisy knowing is bad enough.

Glancing at the screen again, I type out a quick response to my dad. He's been asking me to come out and visit since I missed Christmas with the family. Maybe a day trip out to Long Island is exactly what I need. Too bad I can't afford to take more days off.

I glance over my shoulder to find Tony lingering just outside the lounge door. His big head fills the small glass window. I should be happy I have a new bodyguard because at least this one lets me go to the bathroom alone, but I can't help my stupid, weak heart from missing the overbearing Italian.

Any normal, self-respecting girl would've been happy to get rid of him after the way he ghosted me. How the man could avoid me so well when I live in his own damned apartment is beyond me. I spend nights in my bed wondering if he's filling Caroline's. Because where else could he be at that hour?

I release a frustrated breath and slam my locker door closed. Today will be my first day back at Dr. Winchester's office after my extended vacation, and a part of me is glad to get back into a normal routine. But the other part can't help but think of Mark. What if he follows me there? What if he gets in somehow?

Tony won't be able to shadow me like he does at Palestra because of patient confidentiality, and there is no way I'm admitting what happened with Dr. Mark to my boss. Assuming it's him.

"Hey!"

I nearly jump out of my skin as I whirl around and find a grinning Maisy. "Oh, hi." I clap my hand across my chest to keep my heart from popping out.

"I'm so sorry, sweety, I didn't mean to scare you."

I wave a nonchalant hand like I hadn't almost had a heart attack. "Oh, no worries. You just surprised me." I haul my tote bag over my shoulder and turn toward the door. "I have to run though, I'm back at the office today."

"Oh, right." She swings her designer purse higher up on her shoulder and follows me to the door. "I'm actually leaving too. Doctor's appointment in the Upper East Side. We can walk together if you want."

I eye Tony through the crack in the door as one of the spin instructors walks into the lounge. A stroll with my friend sounds much more bearable than the extended awkward silences with this guy. "Yeah, I'd love that."

She throws me a conspiratorial wink and leans in close, "And you can catch me up on what's going on with you and the sexy Dante."

I let out a frustrated grunt. "Absolutely nothing. He's still avoiding me." I'd filled her in on the tamer details of our laundry room hook up, leaving out the dark and twisty bits. I didn't think Maisy would be into that stuff, and we weren't that close of friends just yet.

"Men are such a-holes." She throws Tony a glare, and my faithful bodyguard falls into step a few paces behind us.

"A-hole." A laugh tumbles out, probably the first one in days, and it feels good. "I don't think I've ever heard you curse, Miss Maisy."

"Yeah, Mrs. Gloria Vanderbilt would definitely not approve. She would've fired every single one of my au pairs if she'd heard such vile language."

I laugh again. "Damn, so you're not just rich because of your ex, you were raised rich?"

She nods. "It's not something I really like to brag about. Growing up in a wealthy family just meant being raised by cold, uncaring staff in a huge house devoid of any warmth and hardly ever spending time with your parents."

"Geez, I'm sorry, girl." My life might have gone to shit because of my uncle, but before that, the memories were good.

"Seriously, you have nothing to be sorry about." She shrugs. "Nothing worse than the poor little rich girl."

I wrap my arm around her shoulder, not only for her, but also for me. With Stella gone, she's done an amazing job filling the void, and I'm beyond thankful to have her. As a matter of fact, if this thing with Dante doesn't thaw out soon, I may ask if she'd be interested in a new roommate. Her house is certainly big enough.

Despite Dante completely ignoring me, I have a feeling he wouldn't take my moving out well. But honestly, I don't give a fuck what he wants. I've been more than understanding, I've given him days to work out his shit. I might not have been a licensed psychologist yet, but I know exactly what he's doing. He is scared out of his mind after showing me his dark and twisted pieces, and now he is desperately trying to push me away.

Well, if he doesn't figure out his issues soon, he'll get what he wants.

We walk in a comfortable silence for a few more blocks, my spinning thoughts more than enough company. Maisy starts to slow and points at a building on the corner of East 76th Street. "This is me."

Thank goodness it's only a few more blocks to Dr. Winchester's, and the cold hasn't quite frosted my nose yet. "Thanks for the walk and the chat."

"Anytime." She turns for the door, but before her gloved hand closes around the handle, it swings open.

Caroline barges out, then freezes when her icy glare catches mine. She stares down at me, her long, aristocratic nose in the air. "Oh, you," she snarls.

"Yup, me." I'm not quite sure what Dante told his ex after he kicked her out of his apartment to spend Christmas with me.

"Maisy, you two know each other?" Caroline's perfectly plucked brows nearly reach her platinum blonde hairline.

I shoot my friend a curious glare. How does she know the enemy?

"We do." She offers the blonde bitch a smile and squeezes my hand. "Rose and I work together at Palestra."

A forced laugh titters out as Caroline presses her hand to her chest. "Oh, that's so cute, Maisy. I heard you got a little job after that shameful divorce."

Crimson blankets Maisy's cheeks, and a swell of anger

blossoms in my core. Maisy is one of the sweetest people I've ever met. No way I'd let this bitch talk down to her.

"Listen, Caroline," I grit out.

"No, it's okay, Rose, seriously." She turns to me, those bright green eyes pleading, then pivots back to the queen bitch. "I just want to start over, Caroline. I have no interest in galas and all the pomp and circumstance of Manhattan high society."

"Well, that explains why you're with *her*." She points her stuck-up nose in my direction.

I clench my molars to keep from cussing her out because I know I can do one better. "Maybe that explains why Maisy's with me, but what about Dante?" I shoot her a sweet smile. "My guess is your frigid cunt just wasn't doing it for him."

A sharp giggle escapes Maisy's lips, but she quickly covers it with a cough.

Caroline's eyes shoot daggers, her murderous glare worth every second of this conversation. "You're a vile-mouthed, uncouth little thing."

"Maybe, but Dante sure seems to enjoy my mouth."

Her nostrils flare, deep red coating her cheeks. "That's not what he said when he came over last night."

The smile melts right off my face, and all the air siphons from my lungs. I stand there gaping as she smirks at me. I tell myself she's lying; she's just trying to get a rise out of me, but I can't help the crushing doubt. Dante has been coming home later and later every night. He easily could have been with her.

"You're a liar," I force out.

"Guess you'll never know, will you?" With a satisfied grin, she barrels by me, hitting my shoulder with her oversized Hermes. She angles her head back and wiggles her fingers at my friend. "Nice to see you, Maisy. Hopefully next time, it'll be in better company."

"Ugh, what a bitch," I mutter as she saunters down the street.

"Sorry about that, Rose." She squeezes my shoulder, her lips pulled into a pout. "I never put two and two together. I'm such an idiot. I knew her and Dante had been on again, off again for a while."

My thoughts fly back to Christmas to how protective he'd been of me, and how easily he'd dismissed her. Then again, he'd done the same to me only a few days ago. What if Dante's obsession with me ended the moment he sank his cock inside me?

It had clearly only been about the thrill of the chase for him.

My heart staggers on a beat. Gawd, how could I be so stupid? He'd made it clear from the first night at Luca's. It was a one-night only thing. He'd gotten what he wanted out of me, and now, I'm old news.

Hot tears prick my eyes. I need to go now before they spill over, and Maisy thinks I'm really nuts. Because what kind of moron falls for an emotionally unavailable, asshole mob boss?

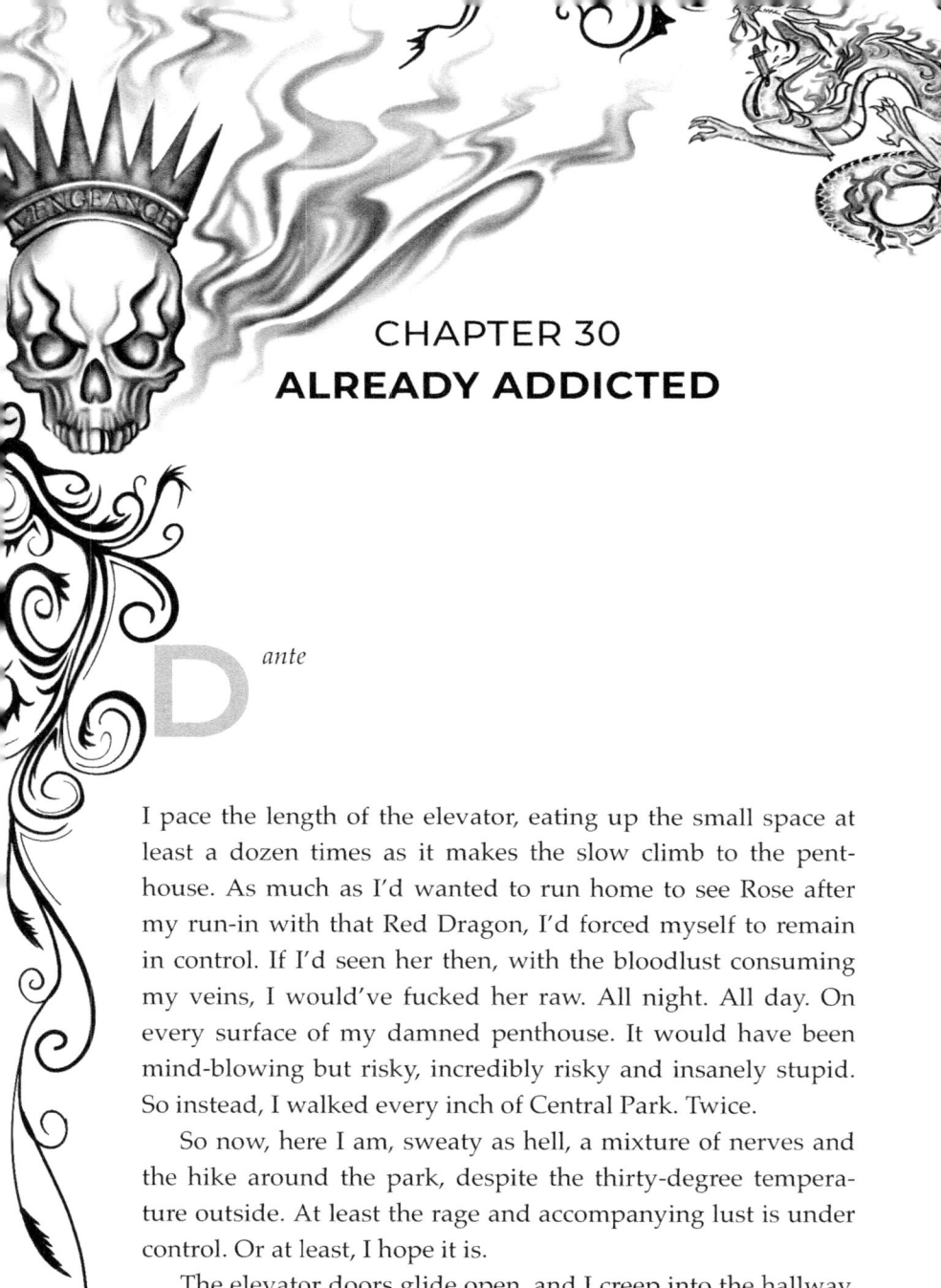

CHAPTER 30
ALREADY ADDICTED

D*ante*

I pace the length of the elevator, eating up the small space at least a dozen times as it makes the slow climb to the penthouse. As much as I'd wanted to run home to see Rose after my run-in with that Red Dragon, I'd forced myself to remain in control. If I'd seen her then, with the bloodlust consuming my veins, I would've fucked her raw. All night. All day. On every surface of my damned penthouse. It would have been mind-blowing but risky, incredibly risky and insanely stupid. So instead, I walked every inch of Central Park. Twice.

So now, here I am, sweaty as hell, a mixture of nerves and the hike around the park, despite the thirty-degree temperature outside. At least the rage and accompanying lust is under control. Or at least, I hope it is.

The elevator doors glide open, and I creep into the hallway, listening for noises in my apartment. Tony stands by the door, a gun clenched in his palm. "All quiet, boss."

"Good," I murmur. "You can go now." It's after midnight, and I'm more than capable of taking care of Rose by myself. Besides, I still have Aldo downstairs for emergencies.

Tony marches toward the elevator, but I reach for his arm before he gets far. He spins toward me, eyes wide.

"Did any of those dickheads at Palestra flirt with her?"

His head dips slowly. "Just a few…. She's a beautiful girl, boss. It's only a matter of time until someone snatches her up." A growl vibrates my throat, and Tony bites down on his lower lip. "Sorry, it's none of my business." He whirls around and scrambles for the elevator, jabbing his finger into the call button.

Reining in my temper, I jerk the penthouse door open. The place is quiet, the warm glow of the Christmas tree pervading the darkness. A part of me is relieved Rose is already asleep. I'm a damned coward, and I'm well aware of it.

I creep into the kitchen and grab a bottle of water from the fridge. I take a long pull, my gaze intent on the ugly little tree. For such a small, scraggly thing, it sure brings a lot of warmth to the place. I rise to my tiptoes to see over the marble island, movement catching my eye.

Rose is splayed across the couch beneath a furry pink blanket. Her girly shit has invaded my penthouse now. It seems like it's expanded in my absence, like she's purposely trying to take over my home.

I inch closer, my traitorous feet moving of their own accord. It's the first time I've seen her in person in days. Sure, I've spent many a night watching her through the surveillance cameras, throttling my cock as I fantasize about the things I want to do to her, but the black and white images never do her justice.

An odd tightening in my chest has me halting a few feet from the couch. I massage the spot, the unfamiliar feeling constricting the blood flow to my withered, weary heart.

A faint sigh escapes, drawing my attention to those pouty,

full lips. For the first time since we met, I imagine that mouth against my own, instead of wrapped around my dick.

I move closer and drop to my knees beside the sofa. Sweeping a lock of blonde hair behind her ear, my thumb lingers on her cheek for a moment longer. Before my brain can process my own stupidity, I bend down and press a kiss to those lips. It's soft and chaste, completely unlike any kiss I've ever given.

Her lips are pillowy and perfect with a faint scent of cherry blossoms. I stand there, just staring at her as she sleeps like a complete *coglione*. My heart swells, the rhythm accelerating with each minute. Am I having a fucking heart attack? What the hell is wrong with me?

Rose's lids flutter and slowly open, revealing those brilliant blue eyes. "Were you with Caroline?"

Her rough, sleepy voice nearly makes my dick hard before I focus on her words. "What?" I blurt, still kneeling beside her.

She blinks quickly, then rubs the sleep from her eyes. "All these nights that you weren't at home, have you been with her?"

My brows furrow, and my head whips back and forth. "No."

"You swear to me?" Those eyes pin to mine, and *Dio*, my heart does that strange shudder again. "I know you don't owe me the truth. I know we aren't anything to each other, but please don't lie to me about this, Dante."

"I swear to you I wasn't with her." I press my lips together not wanting to aggravate the precarious situation, but if she wants the truth, I'll give it to her. Maybe it'll help us both understand why this is so wrong. "But she did call me yesterday. She wanted me to come over and begged me to get back together."

She pushes herself off the cushion and sits straight up against the back of the couch, tucking her knees to her chest. She's wearing a crop top and those damned yoga pants again, revealing every decadent curve of her body. "And what did you say?" she whispers.

"I thought about saying yes." I pause and snag my teeth over my lower lip, staring down at the floor. "I hoped a quick fuck would help erase the memories of your hands all over my body, your sweet pussy wrapped around my cock, those lips —*merda*," I hiss out. "I can't do this, Rosa. I'm not good at any of this shit." I glance up and meet a pair of glistening blue orbs. The ghost of a smile curls her lips, and fuck me, but it's the most glorious thing I've ever seen.

"So, you haven't been with her?"

I shake my head, still kneeling in front of her. "How can I when all I think about is you?"

The full smile melts across her lips.

"I don't know how to do this, sweetheart. I am not a good man, not a good person. I do bad, fucked up things. I've only had you one time, and already I'm addicted. That's not good for either of us. I've struggled with addiction my whole life, and it's not pretty."

Her soft hands frame my face and draw me closer. "I'll help you," she whispers.

"Are you sure? Because it's a hell of a lot more than what you've bargained for."

"I want you, Dante Valentino, and I'll take everything that comes with the dark and savage package." Her lips sear to mine, and it's better than any high I've ever experienced. My fingers dig into the hair at the back of her nape, and I fist the silky blonde locks, tipping her head back. From this angle, I devour her mouth, drawing her tongue into my own. I've never enjoyed kissing a woman like this. It was always just an annoying precursor to the final act of wetting my cock.

With Rose, it's different. The perfect bow of her lips is so sensual, that tongue so wicked, I could spend all night exploring every corner of her mouth.

But this feisty little thing can't wait. She pulls me onto the couch on top of her and reaches between us, hands fumbling with my belt. She's a fiend for my cock, and who am I to deny her? Because *Dio*, I love that she knows what she wants, and she has no problem going for it.

My lips move across her jaw, then find her ear as she drags my pants to my ankles. I nibble on the soft lobe before biting down, hard.

"Ow!" she squeals.

I lick it softly before drawing it back into my mouth. "I couldn't resist." Goosebumps ripple down her bare arm, and seeing that reaction only adds to the thrill.

Reaching for the hem of her crop top, my knuckles brush her soft skin. "You want me to fuck you in front of that ugly ass Christmas tree, sweetheart?" I whisper before I jerk the shirt over her head. She's bare beneath, and my cock instantly hardens at the sight of her perfectly pink nipples.

"Mmm, yes," she groans. Her eyes find mine once her top is on the floor and taper at the edges. "Wait a second, it's not ugly," she hisses.

A deep chuckle vibrates my chest. "Whatever you say, sweetheart."

Her fingers make quick work of the oppressive button-down shirt, and it's like the elephant on my shoulders disappears the moment it hits the ground. I'm just not meant for fancy suits and board meetings. I need to get Luca back here ASAP before I lose my mind dealing with all that bureaucratic bullshit.

Her hands move to my chest, fitting perfectly against the tattoo inked across my skin. Her palms cover the word vengeance. Ironic since it's only when I'm with Rose like this, that the burning desire for revenge falls silent.

Vengeance is king.

With the first part covered, only the king remains.

I push the random thoughts aside before I start waxing poetic. Fuck, what has this woman done to me?

Slipping my hands beneath the waistband of her yoga pants, I yank them off so violently a sharp rip breaks through the hum of ragged breaths and shedding clothes.

"Dante!" she cries. "These are my favorite."

"I'll buy you new ones."

"You better." Her eyes meet mine, amusement sparking in the vivid blue.

Cazzo, this woman has me by the balls. And I'm not sure what to do with that. "Or maybe I won't, and then you'll have to run around the penthouse in only your panties." I rip those off too, the tear resounding between us. She lets out another squeal, but I press my palm to her stomach, keeping her still. "Or better yet, nothing at all so I can bend you over the couch and fuck you any time I want."

She wriggles beneath my touch, her thighs slick with arousal already. "And what will I do when I have to go to Palestra?"

"Like hell I'm letting you out of this house again in one of those ass-hugging outfits. Next time you teach a class over there you're wearing a moo-moo."

She lets out a cackle, her beautiful breasts bouncing beneath me. "You're out of your damned mind, D."

"You have no idea." I drop my head between her breasts and revel in the intoxicating feel of them against my cheeks. Inhaling a deep breath, I draw in her scent, warm vanilla and rose petals like her namesake. I linger for a few seconds longer, enjoying the calm before the storm because the earlier run-in with the dragon temporarily quelled the monster, but he wouldn't stay chained up for long. And once I release him and fully indulge in this thing brewing between us, there will be no returning him to his cage. Because the truth is, when everyone already thinks you're a monster, it's easy to let that monster free.

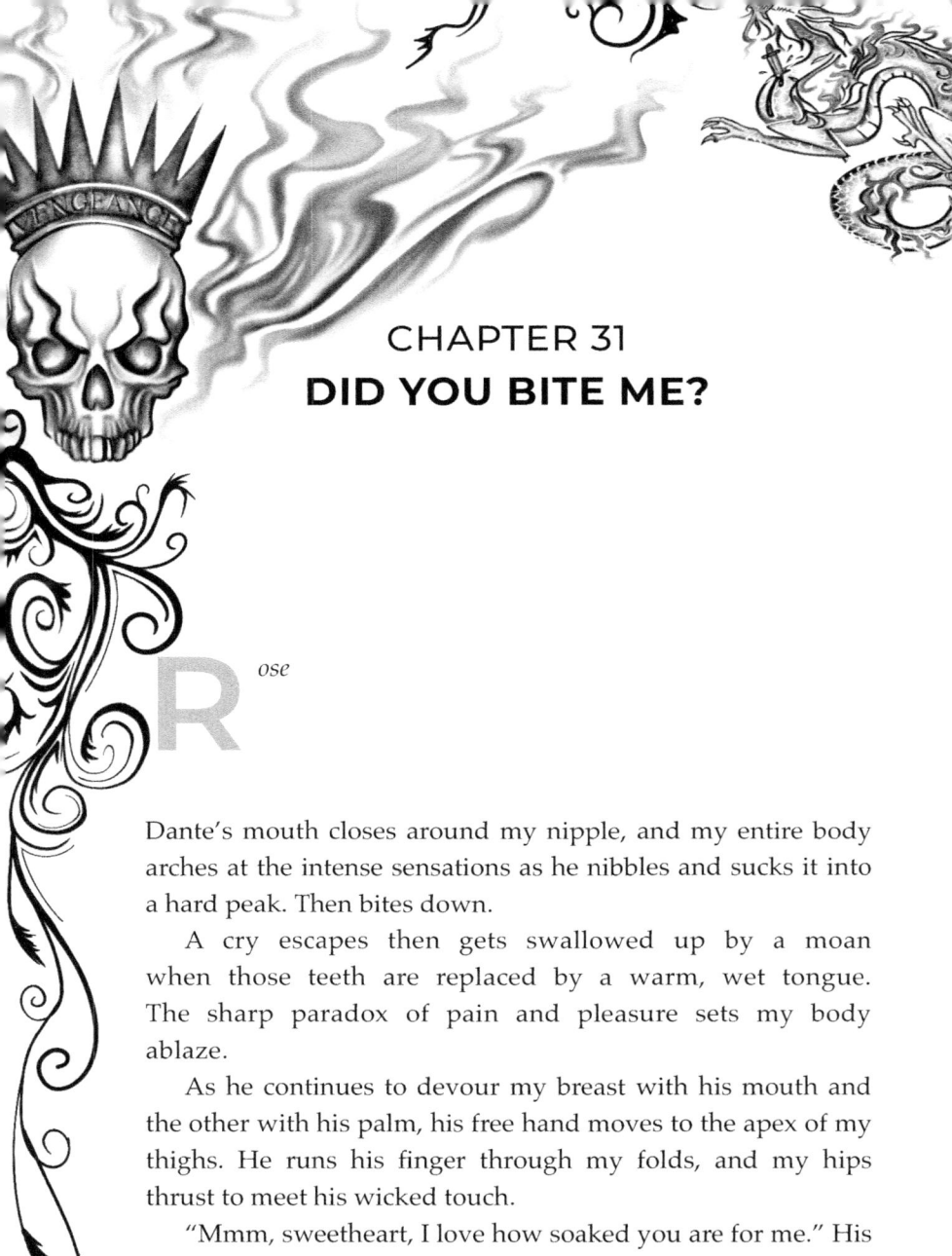

CHAPTER 31
DID YOU BITE ME?

R *ose*

Dante's mouth closes around my nipple, and my entire body arches at the intense sensations as he nibbles and sucks it into a hard peak. Then bites down.

A cry escapes then gets swallowed up by a moan when those teeth are replaced by a warm, wet tongue. The sharp paradox of pain and pleasure sets my body ablaze.

As he continues to devour my breast with his mouth and the other with his palm, his free hand moves to the apex of my thighs. He runs his finger through my folds, and my hips thrust to meet his wicked touch.

"Mmm, sweetheart, I love how soaked you are for me." His thick finger glides across my clit, then circles. "Only for me, right?"

My head bounces up and down.

"If anyone ever touches this sweet pussy, *my* pussy, I'll rip his fucking cock off and make him choke on it. Do you understand me?"

I nod again. A thrill races up my spine at the violence in his tone. It's like catnip to my screwed-up psyche.

"Rosa, do you understand? I need you to say it."

"I understand," I breathe, the ragged sound totally embarrassing. I'd agree to pretty much anything in this moment with that sinful finger rubbing my needy clit.

"Say it." He thrusts his finger inside me, and my hips buck from the unexpected intrusion, then rock against his palm eager for that delicious friction.

"No one can touch my pussy but you."

"That's my good girl." He plunges a second finger inside, curling it in just the right angle. Then he drags that naughty digit wet with my arousal through my folds and further to my back hole.

"Dante...." I stiffen as new, fiery sensations swallow me up.

"Don't tell me I've reached virgin territory, sweetheart?" He rubs my wetness around the tight hole, and pleasure blossoms with every maddening circle.

"Umhmm," I mutter.

"Oh *cazzo*, Rosa, you shouldn't have told me that because now all I can think about is stuffing my cock inside that tight little ass and being the first to make it mine."

A few days ago, and I would've said no way in hell. I'd never felt comfortable enough with anyone to go there. My asshole was unexplored territory, and I had every intention of keeping it that way. But there is something about the gleam of hope in Dante's dark gaze that makes me want to give myself to him in every way possible.

They always say you remember your first, right?

It's insane how badly I want him to be my first something. And even more absurd how much I think he needs it too.

He continues sweeping his long finger back and forth between my two holes, dragging my arousal across those sensitive nerve-endings, and I'm already a second away from an orgasm. He presses his fingertip to my opening, and the pressure is overwhelming, a cry rips out, a tangle of pleasure and pain, and I hurtle over the edge as waves of pleasure crash over me. The vibrations roll through my lower half, rushing all the way down to my toes until I'm trembling.

Holy shit. I've never come so quickly in my life.

A dark chuckle resounds above me, and I pry my eyes open as wave after wave of pleasure vibrates through me. When had I closed my eyes anyway?

"Oh, Rosa, you are so tight, so innocent. We're going to have to work on that ass before I can claim it as mine." He slaps my pussy and I jump, but with Dante's massive body pinning me to the couch, I don't move an inch. "I guess we'll just have to do it the old fashion way." He sits up and jerks his boxers off, freeing his enormous cock.

My core throbs just from the sight of it. I'd only just recovered from our first time on the washing machine; I'd been sore for days. But my stupid lusty pussy doesn't seem to remember any of that right now.

I reach for his hard length, but he bats my hand away and curls his arm around my waist then flips me over. I'm on my stomach facing my cute little Christmas tree.

"I told you I wanted to fuck you in front of that scraggly thing." A sharp sting lances across my ass as the smack rings out over my thundering heart. "Lift that ass for me, sweetheart." He presses a gentle kiss to my burning butt cheek.

A dangerous mix of fear and excitement fills my chest as Dante positions himself over me. He's so damned big I'm scared he'll smother me. He wraps his arm around my middle and cups my pussy. "Mmm, still drenched for me, just like a good girl." He toys with my clit, and I'm already rubbing up against him like a dog in heat. Then his thick head slides through my ass cheeks, and I freeze. The man is an animal, there is no way I can handle his dick.

He folds over me, his big chest blanketing my entire body. "Relax, Rosa, I'm only going to take your pussy tonight." His warm breath sends a chill down my spine.

I release a breath, and he thrusts into me so ferociously I hurl forward. If it wasn't for his hand between my legs, I would've flown right off the couch. Instead, he holds me steady as he pounds into me from behind, his cock spreading my folds until all I can feel is him.

His finger rounding my clit, his cock grinding into my sweet spot, his balls slapping my ass with each thrust, his chest heaving above me, his warm breath spilling over the back of my neck….

Dante. Dante. Dante.

He's everywhere.

And gawd, I can't get enough.

"Don't stop," I pant as he picks up his tempo, his hips rocking harder and faster in time with that finger on my clit.

His free hand finds my breast, kneading and pinching the sensitive flesh. His fingers clamp around my nipple and squeeze. I let out a sharp cry, and he only thrusts harder.

Warm heat bathes my back, and I'm vaguely aware of his tongue licking up my spine. A tornado of sensation consumes me, the pleasure, the torturous ache, it's almost too much. His mouth reaches my shoulder and teeth clamp down on my flesh.

"Ow!" I squeal. "Did you just bite me?"

His tongue moves over the sharp sting, and my back arches in delight.

"Mine," he growls. "All of you. Do you understand?" He fists my hair, yanking my head back so my eyes meet his. "You. Are. Mine."

"I'm yours, Dante," I groan as he rails into me again and again. I can barely hold on, my knees wobbling from the fiery heat racing through every inch.

I'm so close. Another second, and I'm going to unravel all over him.

"I'm going to fill you with my cum, sweetheart. I want to see my seed spilling down your thighs. And one day, I'm going to put a baby in that belly."

All the air catches in my lungs.

I freeze.

And so does he.

The tune of our thundering hearts and ragged breaths fills the heavy moment of silence. He's still inside me, still stretching and filling me to the hilt, but he doesn't move.

I try to think, try to rationalize the words that clearly just burst from his mouth without his control. But I can't. The idea of a future with Dante Valentino is too terrifying. And yet, the idea of none is worse. Add a baby into the mix and it's completely unfathomable.

An endless moment later, I reach between my legs and cup his hand over my pussy. Weaving my fingers through his, I urge him on, rocking against his palm and rubbing my ass against his hips. "It's okay," I whisper.

He slowly pulls out, and for an instant, I'm scared he'll bolt again. But once he's unsheathed to the tip, he plunges inside me once again with renewed ferocity. In and in and in until I can't tell where he ends, and I begin.

I choose to focus on that and not on what he said a few seconds ago because I'm not sure either of us is ready to face that slip of the tongue.

"Mine," he growls again, more beast than man.

I give myself to him completely in that moment, allow myself to be utterly enraptured by this slightly unhinged mob boss. I release every restraint, every fear, every insecurity and allow him to claim me body and soul.

Because I can deny it all I want, but I'm falling for Dante, and I'm going to enjoy every last minute as he drags me to hell.

A second orgasm builds, stronger and more powerful this time. Each thrust pushes me harder, desire curling through my insides until Dante is all I feel, all I know.

"I'm coming, Dante...," I moan.

"Wait for me." He drives so deep inside me I swear he hits my spine, sending a tidal wave of pleasure surging from my core and stretching to every nook and cranny. His cock twitches and his warmth spills inside me, filling me with more of him.

For an insane second, I imagine those tiny swimmers racing to my ovaries and my heart is so full, as full as my pussy with his cock—*No!* I shove the thoughts back along with the unwanted rush of emotion. The baby talk is crazy, absolutely batshit crazy. Neither of us are in any state to take care of ourselves, let alone a child.

Then why is it all I can think about as his arms encircle me, and he pulls me down into his lap? He's still inside me, filling me at an entirely different angle now.

"Mmm, Rosa...." He nuzzles my ear and I lean into him, the hard planes of his chest somehow still soft against me. My head falls back against his shoulder, and I meet that dark gaze. Something I've never seen before flashes across the dark abyss ... insecurity, uncertainty, fear?

The sharp ring of his cell phone shatters the peaceful moment. He mutters a curse before reaching for his discarded pants, bending us both forward. Still inside me. How the man is still hard is beyond me.

He scans his phone and lets out a series of curses, in Italian this time.

"What's wrong?"

Darkness carves into his jaw, the murderous glare sending a chill up my spine. "Some motherfucker burned down your apartment."

CHAPTER 32
USE ME

D*ante*

"How the fuck does that happen?" I shout into the phone.

Aldo mumbles another apology, but all I want to do is reach my hand through the phone and ring the idiot's neck. "We haven't been watching it closely, boss. With Rose at your place, we didn't think it was a priority."

"I don't pay you to think, dumbass."

"Right, sorry."

"Tell me everything." I grit my teeth as he gives me the details, which aren't much. Rose sits beside me, her bare thigh against mine. A slight tremble rushes her body, and I reach for the fuzzy pink blanket and drape it over her shoulders.

I jab my finger at the screen after a few more minutes of nonsense. We are getting nowhere, and I don't have time to waste on excuses. Not when fury is raging through my veins, and I'm about a second away from losing my shit. Crimson edges into the corners of my vision until all I can see is blood.

The blood of my enemies painted across the room. How dare some motherfucker mess with me? Fuck with *my* girl's apartment?

Because this is clearly about me.

No way the arrogant Dr. Mark gets his hands dirty with something like arson. He only wants one thing: Rose. Burning down her apartment doesn't line up with his motives. This is Feng and those Red Dragon fuckers. It's retaliation for the guy I took out in the alleyway. It has to be.

Cazzo. This is my fault. A blast of guilt claws through the rage, but my monster is a ravenous beast. It swallows it up whole until only the insatiable wrath remains. I'm going to rip Feng's head off, but first I'll cut off each and every one of his fingers and toes. Then I'll stuff them in his mouth until he chokes—

"Dante?" Rose's soft voice tears me from sinking deeper into the spiraling darkness. She reaches for my hand and pries my fingers off my phone. I hadn't even realized I was still holding it. Her gaze latches onto the four half-moon bloodied marks on my palm, and she winces. "You're bleeding."

"It's nothing."

"It's not nothing." She stands, pulling the soft, pink throw around her shoulders and marches across the living room to the kitchen. She disappears behind the marble counter and pops up a moment later with a first aid kit. That nosy little thing must've been snooping around my apartment in my absence. I didn't even know that was there.

She marches back, triumphantly, swaying her hips like she owns the place. For someone I just fucked raw only a few minutes ago, she sure has a lot of swagger. The corners of my lips curl as she nears, and my heart does that strange flutter thing. When she folds her legs down beside me, the ballooning rage has all but dissipated completely.

I heave in a breath, searching for that all-consuming anger, but it's simmered to a manageable level.

Rose takes my hand in her lap and dabs the cuts with an alcohol-doused cotton ball. I keep my eyes fixed to her bare pussy just beneath my hand, and I don't even feel the sting. Now that the fury has waned, I realize we're both still very naked. And judging by my hardening cock, I'm more than ready to take her once more. But *merda*, what if I say something completely insane again? I have no idea where the hell that slip of the tongue came from. *And one day, I'm going to put a baby in that belly.* My words echo across my mind, the ramblings of a man drunk on lust.

I don't even want children. Or at least, I never did….

I sneak a peek at Rose who's still quietly tending to my cuts. Any other woman would've freaked out and ran. Hell, if someone had said that to me, I would've been on the next jet out of the country. *Dio*, I'm a complete *coglione*. Fucking idiot.

"So, are you going to tell me what happened to my apartment or are you just going to pretend nothing happened?" Her enchanting eyes turn to mine, and I release a shuddering breath.

How can I tell her I did this? How can I admit that my inner demons got the best of me, and now, her apartment is reduced to ashes as a result of my temper?

"The second one." I throw her a smirk. "Let's just pretend the last ten minutes didn't happen and go back to my room so I can fuck you properly in my bed." It's either that or I go on a bloody rampage and take out half the city.

"Dante…." Her cheeks flush with desire despite her disapproving tone.

Dio, how did you find this woman for me?

Rose places a bandage across my palm and tucks away all the supplies back in the kit. Before she turns away, my hands fasten around her hips and drag her back into my lap, so she straddles me. She lets out a faint gasp as my raging erection brushes her center.

"Stop trying to distract me from the fact that I'm now homeless," she squeals.

"You'll never be homeless, Rosa … but is it working?"

"Yes!" A soft chuckle escapes through her forced scowl.

"Do you want the truth?" The question pops out of its own accord. It's like my damned lips get hijacked every time I'm around this woman.

"Always." Her eyes lock on mine, and *Dio*, the depth of emotion hidden behind brilliant blue steals the air from my failing lungs.

"You, right here, in this moment, are the only thing keeping me from tearing out of here and shooting up all of China Town until I find Feng Zhang and crucify him." My hands curl around her thighs, fingers digging into her soft flesh. "This is my fault. Your apartment was torched because of me. Because of something I did in a moment of rage, and I'm about a second away from doing it again. Because no one hurts what's mine and lives to tell the tale." I draw in a breath and close my eyes. Rose presses her forehead to mine and brushes her nose against my own. I slowly pry my lids open and meet those lively orbs. "And You. Are. Mine. Rosa."

She raises her hips and sinks her sweet pussy onto my cock.

It's so unexpected, a tremor rolls through my entire body as I fill her.

"This isn't your fault, Dante." She starts to ride my cock, gliding up and down my slick shaft but her eyes remain pinned to mine. "If I thought it was, even for only an instant, I wouldn't still be here. But I am. So, use me to quell the anger, fuck me until it's gone. Because you think you're this terrible monster who doesn't deserve to be happy, to be loved, to have a family, but it's bullshit. You say I'm yours now, but you and your monster have been mine all along."

Something shatters inside me. I feel the tear across my heart, rending it in two because I'm so damned torn. I don't deserve this woman. *Dio*, I could live a thousand years and never deserve her loyalty, her admiration, her love, but she's giving it to me anyway. The asshole inside me wants to take it all, but a tiny hidden part knows how wrong it is to drag this woman through hell with me.

"Let's get out of here."

"What?" She falls back on her ass, staring up at me.

I'm so deep inside her I swear I feel her insides, and I've never felt so at home. "I need to get you out of town. I need to get *me* out of town before I do something I'll regret."

"Right now? It's the middle of the night. And I really should go see if I can salvage anything from my apartment—"

I cut her off, pressing two fingers to her mouth. "I'll replace everything you lost, I swear." The last thing I want to do is pull out of her, but I know myself, if I don't leave now, the moment we're done, the rage will return. And if Aldo drives, I can fuck her on the car ride out to Long Island. I gently lift her off me, despite my cock screaming and that pouty lip she's throwing at me. "Pack a bag, we're leaving in ten minutes."

She twirls around, and I smack her ass because *cazzo*, I can't help myself. "Hurry up," I bark as she scampers down the hallway. Then I grab my phone and shoot off a quick message to Aldo, then a second one to Tony.

Me: *I need confirmation it was the Red Dragons that lit up Rose's apartment.*

Tony: *Sure thing, boss. We're on it.*

Me: *And if it was them, I don't want you to move until I give the go ahead. Got it?*

Tony: *Got it.*

I attempt to slide my phone into my pants' pocket until I remember I'm still naked. Glancing up at the clock on the wall, I hiss out a curse as the hour hand ticks past the two. Tomorrow's going to be a hell of a long day. But at least Rose will be far away from the city, far from Feng and far from that MIA asshole, Mark.

That reminds me.

Me: *One more thing, Tony. Any luck with Dr. Mark's credit cards?*

Tony: *Nope. No activity on any of his bank accounts for days.*

Merda. How is this man surviving under the radar like that? Before his disappearance, before Rose's attack, there was no large cash withdrawal, nothing. It isn't possible to get by in this day and age of Big Brother completely unseen. And how was an ordinary, run-of-the-mill plastic surgeon evading *me*? None of this made any sense. Where the hell is this guy?

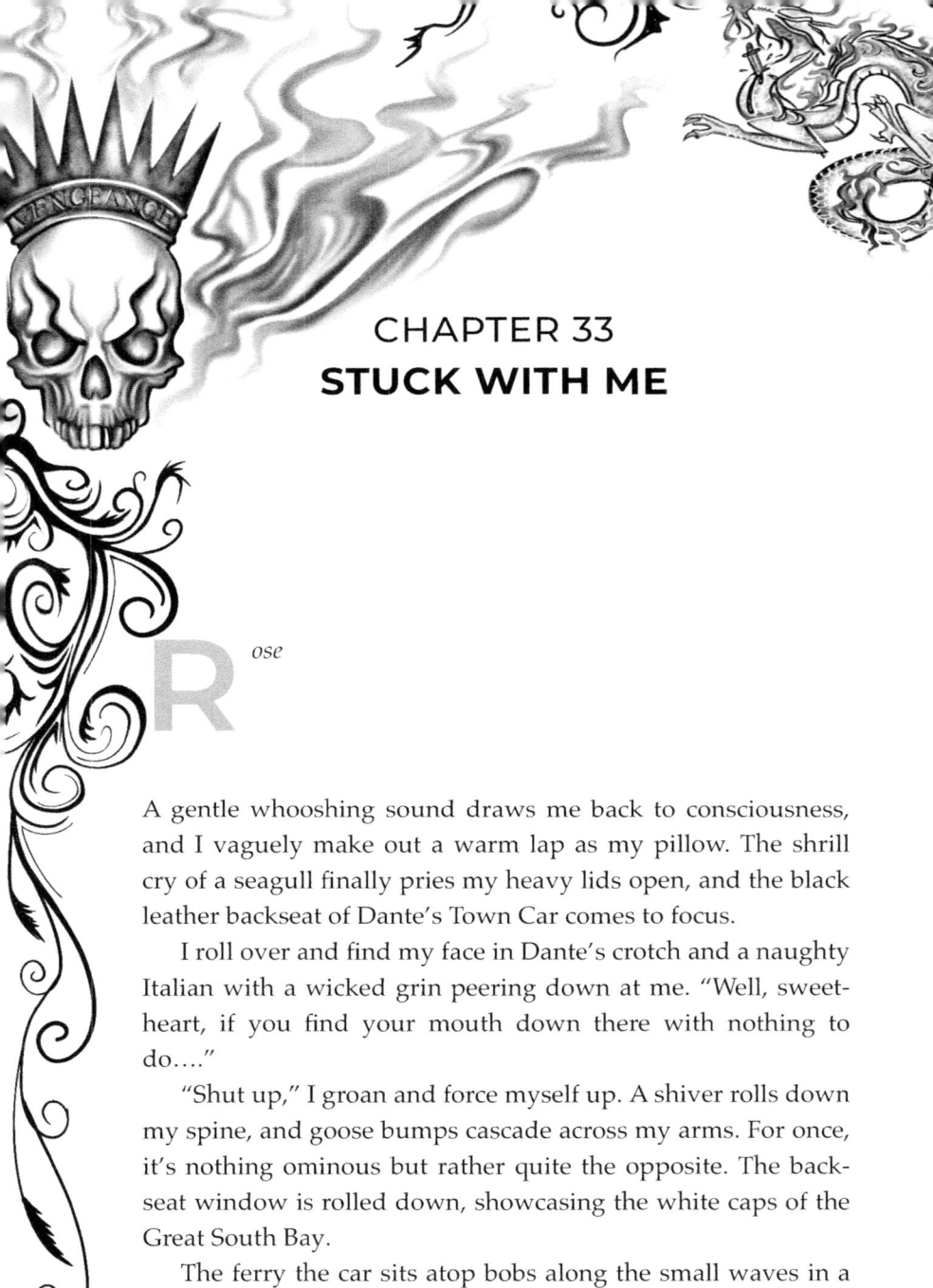

CHAPTER 33
STUCK WITH ME

R*ose*

A gentle whooshing sound draws me back to consciousness, and I vaguely make out a warm lap as my pillow. The shrill cry of a seagull finally pries my heavy lids open, and the black leather backseat of Dante's Town Car comes to focus.

I roll over and find my face in Dante's crotch and a naughty Italian with a wicked grin peering down at me. "Well, sweetheart, if you find your mouth down there with nothing to do…."

"Shut up," I groan and force myself up. A shiver rolls down my spine, and goose bumps cascade across my arms. For once, it's nothing ominous but rather quite the opposite. The backseat window is rolled down, showcasing the white caps of the Great South Bay.

The ferry the car sits atop bobs along the small waves in a gentle rocking motion. I stick my head out the window to get a better look at the sky. A riot of colors streak across the blue, a rainbow of golden ochres and bright magentas as the sun creeps across the horizon.

Gawd, I can't remember the last time I was up in time for a sunrise. Okay, maybe up for an early shift when I worked at that other yoga studio, but never outside to enjoy its splendor.

Studio … ugh, my torched apartment. Thank gawd I'd brought a few personal items along with all my necessities when I'd moved into Dante's house. They were all I had left now … except for the handful of things I'd left at my childhood home in Long Island. The crazy thing was how unemotional I felt about all of it. I should've been devastated, but a part of me is relieved, happy even, to be done with that place. After what happened in there, I don't think I could ever go back.

Dante's head pops up beside me, and I sneak a glance at the fiery mob boss. The typically hard cut of his jaw has relaxed, the deep trenches across his forehead vanished. He looks remarkably calm and at peace.

"Where are we going?" I whisper, scared to break the tranquility of this rare moment.

"To my beach house on Fire Island." His gaze turns wistful as he eyes the small fishing boats scattered across the blue.

The island seems deserted compared to the normal bustle of summertime. Like most of the beachside towns, they're extremely seasonal relying on Manhattanites fleeing the city in the blazing summer months. And it's definitely not summer. Which now that I think about it, shit, it's New Year's Eve. How did I almost miss that? I cast a covert glance at Dante; guess we'll be ringing in the new year together. A mad flutter of butterflies whips at my insides.

Returning my attention to the peaceful scene, I try to hold onto the calm. It's been a long time since I've seen Fire Island so quiet like this. It's eerily beautiful.

As the ferry begins to slow, Dante pulls me back into the car, and the moment of utter peace starts to dissipate. A vein across his forehead flutters, and I want to ask what's caused the change, but I hesitate, wary of making it worse.

"No one will find us here," he mutters. "The house is in Mamma's maiden name, and Luca and I have been adamant about keeping this part of our family's life private."

"Okay. I trust you."

His expression softens, and now I understand what had him so flustered. My safety. A bubble of warmth fills my chest. Something changed between Dante and me in the past few hours. I didn't want to get my hopes up because I couldn't handle the disappointment, but I felt the shift all the same.

The ferry grinds to a halt at the dock, and the rumble of the engine falls away. Dante leans across the spacious backseat and slides open the privacy screen that covers the small window to the front. "You already spoke to the housekeeper?"

"Yup, it's been handled, boss. The girls came, tidied up the place and stocked it with all the necessities, per your request."

"Good." He slides the screen shut and settles down beside me as the car's engine ignites, and the vehicle rolls off the ferry. There's only one other car on the boat with us. Definitely the emptiest I'd ever seen.

"So, what's the plan?" I eye the mob boss warily. This is starting to feel like a couple's getaway, and my stupid, fragile heart is running away with me.

"I'm winging it, as they say." He throws me a mischievous wink. "I already emailed both of your bosses and told them you have Covid, so you'll be out for the week."

"Dante!" I hiss. "You can't do that without my permission."

"Like fuck I can't." He crushes my hands between his, squeezing until I swear I hear the crunch of small bones. I'm so taken by the possessive idiot I don't even flinch. "You don't understand what burning your apartment symbolizes in our world, sweetheart. They're marking you."

A chill skitters up my spine, not at all the good kind this time.

"I didn't want to scare you, and I swear, I'll never let anyone lay a finger on you again, but until Feng is taken care of, we're staying here, and you're not leaving my sight."

I swallow hard; the rage in his tone is nothing compared to the fear lacing it. If he's frightened for me then shit, this must be bad. "Okay," I murmur.

He nods and slides back in his seat, curling an arm around my shoulders. I sink into his hard planes, the amount of comfort his unyielding form brings completely unfair. My lids grow heavy with the steady motion of the car and the lack of sleep last night, and I drift off to sleep again.

"*This* is your beach house?" Rubbing the sleep from my eyes, I stare up at the sprawling mansion along the shore. It's all modern light gray cedar and glass with wrap-around porches on two levels. If it wasn't for the overgrown seagrass and remote location that kept it so secluded, the neighbors could see right into the whole house.

I gawk up at it for a few more minutes before Dante totes me up the white gravel walkway. The ocean is so close I can taste the salt in the air. I inhale a deep breath as he fiddles with the key, carrying our bags on each shoulder.

A swirl of anxiety swims in my gut, worsening with each passing moment. An entire week with Dante here? Alone? Oh, good gawd, help me. I am already desperately falling for this man. There is no way I'll survive this super romantic getaway on top of everything I'm already feeling.

"Ah-ha, got it."

The black door swings open and Dante ushers me inside, dropping our bags and coats at the entrance. I bypass the chic, coastal casual look of the great room and move straight toward the floor-to-ceiling windows which provide an unobstructed view of white powder sand and endless coastline.

My breath hitches at the sight. Even in the dead of winter, the dark blue waters stir something powerful in my soul. I'd grown up on Long Island, too. Not this swanky part but my parents' house is less than an hour away. I'd spent countless summers at the beach. It had been so peaceful, so idyllic, until that one summer….

"You okay, sweetheart?" Dante moves behind me, wrapping his warm body around my suddenly icy one. "I can turn up the heat if it's too cold."

Standing a few feet away from the sliding glass doors, I keep my gaze pinned to the ocean, afraid to turn around and let a tear slip. "No, I'm fine, just tired I think."

Dante spins me around, and the crease between his dark brows deepens. "What's wrong?" For someone so intent on keeping me at arm's length, he's exceptionally attuned to my mood changes.

"Nothing," I force out. "Everything's perfect really." I shrug and try to wriggle free of his embrace, but his arms only tighten around me.

"I meant what I said, Rosa. No one will hurt you again. I will always keep you safe."

"Until you freak out and leave again." The words slip out before I can stop them. I realize my mistake as his smile flips into a frown, but it's too late. I wait for his arms to slacken, for him to dart upstairs, or even out the door.

Only he doesn't move.

Instead, he grips my jaw with his big hand, fingers digging into my cheeks. A murderous glare sears into me, and a shudder crawls up my spine. "I'm not going anywhere," he snarls. "You've unleashed the monster, and I warned you what would happen after that. You're stuck with me now, sweetheart. You're the sweetest drug I've ever tasted, and I'm already completely addicted. No one will take you away from me. *No one*." His mouth crashes into mine as his hands drop to my ass and lift me up. He curls my legs around his waist and walks us the remaining feet to the immense wall of windows. His hand digs into the back of my neck, fisting around my hair.

Then he lowers me to the floor and drops to his knees, taking my yoga pants down with him. I'm bare beneath, and a wicked grin curls his lips. "Oh, Rosa, you are going to be the death of me. But I'll take every sinful moment as long as it means I can die with my face buried in your perfect pussy."

He yanks my shirt over my head and pins me against the window. The icy glass sends goose bumps over my heated skin. I'm cold and hot, blood pounding in my veins as he parts my legs and devours me.

My ass is pressed to the glass, and I thank heavens it's the middle of winter or everyone on the beach would have a front row view of my rosy cheeks. As his tongue strokes my clit, his hand wanders up to claim my breast, and I arch into him as a groan slips free.

"Mine," he growls against my pussy, then dives his tongue deeper. "Mine." He thrusts a finger inside, and I cry out. Then his middle finger rubs my arousal across my back hole, and fire like I've never felt builds at my apex. He plunges his finger inside the virgin territory filling me with all of him. I feel so full, I'm sure I'm going to explode. His fingers claim each hole, his tongue on my clit. "Oh gawd, I'm going to come," I cry.

"No, you're not, sweetheart, not yet." The vibrations of his words on my sensitive flesh nearly send me over the edge. "I'm not finished with you yet. I'm taking that ass with my cock, right now. I can't wait any longer. It'll be mine, only mine."

He runs his tongue across my folds once more before releasing me and spinning me around. I let out a mewl as my breasts and all that heated flesh press against the icy glass. I'm so wet, arousal slickens my thighs, running down the inside of my legs.

"Mmm, perfect," Dante drawls as he bends me over. His pants hit the floor, then his boxers.

His cock strokes my wet folds then moves higher. His thick head brushes my ass, and anticipation tightens my core. He spreads my legs wide and reaches around to stroke my clit. My knees wobble as he starts to circle, and the building orgasm returns anew. "Just relax, sweetheart." His warm breath skates over the shell of my ear. "You're so wet, so ready for my cock."

And fuck, it's true.

I want to experience this with him. I want to give him something that would always be only his.

He grabs a fistful of my hair and jerks my head back to capture my mouth. With my attention on his sinful tongue, he runs a finger through my soaked pussy then drags my arousal to my back hole. He dips a finger inside, and my entire body clenches. He slowly thrusts, stretching me. "Mmm, Rosa. Your sweet little ass is ready for my cock."

Before I can get a word out, his tongue plunges inside my mouth in the same instant he sinks his cock into my back hole. A rush of pleasure and pain consumes me, arching my back as a scream rips out.

"You okay, sweetheart?" He slowly pulls out then thrusts a finger in my pussy, and I cry out again. From sheer pleasure.

"Don't stop," I moan.

His cock fills my back hole, one expert finger plunging inside me and the other circling my clit. Holy hell, I've never felt anything like it. So full of Dante, pleasure seething from every inch of me.

"I'm going to come...."

Pleasure laps through me, swallowing me whole. He thrusts in and out, in and out, slowly and so damned deep.

"Dante," I groan.

"Come for me, sweetheart." He pinches my clit and thrusts his cock at the same moment, my nipples brushing against the frigid glass and the onslaught of sensations bowls me over. I plummet over the edge, a tremor so powerful raging through me, my legs flail beneath me. If it wasn't for Dante holding me upright, I would've collapsed.

As I ride the waves of pleasure, Dante's cock jerks inside me. He moans my name as warmth spills down my legs. "Oh, Rosa," he growls, still fisting my hair. Dragging my mouth to his, he pumps a few more times inside me as his tongue ravages mine. "Oh, Rosa, Rosa, you will be my absolute salvation. That or my utter demise. Either way, I'll die a very happy man."

CHAPTER 34
BETTER THAN HEAVEN

D*ante*

I can't remember the last time I slept with a woman.

Not fucked, but actually *slept* with in my bed, nonetheless. On top of me, more specifically. And to ring in the New Year. That has to be monumental. Rose tried to roll over onto the mattress after the last time I claimed her, but I held her fixed to my body, my cock still buried deep inside her. I liked it there. Wanted to stay forever.

Hours later, when I'd gone soft, I still couldn't unravel my arms from around her soft form. So, I spent the entire night into the New Year like this with her chest against mine, her heart fluttering happily against my own. Who needed New Year's Eve fireworks when we had enough fire in our bed to light up all of Manhattan.

I'd never had a better night of sex or sleep in my damned life. Which of course now has panic flooding my veins.

Rose wasn't wrong yesterday. The feelings this woman

brings out in me have me scared shitless. For years, vengeance, hatred and violence were all I knew. They were all-consuming but simple. Now, I want more.

And it isn't only because of Rose. I'd finally taken the throne as king of Papà's empire, I'd finally assumed my birthright after all these years. But vengeance is bittersweet, and a solitary king is a worthless one. I'd hoped for redemption, for some way to make up for all the shit in my past. For disappointing my father, failing my younger brother, for hurting his fiancée, for screwing up my own damned life. But I've come to a realization: the notion of redemption is for fools. My sins will follow me to the grave and pay for my front seat in hell.

But maybe, just maybe, it'll all have been worth it if Rosa remains at my side in this life.

My thoughts flicker to the past, to the day we buried Papà….

"Someone has to take over Re Industries." Luca stomps across the backyard of our old house in the Bronx. He's fuming, nostrils flaring. The little shit thinks he can frighten me. He's barely twenty years old and already he thinks he knows it all.

He can talk to me about life once he's lived through the hell I've endured.

"I already said no," I growl.

"Are you fucking kidding me, Dante?" He glares at me, jabbing his finger in my chest. We're both still wearing our black funeral suits and the jacket is stifling. I barely contain the urge to rip it off, that and the oppressive tie. "You're the eldest son. It's your birthright to take over the business. Everything Papà worked for all these years, I won't let it go up in flames."

"It's what he *wanted, coglione." The discussion I had with my father all those months ago floats to the front of my mind.* Swear it

on my grave, that you will never assume your roll as heir. I don't want this for you. You're capable of so much more.

"It can't be!" Luca shouts and shoves me back. "If you won't take over the business then I will."

A deep chuckle vibrates my chest. "Like hell you will, fratellino. You don't have the first clue about running an enterprise like Papà's."

"Vaffanculo, Dante. I've been trailing our father for the past two years while you were off at Cornell with those prep school brats. I've been here, not you. And you know what, you're right. You're not the man for the job, I am."

I grab my brother by the collar and jerk him up off his feet. "This is not what Papà wanted for us and especially not for you, coglione. Just let it go."

"Never," he spits before stomping away like a stubborn child.

I was so stupid. If I'd only told him the full truth that day instead of taking off on a wild bender that would throw me into rehab for a month, our entire lives could have turned out differently. By the time I got out, Luca had taken over the business, and my pleas fell on deaf ears. Somehow, they didn't carry as much weight from a raging alcoholic and drug addict.

Porca miseria.

Rose lets out a soft sigh, then stirs on top of me, instantly waking my cock. I press a soft kiss to the top of her head before I can think better of it. *This is boyfriend shit, you idiot. You don't know the first thing about it.* That voice taunts in the back of my mind, and it's not wrong. I don't know the fucking first thing about caring for someone the right way. I'd tried with Luca after Papà and screwed up royally, and even with Mamma, I don't think I've ever gotten it right. She loves me because she has to, but perfect, little Luca has always been her favorite.

Rose's lids flutter, her faint breaths becoming more forceful.

She tips her head back and those irresistible blue eyes meet mine. "You let me sleep on top of you all night?" Her voice is rough and sexy as all hell.

My partial hard-on is now at full mast, poking at her belly. I shrug off her question, doing my best at nonchalant. The truth is I'm totally out of my depths here. So, I do what comes naturally—act like an ass. "I figured it would provide the easiest access to your pussy when you woke up." I lift her hips and drop her down onto my cock. "Happy New Year, sweetheart."

She lets out a cry as I fill her to the hilt. Fuck, she's still wet, probably still full of my cum from last night. I let out a groan as her hips immediately start to rock against mine.

"*Cazzo*, Rosa," I hiss, "You are such a greedy little thing for my cock."

"Me?" She laughs, throwing her head back as she grinds against me. Her breasts bounce with each thrust, and I can't help myself. I sit up and devour those perfect pink buds, first one then the other.

Sitting up, I fill her more deeply, the new angle sending a moan spilling from her lips. "Mmm, Dante… Gawd, you feel so good."

She's the one that feels like heaven.

I grip her hips, guiding her up and down so that the ridge of my cock hits her clit, over and over again. I may suck at a lot of things, but I know how to make a woman come. And luckily for Rose, it's become my mission in life. The curve of her lips, the sparkle in her eyes, the way her cheeks get rosy when I plow into her and coax out that orgasm has become my addiction.

When I close my eyes, she's all I see. I recognize the pattern, and it's terrifying. For once, it's not only for me I fear, but her. Dragging her into my life has only caused her more problems. Now, not only does she have a stalker, but her apartment is destroyed, and Feng is out for her blood.

"Dante?" Her soft exhale draws me back to the present, to the beautiful woman riding my cock like she owns it. And damn it, she does. Her hands frame my face as her eyes lock on mine. With her straddling me like this, her legs wrapped around my hips and my arms enveloping her body, flush against mine, our hearts pounding in sync, the moment is too intimate. It feels too little like fucking and too much like making love.

Panic grips my heart, and I freeze beneath her.

"Don't stop," she breathes.

I lift her off my dick, and she hisses out a curse. So does my dick. "What are you doing?" she cries.

"You want my cock, sweetheart? I want you to beg for it."

She rolls her eyes, but still, she moves to her knees on the mattress. "Please, Dante." A trail of arousal drips down her inner thigh, and fuck, my dick twitches at the sight, eager to burrow back into that warm sweetness.

I reach between her legs and cup her pussy. Her head falls back, and her hips grind against my palm. "Beg harder, sweetheart." I can feel my lips curl into a sinister smile.

"You're such an ass." Her hand moves over mine, forcing my palm against her needy clit.

"Uh, uh, uh." I shake my head. "Beg me for exactly what you want."

"Please, Dante, I want you to fuck me." Her hips roll, still thrusting against my motionless hand. "I want that huge, beautiful cock inside my pussy. I want your fingers on my clit, and mostly, I want that mouth on mine, devouring me. Then I want to come on your cock, and I need you to fill me with so much cum that it dribbles down my thighs."

A shit-eating grin stretches across my face. "That's my good girl, Rosa." I run a finger across her dripping folds, and her groan rents the air. "Now lie down, sweetheart and spread your legs for me. I'm coming home."

She falls back on the mattress, her blonde hair splaying out across the white sheets like a halo. I've never wanted to fuck someone face-to-face so badly before. I typically prefer taking women from behind. It is much less intimate. But not with Rose. I need to see her face as I wring out every last ounce of pleasure.

I thrust inside her, and her back arches as she takes all of me in one go. And *Dio*, it is so hot. I rip my gaze from her flushed face to watch my cock pounding into her pussy. Her lips spread for me, clenching around my dick like it is made only for me. I plunge deeper, my balls slapping against her ass in a beautiful symphony. Taking her from the ass was exciting, unclaimed territory that now belonged to me, but this, this is home.

I slowly withdraw to the tip and Rose's hands clamp around my ass, urging me back inside. "Beg, baby."

"Please, Dante, I'm so close. Please let me come on your enormous cock."

Damn, she's getting good at this. I lift her legs over my shoulders, spreading her wide, so she can take more of me in. Then I plow into her, coaxing another moan out and pick up my pace. Every thrust grows deeper and harder, until our ragged pants fill the air in a synchronized harmony. Running my hand up her body, I knead one of her breasts with my palm while I capture the other with my mouth. Her back arches as I nibble and suck on the hard, pink peak.

"I'm going to come," she cries.

I drive into her with a maddening tempo, and her pussy clenches around my cock so hard, she drags me to the edge along with her. She lets out a moan, my name on her lips and my dick jerks inside her. My lungs seize, and *Dio* it feels like I'm spilling a piece of my soul as I come hard inside her.

Fuck, I don't need heaven anymore, because this right here is a thousand times better.

CHAPTER 35
BEWARE THE FURY

Rose

Dante's moves around the kitchen, much like in bed, are hypnotic. How anyone could make cooking so damned sexy is absolutely beyond me. The bare, perfectly muscled, tattooed torso and low-slung sweatpants certainly don't hurt either. He spins toward the stove, and I'm gifted a perfect view of his broad shoulders and intricate ink designs stamped across his back. The man is a walking piece of art. Even the myriad of scars doesn't detract from his beauty, instead they only seem to enhance the dark brutality of his nature.

I creep around the marble island and stand behind him, clenching my hands into fists at my side to keep from touching him. I have no willpower around this man, and a second later, my fingers trace the map of black ink. He shudders at my touch, and my inner vixen gloats with satisfaction. The man is a god in bed, but I like to think I earned a few of those explosive orgasms on his end. I return my attention to his warm flesh, to the tribal markings, the more intricate drawings of chains, skulls, and a dragon with a knife through its gut. Though I can't see the one across Dante's chest, it leaps to the forefront of my mind.

Vengeance is king.

Stella had filled me in on Luca's side of the family history, but every time my gaze lands on that tattoo I'm tempted to ask more. One-sided stories never supply the full picture, and after spending only a few weeks with this mercurial mob boss, I have a feeling there's so much more to his story. If only he'd open up….

I let out a sigh and dismiss the crazy idea. I should be happy with as much as he's given me so far. It's clear sharing feelings are not part of this man's repertoire.

Leaning into him, I watch his hands as they chop tomatoes and fresh parsley for the frittata I was promised. How those rough, calloused fingers could create something so beautiful is startling. The savory scents fill the air, and my stomach lets out an embarrassing rumble.

With my belly practically pressed to his back, he definitely must hear it. A wicked chuckle rumbles his torso. "*Pazienza*, Rosa, it's coming." He cocks his head over his shoulder and smiles down at me. Not a sneer or a smirk, but an actual smile and gawd, my stupid heart trips on a beat. "Papà always used to say *beware the fury of a patient man*." A rueful chuckle spills out from those kissable lips. "Luckily, I never had that problem. For me, it was more beware the patience of a furious man."

"Well, it's a good thing for you that I'm neither patient nor furious."

"That is very true." He returns his attention to the stove and flicks off the burner. "There, done."

I watch completely entranced as he plates the frittatas, cleaning the edges of the colorful ceramic dishes with a paper towel, then garnishes the eggs with the fresh parsley. He places the plates on the island in front of each barstool then fills our glasses with fresh-squeezed orange juice.

"You never really talk about your papà…" I begin cautiously. "And Stella has told me bits and pieces of your past with Luca and King Industries."

He stares at me unblinking. So I continue.

"Why didn't you take over the King's when your father passed?"

Dante shrugs, darkness curtaining his expressive irises. A long minute passes before he finally heaves out a breath. "He made me promise I wouldn't."

"Seriously?"

He nods, grinding his jaw so that tendon flutters to life. "Papà didn't want this life for us. Before he died, he made me vow to allow the company to perish along with him. I was stupid and pretty fucked up back then, and I never told Luca the full truth until it was too late."

That silences lapses between us again, and I understand the discussion is over. I'm honestly shocked I got that much.

"*Mangia*," he finally says as he slides onto one of the barstools. Eat. My Italian is pretty shit, but at least I know that one.

I just stand there like a complete idiot, hot tears pricking at the corner of my eyes. Between his heartbreaking confession and the fluffy frittata I'm a second away from crying. What is wrong with me? Have I really been used to such assholes that a heartfelt conversation and a freaking home-cooked breakfast bring me to tears?

"Rosa?" My name on his lips, in that sexy Italian accent opens up the floodgates.

I spin away as the tears begin to fall, desperately sweeping them away. Dante is going to freak if he sees me crying. He's going to think I'm getting too emotional, that I'm totally falling for him. He wouldn't be wrong, but he can't know. Not yet, maybe not ever.

The screech of the metal bar stool on the wood floor has me wiping the tears back even more frantically. "What's the matter with you?" His warm breath skates over the shell of my ear.

"Ugh, it's the onions, they're making me tear up."

He throws me a sidelong glance but doesn't argue. Instead, he grabs a napkin from the table and hands it to me. "Sometimes, I have the same problem with the onions. That's why I don't cook often." He shrugs and slides his hand down my arm, lacing his fingers with mine. "Now come on, eat or it'll get cold. Don't get used to this five-star service, sweetheart. It's New Year's Day so I figured I'd whip something special up, but I can't be spoiling you forever…."

I snort on a laugh and follow him back to the island. He takes a bite of the frittata and chews thoughtfully. I wonder if he's fixating on the word forever like I am. *Stop it, Rose*. There is no forever with Dante. Once this mess with Dr. Mark and now the freaking Red Dragons has been handled, I'll have to get back to reality. Dante isn't my boyfriend. Sure, he likes to fuck me, but I'm not even all that sure he likes me. He's my glorified babysitter until Luca and Stella get back in town.

"What's going in that pretty little head of yours?" Dante swings his gaze in my direction, putting an end to my spiraling.

Instead of telling him the truth, I opt for a partial one. "My dad's been texting me about going to see him." It's not a lie. I'd found a half-dozen messages when I woke up this morning. It was like somehow, he knew I was nearby. Being back here on Long Island and so close to my family is weighing on me.

Dante puts his fork down and finishes chewing. "Oh yeah, where does he live?"

I swallow down a big bite, the delicious frittata going down harder than it should have. "Not too far from here, in King's Park." I don't even realize the irony until the name of the town

I grew up in spills out. And here I am with the new king of the Kings.

"Are you close?"

My shoulders lift sluggishly. We had been once. After what happened with my uncle, I'd withdrawn from everyone, men especially. Dad didn't deserve it, but he'd earned the brunt of my pain. "Kind of," I finally mutter.

His dark brows furrow, lips curving into a frown. "I've never seen you speak about anyone with such little enthusiasm. What happened between you and your father?" A hint of anger slices into his tone. It's subtle but after this much one-on-one time together, I've grown to pick up on the hints.

"No, it's nothing like that," I blurt, shaking my head.

"He's never laid a hand on you?" He spins at me, and red-hot fury streaks across the endless midnight of his eyes. "Did he hurt you, Rose? Is that why you didn't want to go to Long Island for Christmas?" His hands clamp around my shoulders, fingers digging into my skin, and he drags my barstool between his legs. "Because I swear to God, if he—"

"No," I blurt. "It wasn't him; I swear."

Shit. I snap my jaw shut, but it's too late.

The fury morphs to rage, and his entire body trembles as he regards me. "Who the fuck hurt you, Rose?"

"It was a long time ago, Dante. It's not worth getting into it."

"The fuck it isn't."

"He's dead," I blurt. A total lie, but I cannot have this man going psycho right now. Not after all the strides we've made.

He blinks quickly and the rage simmers, along with the death grip around my arms.

"I'm fine, he can't hurt me anymore, D. He's long gone."

"Who was it?" he snarls.

"It doesn't matter ... a distant relative." I shrug, the idea of bringing up the painful memories like twisting a knife in my heart. "We used to be close when I was little and…." I let the words fall away. Maybe it had been my fault. I'd been too friendly with him, even flirted a little. I was sixteen going on twenty-one. I'd been stupid, so stupid.

A growl tears me from my spiraling thoughts. "The *figlio di puttana* is lucky he's already dead, or I'd dispatch him to hell myself only after I cut off his balls and shove them down his throat. Then I'd watch the life slowly drain out of his eyes."

A shudder courses up my spine. I'd imagined that very thing more than once, only not quite so graphically. "Thank you," I whisper. No one has ever made me feel so safe, but I'm scared to say the words out loud.

"I can take you to visit your old man, if you want."

I heave out a breath. I really don't want, but I can't put Dad and my stepmom off forever, and going with Dante might just give me the strength I need, not to mention the excuse for a quick visit. "I guess I should…." I take another half-hearted bite of the savory frittata. "Don't you have work to do today or something?"

He shakes his head, the hint of a devious smile tugging at the corners. "I told Clara I have Covid too."

I snort on a laugh and nearly buckle over. The fact that Luca's assistant frightens both Valentinos into submission just makes me giddy. I'll have to learn her trick one day.

"You think that's funny, sweetheart?"

"I do. I really do. That woman has you by the balls."

He throws his head back, and a dark chuckle vibrates his massive chest. "There's only one woman that has me by the balls, Rose, and in a second she's going to have her mouth full of my cock *and* those balls."

My pulse skyrockets, shooting heat between my thighs. Good gawd, that mouth is so filthy, and it fires me up like nothing else. He'd just been inside me only an hour ago, and already I was ready for him again. "That's what you think, Mr. Valentino."

"That's *signor*…."

"Fine, *signor* Valentino." I attempt my best Italian accent. "Only if you beg, of course."

A flash of mischief flickers through those midnight orbs. "That's not how this works, sweetheart."

I hop off the barstool and place it between us. He looms over the white cushion, hovering dangerously. "How about this?" I manage on an exhale, my heart already pumping overtime. "If you catch me, I'll let you fuck me."

Another wicked chuckle fills the air between us. "*Let?* That's funny." He shakes his head, a dark brow cocked. "You liked that game, didn't you?"

My head bounces up and down. It had been the most exciting lay of my life before every one after that with Dante.

He glances at his wristwatch then back at me. "I suppose we could get a quick round in before visiting your family."

I never thought a mere sentence could douse the building flames so quickly. It wasn't that my father had ever done anything wrong. If anything, it was my fault, or my mom's for never having spoken up. All these years and he still had no idea what Uncle John did to me. I had a feeling he suspected, especially after mom….

"Rose?" Dante snaps his fingers an inch in front of my nose.

I blink quickly, chasing away the dark memories. Fuck you, Uncle John. You don't hold any power over me anymore. The only man I need fucking up my life is the grumpy, slightly unhinged Italian leering down at me. I whirl around and race to the sliding glass doors.

"Come get me, D. If you catch me, I'll show you exactly who has you by the balls."

A string of Italian curses explodes behind me as I slide the door open and dart into the brisk morning air. Padding across the sandy deck, I race toward the beach, my silk robe flapping behind me.

The bitter chill in the air cuts through my skimpy clothing, and if it wasn't for the adrenaline raging through my veins, I would've been shivering from the cold. I run faster. The shore is only a few yards away now. Heavy panting echoes behind me, the whisper of feet sinking into soft sand growing closer.

That sweet mix of anticipation and excitement thrums through my veins. Every nerve-ending in my body stands at attention as I take the final steps to the shore. The icy water splashes over my toes, sending goosebumps across my arms.

A massive body pummels into me from behind, enveloping me in that warm, musky scent. "That wasn't much of a challenge, sweetheart." He dips his lips to my ear, his husky voice tickling the shell and drawing goosebumps on top of goosebumps.

"Maybe I wanted to get caught," I whisper back over the crash of waves. Who am I kidding? Of course, I did. What better way to drown out the dark memories than with Dante's cock?

My toes are like icicles, but I remain rooted to the spot with Dante's massive arms around me and the bay stretched out to the horizon. A long moment later, he scoops me into his arms, takes a few steps up the beach and drops me onto the moist sand.

He drags his sweatpants down to his ankles, and I suck in a breath as I take him all in. It's a damned good thing it's the middle of winter and there isn't a soul on the beach, or they'd get a perfect view of that enormous, hard-ass cock.

With the breeze blowing through his hair, and the choppy waves crashing behind his looming form, he looks like an avenging sea god come to the shore to conquer and pillage. *I volunteer*! He drops down over me, wedges his hips between my legs and thrusts his cock inside me.

I gasp at the sudden, overwhelming fullness. Then my legs wind around his waist and urge him deeper, faster, harder. I may have the savage mob boss by the balls, but he has me by the heart, which is infinitely worse.

CHAPTER 36
JUST FRIENDS

*R*ose

I walk up the rocky pathway to my childhood home, a mixture of emotions battling it out across my insides. A colorful red door draws the eyes away from the faded white siding and the gray thatched roof. The house sure has seen better days, much like its inhabitants. I kept my visits to a minimum since Mom passed away, the old colonial holding too many dark memories. Besides, it didn't really feel like home after Dad remarried. Not that I didn't like Janet, it just felt like Mom had been replaced too soon.

Dante nudges me in the side as I reach the bottom step of the rickety, old porch. "I thought you wanted to come visit."

I force a cheery smile and bob my head up and down. "I did—I do. I owe them a visit since I missed Christmas. I haven't seen them since the summer." And the only reason I'd come then was because my brother, Robbie was up visiting from Florida with his family. He'd begged me to come, so I had because I loved my nephews. Not even my big brother knew what happened with Uncle John that summer nearly six years ago. I'd vowed to take it with me to the grave. Until one day, I just couldn't anymore.

I never should have told Mom….

If I hadn't, she'd still be here with us.

"Rosa." I blink, and Dante's nose is an inch from mine. "What's going on with you?"

I shake my head and toss him a wink. "I'm just exhausted from all the S-E-X," I whisper as I march up the steps to the front door.

His brows furrow, like he knows it's total bullshit, but for some reason, he remains quiet. If anyone knows a thing or two about secrets, it's the new king.

"Come on." I reach for his hand with my free one as I press my knuckles to the door without thinking too much into it. Holding Dante's hand has recently become second nature, and I hadn't even stopped to think of the intimacy of it, especially when it looks like I'm bringing my boyfriend home to meet the family.

Shockingly, he wraps his big, warm hand around mine, and immediately the rapid-fire of my heartbeat slows.

The front door creaks open, and Dad fills the entryway. A few whispers of silver hair fall across his forehead, but it seems like he's lost even more in the last six months since I saw him.

"Hey, Rosie!" He tugs me into his arms, and Janet appears a second later just over his shoulder. "Happy New Year!"

She hugs me next, squeezing my cheeks. "You look skinny, Rose. Are you not eating enough in the city?"

"Nah, I'm fine, Janet, thanks." I pull free of her embrace and motion at Dante who's still at the other end of my arm. "Um, Dad, Janet, this is my friend, Dante."

My *friend* slants a glare in my direction the moment the word is out. What the hell was I supposed to call him? My bodyguard? My savior? My roommate? My fuck-buddy? *My everything*. The traitorous thought surges to the tip of my tongue.

He holds his hand out, dipping his head. "Dante Valentino."

"Gerry Holloway." Dad gives him a firm handshake.

"My, my, are you handsome!" Janet's hungry gaze rakes over him.

Oh, gross.

Dante offers a smug smile. "Why thank you, but you are the true beauty here." He reaches for her hand and drops a kiss to the top. Where was Dante hiding this schmoozing mafia gentleman? I'd never seen this suave, sophisticated side of him before. This version reminds me of Luca.

"Well, come in, come in. It's freezing outside." Janet waves us in, and Dad follows a few steps behind me.

"I'm really glad you came, sweetie. We really missed you at Christmas. It just wasn't the same without you and Robbie."

I give him a half-hearted smile over my shoulder. "Yeah, sorry, things just got crazy with the new job."

Dante shoots me a sidelong glance. *Great, busted lying to the fam.* There's no way I'm explaining the attempted rape, my stalker, or anything about my burnt down apartment. Dad would insist I stay out here with them, and I'd rather die than endure that torture.

Janet leads us into the living room, all my mom's personal touches long gone. Being here without her still seems wrong. Even after all these years. It's like Dad wiped away every memory of her the day she took her own life, the day she made the active decision to leave us. That's what a broken heart will do to someone.

Only a few months after I told her the truth about Uncle John.

Sometimes the guilt of keeping the truth from Dad is suffocating. He blames her for taking the easy way out, but he has no idea why she did it. I do.

Dante's arm curls around my shoulder, and a shudder surges up my spine. "You're like ice, sweetheart. What's wrong?"

I offer him that fake smile I thought I'd perfected, but not with Dante, he can always see through the bullshit. Probably because he is so familiar with it. "It's just hard being here sometimes."

He nods as I tick my head at the pictures of Dad and Janet on the walls. Their wedding day, vacations at the Jersey Shore, family trips to Florida with Robbie and his smiling wife and kids, and of course, tons with Janet's kids. I made one fucking picture. Not that I care. I purposely avoid family time as much as possible.

"Sit, sit." Janet motions at the new living room set. It's a gaudy floral print that has my eyes burning from the clash of blinding colors. I plop down onto the couch so at least with my ass on it, I don't have to look at the ugly thing for a moment longer. Dante folds down beside me, bringing our entwined hands into his lap.

Again, I'd forgotten he was still holding my hand. I should've realized because it's the only part of my body not currently iced over.

"Can I get you two something to drink? A glass of wine, some beer, Dante?" Janet's appreciative gaze rakes over *my* hot Italian.

A harsh line slashes across his lips. "No, I don't drink, thank you."

His words strike a chord, and I want to smack myself for not realizing it sooner. He often speaks of his addiction, but a part of me never quite absorbed the full meaning. And it's true, in the months that I'd known the fiery mob boss, I'd never seen him drink a drop of alcohol.

"Two waters would be great, Janet," I answer.

"Really, Rose? No wine for you?" Her brow arches like it's the strangest thing in the world, and I'm a raging alcoholic. On second thought, I guess I do drink a lot when I'm visiting. Only way to numb the pain.

"Just water, thanks."

Dad's gaze flits to Dante, and a faint smile curls his lips. "I don't know this guy, but I like him already."

"Dad," I groan.

"What? Can't I call it like I see it?" He folds down onto the easy chair beside us. It's the only relic left over from Mom's days. "I may not see Rosie much anymore, but I know my daughter, and she seems happy."

"We're just good friends," I hiss.

Dante's hand tightens around my fingers, crushing them in his big palm. I shoot him a narrowed glare barely restraining a squeal.

"Sure, Rosie, whatever you say." He rolls his eyes then kicks the recliner back. Turning to Dante, he stretches out his legs, calling attention to the glaring hole in his sock. So embarrassing. "So, Dante, what do you do?"

"Italian mafia." His dark eyes sparkle with amusement, and the entire room goes silent. My heart stops, and I'm sure my jaw is about to unhinge. A long second later, Dante chuckles, the warm, sultry sound chasing away the chill that had settled into my body since I walked into this house. "I'm joking, of course." He leans across the armrest and pats my dad's hand, a little too vigorously. "I'm a businessman, Mr. Holloway. Perhaps you've heard of King Industries?"

"Why, sure. Who hasn't in the tri-state area?"

"It's our family business."

Now it's Dad's jaw unhinging and Janet's eyes flashing dollar signs as she saunters toward us with our glasses of water. "So, you're *that* Valentino?" Janet squeaks.

"I'm assuming you're speaking of my brother, Luca. He's the CEO, the former most eligible bachelor in New York City. I'm his elder brother. I deal with other aspects of the business."

"He's currently acting CEO, actually," I interject.

"It's only temporary." Dante shoots me a sidelong glance.

"Unless Luca and Stella start popping out babies." I take a quick sip of the water.

"They're not even married yet."

I shrug. The way those two fuck like bunnies I wouldn't be surprised if they had an oops baby.

The rumble of an engine and the crunch of tires spinning through gravel sends my head on a swivel over my shoulder. An old Chevy truck pulls into the driveway, and all the air squeezes from my lungs.

No! What the fuck is he doing here?

CHAPTER 37
SEE YOU IN HELL

D*ante*

A tremor surges up Rose's spine, the reaction so violent her entire body trembles. *What the fuck is going on with her? She's been keeping something from me, and I was okay with it at first. I wanted to give her time so that she'd feel comfortable enough to tell me herself, but enough is enough. If she doesn't tell me what the hell is going on here, I'm going to spank it out of her, and I don't care if her whole damn family hears her screams.*

"Rosa…," I growl in her ear. "What is going on?"

She swallows hard, her anxious gaze pinned to the hallway that leads to the front door.

"Nothing." Tears fill her eyes, and she chokes back a sob.

Footsteps echo down the corridor, the ominous slapping spiking my heartrate.

"*Cazzo*, Rosa," I hiss. "If you don't tell me right now, I swear to God, I will punish you." My own body vibrates with rage at seeing her like this. I've never felt so damned helpless in my life. Clenching my fists, I attempt to soften my tone. "I can't help you if you don't tell me what's wrong."

"I—I can't…."

I glance around the room at her father and stepmother who seem completely oblivious to Rose's total meltdown. How can they be so blind?

The source of the heavy footfalls appears around the corner, and every muscle in Rose's body goes tense beside me. From the corner of my eye, I catch her face pale, a sickly pallor coating her typically rosy cheeks.

I glare up at the male as his gaze lands on Rose, and a spark lights up his gray eyes, a sneer curling his lip. He's tall and lanky with wispy blonde hair, probably a decade or so older than me. Nothing that screams predator.

"Well, hello there, baby girl," he croons. "It's been way too long. When Gerry told me you were visiting, I couldn't help but come by since I missed you at Christmas."

But her reaction to him is nothing short of terror.

Dead, my ass.

She curls into herself, bringing her knees to her chest, and I see it. It's so obvious to anyone with eyes. I don't know how I missed it. How her entire fucking family doesn't see it.

"Dante this is Rose's uncle, John—"

I jump up, cutting her dad off, and drag Rose along with me. "Excuse me, I must speak to Rose in private immediately."

This John fucker watches me, his shifty gaze running to our entwined fingers. Fury pounds through my skull, and if I don't get Rose out of this room right now, I'm going to rip the *pezzo di merda*'s head off without confirming my suspicions.

My hold on Rose's hand is so tight, she squeals as I pull her out of the living room. I have no idea where I'm going but I just head toward the back of the house. She doesn't say a word as we pass closed doors, a bathroom, and finally, I see it. A screen door that leads out to the backyard. It's frigid outside, just what I need to douse the fiery inferno surging through my veins.

I jerk Rose through the door, and a blast of icy air sends another tremor up her spine. She hugs her arms around her middle, and if I wasn't so furious I would've greatly regretted my decision of dragging her out here. I suck in a breath of frosty air and spin at her, my hands clamped around her shoulders.

My eyes fix to hers and instead of the typical lively blue, a vacant gaze stares back at me. "You lied to me," I snarl. "Is that the man that hurt you?"

Her bottom lip quivers, and a sob builds in her chest.

"Rosa, tell me!" I shake her until a tear slides free, then another and another. "Damn it, Rosa, what did he do to you?"

"Stop yelling at me!"

"Then tell me!" I growl, unable to keep the anger at bay.

"He raped me! Is that what you want to hear, Dante? My mother's brother sexually assaulted me repeatedly for an entire summer when I was only sixteen."

"Fuck...." My stomach revolts, the breakfast from earlier threatening to make a reappearance. I stare at her, my eyes so wide they're a second from bulging out of my head. I'm going to kill that man. I'm going to chop his cock off and beat him to death with it. How dare he? How fucking dare he take advantage of a child like that? "I'm going to fucking rip him to pieces." My ramblings burst out unbidden.

"No, Dante...." Her tear-filled eyes lock on mine, the anguish tearing at my heart. "No one knows, not my dad, not my brother, no one."

"Why? Why didn't you send that *figlio di puttana* to jail?"

"It's not that easy."

"What the hell are you talking about, Rose? It is!"

"He's my uncle, Dante, my mom's brother, and we were close. I was young and stupid, and I probably provoked him—"

"No!" I shout, the anger reaching a dangerous crescendo. I shake her again, wanting to force some sense into her. "It's never your fault. Don't you understand that? *He* did this. He's a sick fuck, and he will pay for touching you."

Her head whips back and forth. "I can't do this, Dante. I don't want to re-live the past, unearth all those dark memories. I just want them to stay dead and buried."

Oh, they're going to be dead all right. I'm going to bury that motherfucker alive and stand over his grave, laughing, while he tries to claw his way out.

"No one else can know." She presses her body to mine, desperation in her blood-shot eyes. "Promise me, Dante. Promise me you won't say anything to my dad."

My throat tightens, the desire to wrap my hand around that man's neck and squeeze until his eyes pop out of his head so overwhelming I curl my fingers into a fist until my nails carve half-moons into my palms.

"Please, Dante. I've never asked you for anything, but I need this. I don't want to re-hash the past, I just want to avoid it for the rest of my life."

That look, the fear in her eyes, it's strangling. It breaks something inside me, brings those towering walls around my heart crashing down. There's nothing I want more than to protect this woman, than to spend every minute of my life making sure that nothing like that ever happens to her again.

"Okay," I finally mumble.

"Okay? We don't have to talk about it ever again?"

I shake my head. "We never have to talk about it ever again, but so help me, Rosa, if you ever try to come out here and visit without me, I'll lose my shit. You are never allowed near this house again unless I'm with you. Do *you* understand?"

She nods, her bottom lip snagged between her teeth.

I pull her into my arms and crush her against my chest. She's trembling again, but I'm fairly certain it's from the cold this time. "I know I've said it before, but I swear to you, Rosa, no one will ever hurt you again. I'm here now, and I'll burn down the world for you."

She tips her chin up, the ghost of a smile twitching at her lips. "I like the sound of that."

My hands run down her back and cup her ass because I just can't help myself.

"Now what?" she asks.

"I'm taking you home."

Her eyes light up, the dark curtain receding. "Good, because I need you inside me."

My cock instantly hardens at her words, it's like her voice has a direct link to my stupid dick. I feel like a total asshole after all the shit she's just admitted to me. She must read the surprise on my face because her cheeks go rosy, and she tightens her hold around my waist.

"Right now, when I close my eyes, all I can see is him. I feel his hands on me, and I just—" She shudders again. "I need you to erase it all. I don't want to think about him, I only want to feel you."

My head dips because I completely understand her. I'm about a second away from pulling out my cock and taking her right here on the back porch if it'll erase the pain in her eyes. That'll show fucking Uncle John.

"Get in the car." I release her and force myself to take a step back.

"Where are you going?"

"To give our regards to your family."

She arches a light brow, her lips puckering. "Dante…."

"I'll be on my best behavior, I promise." My fingers wrap around her wrist, and I jerk her mouth to mine. I pry her lips apart with my tongue and kiss her roughly. If she wants to forget, I'll make her forget. After I'm done with her, I'll be the only man she'll ever think about, the only cock she'll ever want, the only hands she'll ever remember on her body. "Now get in the car," I whisper against her mouth, "before I fuck you right here on the porch."

Her head bobs up and down, and she darts down the steps into the backyard. I watch her as she follows the stone pathway along the side of the house and disappears around the front. I pull my phone out of my pocket and shoot Aldo a quick text message to make sure she stays in the car. I don't want her anywhere near Uncle John.

Running my hands over my face, I draw in a steadying breath. Going back in there and facing that fucker while keeping my calm will be the hardest thing I've ever done. My mind flickers back to my days in A.A., and I search for that inner peace.

I jerk the door open and nearly rip it off its hinges. So much for calm. Inhale. Exhale. I repeat the mantra as I stomp down the hallway. When I reach the living room, Rose's dad's eyes lift to mine. I must look terrifying because he seems like he is about to shit himself. And he isn't even the object of my rage. I mean, I do blame him because what kind of a blind idiot doesn't realize what's been going on right under his damned nose?

Which derails my thoughts to Rose's mother. She's gone now, but had she known? I toss the thoughts to the back of my mind for now and focus on the blonde *pezzo di merda* perched on the couch. A smug grin curls his lips, and *Dio*, I'm dying to wipe that smile off his face with my fist. My nails dig into my skin with the strain of keeping the monster at bay.

"Rose and I are leaving. It's been an enlightening visit." I lace my tone with ice, daring one of them to question me. No one does. Swinging my gaze toward the uncle, my eyes shoot daggers. "There's just one thing I'd like to make clear before I go. Rose has come to mean a lot to me, a fucking hell of a lot more than to the rest of you. I plan to spend the rest of my life taking care of her, protecting her. I might not know exactly how to do that, but I'm damned sure I'll do a better job than any of you."

Janet lets out a little squeal.

I fix my dark gaze on Dad next. "Don't reach out, don't call her, don't text her. If she wants to talk, she'll call you. And if she never does, then forget about her. I may not know much about being a father, but you fucked it up big time, Gerry."

Whirling back on Uncle John, I lift my finger in his direction. "I'll see you in hell, *pezzo di merda*."

With a wicked grin, I tip my head at Rose's family and march out the door.

CHAPTER 38
FALLING FOR HIM

R*ose*

A steady rumbling draws me from a deep sleep. Blinking the haze away, I try to roll over, but steel bands tighten around my waist. Lifting my head, I take in the sleeping Italian I'm sprawled on top of. With his eyes closed, he's much less intimidating, that scruffy jaw relaxed instead of its typically clenched state. He looks younger, somehow.

I revel in the rare moment of peace to ogle this beautiful, lethal man. Tracing the map of tattoos on his chest, I slowly dance my finger over the intricate designs. I'm surprised he hasn't stirred; he must have been exhausted after last night. He'd stuck to his promise, fucking me so thoroughly he erased all the dark memories seeing my uncle had unearthed.

Whenever I think the past is finally behind me, it finds a way to surge back. If not Uncle John, now it's this crazy-ass stalker. At least, Dr. Mark has been quiet since my escape from the city. I haven't thought about him at all since that day at

Palestra. Funny how a change of scenery and being fucked senseless for days will take your mind off things.

A smile melts across my face as I take Dante in, asleep and unguarded. My ribcage suddenly feels too tight around my full heart. This man has done the impossible. I'm falling for him. Fuck … who am I kidding? I'm already totally in love with him.

Which is absolutely terrifying.

Men like Dante don't fall in love, they don't get married or have houses with white picket fences. But who says I need all that, right?

Simply being with Dante is enough. My thoughts flicker back to his mid-sex slip up. *And one day, I'm going to put a baby in that belly.* Or maybe we can have it all…. Just the thought of a future with the savage mob boss has heat building between my legs. I slowly inch down his torso until I'm straddling his thighs. His cock sits up at attention; even asleep, he's already sporting a hard-on.

I bend down and run my tongue over the tip. He's salty and musky, a heady combination of us both after how much time he spent inside me last night. A groan vibrates Dante's barrel chest, only spurring me on, and I peek up at him. His eyes are still closed but the rise and fall of his chest has quickened. I lick circles around his crown and start working his shaft with my hand. Cum glistens from the tip and mingles with my saliva, slickening his thick length. Practically unlocking my jaw, I try to take in all of him. His head butts up against the back of my throat, he's so damned huge, but I'm not deterred.

Last night, he was everything I needed and more, and today I'm determined to show him my appreciation. I suck harder, circling my tongue, and use my free hand to cup his balls.

"Mmm, Rosa, what a way to wake up in the morning."

I flash him a toothy smile but don't stop working. They don't call it a job for nothing.

He props himself up on his elbows, those intense midnight orbs drilling into me as I devour his cock. I've never been a fan of the act before but with Dante it's different. The power that comes along with bringing the great king to his knees does something to me.

"Oh, sweetheart, the things you do with that tongue and that mouth, *cazzo*. You're a goddess."

I'm preening like a fucking peacock now as I take him in deeper, sucking harder. His cock twitches, hardening in my mouth and I know he's close. I hum as my head bobs faster, and I drive him to the edge.

He sits all the way up now and fists one hand in my hair. I wait for the pain as he tugs on the long strands, but it never comes. Instead, he massages the base of my neck as I move more quickly.

"I'm going to cum in that pretty little mouth, Rose, and I want you to swallow all of it. Do you understand?"

I nod blindly. I want to taste him, feel his warmth spurting on my tongue. With Dante, the act is intimate, like I'm taking in a small piece of him.

"Are you wet for me, sweetheart? Does tasting my cock drive that sweet little pussy wild?"

"Umhmm," I moan against his cock.

"Let me see, baby." Reaching between my legs, he cups my bare pussy as my head continues to bob. "Mmm, you're soaked, just like I thought." He runs his thick finger between my wet folds, and my hips buck. "You want my finger inside you, don't you?"

Oh gawd, yes, I do. I just can't get enough of him. I nod, meeting his dark gaze with my lips still wrapped tight around his dick.

"Then you'll get exactly what you deserve." He shoves his finger inside me, and a moan erupts, vibrating his entire cock.

"Careful, sweetheart, I'm awfully close now and I want you to come with those luscious lips around my cock so I can feel every ounce of your pleasure."

My heart races as I grind my hips against his palm. He pushes a second finger inside me, and I'm so full of him I'm certain I'll burst. I don't stop sucking and spinning my tongue around his crown as he drives those fingers in and out. In and out. It's devastating and mind-blowing all at once.

His hips begin to move, shoving his cock deeper down my throat. I don't know how I take all of him in, but I'm half delirious between his fingers and the pleasure carved into his jaw, the dark sparkle in his eye. I want to drive him to the edge, I want to be the one to steal the air from his lungs as he comes.

The pressure at my apex is like a fiery inferno, another few seconds and I'll explode. "I'm coming," I rasp out.

"Good," he pants, "because you've got me by the balls, sweetheart."

His thumb grazes my clit, and waves of pleasure crash over me. My pussy clenches around those fingers as tight as my mouth on his cock. I groan against his hard flesh and with one last pump he unravels on my tongue. His warmth spills into my mouth, and I swallow him down as I ride his fingers to the very edge of oblivion.

When he finally withdraws from inside me, I slump down on his chest. Overwhelming emotion tightens my ribcage, and I can barely keep the tears at bay. I have no idea why I'm crying. It makes no sense at all. Maybe it's because for the first time in as long as I can remember, I feel cared for, protected, and adored, hell, maybe even loved.

Dante runs his thumb across my cheek sweeping away an unshed tear. Shit, I hope he can't tell I'm about to cry. How embarrassing. I've become this weak, weepy girl since I met this man.

I have the most overpowering urge to spill those three little life-changing words. *I love you*. I want to say it so bad, but I don't dare. We've come so far, and I'm terrified what that admission would cost me.

Pressing my lips together, I drop my chin to his chest. The rapid rise and fall begins to slow, but I can still feel his heartbeat beneath my hand. Maybe I'm hallucinating but it feels like it's beating only for me.

His eyes lock on mine, a glint brightening the endless midnight. "*Dio*, Rosa, what are you doing to me?"

Batting my lids, I give him an innocent smile. "I don't know what you're talking about."

"You know damn well what I mean. This, us, we were never meant to be." He chews on the inside of his cheek and runs his thumb across my bottom lip. "But fuck, sweetheart, it just feels so damned right."

I blink quickly because with that heavy gaze fixed on me, I'm about a second from losing it. Instead of opening my mouth and risk saying something completely inappropriate, my head bounces up and down. I just hope he knows how much I feel for him. I think he does….

He groans and rolls me onto the mattress beside him. From the corner of my eye, I catch a glimpse at the white-caps and sandy beach stretching out through the sliding glass doors. Going to sleep with the sound of the ocean singing in the background mingled with our ragged breaths is the only way to do it, in my opinion.

Dante climbs on top of me, his erection still heavy on my thigh. "I hate to say it, Rose, but I have to run a quick errand."

"What?" I whine. And here I am getting ready for round two.

He grabs his phone and flashes the screen at me so quickly I can't make out a single thing. "Tony just messaged me this morning. Something came up on the North Shore. It's urgent and since we're out here anyway, I can quickly take care of it."

"Why can't you send Aldo?"

Dante rolls his eyes. "Sweetheart, Aldo can't handle this sort of thing." He presses a kiss to my forehead, and I nearly melt into a puddle from the uncharacteristically sweet gesture. "But I'll be back in two hours tops." He drops his mouth to my breast and sucks my nipple into a sharp point. My back arches at the thrill of sensations. "So don't get dressed. Wait for me in bed because I'm nowhere near done with you."

A ripple of excitement surges up my spine, and another unstoppable smile spreads my lips. "Is that all we're going to do out here, Dante? Fuck and sleep?"

He shrugs, a devilish grin tugging at the corners of his mouth. "We gotta eat too, baby." He crawls down between my legs and drags his tongue across my clit. I nearly buck from the unexpected lavishing. "And I'm starving for that pussy."

Heat races up said pussy and blossoms across my cheeks. Gawd, this man is ravenous.

He pushes himself off the mattress, grunting from the effort.

"Do you really have to go?" I totally whine again.

"Yes, this is personal, sweetheart. But I promise, I'll be back before you know it, and Aldo will be stationed at the front door the whole time. You'll be safe." He ticks his head at the bathroom door as he steps into his discarded boxers. "Take a nice, relaxing bath while I'm gone because you're going to be sore as hell once I've had my way with you."

CHAPTER 39
I'M NOT OKAY

D*ante*

Blood stains my hands, embedded in my fingernails as I march down the pebble walkway. A part of me is loath to scrub it off. I need to remember that *figlio di puttana*, every second of torture I inflicted. The monster inside was ravenous after witnessing Rose's tormented state. It had taken every ounce of my restraint not to strangle the motherfucker right at her dad's house. Then I had to wait all night. Every time I tried to sneak out of bed, a sigh or some other ridiculously cute noise would flee Rose's lips, locking me in place. Then I'd get hard again, and I'd wake her up just to worship at that beautiful pussy one more time.

Now the monster is satiated. The *bastardo* who dared hurt what's mine is dead. I'd watched him endure the slow torture of bleeding out after I'd cut off each of his appendages, starting with that filthy cock. The punishment was too short for my liking, but I hated leaving Rose alone. Even with Aldo.

I'd been gone just over an hour and already, I felt her absence acutely.

Dio, what that woman has done to me….

I'd fought so hard to conquer my addiction, but this one, my obsession with her is one I'll never overcome. Nor did I want to. *Merda*, I want her at my side constantly. Forever. That unfamiliar sensation invades my chest, the tightening of my ribs, the fullness of my heart. I've tried to avoid it my whole life because it scares me shitless. But after yesterday, it's impossible to ignore.

Fuck, I'm in love with Rose.

The realization comes sharp and quick, like a shot to the arm, followed by that euphoric feeling flooding my veins. I. Love. Rose.

My feet move more quickly, in a desperate race to reach the car, to get to Rose. Panic crushes my chest, and I freeze with my hand on the doorhandle. What would I say? What kind of a life can I offer her? My future is as clear as a fog-shrouded night, where every step forward feels uncertain. The only certainty is I can't survive without her.

Just get in the car, you coglione. This time I recognize the voice in my head, it's Papà. He was the only idiot that ever believed in me, wanted more for me. I'd been the one who fucked everything up.

I slide into the Town Car, jab my finger into the ignition and peel out of the driveway. I've already got my guys on the way to clean up the mess. He'll never make his flight back to Florida. No one will ever find dear old Uncle John. I hope you rot in hell, *pezzo di merda*.

Papà taught us lots of things, but the one that stuck the most with me was how to clean up after ourselves. My thoughts whirl to the past, to a conversation with my father when I was just a kid.

. . .

Papà sits in the kitchen, dragging his fingers through his hair, tugging at the ends. A torn envelope and shredded piece of paper lie in front of him. I was supposed to be at soccer with Luca, but I ditched practice and snuck home. I didn't think anyone would be here. There's something about Papà's tortured expression that has me backpedaling. But it's too late. He lifts his gaze to mine and fear tightens my ribcage. I've never seen him like this, so desperate, so tormented.

"Dante, che fai qui*?" he barks as he crumples the paper in his fist. What am I doing here? I almost ask what he's doing here.*

"I wasn't feeling great, so I skipped practice."

His dark brows furrow as he regards me. "Stai bene?"

A stab of guilt invades my chest at the worried look in his eye. "Yeah, I'm okay, Papà, just my stomach or something," I lie.

"Are you okay?" I slide into the chair beside him.

He stares at the crumpled-up note peeking out from his clenched fingers. "No…." He huffs out a breath, eyes still fixed on whatever is in his hands. "I suppose I will have to be, figlio mio.*" He finally looks up, spears me with those dark eyes that I'm sure could read every secret in my black soul. "Listen to me, Dante, you are going to become a man soon. Being a man means taking responsibility for your actions, cleaning up your own messes.* Capisci*?"*

"Yeah, Papà, I understand."

"We all make mistakes, son. Some worse than others, but you meet them head on and you do what's right."

I nod, wondering if he's waiting for me to come clean about skipping practice.

He turns away, stares at that note again and stands. "Go, Dante, go do your homework. I have something important to take care of."

"Yes, Papà." I jump out of the chair and dart down the hallway, all too eager to get away unscathed.

I never did find out what had Papà so spooked. I was only a kid back then, seven or eight at most, but there was something about that scene that remained in my mind all these years.

The sharp squeal of my phone lights up the dash, drawing my thoughts back to the present. I press the green answer button when Tony's name flashes across the screen.

"What?" I bark.

"I got bad news, boss."

"*Cazzo*, what now, Tony?" The only time I ever hear from this guy is when he's got bad news.

"Three of our warehouses in Meatpacking were emptied out."

"What do you mean *emptied out*?"

"All the shit is gone, Dante. All the supplies, machinery, special material for the commissioner's new docks are gone."

"Fuck…. How?"

"The cameras were scrubbed, there's nothing, D. My guess would be the Red Dragons, but it doesn't seem their style. They would've set the warehouses ablaze, not steal the stuff. It just doesn't make sense."

"Who else could it be?" My thoughts flicker back to the Christmas tree lot with Rose. The new player Clara keeps talking about, what was their name? Damn it, I should've been paying better attention.

"Not sure, boss, but Luca's going to lose it when he finds out this is going to cost us the commissioner's project."

"The fuck it will. We'll find out who the hell stole our shit and get it back." There's no way I'm admitting to my little brother I dropped the ball on this multi-million-dollar deal. Losing Caroline's father's new high-rise is bad enough.

"So, you coming back to the city?"

"Yes," I growl. Incompetent idiots can't do anything without me. "What about Rose's apartment?"

"I don't think it was the dragons…."

"You don't *think*? I need you to be sure here, Tony."

"I've got nothing concrete, but no way Feng wouldn't take the credit. You know what a peacock that guy is."

Damn it. He's right. Then who the hell is fucking with me?

The house is quiet as I stalk inside, the steady crash of waves off the balcony the only sound. After that talk with Tony, I need to burn off some of this wrath, and I know exactly how to quell those dark desires. Hopefully, Rose obeyed me and is still naked in our bed.

Our bed? Where did that come from?

I race up the stairs, anticipation quickening my stride. "Rosa? You better be drenched, naked and ready for me, sweetheart." I reach the landing and jog through the double doors into the master bedroom. The bed is empty, sheets still in a tangle.

The bathroom….

I dart past the bed and swing the door open. Empty.

My ribs constrict, undiluted fear squeezing the air from my lungs.

"Rosa!" I shout. She can't be gone. I just talked to Aldo downstairs a second ago. He swore he never left his post, not for an instant.

I force in a breath of air to keep from passing out as darkness encroaches on my vision. The beach … perhaps she went for a walk and Aldo was too stupid to notice. That fuckhead is fired. If Rose was able to get the slip on him, he's useless.

I barrel down the stairs and search the lower floor before whipping open the sliding door. Racing onto the deck, I scan the horizon to the east then the west. The white-sand beach stretches for miles, but with the bitter chill in the air, not a soul dots the tranquil landscape.

"*Merda!*" I snarl. Digging through my pocket for my phone, I jab my finger at the screen. "Come on, Rose, answer. Come on, damn it." Paralyzing fear blossoms, but I shove it back, allowing the darkness to consume it. Fuck the fear. Fear is weakness, anger is strength.

The dial tone taunts me, ringing and ringing.

Nothing.

Dio, if something happened to her, if someone took her … I'll raze the entire island until I find my Rose.

I march back inside and head straight for the front door again. I'm going to fucking ring Aldo's neck. My hand strangles the knob, and I'm about to jerk it open when soft footfalls over my head whip my attention to the staircase.

Rose stands at the landing with earbuds dangling from her ears and a towel wrapped around her bare form.

My heart staggers, then halts, before kicking up again. "Rosa…." I murmur, heat pricking at the back of my eyes.

"Hey, I thought I heard something—"

I charge up the stairs and pull her into my arms, crushing her against my chest. A gasp escapes her lips, and it's only then I realize I'm literally crushing her. I loosen my hold around her torso, and her curious eyes lift to mine.

"You okay, D?"

"No," I growl. "I'm not okay at all. Fuck, Rosa. I'm in love with you."

CHAPTER 40
DO YOU LOVE THIS?

R*ose*

My head falls back, jaw unhinging as I stare up at Dante. I must have inhaled some funky bath salts or something because I could have sworn I just heard the savage mob boss tell me he loves me. I must be hallucinating.

"Wh—what?" I rasp out.

"Where the fuck were you, Rose? I've been searching this house like a *pazzo* … I thought someone took you."

Yup, someone's definitely gone crazy, I'm just not sure if it's him or me.

"Rose, answer me!" He shakes me, snapping my jumbled thoughts back to the present.

"I was in the bathtub." I point over my shoulder to the guest wing. "I couldn't get the water in the master to heat up, so I went in there instead."

"*Dio*, Rosa, you scared the *merda* out of me." He tugs me

close again, and I breathe him in, the mad pounding of his heart pressed against the shell of my ear.

"I'm okay, Dante. I'm right here." Now, back to that I love you stuff … I wait a few more seconds, until his breaths come out more evenly, but the longer I wait, the faster my pulse becomes. Had he meant what he said? Was it just a slip of the tongue like the baby thing? Something we'd just ignore again? "So…," I start, but his mouth captures mine, cutting me off.

He bends down and wraps his arm beneath my thighs, cradling me against his chest. "Where are we going?" I whisper against his lips.

"Back to the tub."

His tongue invades my mouth as he carries me back upstairs, across the landing, through the loft and to the opposite side of the master wing. I'd been in such a hurry to see him, I hadn't even pulled the drain in the tub. It's still filled to the brim with bubbles and the scent of lavender.

Dante sits on the edge of the marble basin with me on his lap and turns on the hot faucet. Warm steam fills the room in seconds, and he dumps another capful of perfumed bath oil.

Then he pries my towel off so I'm bare, cradled in his arms.

"*Dio, sei bellissima.*" His gravelly tone sends heat shooting between my legs. My Italian may be shit, but even my English-only speaking pussy knows what that means. *God, you're beautiful.* And I don't think I've ever felt more beautiful than in this moment.

He releases me only long enough to tug the shirt up over his head, then lifts me up so he can wriggle out of his pants and boxers in one go. And just like that, we're both naked and he's carrying me into the tub.

Dante tucks me between his legs, his already-hard cock brushing against my ass. I lean into him because despite his hard planes and corded muscles, laying against him is the most comfortable place I've ever been.

He dips his chin and rests it on my shoulder, and a

contented sigh slides past his lips. I tip my head back against his shoulder and his arms encircle me. The warmth of his body coupled with the hot, fragrant water is heaven.

His hands begin to move across my torso, rubbing the bubbles over my belly, then up to my breasts. My back arches as his firm hands close around the sensitive area. I want—no, I need to ask about what he said earlier, but I'm too much of a chicken.

What if it had been a mistake? Something he'd blurted in the heat of the moment because he thought I'd been kidnapped or worse.

"Speak, Rosa." Dante's command brushes over the shell of my ear, sending goosebumps raging down my arms.

"Hmm?" I ask innocently as his deft fingers circle my nipples.

"I know there's something on your mind, so just say it." His warm breath ripples down my spine a second before he takes my earlobe between his teeth. He nibbles and sucks, and now, I'm a writhing mess.

If he's trying to distract me, he's doing a damned good job.

His mouth moves to my neck, tongue lavishing its way down to my collarbone. His cock grows harder, like steel prodding between my ass cheeks. His teeth sink into the soft flesh at the base of my throat, and I let out a squeal. Then a dark chuckle echoes behind me, the warm sound filling my insides.

"That hurt, *bastardo*." I attempt my best Italian accent earning me another laugh.

"Don't even pretend you don't love it."

There it is again, the L word!

I steady my nerves and put on my big girl panties, whispering, "I do *love* it."

"Good," he murmurs. Then one of his hands releases my breast and skates down my torso, sinking between my legs. "What about this, Rosa?" He runs his thick finger across my pussy. "Do you *love* this?"

"Mmm, I do." My hips instinctively rise to meet his touch.

"What else do you *love*?" His lips are at my ear, and he dips that finger inside me. I clench around him, eager for that familiar feel of fullness. He starts to move slowly, his cock grinding into my ass as he finger-fucks me with one, then two long digits.

"I love this," I pant.

"Yeah, you love it when I let you come on my fingers?"

"Yes." My hips roll again and again, desperate for the friction that palm provides even beneath the swirling waters.

"How about my cock?" His wicked tone sends heat blazing through every inch of me. He lifts my hips and positions his erection at my entrance.

"I love your cock."

He guides me onto his hard length, and I let out a moan as he fills me. "Especially when it's buried deep in that sweet pussy, right?"

"Yes, Dante," I groan. "I *love* that."

I ride his cock as he guides my hips up and down, up and down along that stiff shaft. Then he reaches around me and finds my clit. I watch as his finger disappears inside me, mesmerized by the insanely erotic image. His cock thrusts into me from behind, finger circling, water lapping all around us.

It's only been a few seconds, and already I'm on the verge. The fire builds and builds, electrifying my senses.

"What else, sweetheart?" Dante's words are muddled in the background over the pounding of my heart.

I move faster, desperate to find that release. As if he can feel my overwhelming desire, his finger circles more quickly, pressing harder against my clit. He buries himself deeper inside me, that thick crown finding the mystical spot.

"Dante…," I moan.

"What else, sweetheart? What else do you love?" He slows his thrusts to a devastatingly languid pace. He's teasing me now, holding me hostage on the brink of orgasm.

"I love you, you jerk!"

He plunges inside me, and I cry out as an explosion of pleasure rolls over me. It vibrates from my clit, down my legs, to every nerve ending in my body. I pant, my head thrown back as the tremors consume me.

Dante jerks inside me a second later, initiating another round of convulsions as his warm cum fills me. The moment his breaths return to normal, I spin around like a freaking contortionist, and somehow, he remains inside me.

His pitch eyes raze over me, the depth of emotion streaking through the interminable darkness stealing my breath. We remain locked in each other's gaze for an impossibly long minute. His chest brushes against mine with each ragged inhale, that tattoo grazing my nipples. Neither of us speaks but we don't really need to say anything. We clearly both suck at this. His mouth finally captures mine, and I'm fairly certain it is only to distract from the intense moment.

But I'm okay with it because I also *love* kissing Dante. I'm pretty sure I could spend the rest of my life doing it.

My eyes snap open and meet glistening midnight orbs. "I want to put a baby inside you," he whispers.

My jaw drops, and I just stare at the insane male I'm straddling. "What?" I finally manage.

"You heard me, sweetheart. I love you, Rosa, and I may not know what the fuck I'm doing with my life right now, but I know that I want you in it forever. And I want that belly full of my cum, and my baby to pop out of that perfect pussy one day."

I snort on a laugh because it's either that or cry. I can already feel the hot tears building. "Are you serious?" I finally choke out.

"Completely." He claims my lips once more, and already he's hard again and thrusting inside me. "Now stop asking questions and let me fuck the woman I love."

Heat floods my cheeks, filling my heart with so much

happiness I think it might burst. It's a damned good thing I'm on birth control because I have a feeling if I wasn't, the impulsive mob boss would be trying to impregnate me as we speak.

Dante and I sit on the balcony on one lounge chair, cuddled up in fluffy robes and blankets. Despite the chilly air, it's perfect.

Almost.

In the last few minutes, I've felt Dante stiffen beneath me, and not in the good way. His muscles seem tense, his thoughts somewhere else. Gathering my nerve, I turn my head back to face him. "Are you trying to find a way to take it all back?"

A rueful chuckle parts his lips before he slowly shakes his head. "I'm afraid that ship has sailed, Rose. Your intoxicating pussy has claimed me for life. She's a wicked little thing."

I'm the one laughing now.

"But there is something I have to tell you."

And just like that, the happy cackles fade away.

"The vacation's over, sweetheart. We have to go back to the city."

CHAPTER 41
I AM YOURS

D*ante*

Aldo brings the duffle bags to the car as I help Rose with her coat. I'm dragging my feet because I really don't want to leave the beach house. The past few days with her here have been incredible, and I'm terrified what will happen once we leave our peaceful bubble.

I'm not stupid enough to think I'll fall out of love with her, but everything seems so much more complicated back in the city. The Red Dragons, Rose's stalker, King Industries, this mysterious new player in town, the tower of paperwork that Clara will have waiting for me….

Merda.

"Don't worry, D, we'll figure it out." Rose rewards me with a smile, as if she's read my dismal thoughts. Maybe she'll let me fuck her in the backseat on the way home. That'll improve my mood.

The rumble of an approaching car sends my hand straight

for the gun at my waistband, while the other shoves Rose behind me. Apparently, I'm still on edge. Instead of a barrel of a gun poking out the window, a familiar car with a familiar face pressed to the tinted glass rolls into the driveway.

"Mamma?" What the hell is she doing here?

The Mercedes SUV, a present from my brother, slows to a stop next to the Town Car and Ma practically leaps out of the vehicle. "Dante, what are you doing here?" She barrels toward me, her gaze covertly lifting over my shoulder to Rose. Her smile is so damned big when she sees Rose's hand tangled with mine I'm scared her cheeks will burst. Ignoring the odd fluttering in my chest, I glare down at my mother.

"You're supposed to be with Luca and Stella. What are you doing here?" A boulder-sized pit of dread sinks to the bottom of my gut. "Oh, *cazzo*, please don't tell me they're back, too?"

"Dante, language!" She swats at me, but she's still grinning like mad.

I realize then I'm still holding Rose's hand, my shoulders sprawled wide in an attempt to protect her from my sixty-year-old mamma.

"No, your brother and Stella have stayed—"

I press my finger to her mouth, cutting her off. No one needs to know where they are, especially not Rose. The last thing I need is to drag her into more trouble. "*Grazie a Dio*," I mutter. Thank God they're not back in the city with the disaster this day has become.

Rose clears her throat and steps out from behind me. "Hi, Mrs. Valentino, nice to see you again."

"You too, Rosa, *bella*. I apologize for my son's rude behavior. And mine, too. I just never expected to find you here. *Together*."

The emphasis on the last word has Rose's cheeks blushing a deep crimson, and *merda*, that look goes straight to my cock.

"We needed to get out of the city for a while," I interject

before Rose can give my mother any of the dirty details. "And now, it's time for us to go back."

"Oh, what a shame, I would have loved to spend some time with you for a little while at least. It's been weeks, Dante." She pinches my cheek like I'm five, and a groan rumbles in my throat. "Do you really have to leave right this second?"

"Do we, D?" Rose pushes out that full, bottom lip, batting sooty lashes, and I'm a goner. Fuck, this love thing isn't for the weak-willed.

"I guess we could grab a quick breakfast together, but then we have to go."

Rose lets out a happy squeal, and Mamma's back to her manic grinning again. She weaves her arm through Rose's like they're old friends and tows her up the steps to the house. Guess I'll be bringing in Mamma's luggage.

As I trudge toward the trunk of the big SUV, I tick my head at Aldo. "We leave in an hour, be ready."

"Yes, boss."

I lower my voice and creep closer. "Any chatter about this morning's incident?"

"Nothing. All quiet."

"Good." I turn toward Mamma's car, open the trunk, and get a good look at the half-dozen bursting suitcases. I shake my head. Nope, not doing it. "Aldo, get Mamma's luggage and bring it inside."

"Will do, capo."

Spinning on my heel, I march back to the house. Leaving those two chatterboxes unattended is just asking for trouble.

Two minutes here, and already Mamma has made herself at home in the kitchen. Rose runs after her as she spouts off instructions, her arms already overflowing with eggs, fresh vegetables, juice and milk containers. Now, she'll see exactly how I learned to make those frittatas. And Mamma will put mine to shame.

"Ah, good, Dante, can you run to the store and buy some oranges?" She sniffs at the plastic bottle in disgust.

"Mamma, it's December. You're not going to find fresh oranges on Fire Island right now. Just drink that. It's organic and fresh squeezed."

She grunts. "The food in America is nothing like what we had back home…." She continues her tirade, but it's drowned out by the shuffle of pots and pans.

While she's distracted, I move behind Rose and slip my arms around her waist. Nuzzling the back of her ear, I inhale her fragrant scent. A giggle escapes, but she doesn't. The gesture comes so naturally I'm caught off guard when a loud squeal rings out behind me.

Mamma stares at us, her eyes so wide I'm afraid they'll pop out of her head. "Oh, Dante, I'm so happy for you. It was about time…." She's smiling and now there's clapping too. "I knew it. That night I saw you two together before we left town—I just knew it!"

I mutter a curse and release Rose before wagging a finger at my nosy mother. "Don't you start."

"Start what? I can't be excited for my first born son? That for the first time in twenty-nine years he looks truly happy? Ugh, after that terrible Caroline—"

"Ma!" I cut her off, and Rose is practically glowing beside me. "You got all of that from this?" I motion between the two of us.

"A mother knows, *figlio mio*, a mother always knows." She turns toward the sizzling pan, the scent of sauteed onions already filling the house. "Go, relax. I'll make breakfast and then you can tell me how this happened. And don't even think you can get away with keeping this a secret, Dante. When two people are in love, only fools can't see it."

Mamma's words echo in my mind the whole drive back to the city growing more ominous with each repetition. Fuck, she's right, everyone's going to know about Rose and me. Even I saw it with Luca and Stella and look where that got them: in hiding with bounties on their heads.

Is it fair for me to put Rose through that?

Clearly, the answer is no, but am I too much of a *bastardo* to care?

Jury's still out on that one.

I run my hand through Rose's hair, a blonde halo spilling across my lap. This woman sleeps through anything. An hour into the ride back and she is out cold, which only gives me more time to spiral into my dark thoughts.

Had I been a good man I would've sent her away. Far away from me, Feng, Dr. Mark, the lot of us. But it is clear I'm not a good man, and for the first time in my life I am okay with that. Because of this beautiful, fierce woman's love.

The chaotic sounds of the city infiltrate the double-paned windows and as much as I hate to tear Rose from the moment of peace, we'll be home soon. Once I drop her off, I need to get to the office immediately. Finding the stolen building materials from the warehouses is my top priority right now. Then, I'll deal with Mark and Feng. I'm done with the Red Dragons. It's time to end this once and for all, and if that means a full-blown war, so be it. It's time to let the monster free….

Sweeping my thumb across Rose's bottom lip, I pry her mouth open. She doesn't stir as I wet my finger then glide it down her chin and beneath her t-shirt. My moist fingers tease her nipple before my palm closes around her breast, and a faint groan flees her lips.

"It's time to wake up, sweetheart." I knead her soft, perfect breast and my cock hardens beneath her head. That can't be comfortable.

Still, she doesn't move.

A wicked grin curls my lips, and I slide my free hand

beneath the waistband of her tight yoga pants. My cock twitches when I find her bare pussy.

"Mmm, Rose, you're going to make it impossible for me to get any work done now that we're back in the city."

She continues to ignore me, her lids still pressed tight together, but already I can feel the rise and fall of her chest quicken. Funny she thinks she can get away with disregarding me.

Cupping her silky slit, moisture pools in my palm, and a thrill surges straight to my dick. "I know you're awake, Rosa, or at least your pussy is. She's already dripping for me."

When I still get no response, I thrust my finger inside her slick entrance, and her hips leap up to meet my palm. Her moan fills the backseat, the sound so powerful Aldo would have to be deaf not to hear. Oh well, he'll have to get used to it. I plan on fucking Rose on every surface we occupy for the rest of our lives.

Her insides clench around my finger, sucking me in with each plunge. Gods, she feels so tight around me. Like she's desperate to hold onto every inch of me.

"Are you awake now, sweetheart?"

Her lids flutter open, a heart-stopping smile stretching across her face. "Umhmm," she murmurs, her back arching off the backseat as I curl my finger to hit *that* spot. Fuck that, why should my finger have all the fun?

I inch out of her, and she lets out a frustrated sigh. "Greedy little thing, aren't you?"

"Only for you, D."

Cazzo, this woman drives me mad when she says stuff like that. I lift her up and drag her tights down to her ankles. I take a minute to stare at that perfect pussy and press a kiss to the soft patch of dark hair.

My cock strains against my pants, frantic to sink into her sweetness. As if she senses the struggle, her hands move to my zipper and free my erection from its cage. Cum already beads on the tip, and I wonder if she weren't on the pill if my little guys would have enough juice to put a baby in that belly. It's the strangest thing, but it's all I can think about lately. Maybe it's my looming thirtieth birthday, but the idea of Rose full of my seed makes me hotter than hell.

Gripping her hips, I yank her on top of me. She sinks onto my cock, and I let out a moan as she takes me in all the way to the hilt. My balls smack her ass as she starts to bob up and down. She's so wet the sounds our bodies make together have me skirting the edge of delirium.

I've never been so turned on by anyone in my life. Is this what love does to you? Maybe I've been missing out all these years. No wonder Luca and Stella are constantly fucking. I fist my fingers in Rose's hair, exposing her neck and drag my teeth across her sensitive skin.

I need to mark her as mine, so everyone knows what'll happen if they dare touch her. Wrapping my lips around her neck, I suck hard. So hard she lets out a squeal.

"Are you giving me a hickey?"

"Maybe," I murmur against her flushed skin. My fingers dig into her hips, and I urge her up and down more quickly as we race along the West Side Highway. We're nearly home, and I need her to come before we get there. I can't get enough of the look on her face, her parted lips, the flush of her cheeks, her ragged moans as I spill into her.

It's so damned addictive, better than any drug I've known.

Bringing a finger to her clit, I massage the swollen nub, and her hips roll more urgently. I can feel the desperation as she inches closer to release. Her pussy tightens around my cock, and I perfectly time my thrusts with her bounces. We move as one, in perfect rhythm. I'm so damned close, raging heat courses through my body, and I won't be able to hold it back much longer. Moving my free hand to the hem of her tee, I tug it off, freeing her breasts. They bounce in time with our rhythm. Her nipples are hard, perfect for sucking. I take one in my mouth and her back arches, positioning my cock in a new angle. A good one from the sounds escaping her clenched lips.

"I'm coming, Dante," she moans.

"I fucking love that sound, sweetheart. Give it to me baby. I want you to come all over my cock."

So she does, like a good girl.

Her head falls back, and her sweet moans of pleasure echo across the backseat. Unexpected jealousy spears my chest at the thought of Aldo hearing her sounds, the sounds she makes only for me. I clap my hand over her mouth, muffling her groans and thrust harder, extending the waves of pleasure. Her pussy clenches around my cock, squeezing the orgasm out of me, and I follow her over the edge.

A few seconds later, my forehead drops to hers, both slick with perspiration. I trap her chin, forcing her starry eyes to mine. "Fuck, I love you, Rose."

She licks her lips and presses them to mine. "So much, Dante," she whispers against my mouth. "Possibly too much for my health."

A deep chuckle vibrates my chest because I couldn't have said it better myself. What I feel for her is so much more than love. It's an obsession, an all-consuming sensation that I can't get enough of.

I'm so distracted by her, I don't even notice when the car slows to a stop. Glancing out the window, I find my motorcycle in the parking spot beside us. Damn, when did we get to my building?

I roll the tinted window down a crack just in time to find Aldo at the other side of the door. "Give us a minute."

"Sure, boss."

"Phew, that was a close one." Rose tries to get up, but I tighten my hold around her waist, keeping her pinned to me. Her curious eyes lift to mine.

"I need to tell you something before we go back to the real world."

Her head bobs, something like fear flashing across those expressive orbs. I don't blame her because I've given her so many reasons to doubt me. "I love you, Rosa, but this thing between us terrifies me. Not because of me or you, but because of all the shit around us. I know I'm going to fuck this up at some point because that's just what I do. And I need you to promise you'll never give up on me, okay? Because before you there was only darkness, and now that I've had a taste of your light, I'd never survive the void again."

The ghost of a smile turns up the corners of her lips, and damn it, I think I made her cry. A tear rolls down her cheek, and I feel like an asshole. I don't want to hurt her, but I'm way out of my league here.

"I'll never give up on you, Dante Valentino. You're mine as much as I am yours." Her mouth captures mine, arms winding around the back of my neck. "I love you," she whispers, and my whole damned body trembles.

CHAPTER 42
IT'S ALMOST TIME

R ose

As we ride the elevator back up to Dante's penthouse, I finally pry my phone from my pocket to check out the string of messages I'd missed on the ride back into the city. A few from Dr. Winchester, a classmate from the university, and a bunch from Maisy. I'm shocked I didn't get any from Dad after that impromptu escape. After the nap and glorious wake up call, I just don't have the energy to deal with half of these. Except for Maisy. I feel bad how I totally went MIA on her. Clicking on the blue bubble, I scan through her texts.

"Apparently, I got a package at Palestra." For a second, I'm excited. Did Dante send me something? Then I notice the time-stamp on the text; nope, it couldn't have been him. It was while we were at the beach house.

Dante eyes me, lifting his gaze from his phone. "What kind of package?"

I shrug. "I don't know. Maisy didn't say, but it arrived two days ago."

"I'll have Aldo pick it up later today."

I cock a brow at the bossy mob boss. "Or I can just swing by and get it myself."

He laughs so hard the asshole buckles over. When he finally straightens, he pins me against the cool metal of the elevator, his dark eyes lancing into mine. "Let's get something straight, sweetheart. You are not only mine, but now, I'm fucking in love with you. That changes things. You can't just go gallivanting around the streets by yourself, and you sure as hell aren't going back to Palestra where all those dickheads can ogle your ass until there's a ring on your finger or my baby in your belly."

Tingles race up my spine at the rough edge to his tone and the image of a big ass diamond on my finger. Until this very moment, he'd only talked about babies. I thought it was a macho, weird need to show everyone his masculinity and virility or whatever, but a ring? Forcing all those girly thoughts to the back of my mind, I refocus on the issue I have with his insane possessiveness. "I'll have to go back to work eventually."

"Like hell you do."

"Dante, I have college tuition, an apart—, well I guess I don't have an apartment anymore, but I have bills to pay, and—"

He presses his fingers to my lips, my own musky scent invading my nostrils. It's hard to remember those incredibly talented digits were inside me less than five minutes ago driving me to the heights of pleasure. I try to focus on that instead of how annoyed I'm becoming. If he thinks I'm going to be his kept woman, he's got another thing coming. And I know that's exactly where he's going with this.

"I'll take care of everything," he growls.

Bingo.

"I'm not okay with that."

"Well, you'll just have to learn to be."

"Dante," I snarl as the elevator doors glide open.

Ignoring me, he stomps toward the door, jabs the key into the keyhole and whips it open. "This isn't up for discussion, Rosa. It's too dangerous for you out there."

"Out where?" I shout as I follow him through the foyer.

"Everywhere!" He twirls around with his arms outstretched, motioning at the bustling city beyond the glass walls. "My enemies are everywhere right now, Rosa, and the minute that they figure out what you mean to me, you'll become a target."

I slap my hands on my hips and glare up at the paranoid idiot. "So, you're going to keep me captive in your penthouse for the rest of your life?"

"No," he growls, bending down so his eyes meet mine. "I'm going to keep you captive in *our* penthouse for the rest of *our* lives."

My stupid heart pinches at his words, despite the flaring irritation. "Dante, you can't imprison me for my own safety." I force a breath in, attempting to calm the raging storm, and a familiar sickly, sweet scent invades my nostrils.

My pulse ratchets up and I take a few more steps into the apartment, past the kitchen island, and my gaze lands on the cocktail table in the living room. I gasp, all the air rushing out of my lungs.

A vase filled with withered, yellow roses.

Dante trails my every step, and a string of curses explode from his mouth as he follows my line of sight. *"Pezzo di merda, come cazzo é possibile…?"*

I should've been scared; I am kind of. But the first thought that pops into my head is: Dante's never going to let me out of the apartment now.

He barrels by me, still muttering curses, jerks the vase off the table, rips the note from the plastic holder and tosses it on the floor before stalking toward the balcony.

"What are you doing?" I run after him.

He's already outside in the frigid air, holding the dead roses over his head by the time I catch up.

"Dante, no! You could hit something or some*one*."

"I don't give a fuck," he growls. "This *bastardo* dies today. I've had enough of his taunting, his stupid passive aggressive bullshit. I'm hunting Dr. Mark down this instant." He tosses the crystal vase over the veranda, and I stare horrified as it plummets down fifty floors and smashes in the middle of Central Park West.

The devil beside me must have a guardian angel on his shoulder because somehow it doesn't hit anyone, just shatters into a million pieces on the asphalt.

"Dante!" I hiss.

He ignores me and stalks back into the living room, searching for the discarded note. The one I slid my boot over. He's already so pissed, I can't imagine what he'll do once he reads whatever the psycho sent.

He's on the floor now, lifting up the edges of the carpet, crawling and cursing. "Where the hell is it?" he snarls. For fuck's sake, this man has lost his mind. I kind of feel guilty now for hiding the card from him.

Keeping it concealed under my shoe, I drop down to the floor beside him. "Dante, it's okay. I'm okay." I frame his anxious face with my hands and force his eyes to mine. "He's just fucking with us, don't you see that?"

"Well, now, I'm going to fucking tear his throat out with my teeth." He snarls at me, baring those gleaming teeth, and for the first time since I met the savage male, I'm scared. Not of him, but *for* him.

"What are you going to do?" I hate the tremor in my voice.

"First, I'm getting a whole fucking herd of my men over

here to guard you, then I'm going to find that asshole if it's the last thing I do."

That icy fear laces around my lungs as I take in the madness swirling across Dante's dark gaze. "Please, don't go. Stay here with me."

"I can't, Rosa." He shakes his head, rage carved into his features. "This has gone on long enough. I should've handled it myself weeks ago."

"I'm scared," I whisper.

"No one will get into the penthouse, I swear it. I'll have an entire army at the front door."

"I'm scared for you, you idiot." I release his face and punch him in the shoulder.

The furious set to his jaw softens a touch, and the ghost of a smile curls the corner of his lip. "I'll be fine, sweetheart. I can handle one *pezzo di merda* plastic surgeon."

"That's all you're going to do, just look for him, right?"

He nods slowly, but his eyes chase to the floor. Clasping my thumb and forefinger around his chin, I force his gaze to mine once again. "Promise me you'll be back in our bed tonight."

The half-smile turns into a full one as he regards me. "You said *our*."

"I did."

Dante jerks me into him and captures my lips with the ferocity of a tempestuous storm. Crashing waves of desire roll between us as his tongue tangles with mine. When he finally pulls back, I'm breathless and panting, and so needy for more.

"Wait for me," he mumbles against my mouth. "I'll be back soon."

I open my mouth to say something, but I can't seem to string together a sentence.

"Promise me you won't move from this penthouse, no matter what."

I swallow hard before finally nodding. Before I can get another word out, he leaps up and stalks to the door. Fear pounds against my ribcage with each step as I watch him walk away. The door slams shut with an eerie ring of finality.

I love you. That's what I should have said, damn it.

He'll be fine. Dante will be fine.

I hug my knees to my chest and curl into a ball. The small card slides out from under my boot at the movement. It's face down on the floor. For a second, I'd almost forgotten about it.

Drawing in a steady breath, I pick it up with trembling fingers and flip it around. My heart lodges itself up my throat as I scan the dark penmanship.

It's almost time.

CHAPTER 43
PAYBACK

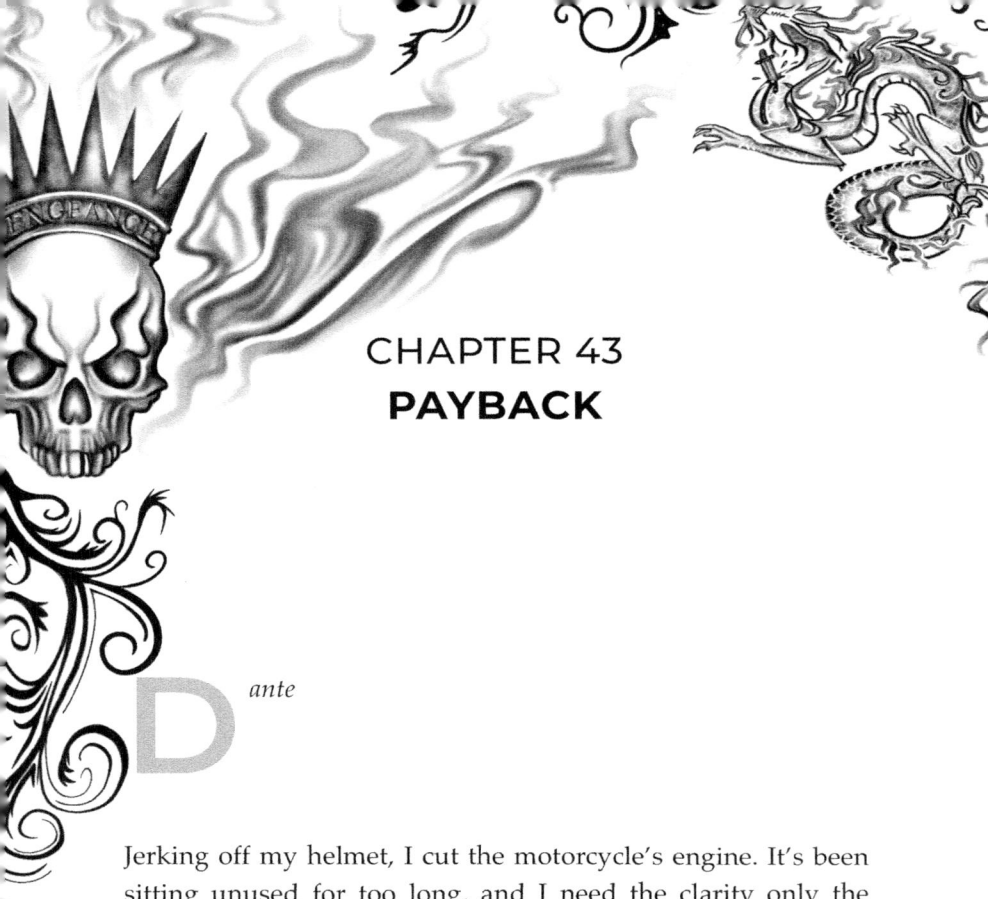

D ante

Jerking off my helmet, I cut the motorcycle's engine. It's been sitting unused for too long, and I need the clarity only the freedom of a bike can bring. I eye Dr. Mark's office across the street. If the *bastardo* is too much of a chicken shit to show his face, I'll just have to smoke him out.

But first … I pull my phone out of my pocket and jab my finger at the call button. "Tony, how many guys are at the penthouse?"

"I've got three at the building's entrance, another two at the elevator, two on your floor, one outside the door and I'm inside with Rose per your instructions."

"Good," I growl. "How is she?"

"She seems okay. She's sitting on the couch staring at that scrawny little Christmas tree. You couldn't afford something a little nicer, boss?"

"Shut up, Tony."

"Right ... where are you?"

"Taking care of business. Keep me updated." I tighten the straps on my backpack, the heavy bulk weighing on my shoulders, before I swing my leg off the bike.

"Will do."

I slide the phone back in my jacket and stalk toward the entrance of the upscale building in the Upper East Side. The doorman eyes me as I approach, then the bulky backpack, and I only earn the faintest tip of his black hat as he offers me a "Good day, sir."

"Dante Valentino," I announce, "I've got an appointment at the day spa on the third floor."

He glances down at an old clipboard and nods. "Yes, here it is, sir. Enjoy your day."

Oh, I will.

Marching past the old man with one hand clenched around the strap of my backpack, I stab my finger at the elevator button. Adrenaline pumps through my veins, fueling the building rage. Now that Rose's calming presence is gone, the beast is tearing at its chains, eager to unleash the fury.

When I reach the third floor, I slip out of the elevator, staying just beyond the watchful eye of the security camera on the wall. Then I wait. Five, four, three, two, one…. The blinking red light goes dark. Thank you, Smitty. Having a tech guy is indispensable these days.

Creeping out of the shadows, I slide the backpack off my shoulder and find the small black kit I'll need to get into Dr. Mark's office. I carefully insert the slim, metal pick into the keyhole, my heart racing as I feel the tension in the lock's pins. Picking a lock is a delicate dance of touch and precision, one it took years to master.

I gently manipulate the pins, and a faint, almost musical, series of clicks and subtle vibrations echo in the quiet hallway. Beads of sweat form on my brow as I give it one last twist. With a satisfying click, the lock surrenders. *Bingo.*

I've had my guys watching the building for days, and as expected the office has been closed since all of this began. The penthouse too has been vacant according to my intel. I still can't figure out where the hell this guy has been hiding.

Jerking the door open, I creep into the waiting room of the extravagant office. With a quick glance up at the security camera, I confirm it's off before I rummage through my backpack and get to work.

Explosives are not my wheelhouse, luckily, I've got a guy for that too. Carefully, I maneuver the small device out of my backpack and place it just under the emergency sprinkler. I only want to destroy Dr. Mark's office, not take down the entire building.

Once I'm finished setting it up as instructed, I stalk out and ready myself to repeat the process in the asshole's penthouse. That motherfucker will burn for what he's done to Rose, or at least everything he loves will.

Now that it's done, a strange calm settles over me. I stand at the corner watching the conflagration as the fire trucks and ambulances barrel down the street. My explosives guy is a genius. I don't know how he was able to keep the blast so contained. But exactly as promised, only Dr. Mark's practice and penthouse went up in flames.

The building is of course being evacuated, but there hasn't been any collateral damage. I hung back just to make sure. I may be a little unhinged right now, but after what this city has survived, no one deserves another skyscraper coming down.

I jump on the back of my bike, strap on my helmet, and head downtown. All this destruction has fueled the monster within, but instead of quelling the rage, it's only spurring it on. That and I still haven't found the psycho stalker and until I do, someone else will have to suffer the burden of my rage.

The scent of sweet and sour sauce and fried wontons floats in the air as I stalk toward the front door of the Red Dragon. The two crimson winged beasts stare down at me as if they know what I've done as I take the steps two at a time. Heated blood and violence pounds through my veins. The adrenaline from setting fire to an entire block of Red Dragon warehouses in the Lower East Side has my heart racing. Now, I understand the thrill arsonists get. I can see how it becomes addictive. The power, the destruction, the feeling of godliness as you stand over a pile of rubble.

My phone rings, halting my strides, a foot from the door. I glance at the unfamiliar number for a long minute before answering.

"Who is it?" I bark.

"It's your brother, you fucking *coglione*. I just heard about all our shit for the commissioner's project being stolen and now the *accident* at the Red Dragon's warehouses. What the hell do you think you're doing?"

Merda. Who the hell spilled? "I've got everything under control, Luca," I hiss.

"The fuck you do. It sounds like it's a dumpster fire over there, Dante. *Sei impazzito?*"

Have I gone crazy? Probably. That's exactly why love has no business in the lives of men like us. "No," I finally growl. "I'm taking care of it."

"Do you have any idea what's going to happen when Jianjun retaliates?"

"He's not going to. I'm at the Red Dragon now."

"What exactly do you plan on doing?"

"Ending this once and for all." I stab my finger at the red button, silence my phone and shove it back in my jacket pocket. It continues to vibrate as I march up the final steps to the restaurant.

A hostess stands behind the red podium, her crimson lips sliding into a scowl as she takes me in. "Mr. Valentino, Jianjun is—"

I cut the woman off, barreling past her. "I'll see myself in, thanks."

She races after me hissing in Mandarin, but I ignore her and march across the dining room, and through the swinging doors that lead to the back offices with my gun drawn. Four guys in matching red cuirass armor and hoods stand in front of a round table. I can just make out Jianjun over one of the guys' shoulders. Next to him sits Qian Guo of the Four Seas and Hao Wei from the outer boroughs. Fucking fantastic, they're all here.

The clang of metal vibrates the air as a flurry of swords are drawn. The old man's going old school now?

"What are you doing here, signor Valentino?" Jianjun's voice is clipped. "Let him through." The dragon soldiers split apart, revealing the table of leaders behind them.

Clearing my throat, I level Jianjun with a narrowed glare, keeping the barrel of my gun pinned to the head of the Triad. "I came to tell you in person in case you hadn't already heard that all your warehouses along 1st Avenue are destroyed."

Muttered gasps fill the room, and my finger twitches on the trigger.

"One of your fucking Red Dragons torched my girl's place. Just think of it as payback." The excuse is weak at best, but I stick with it anyway since I'm still not a hundred percent sure they were behind it.

"What are you talking about?" he hisses.

"The small studio in mid-town? I know Feng was the culprit. He saw us together, and he's trying to get his revenge by targeting what's mine."

Jianjun rises, the screech of the chair legs on the tile elevating my pulse. "I had nothing to do with that."

"And Feng?" I bark.

"I have no idea. We've parted ways."

"What?" I almost lower my gun.

"You heard me. My nephew and I have come to an impasse. I'm tired of the killing. You and your Kings have taken over three dozen souls in the past few weeks. I want it to stop, and he refuses to meet with you, man to man." The two other males nod in agreement.

"Then rescind the bounties on my brother's and his fiancée's heads."

"I've already informed my men that no harm should come to them." He lowers his gaze as he pauses. "However, there is nothing I can do about Feng. He has his own agenda."

"Fucking *cornuto*."

"Now about my warehouses…."

Shit. "I'd say we're even," I interject.

A sharp laugh erupts from the old man's thinned lips. "You and your brother killed my son months ago, now you've murdered half of my men in cold blood, practically destroyed my livelihood, and you think we're even?"

"Listen, Jianjun, I know you liked things better under Luca, right?" I keep the barrel level to his head.

The three males nod.

"The sooner this is over with, the faster my little brother can return, and things can go back to normal. I'm not going to lie; I'm not made for this ruling shit. So, find your nephew, bring him to me, and we can forget all about this unfortunate set of events."

"You're out of your mind," he hisses.

"You're going to be out of your mind in a second, when I blow a bullet through your head."

The guards tense, the flash of swords catching my eye. I draw in a breath to slow my thundering heart. As much power as the monster brings, sometimes I need the calm. I might die today, but I'd take a few of these motherfuckers down with me first, their leader most importantly.

The thought of never seeing Rose's big bright eyes, never touching her soft skin, never feeling her pussy clamped around my cock, clears the haze of anger. I shove the monster back and try to channel my brother's diplomatic flare. What would he do in this situation? "But," I mutter. "I'm sure we can come to an equitable arrangement somehow."

CHAPTER 44
A SURPRISE GIFT

R*ose*

Chilly fingers race down my thighs, yanking me from a restless sleep. My lids flutter before I finally pry them open. A pair of bottomless midnight orbs lance into me. "Dante?" I croak.

"Oh, good, you're awake." Warmth blankets my body as he rolls on top of me, spreading my legs, and wedges his hips between my thighs.

"What time is it?" I glance at the clock on the nightstand. Just past five. "You promised you'd be back…."

"I am back." He runs his cock across my entrance.

"It's practically morning. Where were you all night?" I try to sit up, but he lowers his hulking frame on top of me, stalling my efforts. "I was worried, Dante. Really fucking scared."

"I'm sorry," he whispers against my lips. "I was in the middle of something big, and I knew that if I got distracted that would be it. If I heard your voice, I would've come back running, and I couldn't. This was too important."

"What happened?"

"I think I found a way to get Luca and Stella back."

My sleepy eyes widen, a flare of hope chasing away the haze. "You did?"

He nods and presses his tip inside me.

"Dante…," I grumble. Not that I don't want this, I just need to know what's happening. When he left yesterday, I was terrified he was going to burn down all of Manhattan.

He rocks his hips back, withdrawing, and my lusty pussy lets out a grunt of annoyance. Even at the ass crack of dawn she's ready for him.

"Tell me what happened," I force out.

"I couldn't find Dr. Mark, so I got pissed." He huffs out a breath and braces himself over my body. "I blew up his practice and his hoity toity apartment." He says it so nonchalantly, like he swung by the deli and ordered a meatball sub.

"You did what?" I screech.

"When that didn't pan out as I'd hoped, I went ballistic on the Red Dragons. It'll take them months to recover from their losses." He shrugs again.

I stare at him, my jaw nearly unhinged. "I thought you said you found a way to bring your brother and Stella back?"

"I did, eventually." He smirks and drops a kiss on my forehead. "I never would've done it if it wasn't for you. Surprisingly, you make me a more rational man."

I snort on a laugh. "Really? Because I thought I made you a crazy, possessive psycho."

"That too." His smile widens. "But I realized, you'll never be safe in my world if I don't make it safe for you. Now, I understand why Luca was always trying to wheel and deal with these guys instead of just snuffing them out."

"You do catch more flies with honey than vinegar."

"Aren't you smart?" He boops my nose, and now I'm

smiling so hard I must look like the crazy one.

"So when can they come back?"

"I have a meeting at the office with Jianjun tomorrow to iron out all the details. We're carving out lower Manhattan between the Kings and the Chinese Triad. We'll even make things all official and legal with Luca's lawyer, Jones, in the mix."

"That's great."

"Part of the conditions are that if Feng shows his face, Jianjun is legally obligated to turn him over to me. So, I expect to have things settled with that fucker any day now. With that taken care of, I'll have one less enemy to worry about."

"So, I'm hearing I'll be able to leave the penthouse soon?"

"You must have some cum stuck in your ears, sweetheart, because I definitely never said that." He throws me a shit-eating grin and thrusts his cock inside me. "Let's get that cum where it's supposed to be, in that pretty little pussy."

My hips instinctively roll with his, the movement second nature now. This time the sex is more therapeutic than earth-shattering. Just feeling him above me, inside me, all around me is all I crave. The fear yesterday was crippling. I never thought I'd fall so hard or need him so much.

Closing my eyes, I lose myself in the fiery sensations, in the turbulent storm that is Dante Valentino.

I sit across the kitchen island from Dante as he flips through the pages of the New York Times, and I shovel cereal into my mouth. I'm already dreading him leaving. He promised he'd be back in a few hours after the meeting with Jianjun, but still. My eyes lift to ogle him one more time before he goes. He's stunning in a three-piece navy suit that hugs those broad shoulders and tapers perfectly down to his narrow waist. The devil really does wear Prada.

My phone buzzes, drawing me away from the blatant gawking. I stare at the screen and immediately pick up when I see my brother's name. Robbie doesn't call often so it must be something important.

"Hey, sis."

"Hey, what's up, Robbie? Everything okay with the kids?"

Dante's watchful gaze rakes over me.

"Yeah, they're fine. I was actually just calling to check in on you. How are you holding up?"

Shit. Did he hear about me running out of Dad's place? Did he find out about my stalker? Did Dante call him? A million thoughts swirl through my mind.

"Uh, I'm good...," I finally mumble. "Just got back into the city."

"Yeah, I heard you were out on Long Island visiting. At least you got to see Uncle John before … crazy, huh?"

Ice surges through my veins, and all the air catches in my throat. "Umhmm," I mutter.

"How could someone just go missing like that? I mean I know he's not married and it's not like he has kids waiting here in Florida, but who just disappears without telling anyone? And right after your visit."

My fingers tremble around my phone as I look up and find Dante's gaze still heavy on me. "Yeah, it's definitely weird."

"Anyway, I know you guys were close, so I just wanted to see how you were doing." *Close, ha. A lifetime ago, bro.* Sometimes, the fact that no one realized what my uncle had done to me hurt more than anything else. How was everyone so blind?

Was I that unimportant to everyone in my family that no one noticed how broken I was after that summer?

"I'm totally fine," I finally say. "And you know what, Robbie? I hope they never find that asshole." I punch the hang up button and drop the phone on the marble counter. Then I glare up at the brooding male perched across from me, pretending to read the newspaper. "Dante…."

His brows lift, an innocent expression across that perfect face.

My phone rings again, but I ignore it, refocusing on Dante. "You don't happen to know anything about my uncle going missing, do you?" My thoughts flicker back to the rage in his eyes that day. That pure unadulterated hatred emanating from every pore in his body. I should've known he never would've let that man go unpunished.

"Which uncle would that be?" He smirks.

I nearly jump across the counter, planting my palms on the marble. "What did you do?"

"What had to be done." The smirk is replaced by something far more sinister as darkness etches across his features.

A thrill surges up my spine. "Did you kill him?" I speak the words slowly, the voice not quite my own.

"It's better if we don't talk about this."

"Dante…."

He shakes his head. "We won't have spousal privilege until we're married. Then I'll tell you every last fucking, gory detail of his alleged disappearance." His lips twist in disgust, and my uncle's bloodied, bruised face fills my vision. An image I've dreamt about my whole life.

I'm so enraptured with the thought I almost skip right by the marriage bit. *Almost*. He's mentioned it twice now and each time has my heart punching at my ribs. I vow to bring it up when things settle. For now, I crawl across the counter and leap into his arms. His hands cup my ass and hold me tight against his fine suit. "Thank you," I whisper against the shell of his ear. "I sure as hell hope this never comes back to bite us in the butt, but I appreciate it more than you'll ever know."

Dante runs his hand over the back of my head, threading his fingers through my hair. "I know, sweetheart, I know." Then he kisses me so hard, he steals the air from my lungs.

"I love you," I rasp out. "I love you more than anything."

CHAPTER 45
A BARELY VEILED THREAT

Dante

Clara sits across my desk, her mouth twisted into a disapproving scowl as I go through the mountains of paperwork piled on my desk. She didn't buy the Covid thing, not for a second. The bigger problem I'm facing comes in the form of this Gemini Corp. The new company that sprang up out of nowhere is outbidding Kings Industries in every significant deal across Manhattan.

I'd definitely dropped the ball on that one. Clara had mentioned the name weeks ago, and Rose had overheard Feng talking about them at the Christmas tree lot that day too. I'd been so damned distracted between Rose's legs, I'd fucked up big time. I spent all morning researching the corporation myself this time, and they seem as clean as a new penny. There's no way they're the ones behind our warehouse robbery, right?

Then again, why would they be on Feng's radar if they were so squeaky clean?

Dropping my pen to stare at my computer screen, I scan my inbox for that email from Clara all those weeks ago. "*Merda,*" I mutter. Gemini Corp had been buying land along the docks back when I first took on the role as CEO.

It has to be them…. But why? This seems personal.

I skim the measly documents Tony sent over when I'd had him pull up everything he could find on the new player in town and zero in on the name of the CEO. Or rather *names*. Niccolò and Marco Rossi.

Rossi? Rossi … Rossi. I think back to the big Italian crime families of New York City. The Espositos, my future sister-in-law's family had been one of the biggest, then the Romanos, the Capones. But Rossi doesn't ring any bells.

It must not have meant anything to Tony either, or he would've been on it.

"What did you find?" Clara's sharp voice draws me from my inner musings.

"I'm not sure yet, but there's something going on with Gemini Corp."

"I told you—"

I raise my hand, cutting her off. "I know. You were right, Clara. I fucked up."

A smug smile crosses her Chanel red lips, and I nearly take it back.

"Now we just have to figure out who these *bastardi* are and what they want." My gaze pivots back to the mound of files on my desk, and a groan slides past my clenched teeth. Turning to my brother's executive assistant, I force a smile. "Were you able to re-source the materials we lost for the commissioner's project?"

She nods. "Of course, but the problem is the timeline. We will never be able to break ground per the original schedule."

"I'll talk to Commissioner Gordon myself and explain the situation."

"You're going to tell him we were robbed?"

"No," I growl. "I'll come up with something better."

"As long as you don't blow up our warehouses, I'm happy." Her eyes sparkle at the jab. Clearly, she's heard about the incident at Dr. Mark's practice. Irritation crawls beneath my skin, like thousands of spiders dancing across my flesh. Even with his home and livelihood destroyed the asshole hasn't shown his face. How is that even possible?

I loose a frustrated breath and focus on the calm. "Call these Rossi CEOs and coordinate a meeting, will you? I need to meet these *coglioni* face to face."

"Of course, *signor* Valentino."

Muttering curses, I storm out of the commissioner's office and jump into the limo. "Drive!" I bark at Aldo. He guns the engine, and we weave into mid-day traffic. Of course fucking Gemini Corp put in a bid on the dock's project the second our shit went missing. It only serves to confirm my suspicions that these assholes are not what they seem.

It's a damned good thing Clara's a fucking pit bull, and I've already got a meeting on the calendar with the Gemini CEO in an hour. I'm going to teach that man who rules Manhattan. As Aldo drives us through the gridlock up to Park Avenue, I shoot a quick text message to Rose.

I hate leaving her all day, but I've let so much slide in the past few weeks I'm starting to worry by the time Luca returns there will be nothing left of the old King Industries. And he'll have my fucking head on a platter.

She responds right away, the silly heart emoji at the end of the message doing stupid things to my real heart. *Cazzo*, this love shit is a nightmare.

Now that I've heard from her myself, not that I haven't had Tony checking in every half hour with reports, I can focus on the matter at hand. Crushing Gemini like the fucking low-life scavengers they are. If they rescind their bid on the project, Gordon will have no choice but to wait for us to get the replacement supplies.

My phone buzzes in my pocket, and I pull it out only long enough to confirm my guess. Luca again. He's been calling nonstop since I hung up on him yesterday. I refuse to talk to my little brother until I have good news. Or better yet, when I have Feng's head on a spike. I'm not really counting on Jianjun to deliver his nephew straight to me, but I only hope he sticks to our deal when the time comes.

The car rolls to a stop in front of a towering skyscraper only two blocks away from King's Tower. These dickheads are really asking for it. Do they really think they can step in and take over our city?

Over my fucking dead body.

I march into the modern lobby, all dark, thick-paned glass, clean lines and black-and-white furniture. The name Gemini is stamped across the front desk in bold, gold print. Damn, I hadn't been sure before, but this confirms it, the whole building is theirs.

A woman with a bright smile and a tablet pressed to her chest darts toward me. "You must be Mr. Valentino."

"I am." This is some reception.

"Great, Mr. Rossi is waiting for you in the conference room upstairs. I'll escort you up." She motions toward the elevator bank and guides me to the last one. She presses her hand to the biometric reader, and a green light flashes a second before the doors open. Hmm. High-tech. Once we're inside the sleek contraption, only one button is lit. It whizzes us up to the top floor of the immense building, and my stomach nosedives at the speed.

I'm going to have to get after Clara to update our clearly outdated lifts.

Leaning against the cool metal, I toss the girl what I've been told is a charming smile. I may be a lot of hard edges, but I know how to schmooze when I must. "Have you worked for Gemini Corp long?"

"No, I haven't. I just started about a month ago when they moved to this location."

"Oh, really?"

Her head bounces up and down, reminding me of an over-eager puppy.

"How do you like it?"

"I just love it," she croons. "Mr. Rossi is tough but he's fair, and—" Her mouth snaps closed as the elevator doors glide open.

Damn it.

"Right this way, Mr. Valentino." She leads me through the modern foyer with sweeping views of mid-town and furnishings that match the minimalistic esthetic from the entrance, then stops in front of a black door. "Mr. Rossi will be right in. Please wait in here."

I nod and slip through the doorway as she watches me. The conference room features the same views as the foyer along with a massive table at the center with seats for at least twenty.

How could an operation this significant spring up out of nowhere? Had I really been that distracted since Luca's departure? My brother is going to murder me, and he has every right.

Jerking the leather chair back, I settle into the one at the head of the table. It's a simple power play, and I'm curious to see what Mr. Rossi will do. Also, which one would I get and what is the relation? Father and son? Brothers? Cousins? So many possibilities.

I stare at the clock on the wall as the minutes tick by. The *bastardo* is making me wait, also a power play. Drumming my fingers on the mahogany table, irritation gathers along my brow. If this guy's trying to piss me off, he's accomplishing it. Every moment I spend apart from Rose only fans the flames of fury.

Finally, the click of the door handle sends my pulse skyrocketing. But I keep still, refusing to show how much his tardiness is rankling at my last nerve.

"You must be Dante." A smooth voice fills the room, the deep tenor oddly familiar. I slowly turn to face the dark-haired young male marching toward me. He's got to be around my age, early thirties tops. In a sleek, dark suit and wearing an arrogant smile, he reminds me of Luca. Except for the fucking man bun. *Dio*, I hate those things.

"That's *signor* Valentino," I snarl as he extends his hand. I purposely don't stand, matching his disrespect at using my first name.

"Of course, *signor* Valentino." His fingers wrap around mine, aggressively. I give it to him back and more. "I'm Nico Rossi."

So, Marco must be the father….

"A pleasure." I offer him my most plastic smile before it melts into a scowl. "I'll make it quick, Nico. I came today because it appears we have some shared interests."

He slides his ass onto the table so he can peer down at me. Touché. The man is not a complete idiot. "And what might that be?"

"The commissioner's dock project. I understand you've made a very competitive bid, but the thing is, it's already ours."

His lips twist, bright blue eyes sparking with amusement. "That's not what I heard."

"You've been misinformed then," I growl.

"So, it's not true that the necessary supplies have been misplaced?" A glint of humor curls the edge of his lip, and I clench my fingers into a fist to keep from ramming him through with my pocketknife.

"Not at all true." I pause and spear him with a glare that would have my guys pissing their pants. The fucker doesn't even flinch. "Why? Would you happen to know anything about that?"

"No, not at all, *amico*. Why would I? That sounds like back alley, black market dealings, and Gemini Corporation has nothing to do with those sorts of questionable transactions."

"Of course not." I force another smile, but I'm certain it comes off a twisted sneer.

"I'm sorry Mr. Valentino, but I'm a busy man." *Beware the fury of a patient man*. Papà's words choose that moment to infiltrate my thoughts. Nico looms over me, a thick strand of dark hair coming free from that stupid man bun. "Is there anything else I can do for you today?"

I slowly rise and fold back my sleeves, taking my time until black ink spills out from beneath the pristine white. "Actually, there is," I finally say. "I came to deliver a friendly warning. If you fuck with the Kings, you'll pay for it in blood."

"Thank you, for that barely veiled threat, Dante. I'll keep it in mind." He hops off the table and offers that ingratiating smile. "Now, if you'll excuse me, I have some important matters to attend to. An unexpected visitor showed up a few weeks ago, and I can't seem to leave him unattended for more than a few hours or he gets into no good."

My brows furrow as I process his words. So far, every point of conversation has been succinct and to the point. Why would he offer such random information? "Good luck with that," I finally bite out.

He spins on his heel and marches to the door. It swings open, and the blonde female from earlier reappears. "Melanie, will you escort our visitor off my property?" He takes a step then whirls back. "Oh, one more thing, Dante, if we're doling out friendly warnings, here's one for you: the sins of the father frequently fall upon the son."

The hair on the back of my neck prickles, but before I can get a word out, the *figlio di puttana* marches out, leaving me alone with the smiling blonde. What the fuck does that mean?

CHAPTER 46
UNEXPECTED ALLIANCES

D*ante*

"Pick up, damn it, Rose. Pick up." I stare at the half bar of reception on my phone once I'm out of the elevator and quicken my stride to reach the exit of Gemini Corp tower. Full bars now. It rings again and again, each unanswered tone ratcheting up my blood pressure.

I'm so distracted by the fact that she's not answering, I don't even notice the limo isn't where Aldo left me. Tearing my attention from my phone, I glance down Park Avenue. Now where did that idiot go?

Returning to Rose's smiling face on my screen, I press the call button again. The rumble of an approaching engine forces my gaze up but only long enough to catch a glimpse at the black vehicle. *Finally*.

The voicemail answers again and this time, I leave a message. "Answer me Rose, please. As soon as you get this call me back. It's urgent."

I jab my finger at the red button, then sweep my finger toward the green to try again when the slap of heavy footfalls jerks my attention up. Piercing pain lances into the back of my skull, and I mutter a curse as a hood is yanked over my head. A needle pierces my neck, and my head swims. "No!" Darkness consumes my vision, invading my senses from the inside and out.

"Rose," I mumble before the endless black pulls me under.

Icy water splashes over my face, and my lids snap open. I draw in a ragged breath before another frosty spray crashes over me. Muttered curses spill from my lips as the foggy haze begins to recede, and I recognize the sting of the metal manacles around my wrists and ankles. Sprawling rafters stretch out over my head, and the four walls of an empty warehouse coalesce.

"Whoever the fuck did this is going to pay!" I growl.

"Relax, *signore*." A familiar voice skates across my eardrums.

Twisting my head around to confirm my suspicions, relief floods my system at the sight of Feng Zhang. Better the devil you know, and all that.

"What the fuck do you think you're doing, dragon?" I hiss.

"Chill out, Dante. I just brought you here to talk." He moves around me, and half a dozen men emerge from the shadows. Unlike Jianjun's men, they're wearing modern attire, carrying guns and all still wearing the Red Dragon crimson.

I glance around the warehouse once more and realization sets in. This is the same place we'd had that stand off all those months ago. When the *bastardo* set the price on Luca and Stella's heads.

"So talk, dickhead."

A sly smile reflects across his dark eyes. "I have information for you."

"For me?" This I was not expecting. "Do tell…."

"Those new Italian fuckers in town are gunning for the Kings."

I roll my eyes, adding in a dramatic yawn. "That's not new information, Feng. And what do you care anyway? Why would you help me?"

"I talked to my uncle, and he told me about the deal you struck. It's better than the one I got going with them."

Merda. My two enemies joining forces is the last thing I need right now. "I'm going to need you to be more specific."

"The Geminis approached me a few months ago, right after Luca left town and you took over. They've been paying me to fuck with your business, to keep you busy. But to be honest, I don't like being under the Italian mafia's thumb, and I'm bored."

Pieces of the puzzle slide into place, and I want to smack myself for being so blind. I'd been so busy taking out the Red Dragons two at a time, the Geminis had slipped right by.

"Honestly, the deal you made with my uncle to divide up the southern territory of Manhattan is much more lucrative, so here I am."

"And what do you want exactly out of this truce?"

"Same deal as my uncle."

Immunity and a bigger piece of the Manhattan pie.

"And you won't retaliate for all those Red Dragon lives lost?"

He shrugs. "They were just foot soldiers; they're a dime a dozen."

I hated the idea of it, but having Jianjun and eventually Feng, when he takes his uncle's place, as allies could come in handy especially with this new shit going down.

"If you really want to make amends," he adds, "you can wire money to each of the dead dragons' family members."

Fuck … that sounds like something Luca would do.

"And in return, you'll rescind the bounties on my brother and his fiancée?"

"Sure."

"And that's it, we're even?" This seems way too good to be true.

"That's right, *capo*. Truth is, I don't like this new Gemini asshole. I can't stand you either, but Luca, he's not the worst to deal with."

Even the fucking Triad worships the ground my little brother walks on. I can't say I'm surprised.

"Then untie me and we'll shake on it, like real men."

Feng ticks his head at one of the Red Dragons at his side, and the guy reveals a small metal key from his pocket. He creeps over and unlocks both sets of handcuffs. Feng is either the stupidest person ever, or he's really serious about this deal.

Rubbing my sore wrists, I stand and glare at the man who turned my life upside down in the last few weeks. If he hadn't instituted that bounty on my brother's head, I never would've taken back the throne, never would've met Rose, never would've truly lived.

I hold out my hand and toss Feng a grin. "Come here, you motherfucker, let's shake on it."

Feng takes my hand, and I jerk him into a hug. The guy freezes and half of his men pull out their guns. A wicked laugh rumbles my chest as I finally release him. "Relax, we're all friends now, right?"

He eyes me like I've lost my mind and the truth is, I probably have a little. But he finally nods.

"I'll let you know when my little brother is back in town. For now, if you hear anything useful about our mutual friends, the Geminis, let me know."

"Will do, capo." He shoots me a toothy grin, then spins toward the exit with his men trailing a few paces behind.

Well, this is exactly the opposite of what I expected to

happen today. *Cazzo,* Rose. My thoughts fly back to before I was snatched. Searching my pockets, I find my phone. Those idiots hadn't even taken it off me. I scan the screen, and the punishing weight in my chest dissipates.

Rose: *I'm fine, D. I just miss you. What's going on? You sounded really worried. Also, when are you coming home? I'm bored and horny as fuck.*

Another chuckle escapes as I type out a quick reply.

Me: *On my way. I'll explain everything when I get there. I hope you're naked and ready for me, sweetheart.*

Rose: *Always.*

"Oh, Dante, fuck, Dante, you are incredible." Rose's bottom lip is clenched between her teeth as she rides my cock, her beautiful breasts bouncing with each roll of her hips.

My good girl was soaked and ready just like she promised, and the moment I walked into the penthouse, I dragged her into our bedroom and have been balls deep inside her ever since. I recounted bits and pieces of my day in between mind-blowing orgasms.

"I'm coming," she cries out, and I take over, gripping her hips and sliding her pussy up and down my shaft. Her head falls back, eyes nearly rolling into her head so far back only the whites show.

"*Dio*, you're beautiful when you come on my cock, sweetheart." I pause and nibble on my lip which is still flavored with her musky scent. "Or on my tongue, my fingers…."

"Oh, shut up." She smirks, her chest still rising and falling in rapid bursts. She tries to roll off me, but I close my hands around her hips and keep her locked in place. My dick likes to stay inside her as long as possible. Also, I'm hoping it will make this conversation easier.

The entire ride home it was all I could think about.

"What?" Rose lowers her body flush against mine, those perfect nipples rubbing against my chest. "Your brows are all twisty like an angry caterpillar. Is there something else going on?"

I smirk, the fact that she knows me so well oddly comforting. "I want you to stop taking the pill."

"Dante!" she squeals and swats at my chest.

"What?"

"I'm only twenty-two. I'm not popping a baby out of this perfect, tight little vagina yet."

The laugh roars out of me this time, and there's nothing I can do to stop it. Once the mad chuckling stops, I force a serious expression and pin her in my gaze. "Then marry me."

Her head lifts, eyes so bright they're sparkling. "Are you serious?"

"Yes. I've never been more serious about anything."

"So, where's the ring?" That smile turns downright evil as she flashes me her ring finger.

"It was kind of a spur of the moment decision, sweetheart. Getting kidnapped will do things to a man. The thought of never seeing you again, of never having made you officially mine, made me realize some things."

Her eyes are so shiny now I'm certain I've made her cry again. Not my intention, damn it. "I'm sorry, Rosa. Just forget I said anything, I'll do it better next time, I swear."

She shakes her head, a beaming smile making her even more heart stopping. "Who are you and what have you done to my overbearing, domineering boyfriend?"

Boyfriend. My mouth curls in disgust. That's exactly why I must put a ring on this woman. I'm not a boy, and I'm certainly not her friend.

"You know what, you're right, sweetheart." I sit up and lift her hips, jerking myself out of her. She lets out an indignant squeal. Then I flip her over and lay her across my lap, with her curvy ass sticking up.

"What are you doing?" she cries.

"Say yes, or I'll punish you. I'll spank those perfect cheeks so hard you'll be begging for mercy."

She wriggles against my legs, and wetness seeps across my thighs. Yes, this woman was definitely made for me. All my kinky shit just turns her on.

"I don't know, Dante...." She wiggles as I stroke her ass cheek. "I'm not quite sure if I'm ready to say yes yet."

I lift my hand and land a perfect smack on her left cheek. She lets out a scream then a moan as I lap up her rosy skin with my warm tongue. The sting echoes across my own palm, and I'm reluctant to continue. "Is that a yes, Rose?"

"Mmm, I don't know, D...."

I draw my tongue back into my mouth, and she releases a frustrated groan. "Last chance, sweetheart. It's now or never." Raising my hand, I drop it down, hard, the slap ricocheting over the symphony of our labored breaths.

I'm hard again, and so ready to take that perfectly pink ass.

"What do you say, sweetheart, have you had enough?"

Rose spins around, straddling me, her pupils blow out with lust and maybe, just maybe love. "I've had enough, D. Take me, I'm yours." Her lips crash against mine, and a silly grin stretches so big across my face I can barely focus on kissing her.

"Finally," I growl. "I can't wait to fuck my fiancée."

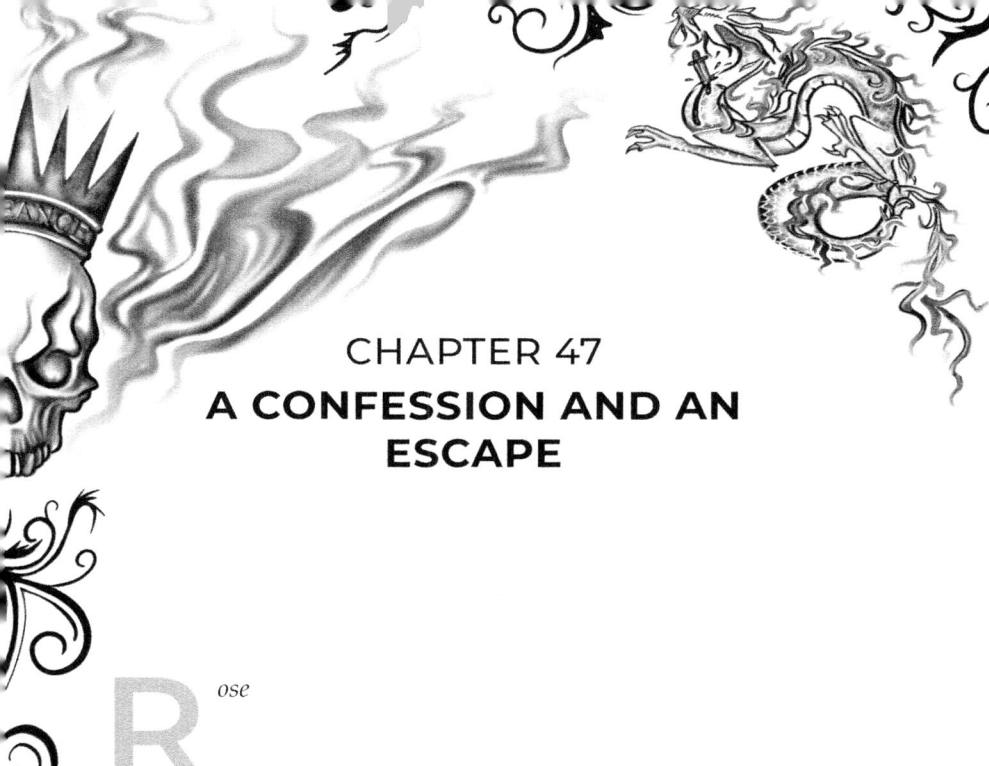

CHAPTER 47
A CONFESSION AND AN ESCAPE

R*ose*

"Can't we just go for a walk at least?" It's been three days since I've been locked up in this damned apartment, and I'm about a second away from losing my mind. I stare out longingly onto the snow-covered trees of Central Park. I even miss the frigid temperatures right now.

Tony looks up from the crossword puzzle and tugs at the curly end of his newly grown-in mustache. He looks creepy as fuck if you ask me. "Sorry, Rose, you know I can't do that."

"Why not?" I whine.

"Because Dante will cut off my balls."

I release an exasperated sigh because I know he's not wrong. Then I stalk to the kitchen and refill my mug of coffee. It's bad enough being stuck here when Dante's with me, but when he's out there doing God knows what, the boredom tangles with gut-wrenching fear.

He swears the situation is looking better with the Red

Dragons, but he's still out there hunting for Mark. The fact that my ex has been able to evade him for weeks just makes no sense. The doc might have been a psycho stalker, but he just wasn't that good.

Then there are the Geminis, and no one has any idea what they're up to….

As I march back into the living room my eyes fall on my tiny tree. It's shed most of the few pine needles it had, its frail limbs are sagging, and the bright colorful bulbs are nearly hitting the floor. As much as I hate to admit it, it's time to put the little guy out of its misery.

My phone squeals, and I jerk it out of my pocket, my heart doing a little dance when I see the number. "Stella?"

"Rose! Happy New Year, a few days late but still!"

I signal to Tony that I'm going to my, well, Dante's room, and he goes back to work on his crossword puzzle. He must be even more bored than I am. At least this is my home and I have some of my creature comforts here.

"So, how have you been?" I ask as my steps quicken down the hall. Dante and I had a big talk the other night and with the possibility of Luca and Stella returning sooner rather than later we decided it was time to come clean about our relationship.

"I'm great, Luca's great, it's been amazing having this time together. But I really do miss home."

"I'm sure you do. I bet you've been fucking like bunnies." A wicked cackle bursts free. "Are you pregnant yet?" My heart lets out a weird flutter as my mouth closes around the word.

"No way. I told you, we have to get married first and with all the stuff going on, who knows when that'll be?" Stella always wanted a big, fancy wedding, and I'm sure Luca will give her exactly that. But she's right, it'll take an entire year of planning.

I stare at my bare ring finger. It's been three days since Dante proposed, or rather forced me into saying yes. That's a complete lie and we all know it, so I decide never to mention that little tidbit to my friend. Proposal under duress isn't the most romantic to normal people.

"Tell me about you! Luca said you're *still* staying with Dante?"

"Um, yeah, there were some recent developments in that area."

"What does that mean?" she squeals, a hint of irritation in her tone.

"There's a lot I need to catch you up on, Stel, but I'm not sure over the phone is the best way. Some shit went down, and I didn't want to worry you, but Dante's really been here for me."

"What happened? Is that stalker creep back?"

Again, I debate going into the gory details. No need to worry my best friend more than necessary. We'd been texting on and off since she left, but I'd kept all the bad stuff to myself.

"Yeah, he resurfaced and was sending me dead flowers and crap."

"Rose! How could you not tell me?"

"You have your own stuff to worry about, I didn't want you freaking out when you're so far away."

"You're my best friend, it's my right to freak out about that stuff!"

"Thanks, Stel, you're the best, and I really do miss you like crazy. I can't wait for you guys to come back." I go on to tell her bits and pieces of what has been going on, leaving out the worst parts for when she returns, and we can talk in person.

"So, you and Dante have grown close?" The disapproval is still clear in her tone.

I'm a big fat chicken so I decide to ease her into this whole me-and-Dante thing and choose not to open with the fact that we're kind of engaged, and he's been begging to impregnate me ASAP.

"Yes," I murmur.

"How close exactly?" Damn, she's got that mom tone down pat.

"I'm pretty much completely in love with him." *Way to keep your cool, Rose.* I want to smack myself when the words dribble out like verbal diarrhea.

"Seriously?"

"Yup."

"And Dante?"

"Yeah, he's pretty much gone off the deep end too."

An unexpected laugh rings out on the other end of the line. "Dante in love?" she finally rasps out. "I thought you guys would just be fucking by now."

"Thanks a lot, bestie."

"I'm sorry, I'm going to need a minute to process this. You know Dante and I haven't had the best history and—"

"No, I don't know what happened between the two of you because you never told me."

"And he didn't?"

"Nope." I pop the P for emphasis.

A long minute of silence surges between us. She finally releases a breath, and anxiety rushes my nerves. "Dante saved our lives, as you know. It's hard for me to reconcile that man with the man that almost assaulted me."

All the air catches in my lungs, and my head starts to spin. "Dante would never—"

"He swore he was only trying to scare me. He thought I was involved with the Red Dragons and that Bo had sent me to spy on Luca. Nothing happened because Luca came home, but…."

"He still tried to attack you…."

"Umhmm." Another long pause, and my heart rails against my ribcage. "I've forgiven him, Rose, and the more I learn about Dante, the more I understand how much he loves his brother. He just doesn't know how to go about it the right way. I choose to believe he was telling the truth, and he would have stopped before things got out of control. He's going to be my brother-in-law, and I couldn't live with that otherwise."

I take a minute to process her words, really let them sink in. After all the shit I've been through with my uncle and now with this stalker, I'm not sure I can handle this. All the happiness I felt a moment ago whooshes right out.

"I'm sorry, Rose. I should have told you a long time ago. I never thought you two would get involved."

Fuck, I'm an idiot.

"Rose?"

I heave in a breath. "Yeah, still here."

"You should talk to Dante, let him explain. Maybe it'll help."

"Right." My chest feels like its caving in on me, my ribs strangling my heart and lungs. Dante had told me so many times he wasn't a good man, but I was so obsessed with him, I just didn't want to listen. "Hey, Stel, I gotta go."

"I'm sorry, Rose, really. I'll call you tomorrow to check in, okay?"

"Okay, thanks." I pocket the phone, my heart in a vice grip. Squeezing my eyes shut, I try to force back the tears as Dante's room blurs around me. I can't be here right now. His scent floods my senses, the dark, masculine furnishings reminding me too much of him.

I race out of his bedroom, and Tony's eyes jerk up to meet mine as I sprint down the hallway. He's still sitting on the couch with the newspaper in his lap. "What's wrong?"

Shit, I probably look like I just had my heart ripped out.

I glance desperately from him to the kitchen, to the living room, to my Christmas tree. "I have to throw that thing out," I blurt. "Dante's going to kill me if it sheds any more pine needles on his floor."

Tony smirks and drops the crossword puzzle onto the couch cushion. "Sure, I can take it out to the dumpster for you."

"No, I can do it. It's so small it'll fit in the garbage chute out in the hallway."

"You sure?" He lifts a wary brow.

"Yup, no problem. She's my baby, and it's time I put her to rest."

He must read something in my frantic gaze because he relents. I rush over to the tree, rip off the remaining decorations and toss the frail trunk and bare limbs over my shoulder. As I carry it past the cocktail table, I leave a trail of pine needles. It's going to drive Dante insane. Good.

"Be right back," I call out over my shoulder.

Opening the front door, I peer out into the hallway. I totally lucked out because instead of the two men usually stationed by the elevator there's only one today. Maybe the other guy went on break or something.

"Hi." I shoot him a wave and an innocent smile, then drag the little tree to the garbage chute. I make a big show of trying to shove it down, then let out an exasperated sigh when it doesn't fit. "Um, excuse me, Marty, could you help me take this downstairs?"

The big guy glances up, and his lips curl into a frown.

"I'm sure I'll be perfectly safe with you escorting me."

His cheeks turn rosy, and he fidgets for a second before stalking toward me. "Here, let me take that for you."

My heart rages against my ribcage the entire ride down in the elevator. Tony will start looking for me any second now. I hadn't given my escape plan much thought beyond this point. I didn't really think I'd ever make it this far. Once I get to the garage where the dumpster is, I could very well run into two more of Dante's men. Unless they're stationed on the lobby level…

The elevator doors slide open, and I'm greeted only by a dimly lit garage. No more Kings. Damn, I totally lucked out. I follow a few steps behind Marty as a fantastic idea begins to form in my head. I nearly got stuck in this little garbage room once before. There's a huge sign warning about not letting the door close behind you because it locks automatically.

And just like that, I've found my escape.

I linger behind the door as Marty hauls the tree toward the dumpster. The minute he turns his back, I pull the doorstop free and slam it shut behind him.

"Hey!" he shouts then his fists pound on the door.

I don't wait another second to spin around and race toward the exit. I'll be surrounded by men in black suits in minutes. The moment I make it out of the garage, the frigid air smacks me in the face. I tug on my measly sweatshirt and break into a run.

I have no idea where I'm going and maybe that's a good thing because it'll make it that much harder for anyone to find me.

CHAPTER 48
YOU CAN'T HIDE

R*ose*

After an hour of aimless wandering, I'm freezing and exhausted. I have my phone but no wallet, and I'm starting to regret my rash decision. At least, I've had some time to clear my thoughts. When I first made my mad escape, every time I blinked all I saw was Dante attacking Stella. My best friend tossed over the couch, crying, his massive body pinning her down. Nausea crawls up my throat at the vivid images my mind has conjured.

Now, I'm just numb.

My phone pings, and I yank it out of my pocket just out of habit. It's been going off non-stop for the past hour. I've declined every single one of Dante's calls and ignored his texts. He must be losing his mind with worry, but right now I just don't care.

Eventually, I'll answer him. I just have no idea what I'll say.

It's not like I magically stopped loving him the moment

Stella told me the truth, it's just that I wish I could. I love him so damned much there isn't much he could do that I wouldn't forgive … but this? God, he's torn my fucking heart out.

I finally focus on the text message from Maisy.

Maisy: *Hey girl, I hope you're doing well. I still have that package for you. I took it home because I didn't want it to go missing at Palestra. Let me know if you want me to drop it off one of these days.*

I stare unblinking at the blue bubble for a few more seconds before I click on the text and force my frozen finger to type a response.

Me: *Are you home? I can come by and get it now.*

Maisy: *I am, that would be perfect!*

Perfect for me too since I've run out of ideas. Maybe after a little chat with Maisy I'll feel better. I dart across the street and continue my walk further west to Riverside Drive. Thank God I'm not far from Maisy's Upper West Side brownstone.

By the time I reach her place, my fingers are so numb I barely feel it when I press the buzzer. She answers a few seconds later like she's been waiting at the door.

"Hey, girl!" She pulls me into a hug, then holds me out to arm's length and scrutinizes my poor choice of outerwear. "You must be freezing! Where's your jacket?"

"I kind of left Dante's in a hurry." I shrug lamely.

"Well, come in, come in." She hurries me in, shutting the cold out behind us. A tremor races over my frozen body as the warmth envelops me. She leads me to the cute sitting area in front of the crackling fireplace and immediately the chill that has set into my bones begins to dissipate. "I've got hot cocoa if you want."

"Yes, that would be heaven."

"Be right back."

I curl onto the couch and rub my hands together to bring

some feeling back to my frost-bitten fingers. I definitely should've put more thought into my escape plan. A few moments later, Maisy reappears with two steaming mugs of hot chocolate and a package tucked under her arm.

I jump up and help her with the cups, placing them on the colorful coasters on the coffee table, then she hands me the white box.

"I wonder what you got." She eyes the package expectantly. Beneath the big red bow, a small envelope sticks out.

"When did you say this arrived?"

"Like a day after you disappeared with Dante." Maisy throws me a mischievous wink. "I can't wait to hear all about that."

While I was at the beach house, I'd texted back and confessed I didn't really have Covid and just needed a little getaway, but I didn't spill many details. Now I just couldn't.

I stare at the meticulous packaging, and the hair on the back of my neck rises. Something just feels off about it.

"So, are you going to open it or what?"

Drawing in a steadying breath, I reach for the little envelope.

"Open the present first, duh!" She steals the note, pinching it between her fingers.

I can't muster the courage to tell her how wrong this all feels. So instead, I pull on the red bow and the box pops open.

A decaying yellow rose sits at the bottom along with a picture I immediately recognize, one I thought had burned down in the fire. It was in a frame on top of my dresser, a smiling image of me, Robbie and my parents. It was the summer before my innocence was stolen and our family was perfect.

Only now, my head has been removed, cut out of our perfect family portrait.

Maisy lets out a gasp as she takes in the creepy gift. But I'm just numb, staring at it like nothing.

"Oh my God, Rose! What is this?"

I release a slow breath and reach for the envelope clenched between her fingers without responding. Scanning the dark scrawling, I shove back the trickle of fear.

You can't hide from me forever.

I should be terrified, but mostly I'm just pissed off.

Maisy stares at the note over my shoulder, her big green eyes so wide they're like a second from popping out of her head. She claps her hand over her mouth and another gasp escapes. "No…."

"No what?"

Her porcelain skin has lightened a few shades, making the freckles really stand out.

"It can't be," she mutters.

"What are you talking about?" That hint of unease comes back with a vengeance.

"I know that writing…." She leaps up and crosses the living room, then jerks at a drawer in an antique, white-washed oak desk. Rifling through the papers, she pulls out a stack of envelopes. Then she races back to sit beside me. Ripping one of the envelopes open, she reveals a letter.

The penmanship is exactly the same as the note clenched in my fist.

"Who wrote those?" I blurt, my pulse skyrocketing.

"My ex, Jasper."

My brows slam together as pieces of a complicated puzzle begin to align. It can't be. Lots of people have similar handwriting, right? "There's been a man stalking me," I mutter. "I think it's this guy I dated for a while, but I'm not sure. His name is Mark."

Maisy's face grows paler still, a sick green pallor tingeing her cheeks. "Mark Jasper…."

"What?" I screech.

She grabs her phone and flips through her photos, going back a year or so. Then she flashes me the screen and all the blood drains from my face, only ratcheting my manic heartbeats.

Dr. Mark and Maisy grinning happily.

"Is this him?"

"Oh shit, it is." I shake my head, my thoughts spinning. How is this possible? "I just don't get it," I finally squeak. "Your last name isn't Rattinger, it's Jordan." And I specifically remember Dante doing a background check on Maisy before he let me spend the night here all those weeks ago. There's no way something like this would slip by him.

"No, my ex-husband's name is Mark Jasper Whitaker. My maiden name is Jordan."

"So how could they be the same man? How could Dr. Mark Rattinger the plastic surgeon be your Jasper Whitaker?"

"I don't know." Tears brim in her eyes, and they're about a second from spilling over.

All I feel is anger. This bastard has been living a double life? Not only was he a crazed stalker, but he was married when we were dating?

A sharp knock on the door sends my heart climbing up my throat. Shit, it must be Dante. I'm honestly surprised it took him this long to find me.

Maisy trudges to the door, and as her hand closes around the knob, a prickle of fear surges through my gut. I leap up and dart after her. "Maisy, no wait—"

The door whips open, and three masked men barrel inside.

Before I can get a scream out, an iron grip winds around my throat, and a hand clamps over my mouth. A faint, sweet smell invades my nostrils, and my mind starts to swim. I kick and punch, but already my movements are slowing, growing more sluggish with each attempt.

Darkness invades the corners of my vision, and in an instant, cold oblivion pulls me under.

CHAPTER 49
FURY IS POWER

D*ante*

"Stay on them," I growl at Tony through the Bluetooth speaker of my BMW as I weave across mid-day traffic. Sticking my finger through the knot in my tie, I jerk at it until it unravels. I still can't breathe. Not even when I undo the top two buttons of my dress shirt. "I swear to fucking God, Tony, if you lose sight of Rose for an instant, I'll personally kill you and every single person you've ever met."

"Christ, Dante, calm down. We're on it. I'm two cars behind them and Mickey's trailing on their right. We won't lose her."

Letting Rose wander around the streets of Manhattan all day was risky as hell, but I had to do it. The moment Stella called me and told me what happened I knew Rose would make a run for it. I had a split second to make the decision, and I'd told Tony to let her go. It was one of the hardest calls

I'd made in my life. My heart kicks at my ribcage, pissed off as all hell.

I raced out of the conference room after that call, leaving Jianjun and Feng with their dicks in their hands. King Industries could go up in flames for all I cared. Rose is all that matters. It had taken every ounce of restraint not to go after her as soon as Stella called, not to try to explain what happened that day.

We had eyes on her the whole time, of course. I'd planted a tracking device on Rose's phone on Christmas Eve when I'd caught her trying to spend the night at Palestra. After weeks of trying to find Rose's stalker, when the opportunity presented itself to use her as bait, I'd made the impossible call. It was the only option left.

A violent storm of unease and fury lashes at my insides as I cut off taxi cabs and maneuver through the deadlocked traffic. I wanted to give Rose some space to deal with what happened between Stella and me. Deep down, I knew it was only a matter of time until she spilled the truth to her friend. It is her right after all. I deserve Stella's hatred and so much more. The fact that she forgave me is a testament to her character, not mine.

And now, someone has Rose.

Because I fucked up.

If I hadn't hurt her friend, she never would've run. Then again, I was the one that made the choice to let her go. If anything happens to Rose, it's on me. My lungs heave from the strain, invisible claws tearing at my organs. I breathe through the fear and focus on the rage.

Fury is power. Fear is for the weak.

Tony and the guys had followed Rose to Maisy's, and he'd alerted me the moment those goons showed up. I never expected an entire legion of masked men. Dr. Mark I could handle, but this was completely unexpected.

Which is why I'm panicking as I finally emerge through the

gridlock onto the FDR. According to the beeping red dot on my GPS, they're heading south. The question is who the fuck are *they*? And why did they bother taking Maisy too?

If they were masked, there was no reason to take another hostage. They could have knocked her out or simply tied her up. Why bring her into the mix?

The monster within scrapes and claws his way to the surface, desperate for violence, ravenous for blood. At least this would finally end today.

My phone buzzes, and I hazard a quick glance at the screen. It's the DMV report on the vehicle that snagged the girls. Of course, it's unregistered, no name, nothing.

Who is this Mark guy, ex-CIA or something?

My fingers tighten around the steering wheel, knuckles white as I follow the GPS. The big red dot beeps cross the screen, my Rosa. *Dio*, if she doesn't forgive me when I get her back, I'll lose my mind.

And I *will* get her back. Failure is not an option.

My gaze flickers to the glove compartment, to the small turquoise box with a bow tucked inside. Rose *will* be fine, and I will make her mine forever.

I jerk the steering wheel to the right and follow the exit toward the Lower East Side. So predictable. It's always some seedy warehouse with these guys. I gun the engine, jamming my foot down on the pedal as far as it'll go.

I'm coming for you, sweetheart.

I race around the maze of shipping containers, my heart like a battering ram and my breath so thin every inhale feels like I'm suffocating. An icy breeze stirs the dark waters of the bay, the lapping against the seawall the only sound for miles. Tony and the guys trailed the masked kidnappers to an abandoned shipping yard on the southern tip of Manhattan.

According to my men, Rose and Maisy are being held just three containers down from where they stand. They're waiting on my word to move. As I reach the designated rendezvous spot, I slow my desperate footsteps and creep toward the blue, rusted-out container. I can already make out Tony's large frame only a few yards ahead.

Pulling out my gun, I move quickly and silently; my nails biting into my empty palm. Those fuckers have no idea the bloodbath I'm about to unleash. A twinge of fear settles between the rage, but I force it back. It has no place here today.

One wrong move, and I lose everything.

Tony cocks his head back as I round the empty container. "Glad you made it," he whispers.

"Any updates?" I bark.

"Nah. They walked the girls in a few minutes ago, so they're at least somewhat conscious now."

When Tony told me they'd carried Rose out of Maisy's place with a hood over her head, crimson had flooded my vision. Their blood. I'd bathe in it once I had Rose back, safe in my arms.

"Good. They'll be the only ones unconscious once I'm done with them." I scan the perimeter and catch sight of heavily armed Kings stationed in every corner. "Everyone ready?"

"Waiting on your word, *capo*."

I nod, my fingers tightening around the grip of my gun. That swirl of suffocating fear mixes with the adrenaline of battle and rages a war in my chest. "Let's move," I growl. "Behind me."

Two guys dressed in black stand on either side of the graffitied red container. Their guns are holstered, and they're chit-chatting like little princesses about the fucking weather. Sitting ducks.

I slip the silencer out of my pocket and attach it to the muzzle of my Glock. A quick nod to Tony, and we're on the same page without uttering a word. With lethal precision, I take aim at the guy on the left and he takes the one on the right. Three, two, one.

Twin gunshots to the head. Both bodies sag to the floor in unison.

I reach the container door first and jerk on the latch. The sharp squeal of the rusted hinge ratchets up my pulse, but there's no avoiding it. I whip open the door, gun drawn, and blink quickly as my pupils adjust to the dim surroundings.

Grabbing the first guy I can make out, I wrap my arm around his throat and jerk him against my chest. The barrel is pointed at his temple. "No one move or this asshole's brains will be all over the floor."

My eyes finally adjust to the darkness, and three bound and gagged figures coalesce from the shadows.

My heart leaps up my throat as they settle on Rose.

"Dante!" she murmurs around the gag or at least I swear I hear my name.

"It's okay, sweetheart. I'm here." I bite back the overwhelming emotion tightening my throat and flex my bicep so I'm crushing the guy's windpipe. Then I refocus on the redhead, Maisy, who I recognize, and the other figure with a hood over his head. I'm guessing he's a male based on his dark trousers and brown loafers.

Another male emerges from the shadows, and Tony pivots the barrel of his gun and takes aim. Sharp blue eyes lift to mine, and I barely restrain the gasp from spilling out. "You?" I snarl.

Nico Rossi steps into the light, a smug grin stretched across his face and that damned man bun bobbing at the top of his head. He struts closer so I can make out his dark three-piece suit, just like the one he wore in the conference room the other day, with a gold chain hanging from his pocket. The *bastardo* moves behind Rose, and pure venom surges through my veins.

"Don't take another step closer to her, you *pezzo di merda*, or

Tony will blow your head off." I do take a step closer, dragging Rossi's man along with me.

"Kill him or don't. I couldn't give two shits." Nico ticks his head at the squirming male in my grasp and shrugs nonchalantly.

So, I call him on his bullshit. I squeeze the trigger and the gunshot rings out, echoing across the walls of the metal container. The girls scream around the gags, and I feel bad scaring them, but it's a small price to pay for their safety. It's time to let the monster free. Rossi's guy collapses to the floor, blood dripping from his head and pooling at my feet.

A flash of anger hardens the *figlio di puttana*'s jaw.

"Since you didn't give two shits…," I mutter, shrugging. We've got Nico surrounded now. Besides the four men flanking me, I've got another dozen lurking outside. It's just him and the guy beneath the hood now.

"Mmm." He moves closer to Rose, and every muscle in my body vibrates with wrath.

"Not another step," I hiss.

"Why not? You don't want to see who our mystery guest is?" Nico throws me an arrogant smile as he moves between Rose and the hooded man. "You really do, I know you do."

"Fine," I grit out, only because I am curious as hell, then I level the Glock at Nico's head. "Then you have two seconds to release my girl before Tony and I put two bullets between your eyes."

Nico's fingers pinch around the black fabric, and he yanks it off. The blonde male's head rolls back, mouth gagged.

"Is that…?" I eye the bruised, sallow, dirt-covered face. "Is that Dr. Mark?"

Nico nods, eyes sparkling with amusement. "He was the perfect distraction, Dante. Once I figured out what *she* meant to you, everything fell into place so easily." He chuckles, his thick, tattooed arms pressed over his chest. "You want to hear the funniest part? This asshole isn't just a stalker and a rapist, he's a two-timer with a secret identity. As it turns out, he was married to the cute redhead while he was fucking your girl."

My carefully honed restraint snaps, and I lunge. I throw a quick jab at Nico's jaw, but he deftly blocks it and counters with a brutal left hook. The surprising impact sends me reeling back, blood trickling from my split lip. "Fuck," I snarl and wipe the blood from my chin.

Regaining my footing, I retaliate with a vicious low kick, aiming for Nico's knee. He evades with a swift step back, then lands a powerful kick to my ribs. I stagger back before unleashing a flurry of punches, each one finding its mark on Nico's face and torso.

He grunts with each blow but never loses his composure. He ducks, avoiding a lethal hit, and retaliates with a knee to my midsection. Gasping for air, I stumble backward, my suit torn and disheveled.

Tony ticks his gun at me, but I shake him off. I'm taking this *bastardo* down myself. This is fucking personal.

Nico seizes the opportunity and closes in, launching a series of punishing body blows, forcing me to protect my torso. It's a calculated move, leaving my head vulnerable, only I realize it a moment too late. Nico delivers a precise, bone-crushing uppercut that sends me sprawling across the metal floor.

Rose's anguished cry spears me right in the heart.

I struggle to get back on my feet, my vision blurred by a mix of sweat and blood. I wipe my face and find Rose's terrified gaze. I toss her a smile, despite the pain and push myself up.

No way this asshole wins today.

Nico lunges with a final, feral strike, but I sidestep just in time. Using the momentum from his missed punch, I grab his arm and execute a perfect Judo throw. Nico crashes to the ground, his face smashing against the unyielding metal.

I jump on top of him and rain down a barrage of punches,

each strike punctuated by the sound of flesh meeting bone. Blood splatters the walls, creating a grisly piece of crimson art across the rusted metal.

"Dante, don't kill him!" Somehow Rose has slipped off the gag, and that sweet tenor seeps through the maddening bloodlust.

I pause, my hand curled into a bloodied fist, and cock my head over my shoulder. "Why not?" I growl. "He dared touch you, he tried to hurt you, Rosa. Why shouldn't I tear up this piece of shit and paint his fucking fancy Park Avenue tower with his blood?"

"Because he's your brother."

Ice frosts my veins, and my gaze bounces back and forth between Rose and the bloodied face on the floor. "No...."

Nico's eyes open to mere slits, the swelling already in full force. "It's true, *fratellino*." A sneer curls his lips, and he spits out a stream of blood.

Little brother? "It can't be." I shake my head and sit back on my knees, my mind and my gut reeling.

"Your papà fucked my mamma and left her pregnant. The great leader of the Kings was a *pezzo di merda*."

"A piece of shit?" I snarl and cock my gun, pressing it to his forehead. "Shut your mouth before I finish what I started."

"It's true, Dante," Rose whispers. "He showed us the blood test."

Maisy nods, her head bobbing up and down.

"So what? This is some sort of revenge plot? You're trying to take down King Industries because Papà didn't love you enough?" A sneer curls the corners of my lips. It's a practiced smile because inside my world is crashing down on me. How could Papà do this? How could he have kept this from us all these years?

"Trying?" He smiles again. "I've already done it, Dante. I've stolen your biggest legitimate accounts right from under your nose. And well, your territory, outside the legal parameters of our fine system, you've fucked that up yourself, giving over half to the Red Dragons. By the time the Geminis claim their stake, you'll have nothing left."

Merda....

My fingers ache to wrap around this fucker's throat and squeeze until his eyes pop out. But Luca ... damn it, Luca would want to wait. He'd want to know more about our twisted family history. Hell, he'll probably want to invite the *coglione* for Christmas dinner.

"And just in case you're thinking about killing me," he mutters, "I wouldn't."

"Oh, yeah, why not?"

"Because my brother will kill yours."

Now it's my fucking eyeballs that are about to pop out of my head. *Cazzo*, there's two of them? Papà, what have you done?

Nico sits up and wipes the blood from his bottom lip. "Hiding Luca from the Red Dragons was one thing, but from me? Finding him and his precious fiancée was easy." He pushes off the floor and dusts himself off. "Touché at finding Rose so quickly though. I was hoping I'd get a little more time with her, and this one." He cocks his head at Maisy, and his nostrils flare. "She's something else."

"I swear to you, Nico, this isn't over. If you so much as touch a single hair on Rose's head ever again, I don't care if you are my brother, I'll carve up your insides and hang them outside of your office. Are we clear?"

A smile curls the corners of his smug lips. "I don't want your girl, *fratellino*. I just want what's rightfully mine. The throne of the Kings and Gemini empires." He struts past me, his shoulder brushing mine as he marches out. When he reaches the door, he swings his head over his shoulder. "See you soon, little bro."

CHAPTER 50
NEVER BE ALONE AGAIN

R*ose*

Rubbing my sleepy eyes, I stare at the glaringly empty spot in the corner where my little Christmas tree stood just yesterday. For such a tiny thing, it sure brought a lot to the sprawling living room. I curl my legs under me and pull the fluffy pink blanket up to my chin.

Dante moves around the kitchen, slamming cabinet doors. The clang of glasses and mugs hitting each other make me wince. Loud noises still make me jump. He hasn't left my side since he carried me out of that container yesterday. Now, he's trying to make me hot tea, but clearly has no idea what he's doing.

We've both been quieter than normal, tiptoeing around the discussion that must be had but we're both too chicken to start. After Nico Rossi's guys grabbed us, my first thought was Dante. I could imagine how the guilt would eat him alive if anything happened to me. How he'd blame himself for all of it. And that fear for him was strangling.

So in that instant, I forgave him. He may have never known if I had been killed, but at least it cleared my conscience. But now, here I am, not dead, and the dreaded conversation still looms between us.

Soft footsteps compel my eyes up to meet a pair of anxious dark orbs. Dante hands me the mug of tea and folds down beside me, the scent of Earl Grey soothing the mad flutter of my heart. Dante's thigh nearly brushes mine, but not quite. I miss his arms wrapped around me, the safety only his strength can bring. He held me all night in bed, pressing chaste kisses to my forehead or to the top of my head. It was the first time since we'd started having sex that he didn't even try anything.

Dante's pensive gaze lifts over my head to the vacant spot in the corner, and a rueful grin curls his lips. "I can't believe I'm saying this, but I actually miss that scraggly little tree."

"I was just thinking the same thing!" I spin around to face him, crossing my legs on the cushion. "Dante…"

"No," he cuts me off. "Let me go first."

I nod, a flare of anxiety coating my insides.

Dante drags his hand through his wild hair and heaves in a breath. "*Cazzo*, Rosa, yesterday was the worst day of my life, and I've had a lot of shitty days." His lips thin as he pauses. "Besides the fear of losing you to that *bastardo*, which there was no way I was ever going to let happen, what frightened me the most was that you'd never be able to forgive me for Stella."

Yesterday, Dante admitted he'd bugged my phone, so he knew where I was the whole time. I should've been enraged, but mostly I was only thankful. If he hadn't, who knows what would've happened.

"What I did to her, *merda*, Rosa, you don't know how often I wish I could go back in time and re-do that entire day. It was the first time, the only time in my life, I've ever laid my hands on a woman. Papà would have disowned me if he were alive. Hell, he would have cut off my hands. *Never touch a woman* was one of his cardinal rules. I just lost it that day. I was so sure Stella was working for Bo, and Luca was too blind to see it. I went too far, but I swear to you, I never would have raped her. Never. I only wanted to scare the truth out of her."

"But Luca walked in instead and beat the shit out of you," I interjected.

He nods slowly. "And I fucking deserved it. I'll spend the rest of my life trying to make it up to Stella."

We remain silent for a long moment as I try to process his words. After really getting to know Dante, it seems completely in line with his character. He's impulsive, reckless, and protective to a fault. "I just wish you would've told me," I finally whisper.

"It wasn't my story to tell, sweetheart."

I get that, I do. After what I went through with my uncle, the idea of having my story out there felt like forcing me to relive the horrible event over and over again. And when I finally did tell someone, my mom, the worst happened.

"My mom killed herself a few weeks after I told her about my uncle." The confession comes out on a sharp exhale. The secret I'd been holding onto for years was finally out, and almost immediately my heart felt lighter.

Dante reaches for me, tentatively, but I gladly accept the warmth of his hand around mine. He squeezes, and I can practically feel his strength seeping into me. "I'm so sorry, sweetheart. I'm sorry you had to face all of that alone."

Hot tears prick my eyes, and I blink quickly forcing them back.

"But if you'll let me, if you can find it in your big, beautiful heart to forgive me," he whispers and inches closer, his warm, calloused palm cupping my cheek. "I swear to always stand beside you from this day onward. You'll never be alone again." Those dark, bottomless irises lance into me, and I've never felt so bare before him.

Or filled with so much love.

I draw in a deep breath and fix my gaze to his. "If Stella can forgive you, then so can I."

A beaming smile flashes across that handsome face and he drags me into his lap, his arms crushing me to his chest. "*Grazie a Dio,*" he whispers against the top of my head. Thank God is right. "I love you, Rosa, and I swear, I will be a better man for you, the type of man you deserve."

I frame his scruffy cheeks and press a kiss to those perfect lips. "You already are," I murmur against his mouth.

Then we get lost in fiery kisses, a tangle of limbs and can't tear off our clothes fast enough.

The doorbell rings and I sprint across the living room, tugging down the indecent hem of the new sweater dress Dante bought me. I swear he only likes it because it sticks to my curves like spandex. Much like my yoga pants.

"I'll get it." Dante barrels by me and reaches the door a second before I do. His overprotectiveness has been on full throttle since Nico Rossi appeared in our lives, and I can't even blame him now. He whips the door open, and Maisy stands in the corridor with Tony just a few steps behind her.

We now have full time guards stationed *everywhere*.

She smiles and holds out a vibrant, purple orchid in a pretty white pot. "I figured you could use it to cheer up the place. Not that it's not cheery, but you know since you don't have the Christmas tree anymore and—"

"It's perfect, thanks so much Maisy." She hands me the beautiful plant, and I set it on top of the kitchen island. It does bring some color to the uber-modern black and white of the penthouse. Maybe I can put some lights on it.

"Yes, thank you, Maisy." Even Dante gives my friend a smile.

Since he refuses to let me out of the penthouse, our girls' night was happening here with my personal bodyguard. I escort Maisy to the sitting room while Dante shuffles around the kitchen. "White or red, Maisy?" he calls out.

"Red, please." She folds down onto the leather couch, admiring the sprawling scenery of Central Park. "This view is amazing."

"Isn't it? I can't wait for the summer. I'm totally going to sunbathe on the balcony."

"Over my dead body," Dante grumbles from the kitchen.

"Ignore him." I wave a dismissive hand. "How are you doing?" I couldn't imagine having to stay in that big house by myself after what happened. Which was why I'd invited my friend to hang out over here.

"I'm okay." She shrugs. "I didn't sleep a wink last night though. Every time I close my eyes I see *him*."

"Oh, Maisy, I'm so sorry. I should've asked if you wanted to sleep over yesterday."

Dr. Mark, a.k.a. Maisy's ex-husband Jasper, had somehow managed to escape in the chaos of the shipping yard. With all the personal drama Dante and I have been dealing with, we haven't even had a chance to deal with the surgeon at large.

"It's okay, I'd hate to be the third wheel."

Dante strolls into the living room with two glasses of wine and sets them down on the cocktail table.

"No way. Maisy is totally welcome to stay with us, right, D?" I throw my almost fiancé a pleading look.

"Yes, of course," he mutters. "I just hope you're not a light sleeper because Rose is quite a screamer—"

I leap up and clap my hand over his dirty mouth. "Stop!" A

dark chuckle vibrates Dante's chest, and I shoot him a narrowed glare. "You're terrible."

"But you love me anyway." He presses a chaste kiss to my lips, and already I want so much more.

"I do, I do love you, Dante Valentino."

CHAPTER 51
MY QUEEN

R*ose*

"Really, Dante? A month-long vacation in the middle of the school year?" I glare up at the infuriating man as he waves plane tickets in front of my face. "And what about work? I can't just abandon Dr. Winchester or my clients at Palestra." I chug down the rest of my coffee and drop it down on the kitchen island.

"I already told you, you don't have to worry about that anymore." His dark brows furrow like I'm the insane one.

That's been his answer to everything these days. *You don't have to worry anymore.* It's been a hell of a long week since Dante's half-brother, Nico, threw our lives into turmoil. Besides all the kidnapping shit, Dante and I had a lot of personal things to work through. When I first found out what he'd done to Stella, it was all I could think about. Then being held at gunpoint and fearing for not only my life, but also Dante's, put some things in perspective.

I didn't think I'd ever be able to forget what Dante tried to do, or even *pretended* to do to Stella. He's sworn to me back and forth that he never intended to go through with it, that he would never force himself on a woman. And I believe him, but just the fact that he used that as an intimidation tactic is what killed me. Especially because of what I'd been through.

I talked it out with Stella a few more times, and then with my therapist. I don't excuse what he did, I never could, but you also don't just stop loving someone because they did something unforgiveable in the past.

And gawd, I love Dante more than anything in this world.

"Good, so you agree to the trip then?" His voice interrupts my whirling thoughts, those dark eyes glistening as they regard me.

"I didn't say that." I lift a challenging brow and flash him the back of my hand. "I still don't see a ring on my finger."

"Did it ever occur to you that maybe there's a reason for this impromptu trip?"

"You're full of it, Dante Valentino. You're whisking me away on this 'vacation' because of your psycho half-brother." And the still-missing Dr. Mark or Jasper or whatever the hell his real name is. How the sneaky surgeon managed to give us the slip again is beyond me. It was probably because Dante was so preoccupied with getting me out of that shipping yard, he forgot about everything else.

It was actually Maisy who'd noticed he'd gone missing. I still can't believe her husband Jasper is my Dr. Mark. It's all so twisted and fucked up. Her ex had been living a lie for who knows how long while they were married. I feel horrible for her and have had her sleep over a few times this week. I hate the thought of her all along in that huge house.

A frown slashes across Dante's lips, and I'm almost sorry to chase away his fun mood by mentioning his new brother. "I'll never let Nico hurt you," he grits out.

"I know." Pushing all the other thoughts to the back of my

mind, my arms lace around the back of his neck, and I pull his warm body flush against mine. "I don't think Nico ever really intended to hurt me, if it makes you feel any better. I think he just wanted to prove that he could."

He grunts, an exasperated sigh fleeing his clenched lips. "I don't know that, and I won't risk your life while we try to find out."

"So, you're just going to leave the throne of King Industries unmanned while you fly me away to God knows where?"

He presses his mouth to mine, a punishing, unforgiving kiss. Then he pulls away, leaving me all hot and bothered. "I've already told you, you are everything to me. I've held the throne, and I don't want it. I'd choose you a hundred times over. I'd let the entire Kings' empire burn to the ground if it meant keeping you safe. Do you understand that?"

I nod, a stupid grin flashing across my face. "So does that mean you're going to change your tattoo?" I sneak my finger through his button-down shirt. "Instead of Vengeance Is King, I think it should say Rose Is My Queen."

A wicked laugh rumbles his chest, vibrating against my own. Gawd, I don't think I'll ever get enough of that sound. "Or better yet, Rose's Pussy Is My Queen."

My lips twist, and I shoot him a good eye roll. "You certainly have a vile mouth, Mr. Valentino."

"All the better to pleasure you with, my queen." His lips claim mine, tongue forcing its way between my teeth. He pulls back with a frustrated grunt, his cock already hard against me. "How about this? I'll sweeten the deal…."

"Oh, yeah? How are you going to make a one-month vacation any sweeter?"

"I'll take you to see Stella." With Nico's appearance, Dante convinced Luca to extend his own vacation with his fiancée indefinitely.

My smile grows wider, and my stupid heart expands along with it. "You will?"

His chin dips to his chest.

Seeing the two of them together would provide the closure I desperately need. Hearing my best friend say she forgives the man I love is one thing, but really getting to witness the two of them together would mean the world to me.

"Okay," I whisper.

"Great. I'll talk to Clara to make the necessary arrangements." Seeing him smile like that does funny things to my heart. "And if you're so adamant about the ring…."

Dante drops down on one knee, and I was wrong before. That funny little jig my heart was doing is nothing compared to the somersaults it's now performing. Those midnight orbs lock on mine, and I'm hopelessly trapped in their dark embrace.

"Oh, my, gawd," I rasp out.

"God had nothing to do with this, sweetheart, maybe the devil though." He offers me a sinful smirk as he pulls the small turquoise box from his pocket. A white bow sits atop, and my itchy little fingers can barely wait.

"Marry me, sweetheart, or I'll have to bend you over my lap and spank the yes out of you until that pretty pink ass matches the enticing crimson of your cheeks when you come on my cock."

I suck in a breath at the vivid images his dirty words have conjured in my mind. Also, now I'm soaked just thinking about it. I'm half inclined to deny him just so he'll carry out his threat. "Well, I can't say it was the proposal all the girls dream about…." I shoot him a smirk as he takes my hand in his big ones.

"I warned you I was no hero, sweetheart, no knight in shining armor. I may not spout out pretty words or poetry, but I'll love you the only way I know how, with all the fire in my dark soul. I'll fuck you hard and often, and I'll probably piss you off with my possessiveness even more, but I'll protect you until my dying breath. You'll be mine forever."

All the air whooshes out of my lungs at those dark, tormented, and beautiful words. I drop down to the ground in front of him, and he finally flips open the box. A gigantic diamond is nestled in the teal cushion, an outer ring of baguettes around the top forming the shape of a crown.

"You are my queen, Rosa, you are my everything."

Tears blur my vision, and I'm nodding like crazy, emotion clogging my throat, and I can't even get the yes out.

"Now hurry up and say yes. If I must be on my knees, I'd prefer to have my face buried between your thighs."

A laugh tumbles free, and I hold out my trembling hand. Dante slides the gorgeous ring on my finger, his warm hand enveloping mine. His eyes never deviate from my own, and I'm completely swallowed up in the dark abyss. I want to drown in it, in him. My chest is heaving, my heart rioting against my ribs.

"There, done." He stands, pulling me up with him. "Now, can I please fuck my future wife?"

I bring my hand up and admire the sparkly ring. "D, with this ring on my finger, you can do whatever you want to me."

"Now that's what I like to hear, sweetheart." He bends down, sweeps me into his arms and marches us toward the bedroom.

EPILOGUE

M^{aisy}

"You know, a limo would've been much more comfortable," Dante grumbles from the back of my Mini Cooper, popping his head between the front seats.

"Oh, shush." Rose swats at him and he sits back, wedged between two enormous suitcases. "I won't get to see Maisy for who knows how long. I want to get in every last minute of girl time."

I catch Dante's eyeroll in the rearview mirror along with the silly grin that tugs at his lips. He's clearly head over heels for my friend, and despite everything, I'm so happy things worked out for them.

"I'm sorry, you guys, I just wanted to help." I turn the volume up on the latest Taylor Swift hit, but it goes up way too fast and too high. "Eek, sorry!" I shout as Dante claps his hands over his ears.

"And you are being very helpful," Rose croons. "I'd much rather you drive us than grumpy Aldo."

Dante grunts from the backseat, and heat flares across my cheeks. I can't seem to do anything right. Driving Rose and her new fiancé to the airport is the least I could do. Ever since the truth came out about my ex-husband, a.k.a. Rose's stalker, I've been weighed down by this overwhelming guilt. How could you know someone for years and never really *know* them? I'm clearly not only naïve and stupid, but I'm also blind.

What other terrible things had Jasper done while we were married? Or before? We'd been together since my senior year of high school and married before my twentieth birthday. Jasper was a friend's older brother, which accounted for our rather significant age gap of fifteen years. When had the charming, tempting older man become the sinister stalker with a secret life?

After he disappeared from the shipping yard last week, I'd immediately contacted my lawyer to get to the bottom of his alter ego, Dr. Mark Rattinger, the plastic surgeon. Jasper had gone to medical school but had opted to join the family business instead. Or at least that's the story I'd been fed. How does one get a medical license under a fake name anyway? It's all so surreal; I still can't wrap my head around it.

Rose convinced me to let Dante handle it, but now that they're leaving town for this pre-wedding honeymoon, I'm worried Jasper will slip through the cracks. And I need answers. Was any of it real? Was our entire marriage a sham?

My throat constricts, and I force the dismal thoughts to the farthest recesses of my mind. I did not offer my friend a ride today to dwell on my dark past.

Turning to Rose, I catch her ogling her ring. I'm not sure she even notices she's doing it, but her eyes constantly flicker to the huge diamond. My gaze drifts to my hands wrapped around the steering wheel, and the pale band of skin on my ring finger. It took a long time for me to take my wedding band off, but the moment I did, I felt free.

"So, you're sure I can have my job back at Palestra when I return?" Rose's hopeful eyes dart to mine.

"Yes, it's totally fine. All the clients love you."

Dante mutters a curse, the deep tone only accentuated with the gruff Italian. I don't need to speak the language to guess what he's saying. Rose has already filled me in on the ongoing argument about her returning to work. I told her to stick to her guns. I'd been so young when I married Jasper, I never had a career. Now here I am at twenty-three, and I have no idea what I want to do with my life.

"Thank you!" Rose cries. "I really like them too, and of course, I adore working with you."

"You mean you love our coffee and lunch breaks."

She smiles. "Yup, exactly."

The signs for JFK appear overhead, and Rose starts to squirm in her seat. "I can't believe we're doing this!" She claps her hands and pivots around to face her fiancé. "Can I please just tell Maisy where we're going?"

"No," he barks, his tone brooking no room for argument.

But she tries anyway. "Please, Dante … she's not going to tell anyone."

"Rosa, it's not that I think she would be stupid enough to reveal our secret willingly. My concern is that *someone* might force her to."

A chill squirms up my back at the implied threat in his words. "But why would anyone think I know anything?" I blurt. After the little bits and pieces that Rose has shared in the past week about the Kings, it's become clear there's more going on in that multi-billion-dollar company than meets the eye, but I kept my mouth shut and didn't ask any questions. Now I'm starting to regret any involvement.

"They won't," Dante growls. "Just stay the course, Maisy. Go through your lawyers and the private investigators. They'll find your ex and send him to jail for the rest of his life where that *figlio di puttana* belongs." A scowl slashes across his lips, and the tendon in his jaw pulses. "If they don't, I'll deal with it when we get back."

"Okay. You're right, I'm sure they'll take care of it." I heave in a deep breath and focus on the exit sign ahead. The last thing I need is to get lost on the way to the airport, which is totally something I'd do. *Everything's going to be fine, Maisy. Jasper is finally out of your life, and it's going to stay that way.*

The frenetic rush of the airport terminal is all at once invigorating and overwhelming. Dozens of people dart by, speaking in a sea of different languages, dragging oversized luggage, and screaming children. I don't know why I insisted on walking them to the security checkpoint. Maybe it's because the loss of my new friend is suddenly starting to hit me. Since the divorce, all the Upper East Side wives I used to hang out with have conveniently disappeared. Which is fine, really. I was always too awkward and clumsy to hang out with the likes of them. They were all so extra, and I'm just me.

Which is why I immediately clicked with Rose.

"Well, I guess this is it." Rose stops in front of the security line reserved for first class passengers. I'd wondered why the great Dante Valentino wasn't flying by private jet, but Rose said something about wanting to stay under the radar. I suppose in the chaotic mass of people at JFK, it would be easier to slip by undetected.

She throws open her arms and pulls me into a big hug. "I'm going to miss you, girl."

"You, too." I give her a tight squeeze before stepping back to stare up at her. At just barely past five feet, I spend most of my time looking up at people. Not great for my self-esteem which is already pretty much scraping the floor. But that's what therapy is for, right? "I'm *really* going to miss you," I murmur.

"I'll be back before you know it."

Dante tugs Rose into his side and drops a chaste kiss on her cheek. "*Andiamo*," he growls. Then he whispers something in her ear that has her cheeks turning fifty shades of red. From what Rose has spilled, the man is an animal in bed. I can believe it too with those bulging biceps, that massive chest and those sexy-as-sin tattoos. I'm getting all hot and bothered just thinking about what a night in bed with a man like that would be like….

True fact: I've only been with one man my entire life.

And again, from what I've discovered, Jasper was no expert in the bedroom. I could count the number of orgasms I've had in my life on one hand. I really do need to get back out there. One day.

"Okay, we have to go, Maisy." Rose ticks her head at the walk-through metal detector and the gates beyond. She pulls me into one more hug, and I catch Dante's gaze lift over our heads. His dark eyes narrow in on something over my shoulder, but Rose is still squeezing me into her chest so I can't follow his line of sight.

Whatever he sees has hard lines carving into his jaw, then something dark flashes across his expressive irises. Rose finally releases me and must notice Dante's wary expression because her eyes follow his to the far corner of the terminal.

"What is it?" she whispers.

Goosebumps ripple across my arms for an inexplicable reason.

"I thought I saw…." Dante's mouth tightens into a thin line, and then he shakes his head. "Nothing." He curls his arm around her shoulder and guides her toward the roped off area. She walks through the metal detector first, and Dante lingers a moment longer before turning to me. "Thanks, Maisy. And be careful, okay?"

My head bounces up and down. "Um, anything I should particularly be careful of?" I'm super proud of myself for getting the whole sentence out without stuttering. I tend to ramble when I get nervous.

His dark brows furrow, and he's still glaring at the same spot. There's a café or something at the end of the terminal. "I'm not sure yet, but I'll let you know if I land on anything." He claps his hand over my shoulder and gives it a squeeze. "*Ciao.*"

"*Ciao,*" I mumble back weakly. I remain rooted to the spot long after the happy couple disappears into the jumble of rushing bodies and spinning carry-ons.

With a sigh, I finally turn around and trudge back toward the exit. Now, I just have to figure out how to get back to my car. Scanning the overhead signs, a dark shadow looms over me. A prickle of awareness surges up my spine, but I ignore it, keeping my eyes pinned to the directions above. I try to get my bearings and disregard the overpowering presence sending my mind into a tailspin.

"Are you lost, little fox?" That familiar deep tenor steals the air from my lungs. I blink quickly as vivid images assault my mind. The hood over my head, the gloved hand covering my mouth, my mind spinning before I passed out. Then that deep, sultry voice as we bounce around the backseat as the van rumbles down the street.

I slowly turn around and meet a pair of blazing blue eyes. A few strands of dark hair have come free from the tie at the base of his neck, framing the hard lines of his sculpted, scruffy jaw and drawing my attention to that cruel mouth. A thin line bisects his upper lip, the scar lending an arrogant twist to his lips.

Nico Rossi.

A tremor cascades through my body.

He must notice it because he lifts his hands innocently and

takes a step back. "Relax, *piccola*. I only stopped by to say hello."

I force my lips into a smile as I scan the hustle and bustle of bodies surrounding us. There's no way he can take me again, not in the middle of a busy airport, right?

"And to apologize for that ugly business last week. I never meant for you to get caught up in it."

My head bounces up and down, all the air tied up in my lungs. Was this who Dante thought he'd seen? It has to have been. I convince myself he's here to check on his half-brother and this truly has nothing to do with me. I'm just at the wrong place at the very wrong time. Like always.

"Um, water under the bridge and all that," I somehow manage. "That's such an odd turn of phrase, don't you think? Like what does that really mean?"

Nico's scrutinizing gaze rakes over me, silencing my inane rambling. *Thank God*. His nostrils flare, and his broad chest expands beneath his expertly tailored suit. Like he's smelling me…. I'm overcome with the most overwhelming urge to smell my underarms. Did I forget to put on deodorant? Why is he looking at me like he wants to devour me?

"Anyway, I have to get going." I wave a nonchalant hand. I can't even lie and tell him my boyfriend or my husband is waiting for me because he already knows I don't have one. He's already met my psycho ex.

I spin on my heel, but thick fingers close around my wrist before I can move an inch. Nico steps into me, his towering frame blocking everything else out. His lips brush the shell of my ear, and another wave of goosebumps domino down my arms.

"See you soon, little fox. Very soon."

Read on for a special sneak peek of Brutal King, the next story in the Kings of Temptation series! And you can preorder it now! The release date is currently set for April 9th, but I hope to bring that up. Each novel in the Kings of Temptation series will feature a sinfully gorgeous King and the woman who makes him fall to his knees.

For a chance to win an ARC and get exclusive sneak peeks of what's to come, join my FB group Sienna Cross's Heartbreakers or my VIP mailing list at https://landing.mailerlite.com/webforms/landing/d8j4z4! You'll get the steamy *Savage King* digital art and the *Ruthless King* prequel story for FREE!

CHAPTER 52
SNEAK PEEK OF BRUTAL KING

Chapter 1 – Come Closer, Little Fox
Nico

Come closer, little fox. Closer…

My heart taps out a frantic rhythm as adrenaline rushes my veins. The mad flutter drowns out the rumble of engines and sharp blasts of horns just beyond the lush tranquility of Central Park. A sanctuary amidst the chaos.

My gaze settles on *her*. The object of my desire, the reason my cock strains against my slacks. The thrill of the chase is seductive, addictive, a narcotic far more potent than any available on the market. Crouching behind the shadows of the towering oak, my prey is oblivious to the predator lurking only a few feet away.

The alluring redhead clutches a white paper bag in her hand, her delicate fingers obscuring the name of the franchise. I only know there's a salad in there because I trailed her from the moment she left Palestra. The exclusive gym is nestled within the bowels of the Plaza Hotel. Thanks to my newfound success with Gemini Corp, I was finally granted entry to the high-end facility. Not only would it provide me with unfettered access to the enticing female, but it would also serve as a strategic location to network with the high and mighty of Manhattan.

The only downside is being forced to endure the occasional presence of my half-brother, Dante Valentino, the insufferable *capo* of the Kings. He and his brother Luca rule the streets of lower Manhattan with their underground dealings, while their aboveboard business affairs are conducted through King Industries. Thanks to a few key moves, Gemini Corp is now poised to overtake both parts of their enterprise.

My half-brothers have everything, while my brother, Marco and I grew up penniless at the merciless hands of the foster care system. Now all of that is about to change.

The crackle of footsteps across brittle twigs returns my attention to the task at hand. The mesmerizing female settles down on a bench, folding her leg over the other. Wisps of brilliant auburn hair lash across her face as a chilly spring breeze sails across the oak trees. I've always had a thing for redheads, but this is different…

The beautiful Maisy Jordan captured my attention three long months ago. I've waited patiently, looming in the shadows but *cazzo*, I can't watch her from afar any longer. It's time for me to make my move.

I step out from behind the thick trunk of the ancient oak but before I make it far, a man appears and with a cheesy smile, sits beside *my* little fox.

A wave of fury lashes at my insides as he strikes up a conversation. She smiles politely, as they discuss the weather. Clearly, this man has no idea what he's doing. She brings the plastic fork to her mouth, and her full pink lips close around the leaves of lettuce. Irrational jealousy flares at the nerve of that fork, of that salad to experience those lips. I've dreamt of them since that day in the container at the shipping yard when I had Maisy at my mercy.

She wasn't supposed to be there. It was my half-brother's

girlfriend I'd been targeting. Maisy had been collateral damage, but only a few hours with that woman and I was hopelessly obsessed.

I've never stalked a woman before, but with every passing day, the roots of obsession grow deeper. I was content with keeping my distance at first, but now, the urge to touch her is overwhelming.

A bubbly laugh jerks my attention to the pair still chatting on the park bench. The guy has his phone out now, and he's clearly trying to get her number. That rage ignites, and my nails curl into my palms.

My feet propel me forward before I can stop myself. I emerge from behind the trees and Maisy's gaze lifts almost instantly. Her deep emerald irises latch onto mine, and a faint gasp escapes those pretty pink lips.

It's the first time I've let her see me since all those months ago at the airport. I'd tracked my half-brother and his fiancé to JFK and again, Maisy had simply been at the wrong place at the wrong time. But so right for me.

I stalk closer and that mouth curves into a capital O. I can just imagine her lips wrapped around my cock, sucking and licking me into oblivion. Fuck, I'm so hard now it hurts.

The blonde guy's head swivels in my direction, and I imagine twisting it farther, until it snaps. The satisfying crunch of bones sending a rush of gratification through my hollow chest.

"Nico…" she whispers on an exhale and fuck me, my name on her lips only fuels the fire raging below my belt. I've never had such a visceral reaction to a woman. Maybe it's the months I've spent watching her, keeping her at a careful distance. It's an entirely new experience for me.

"Good afternoon, little fox." I dip my head into a slight bow, my eyes fixed to hers. To her body's reaction to mine.

Her cheeks are flushed, her chest rises and falls more quickly, her lips parted in invitation. I'm not imagining it, she's startled by my presence but there's something more there too.

The blonde male stands and offers his hand. "Jack Dawson, and you are?"

"Not interested," I growl, my gaze intent only on Maisy.

"What are you doing here?" she asks, the slight tremble in her voice doing illicit things to my cock.

"Simply enjoying the beautiful scenery." I inch closer so that her tantalizing scent reaches my nostrils. It's a heady mix of orchids and warm vanilla. I can only imagine what she tastes like.

Her eyes taper at the edges as if she doesn't quite know what to make out of this situation. She's frightened, yes, but there's more, too. Pressing the plastic lid atop the salad container, she drops her chin. The moment her eyes leave mine that vacant chasm in my chest deepens.

Maisy hastily shoves the remains of her lunch in a plastic bag and stands, swiveling toward the grinning idiot. "It was nice meeting you, Jack, but I have to get back to the office."

"Oh, sure." He rises and holds out his hand again, his fingers closing around her small palm. "The pleasure was all mine. I'll call you tomorrow then."

A light crimson flushes her cheeks, but now I'm the one seeing red. The urge to rip that phone from his hands and smash it into a million pieces is overwhelming. I swallow hard, reining in the ravenous demon.

She starts to walk down the pathway without so much as a goodbye. I move into step beside her, and she quickens her pace.

"Why are you running, little fox?"

"I'm not... And don't call me that."

I lengthen my stride to keep up with her as we approach the edge of the park. I'm nearly a foot taller than her, and still, I'm nearly at a jog. She is most definitely running away from me. "Do I frighten you?"

"Um, geez, I don't know… you kidnapped me and my friend and held us at gunpoint just a few months ago. Why would I ever be scared of you?" She keeps her gaze fixed straight ahead and jabs a chipped fingernail at the crosswalk button.

"I've already apologized for that."

"Somehow that's the sort of thing that sticks with you, Nico. Despite apologies."

The light turns green, and she steps out onto the crosswalk without looking, presumably in such a hurry to escape my company. A bike whizzes by, blasting a bell, and I just get my hand around her arm and jerk her back onto the sidewalk before the bike crashes into her.

She lets out a gasp, her palm flying to her chest and drops the plastic container. The lid pops off and a mess of lettuce, tomatoes, and a myriad of other vegetables splatter across the asphalt. "Slow down, you butthole!" she shouts once she's steadied herself against the metal crosswalk pole.

I don't think I've ever heard an adult use that turn of phrase. It brings an unexpected twist to my lips. My hand is still wrapped around her upper arm, and she's clearly still too flustered about her salad to notice.

"Unbelievable." She bends down, jerking free of my grasp and tries to collect the sad remnants of her lunch.

"What are you doing?" I watch her incredulously as she picks the dirt covered tomatoes and places them back in the plastic container.

"I can't just leave them on the sidewalk. The pigeons will try to eat them, and they could choke."

I don't think a single inhabitant in the city would miss those rats with wings. "I think they'll be just fine." I reach for her again and try to force her up, but she glares up at me, those deep green eyes ablaze.

Fuck, that look. It goes straight to my dick.

"No one asked you to wait." She continues her painstaking

task until every leaf of lettuce and pulverized vegetable is back in the plastic bowl.

I eye her completely mesmerized. After months of watching her, I still don't understand this woman. How this sweet, innocent, rather bumbling female could have been married to a psychopath like Jasper Whitaker is beyond me. She must have a dark side, one I am desperate to find and let loose. And if she doesn't, even better. There is nothing I want more than to corrupt her, defile that purity and drag her into the dark depths of my world.

A deep grumble turns my attention to a now standing Maisy. She stomps across the street, and I barely race behind her in time before the light turns red again.

We're only a few steps from the Plaza now, and I'll miss my chance if I don't make my move. "Have dinner with me tonight."

She spins around, her eyes impossibly wide. "Excuse me?"

"You heard me."

A nervous laugh titters out. "I can't…"

"Why? Because of that Jack Dawson asshole?"

Her brows slam together as she regards me. "No, because you kidnapped me, and to be perfectly honest you scare the bejeezus out of me."

I barely suppress the chuckle that time.

"Now, please, leave me alone. I have to get back to work." She spins away, but my hand catches her wrist before she makes it to the first step.

"Do not go out with that Jack guy."

"Right, whatever," she mumbles over her shoulder.

"I'm serious, little fox. I don't like it when others try to play with *my* plaything."

She doesn't even acknowledge my final comment as she races up the steps of The Plaza Hotel.

Rage simmers in the center of my chest. If I can't have Maisy Jordan, no one else will.

. . .

*** I hoped you liked that little sneak peek :) For more of Nico's story, *Brutal King,* preorder here! And make sure you join my FB group Sienna Cross's Heartbreakers or my VIP mailing list here-> https://landing.mailerlite.com/webforms/landing/d8j4z4! You'll get the steamy *Savage King* digital art and a FREE copy of the *Ruthless King* prequel story, *Ruthless Blood* and see how Stella and Luca first met!

ALSO BY SIENNA CROSS

<u>Kings of Temptation</u>
Ruthless King
Savage King
Brutal King

Ruthless (Ongoing on Kindle Vella)

Lords of Stonewall University (Ongoing on Kindle Vella)

ACKNOWLEDGMENTS

I'll let you in on my dirty little secret… Sienna Cross is my pen name, one I've been been dying to launch for a while now. I never would've even attempted it if it wasn't for the support of my husband. He's the only one in my family who knows about naughty Sienna. Thanks for pushing me to do all the things, honey!

A special thank you to my awesome V.A., Sarah, who has been such a huge help and also vault when it comes to keeping all of this a secret. And thank you to the incredibly talented Samaiya for the gorgeous art. You really make the story come to life! And of course my beta readers, Katelin, Sarah (again!), Jena and my ARC team, you're all amazing! Some of you have been with me for years and I really appreciate all your feedback (thanks for keeping the secret too!)

And the biggest thank you to my readers! I could never do this without you :)
   ~ Sienna

ABOUT THE AUTHOR

Sienna Cross was kidnapped by mobsters, saved by her super-hot step-brother, then forced into an arranged marriage with a billionaire. From there, things got really interesting… She loves to write about dark, morally-gray alpha males and the captivating women that bring them to their knees. For all the inside info, join Sienna Cross's Heartbreakers on Facebook, like her page, and follow her on Instagram and Tiktok. She has a thing for stalkers ;)

www.siennacrossbooks.com

Printed in Great Britain
by Amazon